## Praise for Robyn Bachar's
## *Blood, Smoke and Mirrors*

"For a debut book, this story has an incredibly strong and funny main character ...and a strange and interesting world of characters. ...If I had to grab one word to describe this book, it would be refreshing. Not like a diet Coke or something that's saccharine and only satisfying in the short term, but refreshing like thinking to yourself, 'Oh, that's new, that's different' while reading a plot that could have turned on a dime into well-trod cliché-land. Bachar keeps the story firmly in the present with a quick and witty narrator, and I kept reading."
~ *Smart Bitches, Trashy Books*

"Sigh I'm in love. To me, this is classic urban fantasy done very well. An intriguing thread of romance woven through adds to the story. Magic, fairies, shapeshifters and a very different take on vampires all rolled together with the classic quest for justice. ...This story was well grafted with characters that pulled you in and had you on the edge of your seat waiting for the end. I had to sneak in a little reading at work just to finish as I just had to know how it ended. A big thumbs up from me and I will be looking for more work from this author."
~ *Bitten by Books*

"*Blood, Smoke and Mirrors* contains all the things I love the best in books, great internal and external tension, quirky or slightly flawed protagonists, great dialogue, and a captivating story line. It also has a wonderful world. ...Sign me up for book two."
~ *Long and Short Romance Reviews*

"There are some really fantastic bits of laugh craft in Blood, Smoke, and Mirrors. ...The villain of the novel is the masterpiece. Neither Cat's seriously damaged relationship with her father or the creepy Stepford-Vamp character Laura Barrenheart manages to take attention away from Zachary Harrison, newly turned vampire and slick operator. Zachary's character is truly manipulative."

~ *RT Book Reviews*

# Blood, Smoke and Mirrors

*Robyn Bachar*

SAMHAIN
PUBLISHING

Samhain Publishing, Ltd.
577 Mulberry Street, Suite 1520
Macon, GA 31201
www.samhainpublishing.com

Blood, Smoke and Mirrors
Copyright © 2011 by Robyn Bachar
Print ISBN: 978-1-60928-071-0
Digital ISBN: 978-1-60504-997-7

Editing by Sasha Knight
Cover by Kanaxa

First Samhain Publishing, Ltd. electronic publication: May 2010
First Samhain Publishing, Ltd. print publication: March 2011

# Dedication

To my family and friends, for their support, love and inspiration, and to Sasha, the Wandering Gnomes and the Prairie Hearts, for making me a better writer. You are all made of awesome.

# Chapter One

I hate after-midnight meetings. Anyone who wants to talk to a witch after the witching hour doesn't want to chat about the weather, and my boss wouldn't call this late unless something was wrong. Bad news should be heard after I've had a good night's sleep and a cup of coffee, not after I've worked a ten-hour shift that featured lousy tips and three of the loudest screaming babies I'd ever encountered during my restaurant career. Already I wished I'd done the smart thing and hung up, turned off my cell phone, crawled into bed and hidden under the safety of the covers.

The anxious feeling in my gut made me indulge in my first cigarette in over a month as I left my apartment building. I'd dug the half-empty pack out of the bottom of a purse I hadn't used since winter, and the cigarette tasted stale and bitter. This was my tenth failed attempt to quit—I'd have to remember to cuss Mac out for it first thing at this meeting of his, because it was clearly all his fault. Maxwell "Mac" MacInnes is my boss, the owner and manager of the Three Willows Café. He's also my friend, and has been for several years now—one of the few I have left.

Though it was a warm, muggy summer night, the air outside was much more comfortable than my stuffy apartment. I puffed away on my smoke as I headed down the sidewalk, and the streetlight closest to my building flickered as the bulb exploded with a loud, angry pop. Feeling guilty, I ignored it and picked up my pace.

Most of the windows were dark in the houses I passed, the occupants fast asleep at this hour as they rested up for another day of work. My neighborhood is a nice place in general, though

I don't recommend walking through it alone at night, particularly if you're a woman. Of course I don't follow my own advice, but my case is...unique. Sure, I look as threatening as a grade-school librarian. I'm on the overweight side, I wear glasses, and my mouse-brown hair is most often pulled back into a messy braid or ponytail. My wardrobe consists of T-shirts, blue jeans, and unintimidating white running shoes. I might as well have "Mug me" stamped in the middle of my forehead.

The last idiot who attacked me is locked up in a mental hospital in a room with padded walls, still raving about the *bruja* who cursed him with her demon magic. The official explanation is he suffered some sort of psychotic break. The truth is I hit him with a sort of karmic whammy and turned his own evil against him. It allowed me to escape, but did come with the side effect of leaving my attacker permanently insane. I didn't feel bad about it. I did, however, feel bad that my witch brethren felt I needed to be punished for defending myself.

I turned to head east toward the city as I reached the end of my block, where busy train tracks run through the heart of town. The tracks are generally used by Metra trains as they zip back and forth from Chicago to the western suburbs, though we do get several ridiculously long freight trains that rumble through and back up traffic. Flicking the butt of my cigarette into the street, I checked my watch. Right on time so far. I quickened my pace a bit, eager to reach my destination. I didn't know why he'd called me back into work—he knows I don't like to be at the café this late because I don't approve of the sort of people he lets in after hours. The two nearest streetlights flared and then winked out, and I shook my head and sighed.

"Great." If I didn't get a handle on my temper soon, Public Works was going to have a long night too.

The Three Willows Café closes to the public at ten o'clock on weeknights, eleven on the weekends. We get our most interesting customers after midnight, though. The ones who are allowed in by invitation only and look out of place surrounded by the cheery silk flower arrangements and paisley upholstery. Those'd be the customers I don't generally associate with. I'd rather spend my evenings curled up with a good book and my two cats, not serving drinks to the creepy crowd.

As I approached the café I spotted a tall, wiry figure

standing outside the front door, his back to me as he stared toward the Chicago skyline. It was the fedora that gave Mac away. He always wears a hat of some sort in an attempt to hide his hair loss. The clear night allowed a good view of the bright city lights, but I knew the scenery hadn't drawn Mac's attention. He stood with his arms folded across his chest, tension obvious in his posture, and I crept up behind him.

"What are we watching?" I asked in a loud stage whisper. Mac's shoulders pinched in response, but he didn't turn toward me, keeping his attention focused in the distance.

"Hi, Cat. Just wait."

"Uh-huh. What am I waiting for?" I playfully poked him in the ribs, but he ignored me. Not a good sign. I turned and studied the area, curious as to what had caught his eye. We stood together, straining to hear the undefined trouble in the relative silence of the night. In the distance a car blasted down a side street, rattling windows and waking the residents with its booming music. Though the offender was being an ass, I doubted disturbance of the peace was Mac's main concern.

My lungs began to burn and I realized I'd been holding my breath. With an annoyed roll of my eyes I turned away toward the café doors, but before I took a step I finally heard the sound Mac had been waiting for. Somewhere to the east a long eerie howl echoed through the city, and then I glared at him.

"Oh, please. You called me out here because of those idiots? What do you want to do, pretend like we're the supernatural animal cops and arrest them?"

"One of them got caught by a news camera last week," he grumbled.

"Whatever. A blurry shot of a fat coyote running through someone's backyard is hardly newsworthy. Their environment's endangered, you know, I saw a special about it on one of the nature channels." Honestly, I could care less what the shapeshifters did with their free time. If they got liquored up and pranced their furry tails around in front of the ten o'clock news, that was their problem, not mine.

"It's still a risk."

"Not our kind, not our problem, Mac," I quipped. Shifters are the second-class citizens of magiciankind, and not worth raising a fuss over, in my humble opinion. I moved toward the doors of the café, but Mac's hand shot out and gripped my arm.

"What?" I asked, raising a brow. "Move so I can bus the tables." I nudged him in the gut with the side of the bin.

"Hug first," he countered.

I couldn't argue with that. I set the bin down and hugged him, letting him comfort me. It lifted some of the weight in my chest, and I took a deep breath. "I'm still mad at you," I warned him.

"I know." He nodded and let me go.

Picking up the bin, I walked past him into the room. I breezed from table to table, loading the aftermath of late-night meals into the plastic bin as it balanced against my hip. "You really shouldn't let Maria walk all over you like this. Cleaning up is part of closing. Hot dates are not appropriate excuses for leaving early. And you know she's gonna leave early every night you're gone on your trip. You're lucky I was free tonight."

"Just let it alone. I didn't call you in to clean. You know, you could've at least tried to be civil to him." Mac sounded weary, but I shrugged his suggestion off.

"No, I really couldn't. He's lucky I didn't stab him with a salad fork."

"Cat, what happened to you wasn't Lex's fault."

Yeah, like that was going to fix things. A few words from Mac couldn't heal that wound, especially now that Maureen was gone. She'd been my last connection to my own kind, the only witch brave enough to speak to the disgraced outcast. Now I was truly alone, and I had Lex to thank for that.

"I trusted him, damn it, and he *arrested* me. Lex hauled me off and paraded me in front of those dried-up old hags and let them condemn me just 'cause I wasn't willing to roll over and let myself be killed like a good witch would."

"Because they ordered him to, not because he wanted to. You don't think it killed him to do it?"

"Just drop it, Mac. I don't want to talk about this again."

I heard him sigh, and then he retreated to his office and shut the door behind him. Like a good soldier I marched from table to table, making mental notes on what else needed to be done to set the room to rights. I considered pouring myself a cup of coffee, but the warmer had been switched off and the two carafes were empty. Just as well. I really didn't need the caffeine right about now. Hell, what I needed was a bottle of Bailey's Irish Cream and a carton of smokes.

standing outside the front door, his back to me as he stared toward the Chicago skyline. It was the fedora that gave Mac away. He always wears a hat of some sort in an attempt to hide his hair loss. The clear night allowed a good view of the bright city lights, but I knew the scenery hadn't drawn Mac's attention. He stood with his arms folded across his chest, tension obvious in his posture, and I crept up behind him.

"What are we watching?" I asked in a loud stage whisper. Mac's shoulders pinched in response, but he didn't turn toward me, keeping his attention focused in the distance.

"Hi, Cat. Just wait."

"Uh-huh. What am I waiting for?" I playfully poked him in the ribs, but he ignored me. Not a good sign. I turned and studied the area, curious as to what had caught his eye. We stood together, straining to hear the undefined trouble in the relative silence of the night. In the distance a car blasted down a side street, rattling windows and waking the residents with its booming music. Though the offender was being an ass, I doubted disturbance of the peace was Mac's main concern.

My lungs began to burn and I realized I'd been holding my breath. With an annoyed roll of my eyes I turned away toward the café doors, but before I took a step I finally heard the sound Mac had been waiting for. Somewhere to the east a long eerie howl echoed through the city, and then I glared at him.

"Oh, please. You called me out here because of those idiots? What do you want to do, pretend like we're the supernatural animal cops and arrest them?"

"One of them got caught by a news camera last week," he grumbled.

"Whatever. A blurry shot of a fat coyote running through someone's backyard is hardly newsworthy. Their environment's endangered, you know, I saw a special about it on one of the nature channels." Honestly, I could care less what the shapeshifters did with their free time. If they got liquored up and pranced their furry tails around in front of the ten o'clock news, that was their problem, not mine.

"It's still a risk."

"Not our kind, not our problem, Mac," I quipped. Shifters are the second-class citizens of magiciankind, and not worth raising a fuss over, in my humble opinion. I moved toward the doors of the café, but Mac's hand shot out and gripped my arm.

I frowned down at it. "Hey, what gives?"

"Cat, you know I wouldn't have asked you here if it wasn't important."

"Yeah, and I'm seriously disappointed in your idea of important."

"Wait. Before you go in there, I want to say I'm sorry. This wasn't my idea." Mac looked down at me with sincere sorrow in his eyes, and my stomach did a queasy flip-flop. Tugging my arm free, I pushed through the doors.

Glancing around the room, I surveyed the state it'd been left in. I hate coming in and finding the café in disarray. It feels almost as though someone had thrown a wild party in my apartment while I was gone on vacation for a few days. Tonight the place had been left in a sorry mess. Mac's closer must have skipped out early again. Most of the tabletops were littered with dirty plates, sweaty half-empty water glasses and wrinkled, stained napkins.

A flash of movement caught my eye, and I realized someone was sitting in one of the booths, his back turned to me. Arms folded across my chest, I crossed the room to investigate. When I reached the booth its occupant turned to face me, and as I recognized him a jolt of power snapped sharply in my gut.

Alexander Duquesne, or Lex as I knew him better, was one of the three guardians charged with enforcing magical law and order in the Chicagoland area. When I'd used magic against the thug who'd attacked me, it was Lex who turned me in and got me cast out by the witches' council. Before that, Lex had been my boyfriend, but having your significant other hand you over to the firing squad is pretty much the end of the relationship. I wanted him to look terrible, to be a gaunt, pale shell of his former self, like someone who'd suffered four years worth of terrible guilt for arresting an innocent woman, but Lex was a picture of health, still lean and fit like a track star. Even his wardrobe was the same, from his black T-shirt to the scuffed toes of his boots. His long light brown hair was pulled back into a ponytail, and those gorgeous, ice blue eyes I used to get lost in now watched me warily.

"What the hell do you want?" I snapped.

"Nice to see you too, Cat." His warm, smooth Southern drawl was a bit thicker than usual, which meant he was either tired or stressed.

"*This* is why you called me?" I turned to Mac as he joined us. He took the seat across from Lex, and I scowled down at him. "You have lost your damn mind!"

"It's about Maureen," Lex said, his voice low and even.

My stomach twisted into a tight knot. Maureen O'Driscoll was one of the few people I trusted in magician society, someone I cared about and owed a great deal to. She was also the only witch who still spoke to me, even though I was an outcast.

"Is she okay?" My voice hitched up a notch, and I cleared my throat.

"No, sugar. She died two nights ago." The sorrow in Lex's expression didn't do much to soften the blow, and I shook my head, feeling numb from head to foot.

"That's impossible."

"Cat, she was eighty-four years old," Mac said. The placating tone only sparked my already raw temper.

"So? That's not the point. She's too tough to die."

Maureen was as strong as a tower. A fortress. A mountain. The woman's magic was so potent she could practically be a faerie, and faeries are damn near immortal. In another time she would have been the stuff of ballads, epic bard tales. A legend, like Morgan le Fay. She couldn't be dead.

"She died in the hospital," Lex informed me. "There were complications after surgery. No one was expecting it. Wasn't anything they could do about it."

"Lord and Lady," I swore, shocked. "What kind of complications?"

"Massive blood loss."

"Really." I stared at him with narrowed eyes, instantly suspicious. Someone as strong as Maureen should've been able to heal almost any kind of wound, and I'd heard of too many *accidental* deaths from blood loss to buy that excuse.

"There's no evidence that necromancers were involved."

"Is there ever?" My knees went weak and I dropped into a chair across from the booth. Not possible, it just wasn't possible...and yet it was true. Murdered. Maureen had been murdered by vampires—they wanted her out of the way. *Just like your mother,* a little voice inside my head reminded, and I swallowed hard. After a few moments I found myself dragging out my smokes, and I noticed the corners of the hard pack were smushed from being in the back pocket of my jeans. My hand shook as I lit my cigarette, and I hated myself a bit for it, but after a few calming drags I felt better.

"Thought you quit," Lex said, and I shot him another glare.

"Yeah, so did I. So, you came by just to tell me about Maureen?"

"There's more to it than that. With Maureen gone the region'll need a new Titania, or Oberon."

"Obviously. Who'd she name as her heir?"

"She didn't."

Frowning, I tapped ashes onto the plate in front of my chair, sprinkling a shower of gray over a few cold French fries. That made no sense to me at all. Maureen was a sensible woman, she was sure to have a few dozen copies of her will stashed around, in case of Armageddon or other hideous, unforeseen disasters. Like all faerie names, the term Titania had little to do with the actual job—being Titania didn't make you queen of the faeries. Instead, it was a political position, a kind of ambassador that oversaw relations between our realm and the faerie realm. No responsible Titania would leave her region without a designated heir, it was crazy. There were far too many dark things in Faerie just waiting for a chance to get out and wreak havoc, and just as many things waiting to get in.

I shook my head in disbelief. "But she had kids. Grandkids. Hell, she even had great-grandkids. One of them had to inherit her gifts."

"If they did, no one knows about it. There's no evidence of it at all."

"Damn."

"The faerie council is goin' to accept candidates for the position tomorrow. I think you should be one of them." Lex leaned back in his seat, and I blew a stream of annoyed smoke in his direction.

"That's real fuckin' funny, coming from you," I growled. With a vicious stab I ground the cig out and dropped the butt onto the plate.

"I'm serious. You're one of the few strong enough to take it."

"Cat, you should listen to him—" Mac started.

Rising to my feet, I glared at both of them. "No. Not even if I were the last magician on Earth. Thanks for the news, now get the hell out of my café," I said to Lex, pointing in the direction of the front door. "And you," I continued, turning to Mac. "Go balance your damn books."

Turning on my heel, I marched out of the dining room and pushed my way through the swinging doors into the back room. It probably would've made sense for me to have stormed out and gone home, but this was my turf and I wasn't about to let the likes of him chase me out of it. The Three Willows is my second home.

Lex pushed his way through the doors. "Cat, would you just listen to me—"

"Go to hell." My eyes stung and I blinked with stubborn determination. I was not going to let this man affect me. I turned away, looking for a task to focus on, and settled on a bin full of dirty dishes next to the sink.

"Say somebody did go after Maureen. Whoever did it is probably sponsoring a candidate, and we'll all suffer if the wrong person ends up in the position."

"Probably. They'd have to be a really rotten crowd of possibilities if you're scraping the bottom of the outcast barrel to fight for Team Good." My hands trembled as I started filling the sink with hot, soapy water, and I kept my back to him to hide my unsteadiness.

"C'mon, don't be like that." Lex sighed, and I snorted.

"Like what? Bitter? Hurt? Angry? Sorry, can't help it. Guess you just bring that out in me."

"This isn't about us. It's about what's best for the entire region."

"Which is not my problem anymore, guardian. I don't care about saving the world. Go recruit somewhere else."

His only answer was a strangled sound of frustration. Silent, I stared down at the rising soap bubbles and didn't move until I heard the kitchen doors swinging shut again, assuring me Lex had left. I shook my head and started loading dishes in to soak. Wasn't my problem, I reminded myself. I didn't have a place in magician society anymore. I couldn't sign up for a leadership position.

Needing a new distraction, I picked up the empty bin and turned around to head back into the dining room. Mac blocked the doorway, standing with his arms crossed over his chest.

"What?" I asked, raising a brow. "Move so I can bus the tables." I nudged him in the gut with the side of the bin.

"Hug first," he countered.

I couldn't argue with that. I set the bin down and hugged him, letting him comfort me. It lifted some of the weight in my chest, and I took a deep breath. "I'm still mad at you," I warned him.

"I know." He nodded and let me go.

Picking up the bin, I walked past him into the room. I breezed from table to table, loading the aftermath of late-night meals into the plastic bin as it balanced against my hip. "You really shouldn't let Maria walk all over you like this. Cleaning up is part of closing. Hot dates are not appropriate excuses for leaving early. And you know she's gonna leave early every night you're gone on your trip. You're lucky I was free tonight."

"Just let it alone. I didn't call you in to clean. You know, you could've at least tried to be civil to him." Mac sounded weary, but I shrugged his suggestion off.

"No, I really couldn't. He's lucky I didn't stab him with a salad fork."

"Cat, what happened to you wasn't Lex's fault."

Yeah, like that was going to fix things. A few words from Mac couldn't heal that wound, especially now that Maureen was gone. She'd been my last connection to my own kind, the only witch brave enough to speak to the disgraced outcast. Now I was truly alone, and I had Lex to thank for that.

"I trusted him, damn it, and he *arrested* me. Lex hauled me off and paraded me in front of those dried-up old hags and let them condemn me just 'cause I wasn't willing to roll over and let myself be killed like a good witch would."

"Because they ordered him to, not because he wanted to. You don't think it killed him to do it?"

"Just drop it, Mac. I don't want to talk about this again."

I heard him sigh, and then he retreated to his office and shut the door behind him. Like a good soldier I marched from table to table, making mental notes on what else needed to be done to set the room to rights. I considered pouring myself a cup of coffee, but the warmer had been switched off and the two carafes were empty. Just as well. I really didn't need the caffeine right about now. Hell, what I needed was a bottle of Bailey's Irish Cream and a carton of smokes.

Maureen had been a coffee addict too, but she took it black. No frills, no nonsense, no decaf cappuccinos for that woman. She'd always been sensible, which was why she stuck by me. Maureen thought the council was crazy for sentencing me with such a severe punishment for using magic in my own defense—she even spoke on my behalf. They could've censured me—should've censured me—but instead they chose to cast me out. Apparently the council thought I couldn't be trusted not to do it again and considered me to be too great of a risk. A bad seed, thanks to my necromancer father. It didn't matter to them that I hadn't seen the man since I was ten years old, when my parents divorced. Bad blood was bad blood.

The second round of dishes left the tabletops clear, and I grabbed a bucket from underneath the sink and filled it with warm, soapy water. There were a few spots on the tiles in front of the café that needed some scrubbing attention. Grunting with effort, I heaved the bucket up out of the basin and hauled it out of the kitchen and all the way to the front of the restaurant. Suds sloshed over the side and onto my white sneakers, soaking the tips. My white shoes never stay white for very long. You'd think I'd learn my lesson and buy a more durable shade.

Mud had worked its way deep into the grout between the deep green tiles near the hostess station and underneath the bench we have for customers to sit on while waiting for a table. Grabbing the scrub brush, I knelt next to the bucket and set to work. It had rained more than usual the past few weeks, which for the Chicago area is really saying something—six more inches and I'd consider building a boat and rounding up the animals in the Brookfield Zoo. I attacked the dirt with gusto to avoid thinking about Maureen.

I couldn't picture anyone who'd be able to fill her shoes as Titania. I certainly couldn't do it. I didn't want to do it, damn it. Relentless, I scrubbed faster, grinding the bristles into the grout, until a series of loud pops outside startled me. Glancing up, I saw a spectacular shower of sparks sailing out from the streetlights, raining down like fireworks onto the pavement up this side of the block and down the other across the tracks. Eyes wide, I sat back on my heels, and the brush slid out of my hands and clattered to the tiles.

"Oops," I said. Probably one of the greater understatements

I've ever uttered. It had been years, *years*, since I'd had a magical accident that severe—not since I was a teenager, learning how to control my magic while battling the interference of surging hormones. Aside from the flickering streetlights earlier, I usually have excellent control, so this was especially eye-opening.

I heard the sound of the office door opening, but all I could do was stare out the windows of the Three Willows into the darkness. In an area like ours, which stresses the urban in suburban, the night never gets truly dark. Streetlights, illuminated store signs, headlights and of course the lights from houses all keep the deepest shadows at bay and provide a feeling of security—though it's often false. And I'd just zapped that security.

Mac stood behind me. Still too stunned for even a sarcastic quip, I continued to stare outside.

"Catherine," Mac said quietly.

"Yeah?"

"Maybe you should take a break. Come back into my office."

I lurched to my feet, wincing as my joints popped and cracked. Drying my hands on the seat of my jeans, I followed Mac into his office and flopped down into one of the chairs in front of his desk.

I love Mac's office—any magician would. Mac is a librarian, one of the oldest and most respected of the nine subsets of magiciankind. The walls of his tiny office were lined with shelves that were crammed with books. They're all considered safe for public viewing, since the Three Willows caters to the non-magical majority most of the time. It wouldn't be good for one of our regulars to wander in and find a bunch of spellbooks lying around.

The chair creaked as Mac sat down and leaned back. Deciding this would be an ideal time for another smoke, I dug out my pack and liberated another cigarette from it. I glanced up at him over the flame of my lighter as I lit the end of my smoke. "Sorry 'bout that," I mumbled around it. The cig bobbed up and down between my lips as I spoke, and then I inhaled.

"Never seen that one before."

"Yeah, I'm just full of surprises today. It was an accident."

"I'm sure the city will have a fun time trying to figure out what caused it," he replied dryly. Mac wasn't mad, which was a good thing, but there was something on his mind. We sat in silence as I puffed away. I kept trying to quit for monetary reasons, not health ones. I'm not afraid of lung cancer—all magicians are immune to most diseases, one of the reasons we're so long lived. And hard to kill. If your blood is potent enough, like mine is, you can heal a broken bone in a few days, sometimes even hours if it's something small like a hairline fracture. Of course if you drop a Kansas farmhouse on me, I'll be dead instantly, wicked or not.

"If I'd come to you about taking the position, would you have said no?" Mac asked.

I gave him a sour expression. "Doesn't matter. I don't want it."

"A fact which makes you a good candidate for it. You wouldn't be in it for the power or political gain. You'd do it because it's the right thing to do." Though I didn't agree with him, I had to give Mac credit for the thought. "Why do you think someone wanted Maureen out of the way?"

"Power, probably." It was my best guess, and I slipped my glasses off to rub at my eyes with my free hand. "Maureen was always fair, even when being fair wasn't the popular choice. There are people who'd prefer someone more easily corrupted."

Witches follow a strict rule of harming none with our magic. The other breeds of magician don't come with those kinds of ideals though. Most of the major forms don't dabble in the dark stuff—it's the sorcerers and the necromancers you have to worry about, and thankfully there's never been a necromancer as an Oberon or Titania. Necromancy is the first step to becoming a vampire, and vampires can't interact with the Faerie realm. Pretty silly to appoint a representative who's counting the days until they'll be forced to resign.

"I don't want it, Mac. Besides, the witches would never stand for it. They'd refuse to work with me, and the faeries won't want a Titania who comes with that kind of baggage."

"No, the witches would have to listen to you if you became Titania, and it would prove that they were wrong about you."

"Yeah, right." I snorted at the idea, and then inhaled deeply. "That'll never happen. They prefer martyrs to fighters. As far as they're concerned, I should've let the guy kill me." My crime, the unforgivable act that had gotten me cast out from the ranks of witch-kind, had been to fight back against the man who attacked me. I'd thought using his bad acts against him would keep me free from punishment by the witches' council.

I was wrong.

Mac shook his head. "Then forget about the witches. Think of all the other magicians you could help if you become Titania. You can't hide here forever, Cat."

There must have been an audible thump as my jaw hit the floor. "I'm not hiding from anything. What the hell kind of statement is that?" I sputtered. "You own this place, what are you hiding from?"

"I'm not hiding from a thing. I'm a librarian, this place fits me right down to the ground. I host a neutral gathering place which gives me plenty of information from our more unique customers. Outcast or not, you're a witch, you're meant to use your power to help others. Refilling their coffee doesn't count."

"I can't do it, Mac, I just can't."

"Yes, you can. And don't tell me you don't care, because I know you do."

My smoke had burned down to the filter, and I dropped it into the ashtray. I didn't light another one—there weren't enough cigarettes in Chicago to make me feel better.

"I believe in you, Catherine. You should try believing in yourself for a change."

"I'll think about it."

"You do that." He nodded.

"Right... When are the candidates meeting again?" I asked, trying to keep my tone casual.

"Tomorrow."

"Too bad, I work tomorrow." Shrugging with feigned nonchalance, I stood up.

"Not anymore, you're taking the rest of the week off."

"Hey, I didn't say I was going to—"

"Just in case. Think of it as a vacation."

"I can't afford a vacation. I'll take the day off though, if you're insisting."

Rising to his feet, he rounded the desk and gave me another much-needed hug. Sometimes I wish that Mac was younger, heterosexual and that we found each other attractive. It'd be nice to have a lover who was as good a friend as Mac, someone I could trust implicitly.

"Thanks," I said. Pulling away, I gave him a weak smile.

"You may want to consider some ice cream when you get home. For medicinal purposes."

"Good idea. A lot of ice cream."

Tomorrow was going to be a very long day.

# Chapter Two

The familiar sensation of a cat biting my toes woke me. It's almost as reliable as an alarm clock with the bonus of being far more annoying. Cats are unclear on the concepts of shift changes, weekends and days off. Swearing, I untangled myself from the sheets and sat up in my bed. My little angels, Merri and Pippin, were staring up at me from the floor, waiting to be fed. I used to feed them at night, trying to preserve the sanctity of my mornings, but they took to gobbling down their food and waking me up to demand more anyway. Thusly I was outsmarted by my cats.

"Fine, fine, I'm up," I assured them. Placated, they trotted out into the kitchen to await their breakfast. Glancing at the clock, I swore again—it was a little past nine in the morning. I don't function well before the crack of noon under the best circumstances, and with only four hours of fitful sleep I wasn't at my best and brightest. Coffee, I needed coffee, and lots of it.

I stumbled into the kitchen and made a beeline for the coffeemaker. A furry missile attempted to trip me about halfway through the room, but I managed to avoid it. Coffee first, cat food second. Believe me, the little ginger butterballs weren't about to starve to death. Once I managed to start the coffee brewing I scooped food into the monsters' dishes and got out of their way. While the coffeemaker hissed and spat on the counter I padded toward the living room, intent on checking my email.

The scent of cinnamon hit me a split second before I heard the distinct rustle of wings. One of my unusual gifts is that I can smell magic. I've never heard of another magician who can do it. Strange though it sounds, it's a rather useful gift, especially considering no one knows I have it. Faerie magic smells like cinnamon to me, and it gets stronger as the magic gets more powerful.

I paused in the doorway and blinked at the faerie perched on the arm of my sofa. Enormous silvery white wings glistened and glimmered in the sunlight shining through my front windows. Thick waves of hair the color of newly fallen snow fell forward as Portia bent over the television remote held in her hands. I envy her those hands. Her fingers are slender and delicate, and her pale skin is flawless. Though small in stature, she does not have the willowy, almost anorexic angles many artists seem to favor when painting faeries and pixies, but instead her form is rounded, curvaceous. Aspiring artists also have faerie fashion all wrong—they don't usually go for flowers or diaphanous gowns. Portia likes ripped jeans in a bleached 1980s style, white fishnet stockings, combat boots and torn sweatshirts. I keep waiting for her to update her style, but she must be waiting for it to come back.

The mysteries of the remote have always eluded Portia, probably because there aren't many electronics in her world. "Kitty, make it work!" She held the remote out to me with a petulant frown. "I want to watch the game show."

"It's not on 'til ten," I replied, taking it and setting it down on my end table. Portia has a love of *The Price is Right*. She gets excited every time the announcer yells "Come on down!" and her wings shower the room in ice faerie dust, which is damn hard to vacuum up I might add, in addition to leaving a layer of damp when the frost melts. "It's early, Portia, what's up?"

"Stuff. I'm going to escort you to the big meeting. I'm your sponsor now. You'd better hurry up and get ready."

"Whoa, whoa, I never actually agreed to be in the running. I just told Mac I'd think about it, and I thought I'd just drop by and see who turned out for it."

"Oh, you talked to Big Mac about this too? Big Mac is very wise, you should listen to him."

From the kitchen I heard the soft beeping that alerted me that my coffee was ready, and I turned around and fled the room. The strong smell of cinnamon followed me, signaling that Portia was not far behind. When I entered the kitchen I discovered the cats had vanished, off to work on whatever important feline business was next on their schedule. Reaching into the cupboard over the counter, I grabbed my largest mug and filled it with the beautiful, steamy nectar of life.

"Kitty, you just *have* to be the new Titania!" There was a childish whine in her voice I knew she couldn't help. A faerie's vocal range goes both above and below a human's ability to hear, which is why we can't speak their language, no matter how much a magician studies it. Still, even knowing that fact it was difficult to avoid the instant headache that formed behind my eyes.

"Portia, that's really a lot more responsibility than I'm interested in." I opened my refrigerator and grabbed the bottle of vanilla-flavored creamer.

"But you're good at it."

"Yeah, right, I'm a regular candidate for governor. Hey maybe I'll run for mayor and unseat Daley."

After adding a healthy helping to my coffee I replaced the bottle in the fridge. Turning around, I leaned against the counter and watched Portia as she tried to figure out who this mysterious Daley person was from her perch on the corner of my kitchen table. Faeries don't sit, they perch, and though they look as solid as a human they are far lighter, so I had no worry that my cheap, rickety table might snap under her weight. Hell, it'd be more likely to snap under the weight of one of my fat cats than Portia.

"I'm not a people person," I explained, but she was unconvinced.

"You don't need to be a people person, you need to be a faerie person." She jabbed a slender finger at me for emphasis. "You're perfect for that, your blood's strong. The Silverleafs all love you."

"My blood's not as strong as Maureen's was, not by a long shot."

"Few people are anymore. She was half-blood."

Choking, I nearly spat a mouthful of coffee across the room. Maureen being half faerie would explain a great deal about why she was so powerful, but it did bring up another question.

"Why didn't any of her children inherit it then?"

"Oh, they did."

"Why the hell didn't one of them get named as her heir?"

"Never got trained, might as well have been born straights." Portia sighed, her wings drooping in disappointment.

My mouth opened as I almost asked another question, but I swallowed my curiosity. If Maureen hadn't trained her children, there was a reason for it, a personal reason that was none of my business to know. I'd been to her home a few times, but never met any of her family. It made more sense now—she probably didn't want to explain to them how she knew me.

"She'd want you to do it."

I nodded in silent agreement. Maureen would want me to do it, she'd always believed in me. She supported me when no one else would, she looked after me after my mother died and made sure I went to a witch's foster home, instead of being dumped into the straights' system. I owed her a lot. I owed her this much...

"What time is this meeting?"

"Soon! Drink faster!" she urged, and I took a gulp of coffee.

"All right, all right."

Portia barked orders at me as I hurried to get ready—though I had no idea how to prepare for this sort of thing. I was glad I'd showered when I got home from the café, because there was no time for it now. After shedding my pajamas I stood in front of my closet in only my underwear, wondering what to wear. My wardrobe consists mostly of casual, comfortable clothing: jeans, T-shirts, sweatshirts, that sort of thing. I don't own very many things that fall into the "nice" or "formal" category, as I seldom have the opportunity to wear them.

This trip was just plain difficult to plan for—the first and most important lesson I'd learned about the faerie realm is you must expect the unexpected, and that's nigh impossible to dress for. The rules and laws that apply here don't necessarily extend there. Faerie is a world of pure magic, and that makes it far more fluid than our world. Locations and landscapes shift on a whim. Even time runs differently—remember those old stories about people being snatched up into a faerie mound for a night and when they return home the next morning they discover a hundred years has passed, and everyone they loved has died? All true. Magicians eventually learned that taking a piece of time from our world, first as an hourglass and later as a pocket watch or wristwatch, keeps us grounded in our own timeline when we return home.

"Portia?" I said, waving a helpless hand at the selection.

"Dress for battle. Do you have armor?"

"Yeah, they give you a Kevlar vest when you move into the neighborhood," I joked, rolling my eyes.

"What's Kevlar? Is it shiny? I like shiny."

"Never mind."

"How about something with lots of pockets? For spell components."

Well, at least I knew I'd need to be prepared to do magic. The knowledge was not very reassuring, and likely meant my abilities were going to be put to the test. Spellcasting is one of my many strong points, always has been, but like any witch I have an automatic handicap where it's concerned. Witches require tools to cast spells. We need words, ritual and physical components like wands, daggers, herbs, candles and crystals, to name a few. And we need lots of 'em. A sorcerer can conjure up fire with a thought, but a witch needs to speak an incantation and have a symbol of it on hand, like a match or a lighter. That split-second difference has cost many witches their lives.

I settled on wearing my many-pocketed cargo pants, an army surplus button-down shirt over a black tank top, and my black combat boots. Rifling through the drawers of my dresser, I started pulling out nearly every amulet, talisman and holy symbol I own, stuffing them into my pockets and hanging them around my neck. Next my gaze settled upon my ritual dagger and sword. They both serve the same purpose, performing the same tasks and symbolizing the same things, but each would send a different message to my observers. The sword was a more aggressive symbol than the small dagger.

"Bring both," Portia suggested.

"Both?"

"Yup. Just in case."

"Of what? Barbarian invasion?" I joked. Grabbing the belt out of my closet, I affixed the sword's scabbard and the dagger's sheath to it.

I loaded my fingers with rings, my wrists and arms with bracelets and watches, and then earrings for my double-pierced ears. Next I brushed out my hair and let it fall long and loose down my back. The final touch was my favorite: my top hat. It's a detail that is my trademark, and Portia in particular loves it—

she probably wouldn't let me leave without it. It's black, of course, and Two Tarot cards—Justice and The Moon—are tucked into the satin band.

"You look good!" Portia assured me when I was finished.

"I look like a gypsy going to war." Turning toward my bed, I nodded to the two cats that had been overseeing my progress. "Well, what do you boys think?" Pippin expressed his opinion by rolling over and demanding a belly rub, which I indulged him with, and Merri just yawned. "Gee, thanks."

"Good, let's go!"

Fluttering into the air, she zipped across the room and through the dressing mirror. The glass rippled like water in her wake, and normally I would've expected it to display an image of the place in Faerie she'd traveled to, but instead my reflection stared back at me. Guess I'd have to create my own gateway this time.

"Okay, everybody out," I ordered. Pippin hesitated, wanting more attention, but in a stunning display of actual obedience, both cats hopped down from the bed and hightailed it from the room.

After shutting the door to my closet and to my bedroom, I crossed to the antique mirror. The old dressing mirror stretched taller than me and just slightly wider, and my reflection stared back at me, resigned to our fate. Taking a deep breath, I drew the dagger from my belt and sliced a long, shallow cut across my right palm. The blood welled red, bright and painful against my pale skin, and I placed the palm against the center of the mirror.

*"Between the worlds, I make this door,*
*Safe passage through, as time before.*
*The lock undone, with blood as key,*
*As I will, so mote it be."*

The image shimmered and a ripple spread out from my hand like rings on the surface of a pond. A glow formed and lit the room, suffusing the entire reflection until it was a blank sea of light. I inched my hand away and the light brightened even further, almost to the point of blinding until it suddenly faded. My room was no longer reflected in the mirror, but instead an image of a grassy hill appeared. Fluffy white clouds wandered across the landscape's sky, and the long grass waved in the breeze.

I glanced at the two photos atop my dresser—one of me and my mother on my fourth birthday, and one of me and Maureen at my high school graduation. "Wish me luck, ladies," I said softly.

Squaring my shoulders, I stepped through the mirror.

I've lived in the city all my life, so it's no surprise that the sensation of breathing fresh air is strange and foreign to me. I'm used to exhaust, smoke and other general pollution, and the absence of it makes me wary. To me, it's the ultimate reminder of not being in Kansas anymore, Toto. Aside from the cleanliness, Faerie isn't so different from our world as far as looks go. The grass is green, the sky is blue and the sun shines during the day and the stars at night, though admittedly the constellations are different. I'm not sure why that is, I'm no astronomer, and I haven't had the time or inclination to find out.

With one hand secure on the hilt of my sword, I walked forward toward the hill. The portal closed behind me with a muffled pop, but I paid it no mind. I knew how to get home without it, even though I had no idea where I was. Despite the fact that I've used the same mirror in the same spot for seven years in a row now, it's never opened to the same place twice. I knew the hill was a faerie mound, and if this was where the door had brought me then this was where I needed to be.

"Portia?" I called out as I walked. It was slow going, or at least in comparison to a brisk walk down the concrete sidewalks of home. Like I said, I'm a city girl. I like my roads paved, my messages instant and my coffee to go.

"Kitty! This is so exciting!"

I turned to see the faerie fly over to join me. A cool shower of faerie dust rained down as Portia fluttered above me, and I couldn't help but sneeze.

"Yeah, it's gonna be a real barrel of laughs," I muttered. My fingers itched to light up a cigarette, so I balled my hands into fists and stuffed them into my pockets. No point in being rude to the locals. Yet. "So I take it we're going in the mound. Whose is it?"

"The Underhill clan. They're good people. I have cousins here on my mother's side." She smiled at me, and then plopped down to walk at my side. I'd heard of them—despite the terribly unoriginal name, they had a good reputation for fairness, and more importantly, did not have a reputation for causing trouble in the human world. Some faeries, mostly the clanless ones, just can't seem to resist mischief making. A common activity is breaking human gadgets. Ever wonder why your car battery died for no apparent reason? Find your keys in places you *know* you did not leave them? You're not crazy, you just had the misfortune of being targeted by a faerie with nothing better to do with eternity.

"Am I the only candidate who's going to be at this meeting?"

"One other."

"Only one? That can't be good. Who is it?"

"Don't know. We'll find out soon enough." Portia shrugged.

Too soon, in my opinion. The base of the hill grew closer and closer with each step we took. My stomach dropped down somewhere between my knees and I swallowed hard. I had to be crazy to be doing this. For one, I was too young to be Titania. I wasn't even thirty yet. I didn't want to go into politics. This was just insanity.

There was no visible entrance, but I didn't expect to see one, not yet anyway. Portia and I continued on in silence until I felt her hand on my arm. Stopping in my tracks, I glanced over at her. She launched herself into the air once again and fluttered ahead of me. A low rumble like distant thunder emanated from the base of the hill, and the ground swelled and split. Dirt and uprooted chunks of sod tumbled up and away to reveal a large wooden door covered with intricate carvings of intertwined roots and vegetables. Decorative potatoes, who knew? With a graceful wave of her hand the door swung open, smooth and soundless, and Portia flew inside. I followed behind, struggling to keep my expression neutral and my nerves calm.

The smell of faerie magic almost overpowered me as I stepped through the doorway, so much so that it made my eyes water. Walking into the mound was like stepping into a cinnamon-roll factory set for high production. Portia led me down the hallway, a long corridor with walls of rough earth that were common for the inside of a mound. Tiny balls of light bobbed up and down near the ceiling as though floating in a lazy river, casting everything in a soft glow. I was a little unnerved by the quiet hush surrounding us, broken only by the soft whisper of her wings and the clomping of my heavy boots. Most faerie dwellings are constantly filled with noise—they really dislike silence. In addition to that we ought to have run into members of the Underhill clan by now.

"Where is everyone?" I whispered.

"Just wait."

*Great.* It wasn't like Portia to be ominous, or quiet for that matter. A wave of nausea rolled through my stomach, and I did some mental bargaining with it to keep it steady. Losing my lunch in a strange clan's home would not be a polite way to introduce myself.

Finally we reached an enormous set of double doors, ridiculously large by faerie standards and even pushing the limits of human ones. They were covered in runes I couldn't read, but I knew this had to be their great hall. Portia fluttered behind me and hovered just over my right shoulder, placing her hand upon it and giving it an encouraging squeeze. The doors opened at a ponderous rate, revealing the room in slow degrees. My breath whooshed out of my lungs in astonishment, and I stood slack-jawed and gaped at the assembled faeries. The entire clan had turned out, as well as members of several others. I scanned the crowd for familiar faces and caught the eye of Tybalt, Portia's older brother, and he gave me a big grin. Good to know I had some people on my side.

I could barely make out the other end of the hall. Some days it sucks extra hard to be nearsighted, and it reminded me that I needed a new set of glasses. Squinting, I managed to spy three large chairs—no, thrones. The faeries had brought in their Council of Three to oversee the proceedings. The temptation to draw my sword and fall upon it suddenly seemed like an appealing idea. It would be quicker and far less painful than the fate that would await me when my stupid mouth said the wrong thing and pissed off their leaders.

Every faction of magical society is governed by their own Council of Three. Witches, sorcerers, vampires, shapeshifters, everybody. Larger populations have more than one council, each in charge of a certain region. There's only one faerie Council of Three responsible for dealing with North America, and they were sitting in those chairs. Portia gave my shoulder a bump, and with my heart in my throat I made my way into the hall. The silence here was especially eerie, only the low whispered hush of wings and swishing of tails occupied the room. The sound of tails made me take a closer look at the assembled group. Faeries take the form of whatever they want, whenever they want. Not all prefer the delicate wings Portia sports. Some take on animal features, elemental or even demonic aspects. Whatever catches their fancy, really. I don't think anyone's ever seen the original form of a faerie, if the faeries even remember what they were at all.

I remembered not to stare at the council, which would have been really rude, and kept my gaze lowered to stare somewhere around their feet. They were dressed in their finest, glittering and shining bright enough to be their own light source. As I studied the latest in faerie formal footwear I noticed an additional, unexpected pair of shoes standing behind the council and off to the side: a scuffed pair of black combat boots. Despite my better judgment, my curiosity got the better of me and I let my gaze travel upwards. Black duster, black pants, black shirt—the man almost blended completely into the shadows around him, which normally would've hinted at a sorcerer, but I knew the faerie council wouldn't trust one to stand behind them within fireball range.

It had to be a guardian, and my heart sank as I realized it was Lex. There was a casual air about him as he stood with his hands in his coat pockets, and the rest of his appearance complemented his laid-back manner. Unlike last night, his shoulder-length light brown hair was unbound and extra stubble lined his jaw. Lex was watching me, and he gave me an encouraging smile. Flustered, I tore my gaze away, concentrating instead on the figure kneeling with its head bowed low in front of the trio of thrones.

The person's face was hidden by the hood of a long black cloak. *Yuck, must be a sorcerer.* Sorcerers tend to lean toward wardrobes befitting wizards in fantasy stories—long robes, pointy hats, gnarled wooden staffs topped with crystals and the like. Someone really needs to tell them that they are not Gandalf, and they need to join the twenty-first century with the rest of us. I noticed a slender man in a dark gray business suit standing behind the sorcerer, but I didn't recognize him either.

Once we reached the other candidate I knelt as well, trying to look as graceful as I could manage.

"Greetings, Catherine Marie Morrow," a voice in front of me

intoned. I flinched at the sound of my True Name—usually I go by Catherine Baker. I've gone to great lengths to hide my True Name from the magical world, and here it was being shared in front of every damn faerie in the hemisphere. Great. My reaction was to be expected, but out of the corner of my eye I noticed the black-cloaked figure had flinched as well. I turned my head toward him as he looked toward me. I peered into the depths of that black hood and recognized him, much to my immediate shock, and my brain shut down as my mouth took over.

"Aw, hell no," I growled. Leaping to the side, I knocked him off his feet and pinned him to the floor, and the man glared up at me with a mix of shock and hatred. "'Lo, Dad."

I heard something like the rustling of a thousand wings at once and everything around me went black.

# Chapter Three

Throughout my life there have been several times when I woke up and swore that my entire body hurt. Generally I knew the sources of the agonizing pain: moving furniture, an unusually brisk self-defense class, too much drinking. That pain was nothing compared to the complete and utter ache that dragged me back to consciousness, my mind kicking and screaming in protest the entire way.

I blinked my bleary eyes open and discovered a thick layer of blur covered everything above me. Concussion was my first thought, and I reached up to check the status of my broken head. My fingertips brushed my eyelashes and I realized my glasses were missing, which revealed the source of the blurriness. I fished around me for them but my hands found nothing but cool marble floor in my general vicinity. Slow and cautious I sat up, and the room did a lurching spin around me until it righted itself.

"Glasses," I demanded of no one in particular. One of those multicolored blobs in my field of vision had to be a person.

"Here," Lex said. My glasses were set into my outstretched hand and I put them on. He knelt at my side, and I glared at him. The hall had emptied out, leaving only the three Council members in front of me. Glancing behind me I saw both Portia and Tybalt, their faces grim, and that scared the hell out of me. Then I remembered why I'd been hit with the unholy huge whammy that knocked me out in the first place. I swore a vicious curse and leapt to my feet, rounding on my father who stood silently several feet away with the man in the charcoal suit standing behind him like a shadow. My hand went for the hilt of my sword, and I looked down in surprise when I didn't find it there. Before I could do anything further Lex grabbed my arms and dragged me backwards.

"Calm down," he warned.

"Lemme go!"

"Catherine, no," Portia snapped as she appeared in front of me. The fact that she actually used my first name gave me a moment of pause—Portia'd never done that in the entire time I've known her. I took a deep breath and unclenched my fists.

"Murderer!" I spat at him instead.

"I am not responsible for what happened to your mother," he replied calmly. It was the first time I'd heard my father's voice in eighteen years. Amazing how much he sounded the same.

"Don't give me that bullshit. You let your vamp buddies tear her apart like a piñata, you bastard."

The assembled faeries gasped at the language. Faeries don't swear, or at least they don't approve of the use of "oaths and curses" as they call them. I was too furious to care, and the angrier I am the more horrifying my language becomes. Lex gave my arms a squeeze in silent warning to control myself, but I continued to ignore him.

The memory was still so raw and painful, as though it had happened yesterday instead of over a decade ago. I could still see her broken body on the floor of our living room, her eyes wide and terrified, frozen forever, and still smell the awful stench of blood and death and worse. Fury burned inside me, and the floor beneath my feet trembled with it. There were no streetlights to attack here with my excess power, and that power was looking for somewhere else to escape.

"Lord and Lady, I will make you pay for what you've done." My voice was deadly calm, and as the words left my throat something around me seemed to pop. I knew what I'd done—I'd sworn a vow in a faerie mound, a kinslaying vow no less—and invoked my gods at the same time. I was far too angry to care.

The faeries, however, did care.

"ENOUGH!" The word boomed through the room like a crack of thunder. I felt everyone around me step away as I turned and gave my full attention to the speaker. I knew who she was, even though I'd never met her in person before: Cecelia of the Silver Crescent, a truly stunning sight to behold. A frost fairy like my cousins, she looked as though she had been created from silver and moonlight, with iridescent hair falling almost to the floor and wings that glowed with their own light. Large blue eyes stared at me, disapproving, and I had the good sense to feel guilty under her gaze.

"I think you have interrupted these proceedings quite enough, Mistress Morrow," Cecelia scolded, and I blushed redder than a genetically modified tomato. I would've said I was sorry, but I was certain that opening my mouth would get me zotted into unconsciousness again, and I wasn't sure I'd live through another blast. The faerie folded her silvery hands in her lap and leaned back into her seat, appearing relaxed and unaffected by the fact that I'd been ready to stab the face off my father's head just a few short moments ago.

"Both of you have come here to petition for the open position of liaison between the realm of the Faerie and the Midwestern region of the United States of the realm of Earth. The council will initiate the new liaison during your next full moon. You will be tested during this time to determine your adequacy for the position." Her blasé tone did not make me feel more comfortable, and I was nervous about what they had in mind for testing. It was a good bet I wouldn't need my #2 pencils ready for it.

"Your first test begins now."

I opened my mouth to form the word "Now?" but the floor dropped out from under me and someone blacked the lights out again.

Thankfully this time I was conscious, though the landing might have been more enjoyable if I had been unable to feel it. The breath whooshed out of my lungs as I hit solid ground with a very painful thud. Looking up, I expected to see light shining through the trapdoor that attacked me, but only saw more darkness. I reached down and unsnapped one of the pockets of my cargo pants, blindly grabbing a large hunk of crystal and pulling it free. Holding the lump in my hand, I spoke the incantation to activate the spell stored within it.

The crystal began to glow with a bright white light, surrounding me in a circle of illumination. Sadly there was nothing to see—no walls, no ceiling, no people—just more darkness outside my globe of visibility. I almost called out to ask if anyone was there, but I bit my tongue and decided against it. If there was anyone out there in the black, they probably weren't about to come to my rescue, and were much more likely to try to kill me instead. Holding the crystal aloft, I took a few hesitant steps forward. The floor was rough earth, not the pristine marble of the great hall. Roots from indeterminate plants poked through here and there, and I eyed them, half expecting them to leap to life and attempt to strangle me. When the plants did not become homicidal I continued to walk forward, hoping to reach a wall, or better yet a door.

The silence was eerie, even more so than it had been since first I entered the mound. Tilting my head to the side, I paused and sniffed the air, but everything still reeked of cinnamon and was of no help at all. With a disappointed frown I went back to my slow, cautious walk. Maybe this wouldn't be as difficult as I first thought. Maybe this was just a test to see if I could get myself out of wherever I was, which should be easy enough. All I had to do was leave the faerie realm, and I had the materials to do that on me. I just needed the mirror in my compact and my—

Panicked, I grabbed for my dagger and discovered it was missing, as well as my sword.

"Damn it," I cursed under my breath. Well, I would have to find another way to cut myself then. Something in my many pockets ought to be able to do it.

A slithering, skittering noise interrupted my internal cataloging of my equipment. The strange sound was unfamiliar and startled the hell out of me after all that heavy silence. Whirling around, I searched the darkness, but saw nothing. Nervous, I licked my lips, waving the light around and trying to find the source of the noise, but the darkness remained cold and unmoving. Then again, maybe I wasn't supposed to just find my way out. Maybe I was supposed to find my way out alive after whatever slimy monster out there tried to bite my head off.

I balanced the crystal on the brim of my top hat, giving it a sort of magical coal miner's helmet effect. Centering myself with a deep breath, I felt my shields snap into place with an electric sizzle and a spark of multicolored light. Feeling more secure, I dug through my pockets and produced a matchbook. After a few attempts I managed to get one lit, and I turned myself toward the south (thanks to my magician built-in sense of direction).

*"Light that warms and nurtures life,*
*Pierce the darkness like a knife.*
*Drive back this black unnatural sea,*
*As I will, so mote it be."*

A ball of fire appeared in front of me, growing from the tiny flame at the end of the match into a small sun the size of a basketball that hovered in front of me. Now that I had a decent light source I extinguished the crystal atop my hat and popped it back into its pocket. The warmth of the flames soothed me, and thanks to its light I was finally able to see the room I had dropped into. Like the floor, the walls were rough earth, and the ceiling stretched high above my head. I didn't see my father, which was good because I might've accidentally hurled the ball of fire in front of me in his general direction. He must have been sent to another room, or perhaps a different test. I turned around to examine the rest of my temporary prison, and saw an enormous golden eye staring at me, less than ten feet away from where I stood.

I did what any sensible witch would do in my circumstance. I screamed like a scared little girl.

The eye blinked. Once, twice, and then shifted as the dragon turned its head toward me, regarding me with both golden eyes. "I could have eaten you, you know."

I nodded numbly and stammered, "Thank you for not doing that." I knew dragons existed in Faerie, though I'd never seen one before. Dragons are reclusive as a rule and tend to guard their privacy ferociously, so only the overly brave or overly stupid seek them out on purpose. The creature was huge, taking up a good portion of the room with its bulk. Black scales covered its body, and leathery wings were folded against its back. Smoke puffed out of its nostrils for a moment, and my stomach leapt in panic.

"I only eat virgins though."

I stared at the dragon in disbelief, feeling the inexplicable urge to defend my past sexual history. My mouth worked as I struggled to find an appropriate response, and I thought I saw a glint of humor in its golden gaze.

"Oh," I managed. "Why am I here?"

"Because you wish to be Titania."

"Well, yes, I mean why am I here in this room?"

"Because you wish to be Titania."

"Right..." I suppose I should have expected that and just been grateful it wasn't picking bits of Catherine out of its teeth. Turning around, I surveyed the room again, seeing no obvious exit or entrance. "How did you get in here?"

"The same way you did." The dragon laid its head upon the ground, its tail swishing forward to cover its nose, reminding me of a dog curling up against the cold. I couldn't imagine why the council would have abducted a dragon to stick in the room with me if it had no intention of eating me, and no intention of helping me either.

"Can you leave?" I asked, curious. Dragons were magical beings, but I really didn't know the extent of their magical abilities. Maybe it couldn't teleport, as faeries could, and relied on those leathery wings for transportation when faeries used theirs more as a fashion statement.

"No." It sighed and smoke puffed out from its snout in a great huff, which made me jump. "And I'm missing *Jeopardy!*. It's celebrity week, you know."

"Yeah, Sean Connery's on today too." The absurdity of that statement hit me for a moment and I shook my head. My day was just getting more bizarre by the moment. "Would you like me to help you leave?"

The dragon raised a brow, its expression quizzical. "Can you do that?"

"Umm...maybe?" I guessed. Could I? Sure, I could get myself out of the room by returning home, but I couldn't bring the dragon into my apartment. Aside from the obvious fact that it was bigger than my entire apartment building, dragons are very specifically forbidden from traveling into the human world and have been for several centuries. That's why dragons are known to hoard human loot stolen by other faeries. I couldn't leave the dragon here alone in good conscience, not after it'd been nice enough not to eat me or roast me to a toasty Cat crisp. There had to be a way to do it.

I could try opening a portal to elsewhere in Faerie. I'd never tried anything like it before, but I figured it was hypothetically possible. On Earth you couldn't use a mirror to go from one place to another, only from Earth to another world. There weren't any concrete answers as to why that was, but the general thinking was that Earth simply doesn't have the magic in it to support that sort of travel anymore. Centuries ago a magician didn't even need a pre-made portal like a mirror to world walk, they could use almost anything as a gateway, especially mist or water. Faerie didn't suffer from that problem though; Faerie *was* magic. I should be able to get us from the room to somewhere safer, somewhere I was very familiar with. It was worth a shot, if nothing else.

"Where would you like to go?" I asked after a few minutes. "Does it matter to you if you end up somewhere else in Faerie?"

It shrugged its scaly shoulders. "I can get home from anywhere after I'm out of here."

"Right then. Not a problem." I rubbed my hands together, but then paused. "Well, one more question: Can you shrink? Change your shape at all?"

"No." I could have sworn it frowned at me.

"Bugger," I muttered. "No worries, still doable. Just a li'l more difficult." I did my best to sound much more confident than I felt, because honestly I wasn't sure I could pull this sort of magic off. To get the dragon through the portal I'd have to stretch the edges of the gateway. It was possible in theory, but I'd never attempted anything like it before. I could stretch the glass to fit myself no problem, just needed a bit of blood, but the dragon was huge.

Shaking the doubt off, I squared my shoulders and dropped my shields. As hoped, the dragon stayed where it was and did not attempt to eat me while I was vulnerable. Like it said, it could have eaten me when I first appeared and was stumbling around in the dark, so I just had to trust it wasn't hostile toward me. Digging into the recesses of my memory, I recalled that despite the stories, dragons didn't really eat people, and preferred livestock. Hey, unless you're Hannibal Lecter, wouldn't you pick a steak over the guy down the street?

From my right-hand pocket I pulled out my compact and opened it, setting it down on the ground in front of me with the mirror facing up. I frowned down at my hand, wondering how I was going to cut it open without my ritual dagger, and I glanced up at the dragon who watched me with much curiosity.

"May I borrow the use of one of your teeth, please?"

It blinked, and then chuckled, the noise a deep rumbling that made the ground beneath my boots vibrate. "Of course," it answered with equal civility.

Images of rednecks getting their hands bitten off after

putting them in the mouths of alligators filled my head as I approached the dragon. The beast could swallow me in a few tasty bites if it had a mind to, and I felt a trickle of nervous sweat slip down my spine. It opened its mouth wide as I stepped near, and I stared in amazement at the sharp, dagger-like teeth. Terrifying to behold, but just what I needed. To my credit my arm only shook a little as I reached into the dragon's mouth and drew my palm across one of its incisors. I whipped my palm over to prevent any blood from dripping into the dragon's mouth—just in case—and then trotted back to my compact. Squeezing my hand into a fist, I let several drops of blood fall onto the surface of the tiny mirror and then placed the tip of my index finger against the glass.

*"Winter's bite and moonlit snow,*
*To the land of frost let us go.*
*Castle Silverleaf let me see,*
*As I will, so mote it be."*

Closing my eyes, I formed an image in my mind. A castle surrounded by light gray stone walls, slender towers that stretched toward a pale blue sky dotted with thin white clouds, dark blue banners that snapped in the stinging wind. Familiar strains of music carried on that wind, as well as the sounds of voices lifted in song, laughter and conversation. A forest of barren, snow-dusted trees stretched to the north of the walls, and a frozen river ringed the castle like a moat. I opened my eyes and saw the image in the mirror, each minute detail just as I pictured it.

Rubbing my hands together, I smeared them with warm, slick blood. I reached down and brushed the edges of the image with the tips of my fingers, and taking a deep breath, I tugged them outwards. A sharp crack sounded as the plastic backing shattered, but the image expanded. With painstaking care I drew the edges of the mirror farther and farther out, stretching it like a piece of uncooperative dough across a cutting board. Blood continued to flow from the wound, and I used it to refresh the coating on my hands. All magic is based in blood, and my blood is strong. This, however, required a lot more blood than I was used to.

As I worked I lost track of time, focused on the task before me until finally the mirror that had once been small enough to fit in my pocket took up a space large enough to (I hoped) fit a dragon through. Standing up straight, I wavered a bit on my feet, lightheaded, and turned to my captive audience.

"Well, what do you think?"

The dragon studied the mirror. "Impressive."

"After you," I said, sweeping my arm out in an invitation. The dragon crept over to the image, standing at its edge as though it were a pond the beast was deciding to dive into. Its muscles bunched, and with a graceful leap the dragon sailed into the mirror and through it. Before the magic could fade I leapt through and found myself standing in a snowbank up to my knees, staring at the castle in the distance.

A shadow passed over me as the dragon flew away, a black silhouette against the afternoon sky. "Thank you!" it called out as it whooshed toward the horizon.

"You're welcome," I shouted after it. I held my hand above my eyes to block out the sun and suddenly remembered the cut I'd left open and bleeding all this time. "Uh-oh."

Frantic, I tried to direct the cut to close itself, something I'm normally quite good at, but it stubbornly refused. I realized there was something wrong with my legs as well as they wobbled beneath me. My traitorous body was not letting me enjoy my victory, and a queasy lightheadedness washed over me before the world went black for the second time that day.

# Chapter Four

I awoke by degrees, lost in a sea of hazy dreams and nightmares that vanished as quickly as they appeared. I saw myself as a girl running through a forest and giggling madly as I chased after the white, winged figure that darted between the bare trees in front of me. I heard the cool crunch of snow beneath my boots and felt the occasional glimpse of faint winter sunlight on my face as it peeked through the gray clouds above. *You can't catch me, Kitty-kitty!*

Then I saw the front door of my childhood home. I reached to open it, my hand small and smudged with dirt, and the knob turned easily in my grasp. As the door swung open I heard shouting, strange angry words, and it frightened me down to my core. I crept through the house back to the kitchen, everything around me now seeming sinister in the late-afternoon light. I paused as I passed the bedrooms, surprised to see two suitcases on the floor in front of my parents' room. I hid behind the open basement door, sitting on the top step and making myself as small as possible as I listened to the voices. My father was yelling, my mother was weeping, begging him not to leave.

The dream changed, twisted. I was older. I opened the door of my home and found quiet, an awful silence. I stepped inside and turned to my left, looking into the living room. The smell hit me, the pungent, poignant stench of death. My mother's body lay on the floor, tiny pools of her blood staining the carpet, her face pale like I'd never seen it before and twisted into a mask of terror and agony. Those lifeless eyes stared at me, pleading, warning. Home was no longer safe—her killers had been invited in. Invited by my father, to tear my mother apart and feast on the strong magic in her blood.

Fleeing the dream, my eyes blinked open to stare at the ceiling of my bedroom. I lay crumpled on the floor in front of my mirror, the scent of dried blood and faded cinnamon filling my nostrils. I pushed myself into a sitting position and surveyed my surroundings. My top hat had rolled off and was tipped on its side just out of reach. My unbound hair hung in dirty strings, and I absently pushed it out of the way. As my hand passed in front of my face I was startled by the dark, crispy coating of dried blood that stained it, and then I remembered how I'd stretched the mirror in the earthen room beneath the faerie mound.

"Out, out, damned spot," I muttered, my voice dry and raspy in my throat. Shaking my head, I glanced at the alarm clock on my nightstand and was surprised that it read a little after four. I really hoped it was the following morning and I hadn't missed any days during my misadventure in Faerie. It was entirely possible, considering I felt like I'd been run over by a truck. Stumbling to my feet, I wobbled over to the door and opened it. Spots danced in front of my eyes as a warning that I needed to consume mass quantities of coffee and pancakes, and soon. First I wanted to check the date, so I continued on into my living room and flopped down into my desk chair. I slapped my mouse to wake up my computer, raining flakes of dried blood onto the mouse pad in the process, and waited as the screen took its own sweet time to wake up.

At long last I was able to confirm the date: June 29th, and a refreshing 4:36 a.m. Lovely. At least I hadn't lost any days, just hours. For a few moments I sat in the chair and debated the pluses and minuses of showering first versus eating first. The shower sounded very appealing—I felt like hell, gritty and grungy like I'd been dragged through the mud. Eventually I settled on the shower in order to save myself the time and effort it would take to clean the blood trail I'd leave behind in the kitchen. I only caught myself losing my balance twice and managed to hold onto consciousness the entire time.

Go me.

Dressed in my fuzzy purple bathrobe and matching slippers, I puttered about in the kitchen, fixing my "Huzzah for survival" feast. Instead of coffee I forced myself to brew a strong herbal tea, one I knew had healing properties in it. As usual I decided to comfort myself through the cunning use of fattening food—cheesy scrambled eggs, sausage links and chocolate chip pancakes. And, most importantly, nothing that included cinnamon, which was how I realized I was no longer alone in my apartment when the scent of it wafted down the hallway halfway through my meal. I stared down at my eggs, and decided I was too tired to get up and go to her.

"Portia, it's still too early for the game show," I called out.

A cry of childish disappointment answered me, followed by the pitter-patter of little combat-booted feet. I was vaguely surprised to see Tybalt following behind his sister, as he rarely made an effort to travel to the human realm.

"She said it isn't on," he reminded her.

"It is too on, there's an entire channel of the game show, the guide says so!" Portia waved a copy of this week's *TV Guide* in Tybalt's face to punctuate her point.

"There's more than one kind of game show, hon." Scooping up a forkful of pancakes, I watched her mull that development over while I chewed. Rolling his eyes, Tybalt walked farther into the kitchen and plunked my sword and dagger down on the counter. A wave of relief washed over me at the sight of them—it would have been a serious pain in the ass to buy new ones. Good swords are hard to find, and run damn expensive.

"Do they all give away new cars?" Portia asked.

"No. Some of them do. *Wheel of Fortune* does sometimes." I shrugged, and her eyes widened at the idea.

"There is a game show about the Wheel of Fortune?"

Aside from being associated with Pat and Vanna, the big Wheel is a member of the major arcana of the Tarot deck. Not one of the cards I particularly relate to, but still, something amusing to keep in mind next time you watch someone buy a vowel.

"Is it on now?" she asked, thrusting the *TV Guide* at me.

"Answers first, game shows second." Leaning back in my chair, I took a long gulp of tea. Tybalt took the opportunity to hop up and perch on the corner of my stove, which looked very strange considering he has no wings. He had the ability to wear wings, but I once heard him comment that wings got in the way during a fight.

If I didn't know Tybalt and Portia were related, I wouldn't have been able to figure it out by looking at them, because there's little physical resemblance between the two faeries (or at least there isn't when they're in the forms I typically see them in). The only common feature is the white hair, but Tybalt's hung wild and shaggy around his face unlike his sister's long, glossy waves. While Portia's eyes are deep blue, her brother's eyes are pale green, the color of spring leaves. His wardrobe is what one would expect of a faerie, a more traditional combination of a tunic, tough leather leggings and sturdy calf-high boots. And unlike Portia, who doesn't look like she could swat a fly, Tybalt is never without a weapon, mainly his rapier.

"Okay. First, did I pass the test? Wait, no, first, what the hell was my father doing there? He can't be Oberon, he's a damn necromancer," I spat. "And why weren't there any other candidates?"

"Cat, there's no law that says a necromancer can't do it," Tybalt explained. "It's just never happened before."

"Never? As in never, ever? In the whole history of Faerie?"

"Never. And from what we've been able to tell, the other possible candidates were...discouraged from applying."

"Discouraged, huh?" That couldn't be good. I also wasn't comfortable with the fact that this had never happened before. Never was a word with real impact when used by a race that is essentially immortal. I hesitate from saying completely immortal, because they aren't. Faeries can be killed, it's just hard to do. They do age, but at a rate that's so slow that I don't think one has ever died from old age. They're immune to all diseases, and their blood is pure magic. One hundred percent Grade A magic, not the watered-down variety we humans have, which is why vamps have no use for faeries. Though vampires need blood containing magic to survive, and the stronger the better, when a vamp feeds from a faerie the results are explosive. Literally. The overload fries the vamp's brain and *poof!* Instant death. Real death too, not the corrupted undeath they exist with. I'd pay good money to see that.

"Correct me if I'm wrong, but vamps still can't travel to Faerie, right?" I asked, confused.

"Right." Tybalt nodded. "They can't travel to anyplace decent."

Nodding, I stabbed another forkful of pancakes. The doors were closed to vampires because the Higher Powers (whatever you want to call them) consider vampirism such a terrible crime against nature that they don't want it to infect any other world.

Necromancers can still use the doorways—because they're technically not vampires yet—but necros really aren't welcome anywhere. Most faerie clans remove necromancers from their territory with extreme prejudice.

"Hmm. So, essentially the vamps are making a play for political power with a race who won't talk to them, and that live in a place they can't get to. That makes zero sense. And why now? Something must have changed... Hey, so did I pass? Fail? The heck kind of test was that anyway? One of those 'can you think on your feet' deals?"

I speared some eggs next. Left to her own devices, Portia began poking through my kitchen cabinets, looking for a snack.

"First, tell us what happened to you." Tybalt raised a curious brow. "There's been no official report on the results of the first test."

"Was weird. I got dropped into this room with no lights at all, and I stumbled around for a bit. Tried my glowstone, but it wasn't strong enough, so I put up my shields and conjured a bit of sunlight. When the room was lit I saw this enormous dragon behind me, just watching me. Why didn't you tell me dragons could talk, by the way?"

"Sure they can talk, getting them to shut up again is the hard part." Portia snorted. Fluttering up to reach the top shelf, she pulled down a bag of cookies and shoved her greedy little hand inside. The faerie munched on a chocolate chip cookie, raining crumbs and dust onto my kitchen floor, as usual.

"Good to know. So yeah, it said it wouldn't eat me, and we talked a bit. I figured out it was stuck too, so I opened a portal to just outside Silverleaf and we popped right through. It thanked me and flew off, and the next thing I know I'm back here again." I did my best to sound nonchalant about the stunning display of magic I'd pulled off. Sure it was an enormous achievement for me, but faeries can manage that sort of stuff practically from the cradle, and wouldn't be nearly as impressed with myself as I was. The two faeries digested this information as I polished off my breakfast. Even with the food as fuel I still felt drained from my adventure, and figured it'd take most of the day to recharge my magical batteries at this rate.

"I guess that explains how Dorian ended up burnt," Tybalt said.

"Burnt?"

He nodded. "Aye, we have some people keeping an eye on him. When he appeared back at home he had some wicked burns—he must've decided to fight the dragon instead of helping it."

"Why would he fight it?" As I pointed out before, dragons aren't evil, they just...are. I doubted the other dragon would have found Dorian any more palatable than my dragon found me. Tybalt shrugged, and Portia continued to devour cookies as she moved to perch on the edge of my sink. "I guess he went with a 'shoot first, ask questions later' plan. So what happens next?"

"Don't know that either," Portia piped up. "More tests are planned, but so far we have no information of what and when. You did good though, we're proud of you."

I couldn't help but smile at her praise, even if it was spoken through a mouthful of half-chewed chocolate chip cookie. I wasn't entirely sure what happened, if I passed, failed or avoided whatever intended outcome the Council had. All I knew was that I was alive, and apparently still in the running for Titania. I'd better damn well win, too, 'cause there was no way I'd let my father become Oberon.

"Are you speaking to the guardian again?" Tybalt asked.

I blinked at him, surprised. "Not willingly, no. I wasn't expecting him to be there. Or to show up at the café last night."

"I can make sure he stays away from you, if you like." There was tension in his shoulders, and his hand drifted toward his rapier. I smiled inwardly. Tybalt was the closest thing I had to an overprotective big brother.

"Hmm, I'll keep that in mind." It was a tempting offer. I wasn't sure I could deal with the distraction of seeing Lex with the rest of the drama going on.

After my victory feast, the morning settled into a sense of normalcy, or at least it was normal for me. The faeries kept me company, entertaining me until it was time to get ready for my shift at work. Though I could take the day off, the sad truth is a few sick days begin to cut into my small savings and paying the bills gets a bit difficult. Tybalt wanted to go with me, and I decided that with a color and costume change he would fit in well enough. Tybalt's disguise made him look like the world's palest surfer, with lanky white-blond hair and enormous aviator sunglasses, but it worked. Portia, on the other hand, I wasn't about to trust in the café. Promising her I would do my best to be careful and watchful for danger, I convinced her to go home.

The café had a decent amount of customers when we arrived, despite the fact that it was the lull between breakfast and lunch. I set Tybalt up in a booth with a plate full of pancakes and a *Chicago Tribune,* and then hoped for the best. Squaring my shoulders, I pasted my friendly customer-service smile on my face and began my shift. My section kept me too busy to worry about silly details like the fate of magician/faerie relations throughout the Midwest. As closing approached, we had only three customers left in the café: a young newlywed couple who were regulars seated in my section, and Lex, who'd snuck in at some point and was sitting drinking a cup of coffee over in Maria's section. She'd left early, of course, and I'd been ignoring him in the hope he'd leave, but he seemed determined to stay. Annoyed, I stopped at his table, coffee carafe in hand.

"Want me to warm that up for you?" I asked politely. I couldn't tell him off while I was on duty. It'd be unprofessional.

"Sure, go right ahead," he drawled, smiling slightly. I resisted the urge to pour the coffee into his lap and refilled his cup.

"What are you doing here?"

"Well, I was considerin' havin' some pie with my coffee." There was amusement in those dreamy light blue eyes of his, and I frowned. To my credit, I swallowed my temper and dutifully listed off the pies we had left. He picked apple. How all-American.

I disappeared into the back and Tybalt immediately knew something was wrong. He appeared at my side as I stabbed an innocent pie with a knife that was much too large for the job.

"Lex is in the dining room. Again."

"I can't kill him, we're on neutral ground," Tybalt apologized, and I laughed.

"That's true."

"I can spit in his food."

"No, thank you. Feel free to threaten him though."

After venting a little aggression on the pie, I set a non-mangled piece on a plate and carried it into the dining room. Tybalt followed and took the seat across from Lex as I delivered his slice of pie. Without a word I left them alone and headed back to my section to chat for a bit with the newlyweds, who caught me up on the neighborhood gossip. Apparently the city was still investigating the source of a power surge which had blown out the streetlights up and down Main. Oops. Well, that'd teach me for losing my temper. Finally I shooed them outside and began cleaning up their table. As I headed for the kitchen with their dishes I spotted Mac speaking with Lex and Tybalt, and I knew no good would come of that. When I returned to the dining room Mac was in the process of dimming the lights after flipping the sign in our window to "Closed".

"Something you want to share with me, Cat?" Mac asked from the other end of the room.

Hovering in the doorway, I looked pointedly in the direction of the guardian before turning toward my boss. "With you, sure."

Lex chuckled, and I glared at him. Those light blue eyes studied me over the rim of his coffee cup, and I felt something twist low in my gut, something that was certainly not the nervous flutter I'd been suffering from lately. Silently I berated myself for still being attracted to him. I knew better than to get giggly over a man who'd more than proved I couldn't trust him.

I marched over to his table and stared down at him, and he watched me with quiet curiosity. The unmistakable scent of magic wafted up from Lex, the odd mix I'd come to associate with him. A hint of cinnamon marked him as having faerie blood like myself, which could have indicated anything from witch to necromancer, but he was thankfully lacking in the awful rotting stench that clings to necros. There was a bit of the floral scent I associate with witchcraft, but there was also the musk of a shapeshifter and the sharp alcoholic tang of an alchemist—none of which should be found all together. Magicians don't mix and match their abilities—you're generally born to what you become—but guardians seem to have a bit of everything.

Guardians are essentially the magic police, but they're also like the border patrol too. Any otherworldly beings who decide to vacation in the human world and aren't supposed to—imps, goblins, demons, that sort of thing—get evicted by guardians. If a dragon decided to fly through downtown Chicago, it'd be a guardian's job to escort it back to Faerie, with extreme prejudice if need be. Just one of their many, many responsibilities. They are overworked, but not underpaid. The Higher Powers made sure guardians want for very little.

Placing my hands on my hips, I eyed him. "Why are you here?"

"You."

"Oh, be still my heart." Rolling my eyes, I dropped into the seat across from him and sat next to Tybalt. "To what do I owe the honor this time? Not under arrest, am I? Don't you have to at least let me commit the crime first?"

"You shouldn't have threatened Dorian, Cat," Lex replied.

"She wouldn't have to if the guardians had done their job and punished him for her mother's death," Tybalt countered.

"There wasn't enough evidence to prove that he was involved."

"There was enough for us, but your brethren wouldn't let us avenge Julia's death. There was no honor in that."

"I know, you're right," Lex agreed, holding his hands up in a placating gesture. "Look, I'm not here to arrest you. I'm here to protect you."

"Protect her from what?" Mac asked, startled. He crossed the room and stood at the end of the booth, hovering over us. Lex leaned back into his seat and set his empty cup on the table. I reached into the pocket of my apron and pulled out my cigarettes—I had a feeling I was going to need them.

"Well to begin with, when I found out Maureen didn't have an heir, I started looking into who would step up as possible candidates. Imagine my surprise when your daddy, good ol' Dorian, put his hat in the ring. Now, personally, I don't want to work with Dorian, and I really don't want to work with the woman who holds his leash, which is why I have a vested interest in your health. And someone has to make sure you live long enough to take the tests, because it's bad form to kill a competitor between rounds."

"Glad to hear you're so concerned about my welfare," I said, lighting a smoke. "So where were you when I was stuck in a room with a dragon last night?"

"Dragons aren't your problem now."

"No?"

"Nope. The necromancer council put a price on your head. They want you dead in a bad way. In fact, there's two vamps across the street right now, waiting for you to step outside neutral ground."

# Chapter Five

Just when I thought my day couldn't get any worse. This had to be part of the test, because it was certainly testing my patience, if not my sanity.

"There are two vampires outside, and they are here to kill me," I repeated numbly.

"Actually, there are five vampires outside, only two of them are across the street," Lex corrected, shrugging. "And they sure aren't here for the pie, fantastic though it might be." His nonchalance about my imminent demise was just a tad bit off-putting.

"Great, just great. Now what do we do?" I mumbled around the cigarette, fighting with my cheap lighter as it refused to light.

"Easy, we kill them first," Tybalt said matter-of-factly. "Five vampires should be no problem at all."

"You don't think that's a little extreme?"

"No. Those witches poisoned your mind with that 'do no harm' nonsense. You need to listen to your inner faerie more," Tybalt advised. "If anybody tries to kill you, you're allowed to kill them back."

"Geez, Tybalt." I'd forgotten how bloodthirsty faeries could be, because my cousins always seem so innocent with their game-show fascination and addiction to sweets.

"That's exactly why witches are the smallest percentage of the magician population," Mac intoned.

"No shit, Sherlock." Sad, but true, and I knew just how pathetic that fact was. Back in the olden days when hunters showed up to purge a town of magical influence, witches always held fast to their oath to harm none and refused to fight back.

Better a martyr than a murderer, in their opinion—which of course was the very reason I'd been outcast.

Even though I wasn't ready to throw in the towel and let the vamps get me just yet, I wasn't ready to let Tybalt dash outside and slay them all either. There had to be a better way, a plan that would allow me to get around them with no killing involved, even if they more than likely deserved it. Life is a cycle, a great wheel that turns throughout time: we are born, we live, we die, and (if we are lucky) we are reborn again. Vampires take themselves out of nature's cycle, jamming a hypothetical spike in the spokes to stop the wheel from turning. Their souls are tied to a body stuck in a sort of suspended animation, fueled by the blood of living magicians, and all the while gathering up more bad karma. I don't know much about the underworld—the place where the restless dead reside—but I do know horrible things happen to vampires when they die. The things your worst nightmares are made of.

Becoming a vampire doesn't make a person evil. They become one because they already are. And now every vamp in the tri-state area was gunning for me. Great.

"So, what's the plan?"

"When you're ready, I walk you home."

"That's it?" Sounded too simple to be true.

"That's it." Lex nodded. The man was as blasé about the subject as though there were angry Chihuahuas outside planning to nip at my ankles, instead of a posse of vampires waiting to turn me into a magical piñata.

"Huh. Well I guess I better finish cleaning up then." I slid out of the booth, and Mac looked at me, sadness in his eyes. His expression alone nearly broke my heart, and I swallowed the lump that suddenly formed in my throat.

"You don't have to clean up, Cat. I can handle it," Mac offered.

I did my best to give him an encouraging smile and shook my head. "I've seen you clean. It's better if I do it. Won't take me very long. Just give me a few minutes. Do you want more coffee while you wait?" I asked Lex, in my very best customer-service-first voice.

"Sure, Cat." He smiled, and I looked to my cousin.

"Okay. Tybalt, get Lex coffee."

I turned and walked away. Mac coughed, sounding as

though he was swallowing a laugh, and I picked up a half-full bin of dirty dishes. Hefting the weight, I headed back into the kitchen, and Mac followed. I set the bin next to the sink and started to empty it.

"Of all the cafés in all the world, he walks into mine. Again."

"Well, at least he's one of the best," Mac said. "He comes from a long line of guardians. There's Duquesnes across the whole country."

"Yeah, I know." I began placing dishes into the washer. I'd only met one member of Lex's family, but I'd heard a bit about the rest of them. Besides, I didn't need to know about his family history to know the Duquesnes were model guardians—Lex'd already proved that one when he'd turned me in to the witches' council. Takes a special kind of devotion to duty to turn your girlfriend over to the firing squad.

"Exactly what did you do to piss the vamps off this badly?"

"Oh, a little of this, little of that." I waved a hand dismissively. "Swore vengeance on my father in a faerie mound while invoking the Lord and Lady."

Mac snorted in amusement. "Nice one, Cat."

"I'm nothing if not creative."

I headed out to the dining room and went about the rest of my routine—clearing, cleaning and getting the café back to its pristine glory. While concentrating on the music playing through the overhead speakers, I almost managed to ignore the guardian drinking coffee and the certain death that waited outside, lurking in the shadows my own stupidity had caused when I'd blown out the streetlights. See what losing your temper gets you, kiddies?

As I worked I hummed along with the music until I recognized the song—"This Kiss" by Faith Hill. I stopped so suddenly I nearly tripped over my own feet, and then ignored the guardian's stifled chuckle as I tried to regain my dignity. With a full bin of dishes I retreated into the safety of the kitchen, and when I returned I found Lex and Tybalt enthralled with their battle plans. I almost felt bad for the vampires outside. Almost.

Despite being distracted by his discussion, I felt Lex's eyes on me as I moved through the room. Usually men only watch me when they're wondering where their order is, or if they want their check. I assumed Lex was trying to gauge how useful I'd be in a fight, which is not much. Sure, I own a sword and a few knives, but they are forbidden from drawing anyone's blood but my own (and really, I didn't want to be encouraging my own blood loss in the middle of a fight). I also have been through a few self-defense training courses, but that knowledge would do jack against a vampire. They're just about indestructible, as long as they're well fed. Stab 'em, they keep on coming. Shoot them. Run them over with a car. Drop an anvil on their head.

Okay maybe not the anvil, but as long as their heart isn't completely destroyed or their head severed, vampires just keep coming back for more. It's really damn unfair, and the horror-film solutions for vamp slaying don't do a damn thing. Garlic? Uh, no. Silver? Please, they drape themselves in it since it looks so wonderful with their all-black wardrobes. Sunlight? Unless they get burned red like a tomato with fangs, it's not going to slow them down much. Which leaves us with wooden stakes. Really, any kind of stake (not steak, stake, the difference is important) would work if you managed to totally obliterate the heart in one shot. The tough part is hitting that one shot right on, and the wood does help if you're looking for a lovely splintering effect to do maximum damage.

In short, if you should find yourself in a fight against a vampire, you are really right and proper fucked.

The thought was less than comforting to me.

When my tasks were finished I popped into Mac's office to say goodbye. He did his best to look encouraging as he gave me a hug and a quick peck on the cheek.

"Blessed be, Cat."

"Thanks, Mac. Are you still leaving tomorrow for the conference in D.C.?" There was a big librarian get-together he was going to. I wasn't sure what librarians did when they had a conference. Maybe they all sat in the same room and read spellbooks, or had lectures on the finer points of casting anti-dust wards.

"Yeah."

"Have a good trip and a safe flight. Maybe I'll already be Titania by the time you get back," I joked.

"Maybe. I can get you a snow globe of the White House as a congrats gift," he offered.

"Sure." I smiled. "Love you, hon."

"Love you too. Good luck."

I headed back into the dining room. "I'm ready," I proclaimed, and Lex nodded. "So, what's the plan?"

"I doubt they'll leave quietly, so Tybalt and I are goin' to convince them to let us alone. After they've lost a few limbs they'll get the message and clear out."

I wrinkled my nose at the thought of severed dead-people parts.

"Are you sure we can't just kill them?" Tybalt asked, sounding disappointed.

"Nah, that'd just end up in too much paperwork." Lex shook his head and slid out of the booth. I'd forgotten how tall he was. I'm on the tallish side, so I don't encounter a lot of people taller than me. He was wearing all black as usual, from his steel-toed boots to his jeans to his plain cotton T-shirt and long duster. No one wears a jacket in June in Illinois unless we're experiencing one of our more freakish weather patterns, so I was willing to bet there was more than muscular arms and a tight butt under that duster.

I scolded myself for wondering about the state of Lex's posterior and then shrugged. "Anything else I need to know?"

"Nope. When we step outside, you shield yourself and don't distract us."

"That's it?"

"That's it."

"Great." Excellent plan. It was simple, easy to remember. Probably stupid as all get out, but hey, he's the professional, right? I'm just the target. "Sure you don't want to duck out the back?"

"They won't learn anything that way. Don't worry, you'll be fine."

"Right." I motioned toward the door. "After you, gentlemen."

Squeezing my eyes shut, I hugged my arms to my chest as my shields snapped into place. It was a globe of safety that moved with me, but also made it harder to maneuver, like walking through water. I did my best not to be terrified out of my wits as I walked through the door of the Three Willows. There were no less than five vampires out there waiting for me in the dark, ready to tear me apart and bleed me dry, just as they had my mother and Maureen, two women who were by all accounts much stronger and more knowledgeable about their arts than I. The door shut behind me, and I shivered with fear. I was outside neutral ground. I was fair game.

"C'mon, let's go," Lex said. I obeyed, following behind him. He turned in the direction of my apartment, thankfully, and I hurried to keep up. It's damn hard to move and shield at the same time, and because it takes a lot of concentration it slowed me down.

The silence frightened me the most. A Saturday night in the city should be louder, full of urban noises like cars and cell phones and televisions, but here there was nothing, not even the rumble of an approaching train on the tracks. A slight breeze brushed my face and I caught the scent of vampire magic. It's a peculiar but memorable scent, the smell of the last dying ember clinging to a candle's wick, refusing to be snuffed. Really, that's all vampires are, that last spark of life clinging like hell to this world, terrified to give in to what lies beyond. I knew that smell all too well, remembering how it had mixed with the fear and death in my mother's house, and I panicked. Something squealed high and hideous just out of arm's length, and I turned as a small, skinny woman recoiled away from me, her pale hands smoking where they had touched my shield. Glaring at me from beneath her black bangs, she hissed and snarled something that was either incoherent or a completely foreign language, possibly both, and launched herself at me again. The woman bounced off my shield and was thrown backwards like she'd leapt onto a trampoline, a much louder electric sizzle scorching the air.

"Not real bright, are ya?" I smirked, suddenly feeling much braver than I had any right to be. A small crowd of vampires circled around us, and a quick count revealed a few more than we'd expected, nine attackers in total.

"They really aren't the smartest breed, cousin," Tybalt commented. The faerie brushed his disguised white-blond hair out of his face and eyed the mob.

"Settle down now," Lex warned them. "This woman is under my protection, so you'd better head on home."

"You said there were only five."

"There are," he replied. "The rest are just necromancers."

"Oh great, I feel so much better now."

"Go on, get out of here," the guardian repeated to the crowd, as though scolding a disobedient puppy. They ignored him.

"Step aside, Duquesne, you have no business here," said the vamp who'd bounced off my shields. The overly goth outfit she wore made me wonder if the vampires had lowered their standards for membership. She would blend in perfectly with the late-night Denny's crowd. It was damn hard to take her seriously.

"Now, Merrideth, I just told you that this young lady is under my protection, so if you and your people don't turn around and walk away, we're going to have a problem." Lex slipped his hands into his duster, reaching for whatever weapons he had concealed beneath it and sending a clear message to the crowd that he meant business.

"Maybe I should kill one, Duquesne, just to set an example," Tybalt suggested.

"Don't even think about it, Silverleaf. Just cut 'em off at the knees, that's always fun."

Apparently they took offense to that idea, and without another word they attacked, moving in a dark blur that was hard to see. As the vampires swarmed him Lex drew his weapons in a quick flash of bright metal, swinging a short sword in each hand. Guess that answered the question of why wear a long black coat in June, because swords were a tad hard to conceal without it. The guardian moved with inhuman speed as the fight boiled into the street. I couldn't spot how he was wounding them, but I smelled the stale scent of vampire blood in the humid night air.

Tybalt's rapier appeared in his hand and his clever human disguise vanished as he abandoned all pretense of hiding his true nature. The vampires around him hissed in surprise, and he launched himself at them, moving in a dark blue blur I couldn't follow. I felt pretty useless inside of my safe little bubble, but there wasn't anything I could do to help. I wasn't trained as a fighter, and thanks to my witch upbringing I didn't know any offensive spells. Best I could do was hurl harsh language.

A vampire fell away from the fray in the street, stumbling and then scrambling about searching for something on the ground. After a moment I realized it was looking for the rest of the severed arm that had rolled under a parked car. My stomach heaved and I swallowed hard, looking down at my feet and trying to shove that image out of my brain.

"C'mon now, that had to hurt," Lex teased the armless vamp. "Why don't you just take your hand and go home?"

"Only a flesh wound," the vampire growled as it stretched to reach beneath the car.

Like the worst part of a horror film, it was morbidly fascinating, and I couldn't help but watch. They were stronger, faster and outnumbered him, but somehow Lex held his own. While the vampires were slashed and bleeding, the guardian didn't have a scratch on him. Yet.

"Come out and play, little Cat," a new voice crooned. Turning my attention away from the fight, I found four strangers pacing around the edge of my shields. Necromancers, from the awful smell of them. They circled me like hungry sharks, searching for a weak spot in my shields. Yeah, good luck there. It'd take a lot more than four necromancers to get through my shields, as long as I stood still and concentrated. Unfortunately I couldn't stand there all night, and it'd be a real long walk to my apartment with them trying to sabotage me the entire way. Not a happy thought.

"No thanks, I like it here."

"What's wrong? Afraid?"

Oh, please. Like that was going to tempt me into throwing a temper tantrum and let them jump me. I wasn't falling for that lame trick. I put my hands on my hips and smiled again, more confident this time as I glanced over the speaker. Another sad fashion disaster dressed in black from head to toe, the necromancer reminded me of one of the many reasons why I hate the goth trend: it was created and nurtured by vampires. The woman wore a ridiculous getup of black lace and vinyl complete with spider-web hose and a corset top, doing her best to look dark and mysterious. She'd make a fabulous vampire stereotype when they killed her.

"I'm real scared of that outfit. Was there a sale at Hot Topic?"

Apparently I hit a nerve and she snarled at me. I opened my mouth to toss another witty insult at her, but was interrupted by a distinctly male sound of pain cutting through the tumultuous noise of the fight, too deep to be a faerie's voice. My panic level rose as I smelled the scent of strong magical blood. Lex had fallen to one knee.

Charging into the fray, I rushed to Lex's side. My shields bent perilously inward for a heartbeat before rebounding and hurling vampires out of the way like undead bowling pins. When I reached him my shield stretched and enveloped Lex. My brain paused for a heartbeat to wonder about that bizarre detail, because really it should've bounced him out of the way as well since I hadn't had the good sense to drop them before reaching his side. Deciding to ponder that later, I focused on the set of claw marks slashed across his midsection as I hauled him to his feet.

"This qualifies as distracting me," he growled in annoyance.

"What? You're hurt, you need help."

"Barely a scratch. Ol' no thumbs there, now he needs a medic." He nodded at a nearby vampire who was indeed missing his thumbs and most of his fingers, which were scattered around his feet like fat, pale worms.

My stomach bolted up near the back of my throat and I realized we were in trouble, because I was sure I couldn't shield and retch at the same time. "I think we should let him set an example." I nodded at the faerie-sized blur darting in and out of the mob.

"No, we're not, and I was doin' fine on my own."

"We need a new plan." Poking at his wound, I tried to gauge how severe the damage was, accidentally coating my fingers with his blood in the process.

"Had to call a guardian and your pixie buddy, eh witch? Not strong enough to defend yourself," another new voice commented. I spun around to watch in morbid fascination as the limb-impaired vamp reattached his severed arm.

"And you? Needed a hand?" Lex drawled. "Now you, stay here," he ordered as he glared at me. He lunged toward the vampire, and the two circled each other in a frenzied dance. "You tired yet? You'll run outta blood 'fore I even break a sweat," he taunted the vampire.

"Kitty!" Tybalt called out to me as a vamp landed with a thud at the faerie's feet.

"What?"

"Better idea. Conjure sunlight!"

"What?"

"Just do it. Invoke Apollo, trust me," the faerie ordered.

I shrugged, not sure where Tybalt was going with his request, considering sunlight doesn't hurt vampires like it does in movies. Instead of burning them into a pile of ash it gives them severe sunburn, but hey, I didn't have much else to do while inside my shields, so I decided to run with it. Grabbing my lighter, I held it tight in my right hand, and after sorting through the collection of symbols hung around my neck, I found my sun medallion and clutched it in my left. Holding the button down on my lighter, I turned the flame up to its highest level and held it aloft.

*"Great Apollo, drive your chariot hence,*
*Burning bright for our defense.*
*Life from light, push back the night,*
*Chase the darkness from our sight."*

Honestly, I wasn't quite expecting the result I got. I figured the spell would give me a little bit of sun like the one that had illuminated the room beneath the faerie mound. Instead a small supernova formed from the fire in my hand, a bright white light that blinded me for a moment with its pure intensity. I squeezed my eyes shut as piercing inhuman howls split the summer night. The awful scent of burnt flesh and toasted vinyl filled my nostrils, and I flinched at the heat building up in my grasp. My brain warned me that it would be a smart idea to drop the lighter a split second before it exploded.

I shrieked, shaking my open hand back and forth as lighter fluid and melted plastic rained down on me and scorched my skin. The light died, but I was in too much pain to care at that point. My hand was on fire, I was sure it had to be, even though I hadn't opened my eyes to actually look at it. The pain was all the information I needed right then.

When I was tackled to the ground I realized my shields had dropped in my distracted state. I mentally resigned myself to the fact that my dumb ass had gotten myself killed, and I braced for the inevitable.

"Catherine!"

"Kitty? Kitty!" Tybalt's voice assaulted me as I was shaken back and forth and battered by two sets of hands.

"Fire, on fire!" I squeaked.

"I know," my cousin answered. For a few seconds more the battering continued until finally the assault ended.

"Are you all right?" Lex asked.

"On fire! Hello!"

"You're not on fire anymore, Kitty," Tybalt assured me.

"I'm not?"

"Nope."

Slowly, I opened my eyes, peering down at myself. It wasn't as bad as it could have been, but I had some very nasty burns on my right hand, with a sprinkling of minor ones on my arm and across my torso. Thankfully my clothes seemed to have taken the worst of it.

"Great idea, Tybalt. 'Invoke Apollo.' You lit me on fire, damn it."

"Only a little. You lit the vampires on fire a lot more."

"We need to get her home. My truck's this way," Lex interrupted us. He scooped me up into his arms and began to carry me away like a slender damsel in distress, something I certainly am not.

"Whoa, whoa, put me down, you're injured."

"You distracted me."

"I did not. Put me down."

"Not a chance, honey," he drawled. I briefly considered the childish response of biting him to get my way. The thought of biting reminded me that the area had somehow become vampire and necromancer free.

"Where'd all the dead people go?"

"Ran home to their mamas, I imagine, after the toasting you gave 'em. Never seen that trick before. You'll have to teach me that one," Lex explained, seeming impressed.

"Yeah, it was perfect until you lit yourself on fire too, Kitty."

*Wonderful.* From now on I'd just have to light myself on fire every time I got attacked, and all would be right in the world.

"Hey, Tybalt, that doesn't count as part of the test, does it?" I asked.

"No, but I'm sure they'll give you at least a night to yourself after that last one."

"Oh good."

The three of us approached an SUV. The lights flickered as it chirped and the doors unlocked. The car was black. I suppose I should have expected that.

"What happened to your pickup?"

"Needed a change. This one's a hybrid." When we reached

the SUV, Lex set me on my feet and opened the passenger side door for me. "After you, Miss Baker."

I brushed myself off before climbing into the car, and I noticed I'd picked up even more blood that wasn't mine. "You're still bleeding."

"It's only a scratch."

Frowning, I got into the car and he shut the door. Tybalt let himself in behind me and climbed into the backseat, and then leaned forward to stare wide-eyed at the million-and-one electronic gadgets scattered across the dashboard.

"Ooh, what does that do?"

"Don't touch anything."

"Though I do appreciate the light show, I was doin' well enough on my own," Lex drawled as he plopped into the driver's seat.

"Uh-huh. So those slashes across your ribs are what? A pre-existing shaving accident?"

"Don't worry about it."

Resisting the urge to comment on the idiot macho nature of men, I sat silent while Tybalt pestered Lex about what all the buttons did. It was a short drive to my apartment, and the trip was uneventful. Lex paused to grab a gym bag out of the back of the car before we headed into the building. Once we were safe inside my place I escorted Lex into the kitchen to tend his wounds at my breakfast table. Magicians heal injuries faster than the average human, but even we can catch an infection if it's bad enough. No telling where those vamps'd been. They were probably crawling with all kinds of nasty undead cooties.

"We ought to take care of your burns first," he insisted as I plunked down my first-aid kit.

"I just need a new shirt. This one's trashed."

"No, your hand should be bandaged. Give it here and have a seat." Before I could protest he gently took hold of my injured hand and turned it over to examine it. I sat in the chair he pulled out for me and surrendered to his demand. "Explain to me how you lit those vamps up."

"Is that what I did? I was a li'l distracted by being on fire at the time."

"They're char-grilled. It was great!" Tybalt exclaimed from his perch on the edge of the sink.

"Which, I might add, I've never seen before. You drag a vamp out into the sunlight and it gets sunburned, it doesn't burst into flames. What you did is something out of fiction." Grabbing a tube of antibiotic ointment from the kit, he unscrewed the cap and poised himself to squeeze some onto my burns. "This'll probably hurt."

"Yeah, I figured that. Go ahead." To my credit I didn't shriek when the gob of ointment hit my skin, and I kept my composure while he spread it over the angry, reddened wounds. "Tybalt, the spell was your idea. You ever hear of that kind of reaction happening?"

"Sure, that's why I had you invoke Apollo. Magic sunlight's got a chance to do it when it's properly blessed, and the caster's strong enough."

I stared incredulously at the faerie. "Why haven't you mentioned this before?"

"Thought you knew about it."

"Nobody knows about it."

"It's not my fault you humans forget things so easily. You all used to know about that," he pointed out, a scolding tone in his voice.

"Great. Anything else you want to share with the class?"

The faerie blinked and looked thoughtful for a moment before shaking his head. "No, not really."

"Those vamps didn't die, did they?"

"Nope," Lex replied. "Just ran off like someone lit their tails on fire." Finished with the ointment, the guardian wound a thin gauze bandage around my hand.

"So they're going to be extra mad later, pretty much?"

"More than likely."

"Wonderful."

"They'll be less mad than if we'd killed any of them though, so it's not that bad. And no paperwork. There you go, all set," Lex proclaimed, releasing my hand.

"Thanks. Your turn," I said, as I got to my feet.

"I can take care of it."

"It'll go faster if I do it. Guardians may know a thing or two about first aid, but witches are natural healers. Now let me see."

For a second it looked like he wanted to argue with me, but

then he shrugged. Slipping his coat off, he placed it on top of the table, and it made a loud clunk as Lex set it down. Next he removed the torn, bloodied black T-shirt, and I blushed from the roots of my hair down to the tips of my toes. Lord and Lady, I'd forgotten just how gorgeous that man was—or rather I'd repressed those memories. But hell, I'd seen him naked, so I was sure I could survive a few minutes of shirtlessness without making an idiot of myself.

"What did this?" I focused my attention on the marks. Five evenly spaced slashes had gouged through his shirt and into skin. Just deep enough to need stitches, they looked really painful.

"Vampires can grow claws when they don't feel like using fangs to draw blood. Short, stubby claws your average shapeshifter would laugh at, but they get the job done." Lex grimaced, shrugging again.

I nodded in reply and set about dealing with his injuries. I dabbed at the cuts with a clump of gauze soaked in hydrogen peroxide to clean off the blood. The tough guy didn't even flinch, good for him.

"I'm going to need a few more things to close these up a bit, unless of course you'd rather I break out my sewing kit."

Lex winced at the thought of me stitching him up, and I couldn't blame him. It's not something I'd be eager to try either. "Go ahead, I'll wait."

Leaving the two males alone in the kitchen, I ducked into my bedroom and rummaged through my ritual supplies. Normally I'd light a green candle for healing energy, but I'd had more than enough fire for one night. Instead, I raided my collection of rings and slipped a moonstone and silver ring on each finger of my right hand. Moonstone's not normally associated with healing, but it's my zodiac birthstone, so it gives an extra kick to my magic (something I needed at the moment). The rings and my bandages combined to create a ginormous fashion faux pas, but I didn't care. Returning to the kitchen, I found Lex and Tybalt chatting about the finer points of decapitating vampires.

"Hold still." Squaring my shoulders, I stared at the claw marks, holding my right hand just a hairsbreadth above them. I closed my eyes, concentrating as I visualized the slashes closing from the inside out, the tissue and muscle slowly knitting together. The energy moved in a cool, soothing wave, and I passed my hand across the length of the wound. To my disappointment I realized I couldn't close it completely. I just didn't have the strength left in me, but I managed to reduce the gouges to mere scratches.

"That's all I can do." My voice was hushed and breathy as I opened my eyes and sagged into the chair behind me. I was tapped out—between the exertion of the test, the strain of holding up über-shields, and healing the wounds, I was at my magic's limit.

"Thanks, Cat. I can handle the rest."

"Nah, I started it, may as well finish it." Grabbing a tube of triple antibiotic ointment from my first-aid kit, I leaned forward and smeared a generous amount on the claw marks. "Hey, if you heard about my death sentence, I don't suppose you heard why the vampires want my father to be Oberon?"

"No, that's goin' to take more research."

"It's a power play of some sort," Tybalt stated.

"Yeah, but what sort? We need to figure out what they're up to before we do anything else."

"That thought had crossed my mind." Lex smiled dryly. "I'm going to do some askin' around tomorrow."

"You mean *we* are going to do some askin' around, right?" Frowning at my collection of bandages and the placement of his injuries, I debated how best to wrap them up. The prospect of putting my arms around him to do something as simple as winding bandages turned my face even redder, and I cursed myself for being a blushing idiot. With an annoyed sigh I stood up again and got to work.

"No, I meant just me. I wouldn't advise you leaving here right now. Your apartment still warded?"

"Of course. I have the whole lot triple warded, for everything but faeries." With my relationship to Tybalt and Portia's clan, not many beings from Faerie would try to pick on me, so I don't worry about keeping them out. Clan Silverleaf is respected, powerful and well connected.

"I'm impressed," he said, and his expression echoed the sentiment.

"Yeah, well, I got real into security after..." I trailed off. Lex nodded in understanding and didn't comment. After my attack I'd been extra jumpy, but I'd been twitchy about safety even before that. Not many witches have come home to see a loved one ripped to pieces on the carpet. If my mother had taken more precautions, the vampires might not have been able to get in to attack her, though admittedly it was a very big might, considering my father would have just undone whatever wards she put up. He let those monsters in. Very little feels safe again after that.

"With your wards it's safer for you to stay here," he pointed out.

"I'm not going to lock myself in my room and hide under the covers and hope the monsters go away. I need answers, so I'm going with you. There, all done." Stepping away, I let him inspect my first-aid handiwork.

"Thanks, sugar."

I flinched at the nickname, the scene a little too familiar for my taste. Lex'd spent a lot of time in my apartment while we were dating, because my place was closer to most of his work than his house was. Walking around him, I crossed to the sink, nudging Tybalt aside so I could wash up. As I dried my hands off, I fought the urge to yawn. I was exhausted. I hadn't been this tired in years, possibly never. Throwing around so much big magic put a drain on my magical batteries and I hadn't really given them an opportunity to recharge. If we got into another fight, I'd start to worry about the strength of my shields. Then again, it wasn't a question of if we'd get into another fight, but of when.

"You look like you could sleep for a week," Tybalt said.

"Wouldn't that be nice."

"You should come home with me, stay with the family."

"It's not a bad idea," Lex agreed. "You'd be safe from the vamps in Faerie."

"Yeah, but I'm safe from the vamps here as long as they don't drop a house on my building." I didn't want to run and hide behind my faerie cousins—it seemed like cheating somehow.

"Fair enough. So you'll be leaving now?" Tybalt asked Lex. The faerie folded his thin arms across his chest and watched the guardian carefully. It made me want to give Tybalt a big hug.

"I've been ordered to look after Cat. It's best if I stick close. She does have a nice, comfy couch." He nodded toward my

65

living room.

"And you'd best make sure you stay on that couch, Duquesne."

"Of course." Amusement danced in those beautiful light blue eyes, but Tybalt and I weren't laughing.

"I don't know what idiot assigned you here, but I don't like it, and you'd better be on your best behavior." The faerie glared up at Lex, and then he turned to me and gave a slight bow. "Blessed be, Kitty. Rest well." With a soft pop the faerie blinked out of the room, leaving only me and the half-naked guardian. Well, me, the half-naked guardian and my two cats who had been staring at him since he entered the apartment, watching Lex as though he were the King of all cat-kind and they were awaiting his orders. It made me want to yell "boo!" just to see if they'd jump.

"We ought to get you into bed soon," Lex advised.

I blinked, certain I'd heard that wrong, and struggled to maintain my composure. Certain death was almost easier to face than the idea of Lex spending the night in my apartment.

Placing my hands on my hips, I glared up at him. "Why are you here?"

"Orders, actually."

"From who? Obviously they didn't come from the witches' council. They'd be more than happy to see me dead."

"Now that's just not true. And you know I can't tell you."

"Great, classified information, got it." Deciding I wasn't going to get anywhere, I walked away into the living room. "I'll get you a pillow, and I have extra sheets in the linen closet."

"Cat—"

Ducking into the bathroom, I yanked open the door to the linen closet and began rummaging through it. I didn't think he would need a blanket—it was warm up here on the second floor and my bedroom was the only one with an air-conditioning unit. It was a little comforting to know he'd suffer while trying to sleep in the sauna that was my living room.

"You don't need to go to any trouble," he said from behind me. Startled, I jumped and rapped my head hard on the underside of a shelf. It took a great deal of willpower to swallow the string of curses that came to mind, and I rubbed the bump on my head with one hand as I thrust an old set of gray cotton sheets I'd used in college at him.

"Here. Just...just go."

"Thanks, Cat."

"Don't mention it," I muttered as I retreated hastily to my bedroom. Shutting the door behind me, I crawled directly into bed and hid my head under my pillows. Tomorrow had to be better. I couldn't see how it could get any worse.

# Chapter Six

Though I needed to sleep for a week, I woke up at sunrise. I dragged myself out of bed and stood staring at my closed bedroom door. All I could think of was how to best tiptoe around Lex to avoid waking him. Depressing. Pathetic.

After a record-fast shower I retreated back into my room and got dressed. Considering I had no idea what my schedule was for the day, other than the fact that I would not be going to work, I settled on jeans and a T-shirt that proudly proclaimed that I was an alumni of Three Oaks University in bright green block letters. I tamed my wet hair into a long French braid, guaranteeing it would stay in place for the foreseeable future, and then next on my to-do list was imbibing copious amounts of coffee. I crept into the kitchen and set about making breakfast. Thanks to last night's fight I needed pancakes to recharge, and lots of 'em.

I'd used up half the batter and finished my first cup of coffee when I noticed my uninvited guest watching me from the doorway, a cat standing guard on either side of him. Whatever had gotten into my cats was beginning to creep me out—they were disobeying the feline rules of conduct by showing extreme interest in a human who didn't appear to be allergic to them. They'd never paid any attention to Lex before. I had no idea what they found so fascinating about him now.

"Good morning. Hungry?" I asked as casually as I could manage.

"Starved."

"Help yourself." I nodded in the direction of the empty plate I'd left on the counter. "Extra mugs are in the cabinets up and to the right."

"I know."

Staring at the skillet, I choked down a sarcastic reply. Of course he knew where they were. This wasn't the first morning we'd spent in my kitchen. "Gonna need a hearty breakfast if we have a full day fighting evil," I quipped, steering my thoughts to a new subject.

"It does help." He proceeded to stack his plate full of pancakes and pour himself a cup of coffee. There was something absurd about the rugged, long-haired man drinking out of my bright yellow Tigger mug. Really, there was just something absurd about having him in my kitchen in general. It was a sight I thought I'd never see again, but to be honest I'd never understood what he saw in me in the first place. Even with the rumpled, slept-in, bloodstained clothes, a day's worth of stubble and the wavy, shoulder-length hair, Lex still looked as though he belonged on the cover of one of the many romance novels crammed into the bookshelves in my bedroom. Maybe as a pirate, or a barbarian warlord. And he ought to have a busty wench to accompany him. Not me, a mousy waitress in jeans and a T-shirt. I guess we must've been doomed to failure.

"What's our plan for today?" I asked.

"I still say you should stay here, or let me take you somewhere else safe."

"If it gets real bad I can stay with my cousins, but I'm not letting the evil dead chase me out of my home if I can help it." To emphasize my point I jabbed a spatula in his direction, and he held his hands up in defeat.

"All right, I surrender. I'll have to make some calls, and if nothin' turns up we'll take a drive and talk to some people."

"That sounds deceptively easy."

"Don't worry, it won't be."

"How encouraging."

When I finished the last of the pancake batter, I loaded up my own plate and refilled my coffee before sitting across from Lex. My cats sat side by side at his feet and stared up at him as he ate, until I distracted them by getting up and filling their food dishes. The loud crunching of cats chowing down on dry cat food was the only sound in the kitchen while everyone enjoyed their breakfast. I don't do well with silence, and decided to ask something that'd been bugging me.

"Did the faerie council send you?"

"You know I can't answer that."

"It's the only thing that makes sense. Obviously the witches' council couldn't care less about my welfare. They'd probably kill me themselves, 'cept they don't want to get their holier-than-thou hands dirty." I pushed the plate away from me as I suddenly lost my appetite.

"You're not bein' fair to them."

"Why should I? They weren't fair to me," I countered. "I got cast out for self-defense. *Self-defense.* Most people get off with a warning, 'specially for a first offense. It's crazy."

"I know..." He trailed off, and for a moment it looked as though he was struggling to say something, but then he sighed, shaking his head. "Look, Cat. I don't want to work with Dorian, and I'm sure you can understand that. You'll make a good Titania. It's in everyone's best interest that you stay alive long enough to become it. That's why I'm here."

"I didn't think guardians got to choose sides."

"We don't, in general. These are unique circumstances. No one wants to see the vampires get a foothold in Faerie, and I do mean no one," he said, a dire note hidden beneath the Southern drawl. I shifted uncomfortably in my chair as I pondered his words. As the magic police, guardians ultimately answer to only one power. A higher power.

"Huh. Right then."

Aside from a bit of chit-chat about the weather and other benign topics, the meal was a quiet one. I had no idea what to say to him, and as usual he seemed content with silence—Lex'd always been a man of few words. While I cleaned up dishes and the mess I'd made while cooking, Lex disappeared to take a shower and start on whatever phone calls he needed to make. I wondered who he would talk to, and my mind filled with detective-movie images of a nervous, weaselly snitch whispering secrets into the phone, his voice nearly drowned out with an ominous soundtrack that hinted at impending doom. Probably wasn't far from the truth—I can't imagine any wholesome people being willingly involved with vampires and necromancers—and I bet the vamps bumped off informants as readily as the mob. After all, this is Chicago.

When I'd run out of things to busy myself with in the kitchen, I wandered into my living room and discovered Lex seated on the couch. He'd changed into a new set of clothes, and the old bloodstained ones peeked out from the top of the open gym bag at his feet. This time he'd gone with a pair of blue jeans and a simple, short-sleeved, black button-down shirt. There was a lot of black in that man's wardrobe. I knew, I'd seen his closet. Then again most of the men I knew seemed to prefer black instead of color. It's a magician thing. With the stubble gone and his light brown hair pulled back into a ponytail again, Lex almost looked respectable. Almost.

Frowning into his cell phone, he was arguing with someone in French. I raised an eyebrow. I speak a decent amount of Spanish, because I studied it in high school and college. Both languages have their roots in Latin, which I also have a decent understanding of, so I can get a rough gist of what's being said—only if it's spoken slowly enough, and Lex's heated conversation didn't qualify. Annoyed, he snapped his phone shut and tossed it onto the coffee table in front of him.

"Problem?" I asked. He looked up at me with temper in his eyes, and I shrank back slightly into the safety of the doorway.

"A few. Looks like we're going to have to take a drive."

"Where to?"

"O'Hare. Can I borrow your printer?" he asked, nodding at my computer.

"Sure, knock yourself out. Why O'Hare? Are we flying somewhere?" I'd never been to O'Hare airport, considering Midway is so much closer to where I live and easier to get in and out of.

Lex settled in at my desk. "Not really. Just need to talk to someone there, and we'll need boarding passes to get into the terminal. You'll want to travel light. Don't bring anything that'll scare security."

Well, that pretty much ruled out the majority of my magical trinket arsenal. Deciding my attire was appropriate for the airport, all I needed to do was empty anything questionable out of my purse and I was ready to go. Dumping the contents of my bag onto the coffee table, I separated out all my magical tools— a few suspicious-looking crystals, some sinister vials of essential oils (*Look out, she's armed with patchouli!*), and four or five books of matches. This left me with a wallet and keys.

"Here." Lex handed me a piece of printer paper. I scanned it, frowning in disappointment.

"Boise? Who wants to go to Boise?"

"Nobody, that's why they had seats open."

"Oh." Made sense.

Lex drove, since I am distinctly lacking in possession of an automobile. Once we got on the expressway I noticed the roll of dark clouds approaching in the distance, preparing to ruin the bright, sunshiny day. It was probably a good thing. With any luck the rain would break the stifling heat and give us a few days of decent temperatures. Traffic wasn't too awful, so we made decent time getting out to O'Hare. The first drops of rain began to fall as we arrived.

The airport was enormous. I thought I was prepared for it, considering Midway wasn't exactly a shoebox, but the place was gigantic. O'Hare dwarfed the other airport, and I was immediately glad I didn't have to try to navigate the place by myself. Lex maneuvered us through it, quick and efficient, like he had magical radar that alerted him to the lines with the shortest wait. He must be invaluable at amusement parks.

The crowd seemed to be made up of mostly business travelers, with a scattering of families headed out for their summer vacation mixed in. People clutched their carry-ons as though they expected the bomb squad to swarm them if they made the mistake of setting their bag down for a moment. It made me feel very naked—all I had was a near-empty purse. Lex drew to a halt in a small food court, scanned the area, and then turned to me.

"You want some coffee?" He nodded in the direction of a nearby Starbucks.

"Uh, I guess so." Coffee? We'd come all the way out here for Starbucks? Surely not.

"All right. Go find us a seat, I'll be right back."

Without another word he walked away, and I watched him in a state of fuzzy confusion. Deciding to play along and do as I was told, I picked out an empty table and grabbed a seat. I settled back and continued to watch the crowd. The place felt like a mall with businessmen instead of teenagers. It was very odd. Most of the tables around me were taken up by people in suits sipping coffee while staring intently at their laptop computers—lord forbid they go anywhere without a wi-fi connection, might miss an email while waiting for their flight. A mother and her three children were seated a few tables away, and one of the kids began bawling because her brother stole one of her fries. Another fine example of why I prefer cats to children. I don't have to haul my furry babies around and suffer through feline temper tantrums in public. Not that I'm morally opposed to children, I just didn't foresee any in my future.

"Here you go," Lex said, interrupting my train of thought. He handed me a small cardboard cup of steaming coffee and I sipped it. Vanilla latte, my standard gourmet coffee drink. I shouldn't have been surprised that he remembered, but for some reason just that simple detail made my throat tighten with emotion. Seating himself across from me, he sipped at his own cup.

"Why are we here?" I asked, my voice slightly strained.

"Waiting for someone."

"Okay. Pilot? Flight attendant? Business traveler?" I guessed, and he shook his head.

"Nope. Give it a few minutes, you'll see."

"Great." I leaned back in my chair and decided that questioning him further was going to get me jack in the way of information, so I changed the subject. "Still have those season Cubs tickets?"

Lex chuckled, giving me a grin that made my stomach do a fluttery flip-flop. "Sure do. I haven't been to one in awhile though, been pretty busy."

"Uh-huh. How's Marie doing?" Marie was one of Lex's many sisters, and the only family member of his I'd met.

"Not bad. She's still out in Denver, though our mama's been tryin' to get her transferred back home."

"Why?"

"Well the Duquesnes are based in Louisiana," a voice offered from behind me. "It's tradition that they eventually go home to roost, as it were."

Startled, I turned to see an aged janitor leaning against a mop, his tired brown eyes looking down at me from behind a pair of wire-rimmed eyeglasses. The man wore a plain gray coverall with an ID badge as its only decoration, and I wondered how I'd missed seeing him before. I guess he just blended into the background too well.

"Large family, the Duquesnes," he continued. "French originally, quite an interesting history." The janitor turned his gaze to Lex and then ran a gnarled hand through his wispy white hair as he eyed the younger man. "Figured I'd see you here, sooner or later. Looks like it's sooner. I don't have anything for you."

Curious, I surreptitiously sniffed at the newcomer, noting that beneath the strong smell of bleach was the subtle papery scent of a librarian. Guess that explained why we'd come out here—a librarian would have access to the sort of information we needed, and one who based himself in an international airport would hear all sorts of interesting information. There must be more magicians around us than I'd first assumed. It did make sense. Obviously we don't live by magic alone and we don't travel by flying on broomsticks.

"Nice to see you too, Pete. Pete, this is Cat."

"Pleasure to meet you, Miss Baker."

"Likewise."

"You sure you haven't heard anything?" Lex asked him, appearing unconvinced.

"All I have is speculation. Everyone's talking about Morrow's candidacy, of course, but no one knows the reason for it, or if they do they're not telling."

"What are they saying about his candidacy?" I inquired.

Pete picked up his mop, plopped the head into the bright yellow bucket on wheels next to him and took the seat next to me. "It's Laura's doing, obviously. I doubt Morrow's made a decision of his own since he took up with her, and she's got enough ambition for a dozen vampires. No one knows why she'd make this move though. In life she had no link to Faerie, so she isn't looking to reconnect with her past. She's prone to wild stunts, but this is odd even for her."

Tension pinched my shoulders at the mention of Laura's name. Lovely Laura Barrenheart was the reason my father left my mother and became a necromancer. She's the vampire who mentored him. Laura was not high on my list of favorite people.

"And that's all you've heard?" Lex prompted.

"There's some paranoid speculation that the vamps have figured out how to dilute pure faerie blood enough so they can feed on it and not kill themselves. It'd give 'em a big boost, might tip the balance of power. I don't put any stock in that though." Pete shook his head. "Right now the big money's riding on Morrow to win, since the vampires put a price on Catherine's head. No offense, Miss."

"None taken." Sipping my latte, I resisted the urge to sigh—

I was sighing entirely too much lately. Any more angst and I'd be adding black bodices to my wardrobe and shopping for matching lipstick.

"The vamps have been tight-lipped on this one." Pete rose to his feet and took hold of his mop. "You know what you need to do, Duquesne, if you want real answers to your questions."

There was a grim expression on Lex's face at those words, and a sinking feeling settled into my stomach. Whatever the other option was, it couldn't be pleasant. The guardian nodded and took a long drink of his coffee.

"I was hopin' to avoid that particular option."

I opened my mouth to ask what they were talking about, but all I managed was a strangled gasp as the worst migraine in the history of mankind suddenly threatened to implode my skull. I covered my eyes and blocked out the painful light, whimpering like an injured kitten. Before anything important popped inside my brain I felt Lex's hand grip my forearm. Waves of soothing energy flowed out from where his skin touched mine, driving the invading magical migraine away until I was able to open my eyes again.

"You're all right, sugar," he murmured to me.

I blinked at him as I regained my focus, and I noticed that he stared at something behind me. His hand still gripped my arm as I turned around to see what held Lex's attention, and I spotted my father standing across the room.

Because he was out in public he'd left the cheesy wizard robes at home and wore a simple black suit instead. Three men stood with him, dressed in similar dark suits and looking as though the Secret Service had started recruiting from the Addams family. I knew the strangers weren't the ones who'd attacked me, considering my father was smiling. I tensed to leap to my feet and charge across the room to claw that smile off his face, and Lex tightened his grip on my arm and tugged toward him.

"Cat. Don't."

"What is he doing here?"

"If you promise to stay put, I'll go ask him."

"No way. I have a few choice words for that asshole."

"I'm sure you do. How 'bout we let me do the talkin' then?" Lex countered, his voice soothing.

"Fine, fine," I grumbled. It was a good idea—just because

we'd breezed through security to get in here didn't mean they wouldn't arrest me if I cussed out Dorian and lit him on fire. Not that I could, seeing as I had no fire to work a spell with, but it was a pleasant thought.

"Nice talkin' to you, Pete," Lex said as he rose to his feet. The old man nodded, looking uncomfortable, and hurried to get far away from the scene that was about to unfold. I stayed close behind Lex as we crossed the room, staring poisonous daggers at my father the entire time. To prevent any further attacks on his part I made sure to put my shields up as we moved.

"That was just low. Couldn't resist takin' a cheap shot, could you, Dorian?" Lex said, drawing to a halt. Now that we were close I could smell the magic rolling off the group, and easily recognized them as necromancers from their unholy stench. It was all I could do not to gag.

"What the hell are you doing here?" I asked. "I'm willing to bet you and your buddies aren't taking a trip to Disney World. Unless you're planning a hostile takeover of the Haunted Mansion."

Dorian ignored me, concentrating his disdain at Lex. "Duquesne. I'm surprised to see you here, especially with her. I wasn't surprised to hear you'd chosen a side in this, but a man in your position really should be more careful."

"Just trying to keep things fair. You know it's not legal for applicants to try to kill the competition. It's considered cheatin'." Lex eyed the necromancers. "Assuming y'all even remember what it's like to abide by the rules. Course you've already proved that you've got the paternal instincts of a snake, Dorian."

I choked down a bitter laugh and it came out as a cough instead. Dorian glared at me and I gave him a sardonic smile. "Hey, what happened to your eyebrows? Get a little too close to a fire?"

Apparently his ego hadn't recovered from his toasty dragon encounter and he took a step toward me. Lex moved in front of me, blocking him. "Play nice, now. Wouldn't do to make a scene."

Dorian paused, glaring first at the guardian and then at me. "You won't be able to hide behind him forever. He won't be able to protect you during the next test," he said, his voice low and threatening. "I'm surprised you're trusting him at all, after what he did to you."

"That's none of your business. I'm not worried, but you oughta worry more about yourself. Next time you might lose something more important than eyebrows." I tried to sound more confident than I felt, but it didn't come out very convincing.

"You won't survive this."

"When I become Titania, my first act will be your execution."

"You don't have the spine for it. You're weak, just like your mother. Useless, whining witch," Dorian sneered in disgust.

My temper snapped and my shields vanished in a fizzle of fury as I hauled back and slapped him across the face. "Don't you talk about my mother that way, you—"

Lex cut me off mid-shriek as he clamped a hand over my mouth and hauled me out of arm's reach of my father. I struggled, wanting to take another swing at him, but Lex didn't let go. Several more suspicious men hurried over to join Dorian, and by the lack of color in their ensembles I guessed they were also necromancers, probably a dozen in total. What was this, a convention?

"So this is your daughter, Dorian?" a new voice interrupted, calm and soothing. The posse of necromancers parted like the Red Sea as the speaker approached us. The only one of the group who'd incorporated color into his wardrobe, the man stuck out from the crowd. Though I couldn't remember where I'd seen him before, he looked vaguely familiar. He was tall, well-tanned, with sandy blond hair and a pair of expensive designer sunglasses. "It seems she's inherited your temper. Thankfully she has her mother's looks, lucky girl."

Stunned silent, I blinked at him, wondering how to respond to that as he smiled perfect white teeth at me. It was a strange statement to make, because my father was actually quite handsome. All of Laura's men were. She was like a connoisseur of pretty-boy magicians. From the way it made my father twitch I figured it was meant as an insult to him and not to me.

Lex eased his grip but didn't let me go, eyeing the stranger with sincere concern. I was about to demand to know who he was when I caught the scent of vampire magic. Strange. Sure, vampires could go out in the daylight, but I'd never heard of one actually doing it.

"And you are?" I asked, curious.

"Zachary Harrison, a pleasure to meet you." Extending his hand to shake mine, I reached for it in reflex but Lex grabbed my arm and yanked it out of the way.

"Don't you dare touch her, Harrison," Lex warned. Shocked, I turned and looked up at Lex. I'd never heard him use that tone of voice before.

"I was merely being polite, Duquesne." He chuckled, and then it clicked in my brain why the vampire looked somewhat familiar. Zachary Harrison was a famous real estate mogul—one of those celebrities who's famous for being famous. The man owned a string of high-profile buildings in cities across the country, as well as hotels and casinos throughout the world. Harrison was the subject of tabloids and gossip TV shows—who would be stupid enough to make someone with that high a profile a vampire?

Probably Laura.

Turning my attention back to Dorian, I raised an eyebrow. "What'd you do, ditch your skanky blonde for a new boss? Nah, I bet Laura finally got bored with you and upgraded to a younger, prettier boy toy."

Dorian's face went from angry red to furious, blotchy purple, and he raised a hand to take a swing at me. Lex dragged me another step backwards while the vampire clamped a hand on Dorian's shoulder and yanked him back out of reach.

"Is there a problem here?" A pair of female security guards hurried up to us, looking as though they were three seconds away from tazing our whole unhappy group.

"No, just a small family dispute. While awaiting my arrival my associate bumped into his estranged daughter, and he's very sorry for causing a scene, aren't you, Mr. Morrow?" the vampire assured them.

"Yes, of course," Dorian murmured, looking chagrined.

As the vampire smiled at the two security guards magic billowed around him like a thick fog, and I started coughing, my eyes watering. Blinking away tears, I noticed the women's shoulders sagging as the tension smoothly bled away from them.

"Oh, Mr. Harrison! I didn't realize you were coming through here," one of the guards spoke. "We could have gotten you an escort." If I didn't know better, I'd've sworn she even batted her eyelashes at him.

"Thank you, that's very kind, but it won't be necessary." Harrison favored them with a charming, reassuring smile. "I think we'll be on our way now. Dorian, why don't you go see to the luggage."

After throwing one last glare in my direction, my father slunk away like a dog that'd just been kicked by its master. Wow. I could barely believe my eyes.

"Ms. Baker, Mr. Duquesne, I'm sure you have somewhere you need to be," Harrison suggested regally.

"C'mon, Cat, let's go. Y'all have a nice day." The guardian grabbed my hand and tugged me after him as he walked away. "I'm sorry about that. I had no idea they'd be here," Lex said once we'd reached a safe distance. "You're real lucky they didn't haul you off and lock you up for assault."

"I know, I know... What's our next move for finding out what the vamps are up to?"

"I have someone else we can talk to, someone more likely to have answers. If we hurry we can meet with him today."

"Oh. That's good then."

We headed out of the terminal and back to the parking garage. As a smoker I am opposed to stairs, so we took the elevator up to our level. Everything continued to be normal with our departure, until we stepped out of the elevator and the world dropped out from under us.

# Chapter Seven

For a heartbeat I was afraid I'd been dropped into the same earthen cavern as last time but with a different dragon, one that'd be more open to barbequing me. After all, maybe that had been the point of the original test, and the Council hadn't realized that the dragon they'd plopped into the room with me was an easygoing pacifist who just wanted to watch celebrity *Jeopardy!*

The thought faded as the lights came up around me, allowing me to see my surroundings. The floor beneath me was made up of rough carved blocks of stone coated with a thin layer of dampness that soaked into the seat of my jeans. Though I could see, the light was still dim, produced by a series of torches placed around the room. The air was humid, and the sound of dripping water echoed around me.

"Well, I don't think this is our level," Lex commented. Surprised, I turned toward the sound of his voice and saw him getting to his feet. *He won't be able to protect you during the next test.* My father's words echoed in my head, and yet Lex was here.

"Yeah, definitely not. I think our trip to your next contact is going to be delayed."

Reaching down, he took my hand and helped me up. "Looks that way. Let's find out where we are."

We walked down a corridor toward a better lit area, and as we approached, three doorways loomed into view at the end of it, each crossed with ominous, thick metal bars. A prison? A dungeon? It was difficult to see what lay beyond those doors, so I took another hesitant step forward.

"They are all guilty."

Startled, I turned to my right, and Cecelia of the Silver Crescent stood next to us as though she'd appeared out of thin air, her gaze turned toward the three doors.

"Guilty of what?" I asked.

The faerie woman turned toward me, ignoring my question as she coolly regarded me with her regal stare. "It is up to you to determine their punishments. At least one of these criminals deserves the sentence of death."

"Death?" I blurted. I couldn't call for someone's death, not a stranger. Not anyone—well, with the very deserving exception of my father. Aside from that though, I was against capital punishment in my world, and I wasn't about to start doling out death sentences here.

"You may speak with the prisoners. When you have decided their fate, speak with me again." Folding her hands together, she took a step back, watching me with an air of infinite patience in her perfect posture.

"Okay. Now, though I'm happy I got to bring backup with me this time, why is Lex here?" The faerie woman didn't answer, her expression unchanging. "Great." I sighed quietly. I guessed they were allowing him to be a one-man cheering section, which was fine by me. I needed all the help I could get.

Licking my lips, I approached the first cell. Peering through the bars, I spotted an imp sitting on a cot, its tiny legs swinging back and forth as it stared at a spot on the floor, its bright red skin a startling splash of color in the dull gray cell.

"What did you break?" I asked. Imps are one of the less intelligent creatures of Faerie, and thankfully less powerful as well. If faeries are the embodiment of magic, imps are the embodiment of mischief. They seem to serve no purpose other than causing destruction and mayhem. Despite what you may think, those aren't necessarily bad things. Often a little purification by fire can go a long way in raising awareness about a problem, bringing attention to an area, things like that.

The imp looked up at me with its beady little black eyes, and its tiny shoulders slumped in obvious defeat. "It wasn't that important!" it protested in its high-pitched voice.

"Important enough to get your butt tossed in jail, buddy." I pointed a scolding finger at it. "What was it? Cut somebody's brake line? Cause a pile-up on the Kennedy during rush hour?"

"No."

"Cough it up. Confession is good for the soul, you know."

The imp sniffled and then burst into tears. I suppose I should have felt bad, but I've had enough bad imp experiences to not be fooled by their crocodile tears. I didn't believe it was sorry for whatever it was it did—it was sorry that it had gotten caught. Rolling my eyes, I decided to move on to the next and come back later to find out what the little bugger had done. I didn't have time for crying imps, I needed to go home so we could talk to Lex's next contact and figure out why the vampires wanted their puppet as Oberon.

I moved to the middle cell. This one was much darker than the one the imp occupied. A dank, musty odor permeated the air, and there was something vaguely familiar about it. Frowning, I leaned forward and was rewarded by nearly getting my dumb face scratched off as a furred arm shot through the bars and swiped at me with a set of wicked claws.

"Cat!" Lex shouted. Dragging me out of harm's way, he held me tight against him as my pulse thudded loudly in my ears. Cackling laughter reminiscent of a hyena's call sounded from the darkness of the cell, and I glared at it.

"Cute, real cute," I growled between gritted teeth. A snuffling noise answered me, and a stubby snout approached the bars, sniffing in my direction like a dog. It was some sort of canine, caught halfway between human and beast. Pale gray eyes stared from above the snout—they were human and not animal eyes, and a gleam of madness shone in them. Despite the fact that shapeshifters are controlled by wild magic, most of them are very stable, sane people. However, when wild magic is loosed on a weak, fractured mind, the results are catastrophic. Shapeshifters are not creatures of Faerie though, and belong to Earth. If this one was being held here, it must have done something to harm a resident of this world.

Lex released his grip and stood by my side, and together we stared at the shapeshifter. "That one's lost. It's got no control left."

"I know," I answered him and then addressed the shifter. "So what'd you do to get tossed in here?" I barely heard the click of claws on stone as the shifter moved, pacing up and down the row of bars as it watched us.

"Witch..." it whispered in a soft hiss. A chill ran down my spine and I couldn't help but shudder. I swear it laughed at my reaction. "Witch. I am guilty of no crime."

I raised an eyebrow at it as the shifter continued to pace. "Okay. What do they think you did?"

"They think I hunted the hunter, but I did not." The shifter snarled with a snap of its teeth. "The hunter hunted me, I defended myself. That is no crime!" It shrieked, an inhuman howl worthy of a werewolf movie that echoed off the stone walls.

"Hunter?" There were those who hunted shapeshifters exclusively, for a variety of reasons ranging from the benign to the malicious. Attacking a human or magician hunter wouldn't have landed the shifter here, though. "Do you know what it's talking about?" I asked Lex.

"It killed a guardian," he replied, his voice hollow. "That's the shifter that killed Thompson."

"I had to, it would have killed me," the creature snarled.

"What's the story here?"

"Thompson was a guardian in Arizona. He was killed while tryin' to enforce a warrant on that shifter. Happened last week."

Like in an old western movie, the good guys weren't supposed to kill an outlaw unless it was wanted dead or alive, or just plain dead. If the shifter had a death warrant, yeah, I could see why it would have fought back that ferociously. The question then became how had it earned a death warrant in the first place?

"What'd you do that they sent a guardian after you?"

"I was a very bad dog. Come a little closer, and I will show you."

"Thanks, I'll pass." I shuddered, glad I was out of arm's reach. The wild magic had broken this one. I didn't have to know the details of its crimes to know it had committed at least one inhuman atrocity, if not more. It simply couldn't help itself—it had all the instincts of an animal and no control over them.

I moved on to the final cell and saw a thin, scrawny teenage girl seated on her cot, her arms wrapped around her legs. She looked up at me with red-rimmed eyes, her gaze heavy with fear and sorrow. The sight of her made my heart ache.

"Oh, honey, what's wrong?"

"I'm sorry." She hiccuped. "I just wanted him to like me, I didn't—" The girl's eyes filled with tears and she swallowed down a sob. "I didn't know."

"What didn't you know?"

"I didn't know he was allergic to the pollen."

"Pollen?" For a moment I pondered that, wondering just what sort of magic the girl had used on the poor boy. If a flower was involved, it was probably used in a potion, and love potions were the most popular recipes. However, there was only one love potion I'd heard of that contained an ingredient that would catch the attention of the faeries.

"Was the pollen from Medb's flower?" I asked, and she nodded miserably. Medb's flowers grew only in Faerie and were famous for their ability to control the minds of men. "You're an alchemist?" The girl nodded again. "And the boy's not a magician?" Another nod. Poor kid, talk about dumb luck. It was hard to tell what magical ingredients a straight will have an adverse reaction to, particularly in the age of allergies.

"He's...he's in the, the hospital." At least the boy hadn't died, that was a good thing. If a healer could sneak in to see him, the kid could probably be put to rights, no permanent damage caused.

"You know love potions don't cause real love, don't you, honey?"

"I just wanted him to notice me. I thought if he did he'd see that I'm so much better than that stupid Jennifer."

Ah, young love. I hadn't suffered from a real debilitating crush until college, myself. Probably because I was convinced that men were the worst kind of scum and should be avoided like the plague. It took some time and therapy for me to realize that it was unfair to blame all men for the crimes of my father.

"Even if he did notice you because of the potion, it wouldn't be real. It wouldn't last. True love's a rare thing, you know? Can't put it in a bottle."

She nodded, sniffling miserably, and I hoped she understood what I was saying. I couldn't see how this poor kid could possibly be deserving of a death sentence. Hell, she ought to be considered not guilty by reason of mental defect (said defect being teenage hormones).

Lex put a hand on my shoulder, and I turned toward him. "There's somethin' she's not tellin' you." I frowned at him, curious, and watched as he studied the girl. "A severe allergic reaction isn't enough to get her tossed in next to the likes of that shifter."

"Oh. Good point," I replied sheepishly. Sure, it seemed pretty severe to me, because for a witch interfering with the free will of another falls into the category of harming someone. Alchemists don't suffer from those kinds of moral issues though. They're a mercenary lot, ready to stir a spell for the highest bidder with no questions asked.

"What's your name?" I asked, focusing on her again.

"Jane."

Ugh, plain Jane, no wonder she lost out to a Jennifer. "Jane, did something else happen?"

Squirming, she turned away and stared at the opposite wall. "Not to Todd."

"Okay?" I prompted, waiting for an explanation. Jane refused to elaborate, continuing to stare sullenly at the wall.

"What happened to Jennifer?" Lex asked.

"Her hair fell out."

That was odd. True, it was the sort of spiteful thing I expected from a teenage girl, but it also wasn't a very big crime. "Was whatever you gave her *supposed* to make her hair fall out?"

"No. It was supposed to kill her."

"Right then," I said. Guess high school really is tougher these days. Without another word I turned and headed back to the first cell, giving the shapeshifter a wide berth. The imp had returned to staring dejectedly at the floor. "Okay. Tell me what you broke."

"I broke the metal bird."

"Metal bird? What metal bird?"

"The big silver one with the red and blue stripes."

A sinking feeling formed in the pit of my stomach. *Oh no.* "An airplane?" The imp nodded. "Lord and Lady," I whispered. "What did you break on the airplane?"

"A big round thing."

I really hoped it meant a wheel and not an engine. "What happened to the airplane after you broke the big round thing?"

"The round thing started to smoke, big black smoke, and then it went boom!" There was a note of manic glee in the imp's voice. "And then the metal bird fell out of the sky and there was an even bigger boom!"

A nauseous, lightheaded feeling washed over me as I realized just what the imp was guilty of. The little bastard had brought down a plane—not just a "oh the landing gear failed" kind of thing, but the sort of fiery explosion that the more bloodthirsty cable news networks like to show over and over again. I hoped it was a small plane, but a lot of the big airlines had red and blue in their logos. No matter what size the plane was, the imp's tampering caused the death of innocent people. With that in mind, the imp's punishment seemed like a no-brainer, so I didn't know how it could be considered a test of my abilities. There had to be some sort of catch I was missing—

Lord and Lady. Mac's plane left that morning.

"When did this happen?" I asked the imp, a spike of fear slicing through me.

"Just now."

"Like when? This morning? Ten minutes ago?" The imp shrugged its tiny red shoulders. "Where did it crash? Where was it going?"

"I dunno. Somewhere in the human realm."

Frustrated, I turned and walked over to Cecelia. "What plane was it? When did it leave?"

The faerie woman raised a regal eyebrow. "Will the answer affect your decision?"

"*Was it Mac's plane?*" I nearly shouted, at the end of my patience.

She seemed to ponder my question for a long, tense moment, and then she nodded. "Yes, it was."

It felt as though the air had been sucked out of the room, and I struggled to breathe. My knees wobbled beneath me as I stumbled backward. "Imma be sick." Turning, I caught a glimpse of Lex's expression—the color had drained from his face, and his mouth was set in a grim line. My legs threatened to give out and collapse beneath me, but before they did he grabbed me and pulled me into his arms. I closed my eyes and rested my forehead against his chest, letting him comfort me as I broke down into hysterical sobs. Lex murmured to me, stroking my hair as I struggled to pull myself together and regain my composure. Eventually I pulled away to dig through my purse for some tissue.

"I'm better now, thanks," I murmured as Lex released me. "You have any advice here on possible judgments?" My voice was as raw and as weak as my knees had been, and I winced at the sound of it.

"You're gonna have to put that dog down, it's worse than rabid," he replied, and I nodded. "I don't know what to tell you about the imp, you're gonna need to decide that for yourself, but I think the kid might be redeemable. Teenagers are brain damaged that way, they do stupid things."

"Maybe." I had a pretty good idea of what judgments I was going to hand out, but I had a few questions first. With slow, uneven steps I approached Cecelia.

"Have you decided the fates of these criminals?" she asked.

"I have."

"Very well. What do you decree for the imp?"

Of course she had to ask about that one first. Great. Well, it was a tough call. Yeah the little terrorist bastard deserved death in a good old-fashioned law of Hammurabi kind of way. But then again imps just don't realize what sort of havoc they cause when they tamper with machinery on the scale of an airplane, because they're not exactly problem-solving critters. Most of them stick to the small stuff, but when they escalate to something on this scale there's really only one thing you can do to stop them. You can either kill them, or you can send them somewhere they can't cause any more trouble.

If I wanted be a good witch, I'd spare its life by banishing it to the Gray, a realm without warmth, sound, or color, where it would spend eternity tormenting beings that deserved it. It's Hell, essentially, or at least a version of it. But I'd already proved that I wasn't a good witch, and right now I wasn't feeling merciful.

"Death."

"Done." Cecelia nodded, and the little bugger gave a piercing shriek of protest and vanished from its cell. I was glad that it vanished. I wasn't sure I could deal with watching it die. There was a part of me that was afraid I'd enjoy it.

"Your decision for the wolf?"

"I have a question first. Can you cure it? Remove the wild magic from it, I mean. Make it not a shapeshifter." Strange as it sounded, I couldn't blame it for "hunting the hunter", as it put it. If its crimes were all due to its "bad dog" nature, it might be possible to save it. I'd never heard of such a thing, but faeries have incredibly powerful magic.

Cecelia almost seemed surprised, but then again her expressions were so controlled it was hard to tell. "I can, yes. You must promise not to speak of it. I have no desire to deal with other shifters seeking a cure."

"Okay, you have my word. I want it cured then, and sent to a mental-health facility where it can be treated."

"Done."

The intelligent part of my brain warned me not to watch what happened to the shifter, but curiosity got the better of me and I turned toward the cell. I don't know what I was expecting, probably that it would vanish like the imp had and I wouldn't get to see the beast sucked out of it. Instead the shifter loosed a piteous howl, the sound echoing around us as the creature crumpled to the ground in an angular heap of furred limbs. I half expected it would dissolve into the form of a naked human like in the movies, but instead there was a whirl of red energy that swirled up and out of it, ending in a bright white flash that blinded me for a moment.

When my eyes adjusted, I spotted a dirty, nude figure curled up on the floor of the cell. It stirred and sat up, and I blinked in surprise as I realized the shifter was female. A blonde-haired, blue-eyed woman stared back at me—and young too, even younger than me. Someone who should've been in college, not tearing guardians limb from limb. She glanced down at her hands and then back up at me, her eyes large and frightened.

"What have you done?" she asked, her voice still rough.

"Saved your life. You're welcome," I said, my voice hollow. I didn't feel particularly excited about it, I just wanted to go home and cry for a few hours.

"But you've taken my wolf. I'll have no pack, no people."

"You'll get used to it. I did."

Without another word she vanished, and I turned back to Cecelia.

"And the alchemist?"

"Well..." That was a bit trickier. I glanced over at her cell and saw Jane staring back at me anxiously. "A year of being barred from Faerie," I began, and was interrupted by an indignant teenage shriek. Alchemists get many of their ingredients from Faerie, so this would seriously hamper her ability to make potions. Ignoring her, I continued with my decision. "During that time she can spend her extra energy doing community service, preferably in a hospital setting, so she can learn the benefits of healing others instead of interfering with them. Therapy is definitely in order too. Lots of it."

"Done."

"That's not fai—" Jane started, but was cut off as she disappeared. She was probably sent to her room at home, where no doubt another punishment from her parents awaited her.

I raised a weary eyebrow at Cecelia. "Do we get to go home n—"

The floor disappeared from beneath me again and I found myself falling through darkness. Lex and I landed in a clumsy sprawl on my bedroom floor in front of my mirror.

"—ow?" I finished lamely. "Ow."

"Sorry 'bout that," Lex said as he tried to untangle himself.

"Hey, they're back!" I heard an excited voice call from my kitchen. I looked up in time to see Tybalt dash into my room, Portia right behind him.

"Kitty!" the two faeries happily exclaimed in unison. At least someone was having a good day.

# Chapter Eight

Piled into my apartment's small kitchen were two cats, two faeries, one guardian and a partridge in a pear tree. Okay, maybe not the partridge, but I feared my apartment was nearing its maximum legal capacity. Merri and Pippin continued to stare at Lex, as though they found his every move intriguing. Crazy cats. I was half tempted to get out their catnip mice so they'd go do something else, but that would require moving, and I was just too damn depressed and exhausted to do anything but sit. I didn't want to do anything at all.

It was dark and raining outside. Though it seemed to us as though only minutes had passed, hours had flown by during our time in Faerie, which is about par for the course. I made a few phone calls to Mac's family and confirmed it was his flight that'd crashed. They promised to let me know when the memorial service would be. I felt numb and helpless, knowing there was nothing I could do but wait for my chance to say goodbye to my friend. First Maureen and now Mac—I had no one left, aside from my faerie cousins, who were doing their best to distract me. Especially Portia, who was opposed to negative emotions of any sort and was determined to keep my spirits up.

"You're doing good, Kitty," Portia congratulated. "There should only be one more test from the Council too. Piece of cake."

"Do you two know why Lex was brought with me for it?" I asked.

"Well, he's your guardian, silly." Portia rolled her eyes at me as though it should've been obvious.

Confused, I turned toward Lex. "Does that make any sense to you?"

"I haven't heard of it happening before, but I'm not exactly an expert on the subject. This situation isn't normal to begin with. There've been a few attempts to kill off the competition in the past, but usually they're subtle about it instead of outright puttin' a price on your head." He shrugged unknowingly. "Maybe Cecelia thought it'd be rude to separate us."

"Anything's possible at this point. I'm glad you were there." I wasn't sure what I would've done if Lex hadn't been there, if I hadn't had him to comfort me and calm me down when I heard about Mac's death. I glanced at Tybalt, noticing he was strangely quiet on this subject. Well, if he had something to say I'm sure he'd speak up, so I decided to move on. "We're going to talk to your other contact tomorrow morning?"

"Right. We could probably see him now, but it's not safe for you to be out at this hour."

"I won't argue with that, I've had enough drama for one day. Who's this contact of yours? It didn't sound like you were eager to talk to this person when Pete brought it up."

"That's because it won't be cheap—he sells information for a high price. I try to avoid dealin' with him unless it's absolutely necessary."

"Another librarian?" Many librarians, like Mac, prefer the free exchange of information, but there are those who prefer to barter and those who prefer to charge outright.

"In a way. We'll worry about that tomorrow. Now, we have two problems to deal with tonight. Food and entertainment."

I smiled, the first real smile I'd had all day—apparently Lex had the same plan of distraction as my faerie cousins. "Well normally I'd say we should order some pizza, but I'm afraid the poor delivery guy wouldn't make it here in one piece."

"Agreed." Lex nodded.

"You want food? I can make food," Portia offered. A feast popped into existence atop my kitchen table, a stunning array of dishes crammed together, and I swear I heard the table's legs groan under the weight.

"I wish my cousins were this handy," Lex commented, impressed. "You must be great at parties."

The selection was mainly made up of foods I like, the sort of greasy, fried American fare we serve at the Three Willows. Though I didn't have an appetite I forced myself to eat, knowing I needed to keep my magical strength up. Portia regaled us with lively tales of the past exploits of the Silverleaf clan during dinner, and I was grateful for it. When we'd stuffed ourselves full, Portia made everything disappear as easily as she'd conjured it, and we moved into the living room.

For the entertainment portion of our evening Lex bravely—or perhaps foolishly—decided to teach the faeries how to play Texas hold 'em poker. The only cards I own are Tarot cards, but he'd brought a deck of playing cards with him in his gym bag, and we used pretzels and chocolates as poker chips. The man displayed the patience of a saint as he tutored my cousins in the basics of the game—I'd learned it when we'd dated, though we'd bet clothing instead of snacks.

Tybalt was enthralled, but Portia was slow to warm to the idea until she figured out how to cheat by magically marking the cards. Poker ended soon after that, and we turned to the Game Show Network for entertainment. Few things are quite as entertaining as watching millennia-old frost faeries shout "No deal, Howie!" at your television screen.

It was a welcome break, and I could almost imagine this was a normal night of fun with my cousins. The addition of Lex didn't hurt, but it added to the strangeness. He was acting like the Lex I remembered—funny, caring, charming. I wanted to stay angry with him, but having him stand steadfast by my side today made that difficult. He was there when I needed him, which felt weird after what had occurred between us in the past.

A little after midnight I kicked the faeries out and sent them home so Lex and I could get a good night's sleep before our big day tomorrow. Not that I predicted being able to sleep with the cold dread that'd settled into my stomach, but I was willing to give it a try. I gathered up the empty drinking glasses and the bag of chips we'd devoured, and brought them into the kitchen. When I returned to the living room for the second round of mess, I found the lights had been switched off. Barely visible, Lex stood at the window, staring into the night as he held the curtains aside.

"You need to see this."

"What is it?"

"Might want to put your shields up in case they try to take a shot at you," he advised as I crossed the room. With a deep breath I put my shields in place, feeling the energy snap around me and then continue its new odd habit of stretching to include Lex.

"How are you doing that?" I looked up at him, confused.

"Doin' what?"

"You keep getting through my shields."

"Huh. Probably 'cause your subconscious knows I'm not going to harm you, so there's no need to keep me out. Those vamps outside, on the other hand, they're probably not here to play cards." Lex pointed into the darkness, and I looked out the window.

"I don't see anything." Squinting, I pushed my glasses up on my nose and strained to see what he indicated. My eyes slowly adjusted to the rainy night. The streetlights had been doused, and this time it wasn't my fault.

"There." Stepping close to me, he gestured again. "Two in gangways across the street, one behind that oak tree." Following Lex's lead, I managed to spot three figures hiding in the shadows, and they were definitely not my neighbors.

"What are they doing?" I asked, my voice dropping to a tense whisper.

"Waitin'. They can't get in, so they're waitin' for us to come out. Sooner or later they'll get impatient and figure out a way to force their way in. In fact, I'm surprised they haven't tried to set your building on fire and smoke us out."

"They can't, I have a ward against that too. Fire here can't grow any bigger than a stove burner."

"Damn, you are good. Still, with those vultures outside it's not safe here anymore, Cat. You'll have to stay somewhere else from now on." With his point made, he let the curtains fall back into place, plunging the room into darkness, with only the light from the kitchen to see by.

"You're right," I reluctantly agreed.

"You could come stay with me."

"With you?" Surprised by the suggestion, I turned to look up at him. We were standing so close I could feel the heat of his body and the light brush of his breath against my face. Nervous, I took a deep breath and unintentionally inhaled the familiar, unique scent of him. My heartbeat drowned out the steady patter of rain against the windows. With an amazing display of willpower I resisted the urge to bolt, knowing I'd only trip over something (like the cats that were still standing guard over Lex) and break my neck. Instead I took a slow step backward. "Why, you think it'd be easier to babysit me on your own turf?"

"I'm not babysitting you. Really, I'm protecting them from you," he teased. Grinning, he reached up and tucked a stray lock of hair that'd escaped from my braid back into place behind my ear.

"Thanks, that makes me feel so much better," I joked, a blush heating my face.

"I try. But seriously, Cat, I'll be here as long as you need me." Lex looked down at me, seeming sincere, and I shook my head at him.

"Don't, Lex. You're only here on orders. You'll be gone and on to the next as soon as this assignment is over."

"What if I don't want that?"

"What if I do? I'm all for the life-saving thing, but I don't want you in my life again."

"Are you sure of that?"

Scowling, I took a steadying breath and prepared to launch into an explanation of the myriad reasons why I wasn't about to go through another round of heartbreak with him, but before I could speak he leaned down and brushed a kiss across my lips.

A warm tingling suffused my body as soon as our lips met, the sort of electric reaction I usually associate with casting magic, but much, much better. He was hesitant at first, probably afraid I'd slap him or zot him with a spell, but when I didn't object he slowly began to deepen the kiss. My knees went weak as my good sense vanished, and I slipped my arms around him to steady myself. Lex held me close as he continued to kiss me, and I leaned into him. I'd forgotten how well we fit together. He sighed, as though my lips were delicious and he savored them.

"This is a bad idea," I murmured.

"No, this is a good idea." Lex nudged me back toward the couch, and I sat down in a less-than-graceful flop. Next he joined me and drew me into his arms.

"Oh yeah? How?" My hormones were obviously happy to see him, but I still had a little bit of brainpower left, enough to be skeptical of the situation.

"Because letting you go was a bad idea. I don't want to make that mistake again." His voice was low and strained, and I wished it wasn't so dark so I could see his expression. I sighed, a mix of old pain and new uncertainty, but he kissed me again and I stopped arguing.

I relaxed into the embrace, returning the kiss passionately. I felt better instantly—safe, warm, desired. Lex stroked my braided hair and let his hand rest at the small of my back. I ran my own hands up and down his back, debating whether or not it would be a good idea to tug his shirt off, but then I felt him unhooking my bra. My pulse jumped, and my magic decided to take that opportunity to wreak havoc on a pair of unsuspecting table lamps. With an electric sizzle followed by two sharp pops the light bulbs flashed and exploded. Startled, we jumped apart, the mood broken. We stared at each other, and I felt a guilty blush heat my face.

"Cat—" he started, and I held a hand up to stop him before he could say anything further.

"I don't want to hear it. I'm going to get some new bulbs, and we're going to pretend that never happened." Thoroughly irritated with myself, I retreated to the kitchen, fumbling to rehook my bra as I went.

"Don't worry about the lamps, we can fix them tomorrow. Cat, please talk to me." He paused, hovering in the doorway.

"No. Nothing's changed between us, I still can't trust you." *And apparently I can't trust myself with you either.* Rummaging through the cabinets, I banged doors open and shut as I looked for light bulbs. I was sure I had them somewhere.

"Is that why you ignored my advice in the test today? You don't trust my judgment?" Lex asked, sounding more than a bit offended. The change in subject threw me.

"No. I couldn't kill the shifter, not when I could help it. Or her, rather," I corrected. Hadn't been expecting that one, considering the few shifters I'd met at the café had all been men. "The imp had to go though, 'cause I figured that while you might be able to remove the wild magic from a shifter, you can't un-imp an imp."

"That shifter has a death warrant out on her."

"And were any of her crimes committed before she was infected?" I pointed out, and he shook his head. "I didn't think so. See, you haven't changed, you're still Mr. By-the-Book. The first time I screw up something as Titania you'll go running off to rat me out to the faerie council, because you can't risk jeopardizing your position as a guardian. Well I learned that lesson, and I'm not eager to repeat it."

"I didn't have a choice, Cat."

"Yes, you did. I told you about the attack in confidence, because I was scared and I needed comforting from the man I loved, and you had to go all *Law and Order* on me and turn me in." Slamming a cabinet shut, I crouched and started looking through the clutter under the sink.

"You're not bein' fair. I'm not the bad guy here. You caused harm with your magic, and yeah, I couldn't let it go, but I never dreamed the witches' council would treat you so unfair. I tried to convince them to change their minds. I even testified on your behalf, just like Maureen did."

"You did?" Pausing in my search, I turned and looked up at him in surprise. I didn't know he'd tried to help me. I always thought he'd testified against me, that he'd washed his hands of me when he'd found out I wasn't a law-abiding citizen.

"Course I did. I would've told you about it, 'cept you weren't speakin' to me at the time."

"Oh." Feeling numb, I tried to convince myself it didn't change how I felt about him. Out of the corner of my eye I caught a glimpse of the package of bulbs behind a bag full of plastic grocery bags. Reaching back, I grabbed them and then got to my feet. Crossing the room, I handed the bulbs to Lex.

"I never meant to hurt you, Cat."

"And now you want to pick up where we left off, like nothing ever happened?"

"Somehow I doubt you'd ever let me forget," he replied dryly. "I'd like you to forgive me, though, and give me a second chance."

Lex stared down at me as he waited for my reply, and it felt as though he was looking right through me. Did I want to try again with Lex? The physical attraction was obviously still there, but was that enough? I could hear Mac's words nagging at me in the back of my head: *What happened to you wasn't Lex's fault. You don't think it killed him to do it?*

"I don't know if this'll work. I'm not ready to make any promises, but...I suppose we could try."

Lex nodded, appearing to accept my reply. Reaching around me, he gently lobbed the box of light bulbs onto the kitchen table, where it landed with a soft bump. He turned his attention back to me, and I caressed his cheek, running my fingers along the stubble of his jaw and down the side of his neck. I slid the tie out of his hair and let it fall around his shoulders, and then I grinned.

"Then again, I'm not sure this is a good idea. I always hated that your hair is nicer than mine," I teased.

Lex laughed, and the sound made my stomach flutter. I squeaked in surprise as he picked me up and carried me into my bedroom. The stomach flutter kicked into high gear again, but it was replaced by a rush of heat as Lex set me back on my feet and kissed me. I clung to him, this time deciding not to hesitate about pulling his T-shirt off. He tossed the garment to the side and reached for mine, which joined his on the floor, along with my bra. His hands skimmed up my sides and cupped my breasts, and my knees nearly buckled as he ran his thumbs over my nipples. I moaned and grabbed hold of his waist for balance, and he kissed me again.

My hands moved to the fly of his jeans, and then I paused. "Oh, shoot."

"What? What's wrong?" Lex asked, frowning.

"Condoms. I don't have any. Well, I do, but they're four years old, they can't still be good. Damn it."

"Four years, huh?"

"Yeah, I haven't... I haven't been with anyone, not since we broke up." Sheepish, I blushed red enough to glow in the dark—I hadn't meant to admit to that. It made me sound like an idiot girl who'd been pining for him all this time.

"No one else seemed right?" he asked quietly.

"How'd you kn—? Wait, you haven't either?"

"I had a few dates here and there, but it never went anywhere. After awhile, I figured out that I kept comparin' them to you, and no one measured up."

"Really?" I could hardly believe it. Sure, I hadn't been interested in anyone, but I'd only had a handful of relationships before Lex, so it wasn't much of a change. Lex, on the other hand, had plenty of girlfriends before he met me, so I figured he'd moved on.

"Really. I do have some in my bag though." I raised my eyebrows at that, and he grinned. "Wishful thinking, I guess. Was hopin' there might come a time when I wouldn't have to sleep on your couch. I also brought a first-aid kit, in case things went the other way and you decided to stab me or light me on fire."

Shaking my head in amusement, I laughed. "Always good to be prepared."

"I'll be right back."

While Lex was gone, I wriggled out of my jeans and panties, and then turned down the air conditioner so it was a little less chilly. I barely noticed the room's temperature though, my entire body warm and tingly now. Nudging the covers aside, I sat on the edge of the mattress, waiting.

When Lex returned he set the box of condoms on the nightstand, and I again reached to undo his jeans. I stripped him, and I only had a moment to admire the sight of his gorgeous body before he joined me on the bed. We kissed each other hungrily as we slid beneath the thin blanket—eagerness was wearing away our patience. My hands roamed over him, reacquainting myself with the feel of his lean muscles. Lex'd acquired a few new scars since we'd last been together, and I wondered how he'd gotten them—I'd ask about them later.

He lowered his head to my breasts, and my back arched as he ran his tongue over one nipple and sucked it into his mouth. I moaned his name, running my fingers through his hair. Impatient, I guided his face back up to mine for a long, lingering kiss. "Lex, please," I murmured. My hips ground against the hard length of him, leaving little doubt as to what I was asking for. Kneeling above me, he reached for the nightstand, and after a few moments we were ready.

Lex kissed me again as he entered me, and I gasped, holding him tight. His pace was fast and frantic as he thrust into me. Later we'd have time for tenderness, but now our rhythm was all raw heat and need. Moaning, I clung to him as I climaxed, but he didn't slow, allowing me no time to recover. Instead, he continued to kiss me, my lips almost bruised from the force. Lex moved to my neck, trailing kisses up and down my throat and then murmuring my name against my ear. I shuddered, feeling another wave of pleasure building.

"Don't stop," I nearly shouted. I felt him come the same time as I did, both our bodies shaking from the force of it. I held him close, and the scrape of his stubble rubbed against the skin of my throat as we regained our breath.

"I missed you."
"I missed you too, sugar."

# Chapter Nine

There were more gadgets, bells and whistles in Lex's SUV than there are on the space shuttle. After five minutes I began to understand Tybalt's fascination with them as I resisted the temptation to push buttons just to see what would happen. As though sensing my torment, Lex reached over and captured my left hand, holding it in his. I smiled at the sight of our entwined fingers. It was very high school, but still sweet.

We were headed for LaGrange, a suburb that's not too far from my apartment. LaGrange is the sort of place I'd want to live in if I had kids. The area is nice, plenty of shopping, old Victorian houses, decent schools. It's got character, something some of the newer, trendier suburbs with their identical Borg-cube subdivisions are severely lacking.

"Who exactly are we going to meet? A librarian?"

"Of sorts."

"Of sorts? Does that mean not a librarian? An alchemist with delusions of grandeur?" I frowned—you're either something or you're not in the magician world, you can't mix and match your skill set. Sure, I could try summoning something, or stirring up a potion, but I wouldn't be nearly as good at it as an actual summoner or alchemist. In fact, there was no guarantee I could get their spells to work at all. This is one of the reasons why the different factions don't intermingle very often: not much in common, not much to talk about.

"Means he was a librarian, now he's something else."

"Like what? A Republican? Just spit it out, Lex. I'm not as clever as you think I am." I sighed.

"Simon is a chronicler. It's the librarian version of vampire." My frown deepened even further, because that didn't make any sense.

"Librarians don't become vampires."

"As a rule, they don't. Simon's Order is unique." Lex glanced over at me. "Most people haven't heard of them, and they like to keep it that way. I figure since you're about to become Titania you need to know these things, but you also need to know this information shouldn't be shared. Understood?"

"Right, totally classified." I nodded. "But if the vamps have a hit out on me, isn't going to one's lair an inherently bad idea?"

"Not this vamp. The Order has a strict policy of noninvolvement. They observe, record and broker information."

"Oh, good to know. Friend of yours?"

"Simon doesn't have any friends that I'm aware of," Lex replied, and I fidgeted in my seat. I so did not want to go have a chat with a vampire right now, or ever for that matter. And not just a vampire, but a "special" vampire. A friendless vampire. Lucky me.

"And this is the last-resort contact that you didn't want to talk to?"

He pondered that for a moment before nodding. "I wanted to avoid talking to him, if possible, but he's our best bet for finding out what Laura's up to."

"Why did you want to avoid him? Aside from the obvious dead-guy reason."

"Because he's expensive."

"I didn't bring my checkbook." Not that I could write a check even if I did. Anything more expensive than a fast-food meal would probably overdraw my account right about now. My financial future was looking pretty bleak too, considering that with Mac gone I was out of a job.

"Don't worry about it, I'm buying this round." Lex flashed me a reassuring smile and I rolled my eyes.

"Right then. So, what really happened to your pickup truck? You loved that thing."

"Dragon," he answered.

"Get out. Serious?"

"Serious. It didn't go home quietly, totaled the pickup. I'm gettin' used to this one though. Not bad, for an SUV."

"Glad the dragon I met was polite. Though he did say he

wasn't going to eat me since he only eats virgins." I smiled dryly, and Lex laughed. "I'm still not sure why I let myself get dragged into this mess."

"You saw what needed to be done, and you did it. You're a tough one, Cat. You'll get through this." Lex squeezed my hand, and I smiled.

"At least one of us has faith in me. Hey, how's Nick doing?"

Though Nick was a New York guardian, he was one of Lex's closest friends. They were about the same age and had the same tastes in movies, music, and all-black clothing, but Nick had a rowdier sense of humor than Lex did. Lex sighed, his expression somber as the playful light disappeared from his eyes.

"Forgot you hadn't heard about that. Nick was killed in the line of duty, 'bout a year ago now."

"*What?* What happened?"

His fingers tapped a tense beat on the steering wheel as he considered his answer. "You familiar with Poison Apples, the band?"

"Yeah, a little bit." They were a rock band, and I lean toward folksy chick music, but I'd heard of them. I remembered something about them in the news a while back, but because I wasn't a fan I hadn't paid attention.

"They're an all-magician band, so they have a unique fan base. Ivy—she's the lead singer—picked up a vampire as a stalker, real sick psycho, and Nick was assigned to protect her. Well, you know how girl-crazy he was. He got too wrapped up in her, and it made him sloppy. Got him killed. The vamp tore the girl's throat out and then took Nick out, but he'd done enough damage to it that the bastard died too." He spoke in a flat, tired tone that hinted he'd told the story too many times. Lex stared straight ahead, concentrating on the road, and there was a tightness around his eyes. I knew that expression all too well. It takes a lot of practice and control to pretend to be nonchalant about a loved one's murder.

"Oh, Lex. I'm so sorry." I rubbed my throat lightly with my free hand, thinking of my mother. It's a horrible way to die. Lex spotted the gesture and shook his head.

"She lived, Ivy. They say she probably won't sing again though. You know, Cat..." he started. Continuing to drum his fingers on the steering wheel, Lex looked as though he were considering his words carefully. "Never mind. Don't worry about it, we're almost there."

The SUV turned off the street we had been driving on and bumped down a less-than-pristine stretch of paved road, something that immediately caught my attention. A city girl is always suspicious when surrounded by trees, and it looked as though we were entering a forest preserve. We continued forward until the street behind us disappeared, and we rounded a bend to emerge into a clearing, approaching a huge, lonely house. It was in a sad state of disrepair—the faded paint peeled, the shutters hung from their hinges, dirt coated the stairs and porch. It looked like a haunted house from a bad horror film, and probably drew amateur ghost hunters from all over the area. All the scene needed was a creepy old family graveyard in the back, but thankfully there was none to be seen. Strangely out of place, an expensive black sedan was parked next to the building, likely miserable without a garage to hide in.

"What, does he have some sort of religious objection to hiring a groundskeeper?" I blinked as we pulled up to the front steps.

"Nope. Just likes to keep the neighbors at bay."

"Yeah I imagine it works on salesmen too." I hopped out of the car and walked toward the house, hesitating at the stairs as an image of my foot crashing through rotted wood danced through my head. For a moment Lex paused next to me, studying the sedan, and then he shrugged.

"Don't worry, I've got you," Lex said, taking my arm and leading up the steps before I could protest. When we reached the front door he opened it without knocking. I followed, feeling awkward at entering without an invitation. The interior of the place wasn't any more appealing than the outside. Cobwebs hung thick on the doorways, and faint sunlight filtered through windows that had been boarded up from the inside.

"Geez, who's his decorator? Béla Lugosi?" I wrinkled my nose. Lex chuckled as he led me down a hallway into what might have once been a kitchen. Opening a door, he began to disappear down a flight of stairs into the darkness of what had to be the basement. The scent wafted up toward me on a slight draft, the slight ozone smell that follows when a match refuses to be extinguished.

"Oh hell no." I stopped, shaking my head emphatically. "I've seen this movie. There's no way I'm going down those stairs."

"C'mon, Cat." Lex paused and turned around, holding his hand out to me.

"No. I'll wait in the car, thank you."

Sighing, he came back up the stairs and stood in front of me. "I'll throw you over my shoulder if I have to, but I'd rather not. Won't make a good impression on Simon, and you want to make a good impression on him."

I snorted. "The only impression I want to make on a vamp involves a sword."

"Do you trust me?"

Now there was a loaded question. Before last night I would've answered with an immediate no, but now... "Yes," I grudgingly admitted.

He held out his hand again and I took it, letting him guide me down into what my instincts were screaming at me was certain danger. It reeked of vampire magic—the place was completely saturated in it like nothing I'd ever experienced before. Then again I'd never set foot into a lair before. I'm not that stupid. And yet here I was, being led into the proverbial lion's den. I had to wonder if my I.Q. had dropped dramatically in the past few days.

When we reached the bottom of the stairs, we stood in the near total darkness. The only light in the room shone down from the open door at the top of the stairs. It was a tiny, cramped space, the kind that frequents the nightmares of claustrophobic people. I clung to Lex's hand like a scared little girl.

"Okay. Now what?"

As though on cue the door at the top of the stairs swung shut with a bang and plunged the basement into total darkness. I jumped, adrenaline shooting through my veins in a frightened rush, and Lex's grip tightened in what I assume was a futile attempt to comfort me. Off to our right, a door I would've sworn had not been there moments before opened. A figure stood outlined in the doorway, the soft diffuse light of candles glowing behind him. Though I wouldn't have thought it possible, the vamp smell became even stronger, and I sneezed twice in reaction.

"Duquesne," the figure said, inclining his head slightly.

"St. Jerome."

"This must be Miss Morrow, I presume?" I noticed a slight accent when he spoke, a bit of British. The vampire tilted his head to the side as he looked me up and down, an expression of detached interest on his face. If not for the odor assaulting my nose, I would have thought sorcerer on first seeing Simon. He was dressed in the type of long, full robes so many sorcerers seem to prefer. Black of course—in fact I don't think I've ever seen a sorcerer wear robes of another color. I've never seen a librarian dress like a *Lord of the Rings* reject though, so either this vamp was a fan of fantasy fiction or he was actually old enough that his attire had at one point been socially acceptable during his lifetime. I was banking on the latter rather than the former.

I hesitated, unsure of how to reply. The few times I've briefly spoken to vamps in the Three Willows generally involved the words "bugger off, fang face," so I wasn't sure what to say. Somehow, "Hello, please don't eat me," didn't seem like a polite way to start a conversation. I settled on a weak smile instead, and the vampire nodded infinitesimally in reply.

"Come in." Turning around, he walked away, and we followed him through the doorway toward the source of the buttery golden light. After proceeding down a short hallway we entered an enormous library.

"Wow." The word slipped from me in a surprised whisper. I clamped my hand over my mouth before I could make any other brilliant comments and simply stared in awe at row after row of bookshelves. Not since college when I'd taken a tour of the stacks of the main library had I seen a room with so many books. Mac would've fainted if he saw this place, and then awoken crying tears of joy. It made me miss him terribly.

Simon made his way to an enormous, elaborately carved wooden desk in front of a large fireplace. Two more vampires stood in front of the desk, watching us with great interest as Lex and I approached. A man and a woman in conservative business attire—it was refreshing to see a female vampire without dark eye makeup, dressed in real, grown-up clothes, and with her natural hair color too. All three vampires appeared to be in their mid to late thirties, and I wondered just how old they actually were. Our host sat down in a chair that was decorated as intricately as the desk, enough that it was almost a throne really, and nodded toward the other two vampires.

"Duquesne, I believe you've met Mr. and Mrs. Black," Simon commented. Black? Ugh, completely unoriginal vampire name. Do they require you to pick a new, cliché name when you sign up to be a fang-face?

"Nice to see you again," Mr. Black politely greeted Lex. "Miss Morrow, it's a pleasure to meet you. I am Michael Black, and this is my wife Emily."

"Hi," I said, smiling nervously. If it wasn't for my magic-sniffing ability, I wouldn't have taken him for a vamp just by sight—he looked too normal. Conservative haircut, average height and build, there was nothing remarkable about him that screamed "hello, undead!" like the other vampires I'd encountered.

"We've heard so much about you," Emily added enthusiastically. That couldn't be good. It was already disturbing enough that the vampires were being obviously rude by using my True Name, when I was sure they knew the one I go by. "Your story is really quite interesting. I'm a bit of a writer, and I was wondering if I might speak more with y—"

"We'll leave you to your meeting," Michael interrupted his wife. With a polite smile Michael took her arm to lead her away, and I noticed she didn't look happy to be leaving.

"Perhaps I could email you?" she called over her shoulder. Before I could answer, the pair disappeared through a side door instead of leaving the way Lex and I had entered. I bet this place was a maze of rooms.

"Please have a seat."

Lex and I took the chairs on the other side of the desk. Leaning back in his throne, the vampire steepled his fingers as he regarded us. Now that we were in better light I was able to get a closer look at him. Simon's features were thin, similar to the starved scholar look Mac tended to get when he was too involved in studying a new text and forgot to eat. Waves of chestnut hair fell just past his shoulders, framing a thin face with a strong nose and calculating blue eyes. Simon was attractive in a bookish sort of way, if you didn't mind the fact that he could probably drain you dry without batting an eyelash or giving your death an afterthought.

"I would very much like to know the spell you used on the vampires who attacked you, Miss Morrow."

"What spell?" I frowned, momentarily at a loss. Technically

I hadn't cast a spell *on* the vamps outside the café, I'd cast one *near* them. "Oh. That spell," I said, sounding as stupid as I felt. "I don't remember the words to it. I was trying for a ball of light and it ended up...bigger."

"You did not throw the fire?"

"No. Though in retrospect that would have been a smarter idea than letting it explode in my hand."

Simon frowned, appearing disappointed. "You don't remember any of the words at all?"

"Just something about Apollo, that's about it."

His brows rose at the mention of Apollo, but then he shrugged. "Pity. A reaction of that sort with the circumstances described has not been recorded in three hundred years. I would like to study the incident further, perhaps another time. I must congratulate you on your success with the first two tests. You've far outperformed your competition."

"Do you know how he did on the second test?" I asked, curious.

The vampire nodded. "It is fairly common knowledge. I won't even charge you for it. In true necromancer style, Dorian decided on death for the three criminals." He turned to Lex. "I assume you came here for more interesting information though, Duquesne. I'm surprised you ran out of other options so quickly."

"What do you know about the current situation?" Lex asked, ignoring the barb.

The vampire smiled thinly. "I'm afraid you'll have to be more specific."

"All right." Lex sat up straighter in his chair and leaned forward. "Why is Laura making a play for the position of Faerie liaison?"

"Ah, much better. More costly as well, as I'm sure you know," Simon replied.

"I'm willing to pay the price we agreed on." There was a stoic determination in Lex's voice, and it made me nervous. Just how much money did this guy charge? Lex was comfortable financially, all guardians are. I'm not sure where the money comes from, but I know it's meant to prevent them from being tempted by bribes.

"Excellent. Now then, you assume that it's Laura. Why?"

"Because Laura practically owns my father," I grumbled, "and she's on the Council." Lovely Laura Barrenheart (I sincerely doubt that's her real last name), the only female vamp on an American Council. She's also the vamp who turned my father into a necromancer, and promised to turn him into a vampire—a promise, I might add, she obviously hasn't delivered on yet.

"While that is certainly true, I don't believe she is behind this. Laura is very ambitious, but simply not creative enough to concoct a radical plan of this sort, despite the fact that it is a play for power." Simon shook his head. "This manner of move I would expect from a younger vampire, one who has not had the time to accept the way things are and become settled in the routines of the others. Also, it needs to be an individual who has enough influence to convince Laura to act. There are few who fit that description."

"Who do you suspect?" Lex questioned.

The vampire paused, gazing first at Lex and then at me, as though carefully considering something. "Zachary Harrison."

Lex swore under his breath, and I silently echoed the sentiment. Guess that explained why Harrison was in town. He wanted to personally oversee the outcome of the tests.

"You have a file on him?" Lex asked.

"I do."

"Can I get a copy of that?"

Simon appeared almost surprised for a moment, but then nodded in agreement. "Of course."

"This still doesn't answer the question of why. Why do this?" I asked, confused. "Vamps can't get into Faerie. Why jockey for a political position with a race that won't talk to you, and to a place you're not welcome in?"

"Perhaps they are seeking to change that," Simon replied.

"How?"

"Among the realms magicians can travel to, Faerie is unique. It was created after the powers-that-be closed the doorways to vampires. The doors of Faerie are closed to vampires by choice, by the will of the Councils of Faerie. Change that will, and the doors will open."

"Yeah right, like the faeries will just forget the whole unforgivable-crime-against-nature thing because of a little politicking. No offense," I added quickly. Probably not a good idea to remind your host that he was an evil abomination spurned by the gods.

"None taken." Simon smiled thinly again. "I am not a vampire. I am a chronicler."

"What's the difference?" I asked, and then winced. Tact is not my strong suit.

"Necromancers become vampires, though they find the term offensive."

"Oh good, I'll keep using it then. So, why go to Faerie? They can't even feed there."

"Maybe that's not the point. They might just want to open up a dialogue," Lex commented, looking concerned. "My sister in Denver has been monitoring the vamps in her area. They've been making overtures to the shifters, looking to form some sort of alliance."

"I've heard something of that as well."

"So they're extending the hand of friendship to the other magical races. No good will come of this."

"That's quite pessimistic, Miss Morrow. Did you have additional questions?" Simon asked Lex.

"I need confirmation. Who put the mark on Cat's life?"

"You already know the answer to that one, Duquesne."

Lex swore again, and a sinking feeling settled into my stomach. Now that had to be Laura. I'd threatened one of her minions, one she valued as well. She wouldn't take that kind of insult lightly.

"My advice to you would be to take her somewhere they cannot reach her until the trials are complete."

"I know." Lex nodded in agreement.

"Like Jamaica?" I asked. Can't be a lot of vampires on a tropical island, after all. I could use a nice, relaxing vacation too. Both men chuckled at my idea, and Lex shook his head.

"Sorry, sugar, you'll have to settle for something less exotic than that."

"Great. Well, now what?"

"Now there is a matter of payment to settle." For the first time I sensed genuine emotion from him, an eager interest.

"Cat, you go on up to the car, I'll be right there," Lex said, standing up. I was instantly suspicious, and more than a little insulted. What, it was male chauvinist time and the woman wasn't allowed to know about important details like the bill?

"Why?" I asked, folding my arms across my chest.

"Because I'm askin' nicely."

"I appreciate that, but I want to know why I'm being left out of this part of the discussion."

"I believe the guardian would rather you not witness this." Simon rose to his feet and walked around to the front of the desk, standing next to Lex's chair.

"Witness what?" I frowned. I caught a strong wave of the smoky scent of vamp magic, and my jaw dropped. "Oh no way, are you crazy?"

"Cat—"

"What the hell kind of deal is this? 'The Merchant of Venice' package?"

"An interesting analogy, but I assure you it is not a pound of flesh that interests me." Simon smiled, and there was an unmistakable predatory glint to the expression.

"Have you lost your mind?"

"Cat." Lex held out a hand toward me in a placating gesture, and I shot to my feet, backing away from them both. "Simon and I negotiated the payment before we came here."

"Well I didn't know that, and I wouldn't have let you come here if I did," I protested, still in shock.

"Which is why I didn't tell you. Go on up to the car, I'll be behind you in a minute."

"No."

"Let her stay then, it doesn't matter to me," Simon suggested.

"No, you can't do this, Lex. This is my fault, you shouldn't have to pay for information I need for my problems." My voice cracked as it raised a panicked octave.

"Would you pay it then?" Simon asked, gazing at me contemplatively.

"Would—what?" I blinked. My train of thought ground to a screeching halt. Had I finally gone crazy enough to willingly offer my blood to a vampire? Or chronicler, rather. Whatever.

"No, she isn't," Lex said firmly. My mouth worked but no sound came out as I struggled to deal with the very concept of it. If I had given the matter more thought, I would have known the price of Simon's help. We had no information to give him, and what else would a vampire place high value upon? The idea of letting him drink my blood was terrifying, disgusting, horrible beyond words.

But this was *my* problem. I agreed to petition to become Titania, I threatened my father, I lit those vamps up outside the Three Willows. This was my burden to bear, and I couldn't let Lex suffer for it.

"Yes, I will," I said in a small, frightened voice.

"No!"

"Done." The vampire smiled. Furious, Lex leapt to his feet and for a strained moment looked as though he was going to take a swing at Simon, but he barely managed to keep himself in check, his body trembling with the force of his self-control.

"She doesn't know what she's doing, she can't make this bargain," Lex said, almost through gritted teeth. The peculiar mix of scents that made up guardian magic rose around him, and his face flushed with anger.

Simon smirked, appearing as though he very much enjoyed watching the guardian's discomfort. "Just because she hasn't been bitten before does not mean that Miss Morrow cannot understand the bargain. In fact, considering her past, I'm sure she has a keener understanding than you do. Don't worry, I assure you that I won't harm her."

"I know you won't harm her, that's not what concerns me."

"Then you should have stipulated the conditions of payment more carefully when you contacted me. Bluster all you want, Duquesne, she has agreed, and you can't undo it. Think of this as an educational experience for you both—you'll be more careful with your bargains in the future, and Miss Morrow will have the benefit of learning what it's like to be bitten in a safe environment."

The two men sized each other up, and I sneezed once and then again as the smoky vampire scent returned, saturating the air around us and mingling with the haze of Lex's magic.

"Fine, whatever. Can we just get it over with?"

"Of course." With liquid, otherworldly grace the vampire glided toward me and I stared at him, petrified with terror. Images of my mother's broken body assaulted me, of her eyes frozen in an expression that urged me to run, to flee from the monsters which would be looking for me next.

I wasn't sure what I expected him to do. Outside of horror

films and *Buffy the Vampire Slayer* I'd never witnessed a vamp feeding before. Simon circled around behind me. He was tall, even taller than Lex, and I tried to look at him but he stopped me by gently turning my head toward Lex instead. Helpless, I watched as anger and frustration thrummed through him. I was going to be lectured after this, I could tell—provided of course I didn't die on the spot from a fear-induced heart attack.

My hair was tied back into a loose braid, and I felt the vampire smooth it away from my neck as he tilted my head to the side, running his slender fingers tantalizingly slow down the side of my exposed throat. His touch was cold, and there was no warmth from his body as he pressed himself against me, bending down to hover above my pulse. Simon chuckled, and I felt his breath brush against my skin.

"What's so funny?" I asked, my voice high and sharp.

"I was correct, wasn't I? You've never been bitten before," he whispered. I swallowed hard and nodded. "I'll try to make this memorable then. Be sure to watch your guardian. His reaction is going to be most entertaining."

Like a techno-dance beat my pulse throbbed deafening in my ears as I tensed for the coming strike, squeezing my eyes shut. There was a sharp moment of pain, like the quick slice of a knife, that made me gasp, and I fully expected agony to follow it. Much to my amazement, the sensation was pleasant—a warm fuzzy glow that reminded me of adding a shot or two of butterscotch schnapps to my mug of hot chocolate on a winter's night. It was confusing—pleasurably confusing, but still not making any sort of sense to me. This was supposed to be awful, wasn't it?

I opened my eyes and looked at Lex. His hands were clenched into tight fists, as though he was waiting for something dire to happen. I started to comment on how it wasn't so bad after all and reassure him I was okay, but the breath was stolen from my lungs as the experience went from "not so bad" to "*oh dear God*".

A rush of lustful heat spread from my throat in a wave of ecstasy that flooded me down to my toes. I inhaled, the noise a strangled gasp that sounded impossibly loud, and my legs went weak beneath me as my eyes fluttered shut. The feelings were incredible, like nothing I'd ever experienced before. It was one long orgasmic sensation that suffused my entire body, a pleasure so sharp it skirted the edges of pain. Through the haze of sensation I dimly heard Lex thoroughly cursing Simon in both English and French, questioning everything from his looks to his parentage to his sense of honor, but I couldn't understand why. This was amazing, incredible. It now made perfect sense to me why so many magicians willingly signed up to be a vamp's dinner, and I began considering life as a buffet. In fact, I began considering a whole lot of things I normally would never think of doing with a complete stranger, but my girl parts were campaigning that we entertain guests. And they wanted to entertain said company *right now*. Perhaps bent over the desk, or even right then and there on the floor.

I moaned, never wanting the feeling to end, and something about that desire triggered a warning in my mind, a primitive instinct that sent a spike of adrenaline shooting through that lovely oblivious fog. I was weak, lightheaded, and my legs were about to collapse out from under me. Things were wrong, very wrong, and I attempted to struggle free of the bite.

"That's enough, let her go," Lex ordered, but the vampire ignored him. Simon grasped my upper arms, firmly holding me in place against him as he continued to drain me. I tried to fight, to pull out of his embrace, but I no longer had the strength. My eyelids felt heavy and slipped shut. When I was on the very brink of unconsciousness he stopped drinking, and then handed my limp body over to Lex. He pulled me into his arms, still growling curses at the vampire who laughed lightly.

"I have misjudged you, Duquesne," Simon commented, his voice sounding faint and distant to me. "I thought you were an intelligent man, but anyone who would willingly let such a rare treasure get away from him is naught but a fool."

Though I would've loved to have heard Lex's reply, the darkness rose and swallowed me, and everything went cold and black.

# Chapter Ten

Okay, I was getting real tired of this being-knocked-unconscious thing, even though this particular incident hadn't involved me being hit in the head with an almighty whammy, and instead involved suffering severe blood loss. Again. Lord and Lady. Really embarrassing blood loss too. I'd volunteered myself to be molested by a damn vampire. I must be losing my mind. Totally. Completely. Irrevocably.

The sensation of two purring machines sleeping curled up on my feet woke me this time, and I was pleased they hadn't decided to nip me awake. Groaning, I blinked my eyes open, but much to my surprise I did not see the familiar surroundings of my apartment. Nor was I in the vampire's library, or Lex's SUV, which I also would have expected to wake up in. The setting felt familiar to my fuzzy, addled brain, and I struggled to place where I was. I was beneath the covers of an enormous, orgy-sized four-poster bed, with Merri and Pippin napping happily on my feet. Thick navy blue velvet fabric stretched in a canopy above me, falling in curtains around the bed. To my right the curtains had been pulled aside, tied back with a silver cord. Silver. The word finally triggered the correct memory: Castle Silverleaf, in Faerie.

"Portia?" I called out, and was answered by the sound of excited fluttering wings.

"You're awake!" The faerie plopped herself down on the edge of the bed. "Here, drink this." With one hand she guided me into a sitting position while she handed me a silver chalice with the other.

"What is it?" The liquid was cold and looked a bit syrupy, a far cry from my usual mug of morning coffee.

"Pink drink."

Not a good sign—the pink drink is a super energy drink for magic users, like Red Bull on steroids. It's hard to find and costly to make, so if I needed it I must have been in sorry shape. Grimacing, I began to sip the beverage. Chugging the pink drink is a bad idea—it can make smoke come out your ears. Literally.

"How'd I get here?"

"Lex brought you. I went back to your apartment for the cats, and Tybalt brought your equipment."

"Thanks, Portia, I appreciate that." I winced with guilt at the mention of Lex. He'd looked mad enough to shoot laser beams from his eyes before I'd fainted. "Where is Lex now?" I asked, doing my best to sound only casually interested.

"Out in the courtyard sparring with Tybalt. Tybalt wanted to bring your clothes too, but I made you new ones so you wouldn't need them anyway. Better ones too. They're so pretty, you'll love them, look!" Launching herself into the air, she zipped across the room and out of my line of sight. Glancing down at myself, I realized for the first time that I was dressed in a frilly white nightgown, the stuff of Victorian fantasies—long sleeved, high collared, with enough itchy fabric to clothe three people. Shaking my head in disbelief, I cautiously got out of bed to investigate Portia's source of high-pitched glee.

With her wings working a mile a minute the fairy hovered in front of a large wooden wardrobe filled to capacity with dresses. They were the sort of fashion popular in fairytale movies and upscale Renaissance faires. Ribbons, silk, satin, intricate embroidery, lace. It was a virtual hit parade of women's fashion throughout the ages, featuring only the softest, most feminine, flattering and formal. I paused, frowning at Portia dressed like a 1980s punk princess in her halter top, ripped stonewash jeans and combat boots. Elaborate gowns were not her style, and they certainly weren't mine. Hell, I didn't think there was one dress in my closet at home. Probably not any skirts either.

"Look!" Portia gasped, holding out a gorgeous scarlet dress with golden embroidery of leaves and suns. The much-neglected girly part of my brain leapt up from the dark, dusty corner of my mind I'd kicked it into with my white gym shoes, and it did an excited dance of approval.

"Wow. I can't wear that, it's too nice. I'd only end up getting it dirty or bleeding all over it." I shook my head.

Undeterred, Portia held the garment up in front of me with a contemplative expression on her face. "I think the color would go well with blood...maybe something darker," she decided, oblivious as to how morbid her statement sounded. Turning back to the selection, she sorted through gowns, looking for a more suitable dress. "And I have jewelry, and we can style your hair, and I have all kinds of shoes for you to pick from, and—"

"Whoa, whoa, slow down there. What's with the sudden desire for a makeover party?"

"Well, you're going to have to get used to it *sometime*, Kitty. When you're Titania you'll have to go to big formal gatherings like banquets and masquerade balls and you need to dress pretty, like a lady." She lectured me matter-of-factly, her serious tone unusual for the playful faerie.

"Great, something else to look forward to. Okay, fine. I'll wear a dress. A plain dress."

Squaring my shoulders, I endured my torture like a good soldier, sipping my pink drink and regaining my strength as I let Portia have at me. She buzzed and chattered around me as though someone had crowned her my Extreme Makeover Fairy Godmother. After a great deal of agonizing, she settled on a deep forest green satin gown with silver knotwork embroidery along the neckline and hem and a matching cloak, and then made my hair her next project after getting me dressed.

I honestly don't know what magic she used on my hair, but with a few strokes of her brush and the strategic placement of several decorative silver combs, Portia managed to tame my mane more effectively than I ever had in my entire life. Amazing. By the time she finished with me I hardly recognized myself in the mirror. The only things I'd been allowed to keep were my glasses, so I wouldn't be blind, and my wristwatch, because without it I'd slip out of Earth's timeline and that would be really, really bad.

"Eat your heart out, Liv Tyler," I murmured as I twirled around to ensure it was truly me reflected in the looking glass. Though I would have thought it impossible, Portia had transformed me into a fine lady—at least in appearance if not in spirit. As much as I hated to admit it, I felt better. A lot better, by leaps and bounds, and the realization brought tears to my eyes. It had been a long time since I'd given any real thought to the way I looked. I'd forgotten that beneath the messy hair and behind the glasses I was kinda pretty. Maybe even beautiful, but I doubted my self-esteem would ever be healthy enough to buy that.

"Thank you, cousin." I hugged her, carefully avoiding her wings.

"Let's go show Lex how beautiful you look," Portia insisted. If my girly instincts hadn't been enjoying their big day out by preening in front of the mirror, I might have picked up on the mischievous glint in her eyes, but the majority of my brain was taken up by "*ooh, shiny*" at that moment. Portia led me outside, though I could easily have found the way by myself. Castle Silverleaf is like a second home to me, and Portia and her clan are the only family I have left. I hold the title of cousin within them—which is a big deal for a human—and I can trace my faerie blood to the Silverleafs a few generations back on my mother's side.

Family blood ties create most of the contact between humans and faeries. Faeries once lived in our world, but they left to form their own sometime in the distant past. The sheer magnitude of power required to create Faerie left them drained as a people, and inherently changed as well. While they are almost impossible to kill, age incredibly slowly, and are immune to all manners of disease, they are also sterile—at least where each other are involved. A full-blooded faerie child has not been conceived since the split, but they can impregnate and be made pregnant by humans. As a mixed-blood, my ties are to Portia, Tybalt and the Silverleafs. In many ways Castle Silverleaf is the only real home I have.

The pale winter sunlight glinted on Portia's delicate, silvery wings as we emerged into the courtyard, and normally I would have been jealous, but with my stunning dress and my fabulous hair I felt pretty damn good about myself. The ringing, clattering, swooshing sounds of frantic swordplay could be heard even before we set foot outside, and I spotted the two combatants locked in their battle. From the look of it Tybalt was winning, but really that was to be expected, considering he had a millennia or so more experience than Lex did. To his credit, Lex was holding his own, even managing to press the faerie back toward the stone stairway Portia and I were descending.

"Get 'im, Tybalt!" I shouted in encouragement. Lex glanced up at the sound of my voice and did a double take. Tybalt took advantage of the guardian's momentary distraction and swept Lex's feet out from under him. Falling flat on his back, Lex grunted in shock. Triumphant, Tybalt kicked the sword out of Lex's hand.

"You cheated." He coughed, staring up at the faerie standing over him.

"Not my fault you let yourself get distracted by a lovely lass," Tybalt argued, grinning, and then he turned to me. "I see you finally allowed my sister to adjust your wardrobe. You look very elegant." He gave me a courtly bow, and I did my best attempt at a curtsey.

"Why thank you, cousin."

"Were you planning on attending a ball, Cinderella?" Lex drawled, a sour note in his voice. I had the distinct impression he wasn't happy to see me, but I wasn't about to let him ruin my princess vibe.

"I just might. I think we can rustle up a pumpkin and some mice for my coach and four." I turned to Portia for confirmation. "I already have my Fairy Godmother here."

"A ball? Yes! We should have a ball, that's a splendid idea! To celebrate our cousin's ascension to Titania," Portia exclaimed. Her eagerness nearly popped my eardrum, and I resisted the urge to tell her to use her indoor voice. Sadly, faeries don't have one.

"But I haven't gotten the position yet." I was more than a little afraid of the eager gleam in Portia's dark blue eyes. Portia loves parties. I should've been more cautious with my reply. Damn.

"Then this will be a show of support. I'll handle everything, don't you worry," she assured me, and vanished in an excited puff of frost.

"No good will come of this."

"Guess it's a good thing you're already dressed as the belle of the ball." Lex chuckled at my dilemma as he pushed himself to his feet.

"Yeah, laugh it up, she'll be after you next, trying to dress you in a doublet and hose. Just you wait." I shook a finger at him in warning, and Tybalt snickered.

"You'd look good in some nice pastels, guardian."

"Not a chance." Lex shook his head firmly. "Well if there's goin' to be a party, I guess I'd better go catch a shower. See ya 'round."

I frowned at his back as he wandered away, feeling rejected. Didn't I at least deserve a hug after being a blood bank? Well...I wasn't about to let it bother me, just like I wasn't going to pay any mind to the fact that as he walked away Lex looked as good from behind as he did from the front. Tearing my gaze away from that perfect posterior, I turned to Tybalt, who was watching me pensively.

"Come walk with me, cousin." The faerie led me to a familiar spot up on the wall of the keep, a walkway that would have been patrolled by the castle's defenders, if there'd been a need for them. There hadn't been a war in Faerie...ever, actually. I think they must have left those tendencies behind on Earth. Tybalt often came up here when he needed to brood, which true to his namesake was a fairly regular occurrence. With nervous care I brushed away the snow and hitched myself up to sit on the edge of the wall, smoothing the skirt of my gown into place around me.

"So you two are back together now?" Tybalt asked without preamble. I blinked in surprise, startled.

"I suppose so."

"You don't sound very sure of that."

"I said I was willing to give it another try. I don't know. I'm still not sure what he sees in me. Lex needs the kinda girl who'll bake cookies for his kids and be on the PTA council, and in guardian terms I'm practically an ex-con."

"Don't be silly," he scoffed.

"It's only a matter of time before I screw up again. Tick tock. In fact he's already mad at me again."

"Because you were foolish and let a vampire feed from you."

"A chronicler, not a vampire."

Tybalt rolled his eyes. "The difference is purely academic. You're just making excuses. Kitty, I know that you know not all men are base villains like your father, and I can generally tell the good from the bad, which is why I tried to talk your mother out of marrying Dorian."

"And?"

"And despite the fact that he hurt you, I've come to think that Lex is a good man. He cares a great deal for you. He stayed by your side from the moment he brought you here until I dragged him out into the courtyard for some fresh air."

Squirming, I fidgeted with the fabric of my skirt. "We're a bad match. I already failed once at being a guardian's girlfriend. I don't play by the rules enough for him."

"I'm not so sure. Magic needs a balance—masculine and feminine, lord and lady, order and chaos. I think if you worked at it, you could make it a good match. You're obviously attracted to each other, since I hear you've been, ahem, kissing again."

From his expression it was obvious Tybalt was referring to a little bit more than kissing, and I thought I'd die of embarrassment. "He told you that?"

"Of course not. Your blush just did though." Tybalt grinned mischievously and I couldn't believe I'd actually fallen for that trick.

"One night doesn't mean anything."

"Oh no? Then why does he watch you like a man in love?"

"You're being overly dramatic." It really wasn't much of a stretch though, because we'd been in love before our relationship had gone down in flames.

"I'm not blind either, cousin. Well, I'd better go and stop Portia before she throws you a parade. You'll want to find another dress, I'll wager. She's going to insist you wear something even fancier to your party."

The blood drained from my face at the idea of wearing an even fancier gown, and I nodded as Tybalt walked off. Deciding I'd better pick something before she did, I made my way through the castle and tried to ignore the fact that the noise level had raised a few decibels with general excitement at the prospect of a party. Faeries *love* to party—they love food, they love booze, they love music. Wine, women and song is a nicer way to phrase it, but the plain truth is faeries are as rowdy and fun-loving as the Greek community on a Big Ten campus.

When I returned to my room, I stood standing in front of the intimidating array of outfits, having absolutely no idea what I was doing. Like I said, dresses are not my style. I pick my clothing based on comfort, durability and machine washability. I don't iron. I don't dry clean. I wasn't even sure how to get into most of these outfits, much less the undergarments that went with them. There were no less than three corsets, and the mere sight of them made me want to run screaming from the room.

As I contemplated which one would be the least torturous I found my mind wandering. Lex's favorite color (aside from black) was red, and there were several dresses in various shades of it. Would he like me better in the dress with the ridiculously low-plunging neckline, or the anorexically tight dress that would push my girls up so high the tops of my breasts could almost brush the bottom of my chin? The train of thought continued on to consider if the bright scarlet fabric emanated a woman-of-ill-repute vibe.

"Ooh, ooh, the pink one!" Portia squealed from behind me. "Pick the pink one, he'll just *love* it."

"Pink?" I frowned. "Not going to happen. This thing is a nightmare dipped in Pepto-Bismol."

"It's pretty." Portia pouted as she hovered over me, literally.

"It's got ruffles! I don't do ruffles." I shook my head in a firm no. The faerie sighed, the weight of the world in her tone, and poofed the offending dress out of existence in a puff of shining dust. "Is there slinky? Maybe slinky that flows into a twirly-skirt-type thing?" I suggested in my "I know nothing of fashion" speak. "And maybe long evening gloves. I like those, the silky kind."

Portia nodded, pressing a petite finger to her lips as she plotted. "What color?"

"Black."

"Not black. Black is not a color."

"Geez. Red? Like garnet red maybe?"

"I can work with that. Stand still." Tilting her head to the side, she paused for a moment, and then I felt a tingling rush of prickly heat flash across my body in the blink of an eye. Glancing down at myself, I discovered the green and silver gown had been replaced by sleek scarlet silk. I gasped, my torso now constricted by an oxygen-depriving torture device that had to be a corset.

"Ow! Bloody hell, Portia, I can't breathe."

"You don't need to breathe. You look fabulous, see for yourself."

At her direction I turned toward the mirror and blinked. The evil device had sucked me in and fluffed me out, giving me ample cleavage and the illusion of a slender waist. Slowly I approached my reflection and did a series of half turns, amazed at the effect a little torture had on my figure. Maybe breathing was overrated after all. The skirt of the gown fanned out just under my knees, flowing with a fluid grace every time I moved. Strapless, the gown bared my shoulders, and matching silk gloves stretched up my arms and ended just above my elbows, marred only by the bump of my wristwatch concealed beneath one.

"Wow," I said numbly.

"Am I good or what?" Portia grinned, and I nodded in mute agreement. "We should do something about the glasses."

"Don't touch the glasses."

"But they don't ma—"

"You're not touching the glasses." With my luck she'd accidentally screw up the prescription and I'd spend the night stumbling around half blind.

"Fine. Okay, now we just need to do your hair, and I was thinking maybe a diamond and ruby choker with matching drop earrings, and I have such perfect perfume, you have no idea, and a matching evening bag studded with crystals..."

The music floated up around me as I approached the grand ballroom, and I paused at the unique combination of snow falling indoors mixed with a multitude of small, crystalline spheres that waved and danced in the air like soap bubbles blown by a child on a summer's day. They caught the soft light and reflected it in rainbow patterns throughout the hall. As always it was cold, and I wished Portia had thought to add a wrap of some sort to my ensemble.

I almost felt like Cinderella about to enter the ball as I walked down the stairs, but there were too many important differences keeping me from embracing that story. This party was held in my honor, and I already had a place here, a home. I wasn't a poor scullery maid looking to escape her dreary life— not that my life was glamorous, but it'd certainly been exciting the past few days.

I needed the support of my clan, and I needed their protection from the vamps that wanted to tear my throat out before I could become Titania. The purpose of this party was politics, and the fact that a guardian with a sexy southern drawl was probably somewhere on the other side of those huge double doors meant nothing to me. Honest.

Standing straight and proud, I approached the doors and breezed through them confidently when they swung open for me. The room was beautiful, as expected—the Silverleafs don't do anything halfway. More falling snow and crystal bubbles floated overhead, mixed with multicolored balls of light that darted to and fro in time with the music. Though they have a love of all varieties of music, a classical selection had been picked for the occasion, a symphony of strings, reeds and percussion instruments weaving together to form an entrancing waltz. Not my typical style of music, though I do have an appreciation for some classical pieces.

A woman in a rich purple gown glided up to me, her face lit with a bright smile, and it took me a moment to recognize Portia without her wings. The confusion must have shown on my face, and she giggled at me.

"They ruined the line of the dress so I took them off," she explained as she took my arm. "The wings get in the way when I'm dancing too. I'll put them back on later."

"Oh. Well, that makes sense then."

With Portia on my arm I surveyed the room. A large percentage of the clan had decided to attend, both full-blood faeries and mixed blood mortals like myself, creating a virtual sea of glittering finery that moved and hummed with excitement. There were several familiar faces in the crowd, but I continued scanning it until I realized what I was doing and then mentally kicked myself for looking for Lex. Apparently he was still upset, and a cold knot of guilt formed in my gut. Yeah, he should've told me what was going on, but it couldn't have been easy watching a vampire paw at the woman he'd spent the night before with.

Pretending everything was all right in the world, I allowed Portia to lead me around the room. I smiled, I laughed, I chatted, I nodded, and smiled some more. I danced when asked, and eventually sat down and had a glass of wine with a circle of Portia's friends, listening to their gossip.

I didn't enjoy myself. My eyes kept wandering over the crowd, looking for a long black coat and listening for a familiar drawl. The tension caused the urge for a cigarette to loom larger and larger in my mind, until finally I decided to sneak outside for a smoke.

The faeries wouldn't have cared if I smoked indoors. I

could've smoked an entire pack like a virtual chimney in the middle of the room and it wouldn't have fazed them. Faeries are immune to disease, so they had no worries of cancer from secondhand smoke. But I'm used to living in a world where smokers are right up there on the popularity list with lepers and felons, so when I feel the need to light up I find somewhere to hide. Excusing myself, I slipped out of the ballroom and then outside into the courtyard.

The moon hung high above in the night sky, and I took a moment to stop and stare. There aren't as many stars in my neighborhood, where the constant light from the city drowns them out. My first night in Faerie I spent hours just staring up, mesmerized by the sight of all those stars and how large and bright the moon was. The moon is important to me and my magic. It's the second tarot card I wear tucked in the band of my top hat, the planet that rules my sign of the zodiac, Cancer. Now it was a bright, shiny reminder that the full moon was approaching, and the time left before the third test was running out.

Ducking into a shadowed archway, I dug my pack out of my tiny handbag and grabbed a cigarette. My hands shook from the cold as I reached for my lighter and fumbled with it. This was the replacement for the one that had exploded in my hand, and I hadn't broken it in yet. I have a love/hate relationship with my lighters: I love to smoke, they hate to light. The long gloves weren't helping matters either.

"Sure you're allowed to use one of those after what happened last time?"

I glanced up to spot Lex as he wandered toward me across the courtyard. Under his long black coat he wore a black button-down shirt tucked into black slacks. He would have blended right in to the darkness if the moonlight hadn't been so strong. I gave him a dry look as I continued to fight with the lighter, and then the flame finally caught, allowing me to light my cigarette.

"We're safe as long as no vamps try to jump us," I assured him after I took a long drag.

"Then I guess there's nothin' to worry about. Didn't your fairy godmother think to give you a coat?" He slipped his duster off and draped it over my shoulders. The coat was heavy, and I resisted the urge to poke through it and search for hidden pockets and concealed weapons.

"No, and she'll freak out if she sees me in something that doesn't match this outfit."

"You look beautiful."

"It's not bad." I brushed self-consciously at my gown. "Though I think I'm going to buy Portia a set of Barbies so she'll play dress up with someone else next time."

We stood together in strained silence for several moments as I smoked my cigarette, and then he finally spoke up again. "Smoking is bad for you, you know."

"I know. I tried to quit. A few times. Besides, trying to become Titania's been bad for me too, and yet I signed up for that."

"You'll be good at it."

"Should I live that long, I suppose," I replied, trying to sound flippant about my imminent demise.

"I won't let anything happen to you." The sincerity in his gaze sent a tingle down my spine, and I nodded.

"I know you won't. I'm a big girl though, I can take care of myself. More or less." Trailing off, I itched at the side of my throat with my free hand, remembering the sharp slice of fangs piercing my skin. "Lex, I'm sorry. I didn't know what would happen."

"You should've left Simon's lair when I asked you to." He scowled and pointed an accusing finger at me for emphasis.

"My problem, my responsibility." I exhaled a long stream of smoke in his direction, and he waved it away in annoyance.

"It was my idea to bring you there, the payment was mine to make."

My face turned nine shades of red as I blushed, and I was thankful for the concealing darkness of night to hide it. I ground out the cig under my ridiculously impractical high-heeled shoe and immediately lit up another smoke. "So it's okay if the big, bad vampire molests you but not me? Forgive me if I'm not convinced by that."

"He wouldn't have done that to me. I'd already agreed on terms with him."

I blinked, not understanding. "Wouldn't have done what to you?"

Lex sighed, folding his arms across his chest. "It's my fault, what he did to you—I should've been more careful in namin' conditions, but I never thought you'd volunteer to be bitten. Vampires—and chroniclers—can vary the pain or pleasure in their bite. Simon wouldn't've made me experience what you did, because he's not attracted to men, so I didn't think to mention it when I agreed on the price. He bespelled you in order to hurt me. I'm sorry. You're right, I should've told you what the price was."

"Wait a second, he did it to hurt *you*?" I blurted in disbelief. "*I'm* the one who got molested, how did that hurt *you*?"

Stepping away from his spot in the doorway, Lex moved toward me, almost pinning me against the wall. He snatched the half-finished second cigarette out of my hand and flicked it out into the middle of the courtyard. Frozen and wide-eyed, I stared up at him, and he placed a gentle hand upon my cheek and ran his thumb across my lips.

"It did," he said, his voice low and strained. "What happened to you was my fault. Just like...it was my fault you were attacked that night. I should've been there. I was going to stop by the café, drive you home, but I got a call. If I'd been there, I could've done something."

My heart sank—I'd never thought of it that way. "Lex, it wasn't your fault. You know my neighborhood, it could've happened at any time. You couldn't be there all the time."

"I wanted to be."

Swallowing nervously, I struggled for something to say as I tried to decipher his expression, but my thought process ended when Lex kissed me.

I closed my eyes as he drew me into his arms. One of Lex's hands slid up my back beneath his borrowed coat, while the other tangled in the upswept mass of curls Portia had styled my hair into. My hands rested against his chest as he pressed me close to him, and I moaned low in my throat. Lex made a noise in response that sounded surprisingly like a growl, and it startled me enough that I pulled away from him.

"Catherine," he whispered against my ear. As he trailed kisses down the side of my throat it triggered a sudden flashback to the sensations of being bitten, and I tensed in reflex. "I'm sorry," he apologized, misreading my reaction.

"For what? Kissing me? Don't apologize for that. I'm still a li'l annoyed about the macho 'I should've fed the vampire' thing, but the kissing I won't complain about."

Encouraged by my words, he grinned and then kissed me again, long and thorough, until I was so intoxicated by the feeling that it made me weak in the knees, and I had to tighten my grip on the front of his shirt to steady myself. With my gown and my high-heeled shoes I felt a bit like a girl who'd snuck away from the prom in order to make out with the school bad boy under the bleachers.

Oblivious to everything but Lex, I lost track of time. I'm not sure how long we stood there in the archway.

"Is your room close?" Lex asked when we pulled away from each other.

"Fairly."

"How 'bout you give me a tour?"

"I suppose I could arrange that."

Taking Lex's hand, I led him through the castle to my bedroom, doing my best to appear calm and collected on the way there. When we arrived Lex shut the door behind us and glanced around the room. "Nice. Bigger than mine."

"The benefits of being family." I set my evening bag down on the dressing table. My heart beat wildly, though I knew there was no good reason for it—I wasn't a virgin, this wasn't our first time. "I believe this is yours." Slipping the coat off, I held it out to him, and he grinned as he took it and nonchalantly tossed it to the side. The coat landed on the floor with a muffled thunk, and I laughed, shaking my head in amusement.

"I don't think I'll be needin' that."

Peeling off the long gloves, I plopped them on top of the bag, flexing my fingers once they were free. Coming up behind me, Lex slid his arms around my waist and nibbled the back of my bare neck. Impatient, he spun me around to face him and kissed me long and hard.

I nudged him away, needing to catch my breath, and decided to take the opportunity to remove his shirt. One by one I undid his buttons and tugged the garment out of his pants. Pushing the shirt off his shoulders, he moved his arms to let it fall to the floor behind us. Reaching up, I freed his hair from the tie that held it back, and it hung loose around his shoulders. Immediately wrapping his arms around me again, he slid his hands up the back of my gown and then paused.

"I'm not sure how Portia got me into this dress. I have no

127

idea how to get out."

"Hmm. Hold extra still, sugar," he warned. I frowned, and he drew a knife from the sheath on his belt and promptly sliced a long cut down the back of the gown, through the lacing of the corset underneath. "Sorry, but I don't have time to find the manual." Lex tugged both garments off, leaving a pool of scarlet silk around my feet as I stood in nothing but a pair of lacy red panties and the evil high-heeled shoes.

"Fine, I'll blame you then when Portia looks for someone to murder for ruining her dress."

"I think she'll agree it was worth the sacrifice."

Stepping out of the dress, I kicked the shoes aside and grabbed the buckle of Lex's belt, dragging him back toward the bed. He nudged me back a bit as I sat on the edge, and I scooted toward the pillows. Before I was out of his reach, Lex took hold of the panties, sliding them off as I moved.

Stretched across the bed, I laid my head back among the pillows and moaned as Lex kissed a line up my inner thigh. One hand caressed its way up across my stomach and fondled my breast as his mouth teased the edge of my sex. I gasped, squirming slightly in anticipation as I felt the warm pressure of his tongue parting my lips. Lex moaned against me as he licked and nibbled at my clit. Arching my back, I ran my fingers through his hair as he tormented me with his tongue. A sharp wave of pleasure surged through me, and I cried out.

Lex drew away, and when I managed to catch my breath I grabbed his shoulders and tugged him upward. I kissed him, slow and savoring, feeling the heat of his body close to mine. I fumbled with the buckle of his belt, and managed to unzip his pants. Lex tried to tug both his pants and boxer briefs off at the same time, which really didn't work well at the awkward angle he was in as he hovered over me. I smirked, shaking my head, and he grinned.

"Hold that thought." Moving to the side of the bed, he quickly stood and removed the rest of his clothes. I ran my eyes over his naked body appreciatively—he really was all muscle, sleek and toned like a swimmer. Shivering from a combination of anticipation and the chill of the room, I ducked beneath the covers, and Lex joined me. As he lay beside me I ran my hands up and down his body in a slow caress. Reaching up, I drew Lex to me and kissed him, sliding my other arm around him as he moved to hover above me.

My arms encircling him, I watched him with a mixture of eagerness and anxiety. Lex gazed down at me, his eyes dark with desire. I could feel the hard length of him poised to enter me, and I shivered. He paused, and without a word thrust into me hard and deep.

"Lord and Lady," I gasped.

He moved slowly at first, a careful pace that allowed us both to savor the experience. Lex murmured endearments to me in French, and I had only a vague notion of what he was saying. It didn't really matter, because the sound of his voice alone was enough. He began to quicken his thrusts, and I matched his pace. Lex kissed me hungrily, as though he would devour me, and I felt an overwhelming wave of climax building.

I writhed beneath him, wanton and eager, until I let out a scream of ecstasy. My heart raced, and I let the sensations wash over me as we both slowed. He glided in and out of me with a lazy rhythm, enjoying my every whimper and sigh. Then when he decided I'd recovered enough, Lex pulled me even closer to him. This time he was relentless, and I came twice before he lost control. Shuddering and gasping he filled me, my name almost a prayer on his lips as Lex collapsed forward onto my chest.

Spent for the moment, we lay quietly in each other's arms. I nuzzled his neck, and he tried to stroke my hair but was foiled by my elaborate hairstyle. Lex moved and lay next to me, propping himself up on one arm as he gazed at me.

Caressing my cheek, he kissed me softly. "I love you, Cat."

My breath caught in my throat, and I blinked back tears. There was a small part of me that still wanted to hate him forever for handing me over to the witches' council, but I couldn't. "I love you too. You know, I think this may be the best party I've ever been to."

Lex laughed, and then grinned. "Night's young, Cat. There's plenty of party left."

# Chapter Eleven

"Why do you own a sword if you have no idea how to use it?" Lex asked as I missed stabbing the practice dummy by at least three feet.

Dusting myself off, I raised my chin indignantly and glared at him. "Because it's a ritual tool, and it's not meant to spill blood other than mine. It's a symbol, not a weapon."

Lex and Tybalt turned to each other and sighed, both muttering, "Witches," in the same disappointed tone of voice.

"Hey!" I scowled. "It's not a bad thing to try to do no harm."

"Not when there's a hundred or so vampires out lookin' to end you, darlin'," Lex argued, and I rolled my eyes.

"I don't see how this is going to help prevent that." Waving the rapier in a series of swishing arcs, I eyed it dubiously. It wasn't the most intimidating weapon I'd ever laid eyes on. I'd feel more secure with a claymore, except for the tiny detail that I couldn't lift one. Okay, that's an exaggeration, but the rapier was faster and less likely to unbalance me.

Sure, I was safe behind my shields—as long as I remained conscious. A determined vampire could sit and wait for hours, even days, for me to pass out from exhaustion, and though I'd been bending the rules of witchcraft lately, I wasn't about to start lobbing around fireballs like a sorcerer. I didn't think I could even if I wanted to. With that in mind, Lex and Tybalt decided to teach me how to properly use a sword. Though really there was nothing proper about my technique, as I had all the grace of a dying wildebeest. It didn't help that my muscles were already aching to begin with, from activities that had nothing to do with self-defense and were far more enjoyable.

"You'd be surprised what a weapon can do with the right

enchantment," Tybalt said as he strode over to stand next to me. "Easy now." The faerie placed one hand over my grip on the hilt of the sword and then placed his other hand at the small of my back. "Here." He guided me toward the target. "You stab here, aiming for the heart, as many times as you can manage. This sword is a piercing weapon, so you'll not be severing any heads with it. Just concentrate on doing as much damage to the heart as you can, as quickly as you can. Those bastards heal wicked fast."

Gingerly I poked the poor, straw-stuffed victim in the chest. "Like this?"

"Only if you plan on annoyin' him by ruining his shirt," Lex drawled.

"Hey, no comments from the peanut gallery." I stuck my tongue out at him, and he smiled.

"Here, you need to lunge forward." Tybalt tapped me gently on the back, and I felt a rush of power zip through me, guiding my muscles to react perfectly as I moved forward and expertly stabbed through the dummy.

"Wow. I just need to keep you standing beside me and everything will be fine." I grinned, withdrawing the blade.

"I would if I could, Kitty." He patted me on the arm, and stepping back, he nodded toward the target. "Now try it again."

Over and over I practiced with the rapier, first with the target and then moving in slow motion in duels against Lex and Tybalt. Although I knew if I was stuck in a situation with the weapon as my only defense I would more than likely end up dead, it was still somewhat comforting to have a little more practice and knowledge than I had before. By the time we finished, just about every muscle in my body had begun to protest, and I was glad to finally replace the weapon in the scabbard at my belt. The rapier was longer and thinner than my short sword, and its weight felt unfamiliar, but my dagger was sheathed in its usual place on the belt and that gave me a measure of comfort. I was dressed and ready for battle: blue jeans, combat boots and top hat. The only new development had been a loose, long-sleeved white shirt. Made from a tough fabric, it was warm, slightly scratchy, and had a thin cord that laced up the cuffs and neck of the shirt. I felt like a reject from the Renaissance faire, but the faeries had assured me my outfit was fine.

"You look tired," Lex commented. Tybalt wandered off, intent on some mysterious business of his own, leaving Lex and me alone.

"I am tired. Aren't you tired?"

"I'm used to this sort of workout." He smiled, and I nodded.

"True. I'll probably have to get used to it if I'm going to be Titania. Did Maureen have to put up with this sort of thing?" I couldn't picture the matronly old woman with sword in hand, fending off a group of evil ne'er-do-wells.

"Maureen was more of a shillelagh sort of girl. I watched her club a few uppity goblins in the head with that stick of hers." Lex laughed at the memory. "She was quite a woman. I'll miss her company."

"I still can't believe she didn't name an heir."

"She couldn't. Her husband wasn't a magician, and he forbade her from teachin' magic to their children. Even after he died she kept the secret to herself, though she had plenty of grandchildren she could've trained."

The idea was shocking to me, but sadly it was not unheard of. How awful, so much talent wasted... Rubbing at a sore spot between my shoulder blades, I winced in pain. "I think I'm going to soak for an hour or two."

"Need someone to wash your back?" Lex asked, wagging his eyebrows suggestively.

"You'd only help in making me dirtier instead of cleaner."

"And you'd enjoy it."

"I'm sure I would, but you're still not invited," I insisted. I needed some time alone to think.

Though clearly disappointed, Lex still saw fit to give me a parting kiss that left me breathless. I nearly changed my mind about his offer and dragged him back to my room, but I managed to stick to my guns. Set in my resolve, I felt steadier by the time I closed the door of my room behind me. Stripping off my clothes and equipment, I shivered in the cold of the room, hugging my arms to my chest as I prepared the bath. There are many advantages to living in a faerie castle, because it's made of magic like everything else in Faerie. When I entered, it had been a simple bedroom, but with the few words of a spell and a bit of effort I conjured up a fireplace complete with cheerily crackling fire where a bare stretch of wall had previously been. Near the fire I chose a patch of floor and created an enormous marble bathtub the size of a Jacuzzi, filled with bubbles and steaming water.

It's good to be a witch. Well, it's good to be a witch, better to have faerie cousins with their own enchanted castle.

I climbed in, my aching muscles instantly soothed by the water's warmth. Pippin, the more adventurous (and probably less intelligent) of my two cats, hopped up on the narrow edge of the tub and batted excitedly at a foamy white pile of bubbles.

"If you fall in, I'm not rescuing you," I warned him. True to form he ignored me and continued to reach for trouble. Closing my eyes, I decided to ignore him back and concentrate on my biggest problem, the last test. *And Lex.* No, Lex was not a problem, Lex was something else. We'd work that one out later.

I was fairly certain I had passed the first trial. It sounded as though Dorian had foolishly attacked his dragon. I'd worked with mine, and I felt that had been the right choice, or at least I was sure that attacking it would have been the wrong choice. Sure I wasn't an expert on dragons, but I'd known enough of the facts to trust that it wouldn't hurt me, and it hadn't. As the liaison between the human world and Faerie, it would be important to be able to solve problems with strategy and not just nuke the scary things on sight.

The second test had gauged my ability and willingness to judge the guilty and decide their fate. I had the impression that the Council wanted to test my willingness to make the hard decisions. Witches heal, we don't harm. We encourage life, not death, and a Titania can't be that softhearted. Of course, as an outcast witch, I didn't have to struggle as much with that particular moral dilemma, which was reflected in my decisions. I didn't feel bad about killing the imp—in fact, with the loss of Mac gnawing away at my subconscious, I almost wished I could've killed the little bastard more than once.

Lex was still a bit annoyed at me for not killing the shifter, but he'd get over it. I just wanted to know why Lex had been there in the first place. Would he be along for the ride with the last test? If he was, what did that mean? What would the Council ask of me next? There were so many options, countless possibilities. I couldn't prepare for all of them. Hell, I couldn't prepare for even one or two. All I would end up doing would be to make myself sick worrying over what-ifs. Everyone around me trusted that I would make a good Titania. I needed to trust myself.

Which left me with only one problem to deal with: my father. I'd sworn to make him pay for what he'd done to my mother, and now I was oathbound to do so, and by the gods I meant to. Dorian Morrow deserved death. A painful, tortuous death. To abandon your wife and child in the pursuit of empty power was one thing, but having your wife killed so she would no longer "annoy" you with her demands of love, attention and child support was another matter entirely. I knew, I'd always known, that if I'd been home that night I would've been killed as well. The only reason I was alive was thanks to the fact that I'd been at a slumber party with some friends from school.

Tough enough for a kid to deal with the fact that Daddy didn't want her anymore, but knowing Daddy didn't even want you breathing was worse. They would've come back to kill me, I'm sure, if Maureen hadn't shown up and taken me away. I would've ended up in the foster care system if Maureen hadn't pulled a few strings and found a witch to look after me. My life would have been so different if she hadn't been Titania, and the vampires had murdered her as heartlessly as they had my mother. For their pursuit of empty, selfish, dark power.

Dorian Morrow deserved to die. The question was, could I kill him? Could I decide his fate as readily as he had decided mine and my mother's? Would avenging her death make me a monster like him? Or was it justice, a fitting end?

Before I could ponder the topic any further my door opened, and I opened my eyes as Lex stepped into the room and shut the door behind him. "Hey, I thought I told you that you weren't invited," I commented, raising an eyebrow.

"Sorry, sugar, 'fraid I have to interrupt. On business." Though his intention was business he was definitely distracted by the sight of me in the tub. I couldn't blame him, because I was just as distracted by his presence in the room.

"Not good, is it?"

"No." Crossing the room, he sat on the edge of the tub.

"Exactly when will it be time for good news?"

"Soon, I hope." He smiled softly, and it made me feel a little better. "I stepped out to make a few calls."

"Out?"

"Of Faerie, for a few minutes. No cell phone reception here."

"Yeah, I'd imagine not. So what's the story?"

"The vampires doubled the price on your head after the last test."

"Ick. Why? They can't get near me here. All the money in the world can't buy them a ticket in."

"The vampires can't get in, no, but there are necromancers who can, and more than enough sorcerers as well, and they're always interested in makin' a fast dollar. 'Specially if it hurts someone else, like a witch."

"But they still can't get in here, they won't get past my cousins." My voice didn't quite hold the note of surety in it that I hoped for. Any assassins would have to get through the Silverleafs to get to me, but my clan wasn't exactly prepared to go on high-security alert. They'd never been attacked in their home—that was the main appeal of Faerie to its inhabitants, and the reason for its creation.

"Probably not, but it's possible, and it's something to be concerned about. The necromancer council wants you out of the way before you can take the third test, because if you become Titania they can't touch you again without startin' a war. I've spoken to Tybalt. He's alerting the rest of the clan to be on guard."

"Okay. So all I have to do is survive until the final test."

"Right." Lex nodded in agreement, and after a moment's hesitation tugged his T-shirt shirt over his head and tossed it onto the floor. He untied his boots and pulled them off, adding them to the pile.

"Hey, you said you were here for business," I pointed out.

"I did. I've delivered the news, and since you might be in danger here it's my sworn duty to stick right by your side from here on out. It's a tough job, but I'll suffer through it." With a great sigh, as though the weight of the world had been placed upon his shoulders, he continued to strip, and I laughed at the mock-serious expression on his face.

"You poor thing, how will you survive?"

"With courage and stamina, darlin'," Lex replied. I was only able to enjoy a glimpse of the lovely sight of naked Lex before he joined me in the water. "This is a very girly set-up you've conjured, Cat. Is that perfume?" he asked, sniffing the bubbles warily.

"Jasmine."

"That's used in love spells, isn't it?"

"If you're an alchemist. Witches don't generally approve of love spells," I reminded him. Lex moved toward me, and I placed my palms against his chest to prevent him from getting any closer. "Slow down there, buddy. You and I need to talk."

"'Bout what?"

"About this." I gestured at the tub, the bubbles and the nakedness. "Us. I want to know what your intentions are. Specifics."

"Specifics, huh?" Sitting back, he gave me some space. "All right. Where do you think we'd be right now if you hadn't been attacked?"

I frowned at him, hugging my arms to my chest. It was something I tried not to think about, all the "what ifs" and "might have beens" with Lex—it was just too painful. Until he showed up in the Three Willows to tell me about Maureen's death, I honestly thought I'd never see him again. But before my attack, our relationship had been wonderful.

"Married, maybe," I admitted cautiously.

"Just maybe?"

"Okay, married, a house in Des Plaines, with 2.5 kids and a Golden Retriever. Is that what you want to hear?"

"Yes." He took one of my hands in his, and I felt a tingle rush up my arm.

"Geez, don't do that." Frowning, I pulled my hand away and watched him closely.

"I'm not doing anything, not really, which is my point. We're connected, you and I. On more than one level. I feel something just bein' near you."

Silent, we studied each other. It explained how he managed to get through my shields. We were connected; my magic wanted to protect him as much as it wanted to protect me. The idea was scary and exhilarating, and I shivered despite the warmth of the water.

"So what happens when this is over, when things go back to normal? Or at least relatively normal?" I asked.

Moving toward me, he drew me into his arms and kissed me. "I'll take you home to meet my mama, and the rest of my sisters." Lex grinned roguishly as my eyes widened in surprise. "Don't worry, you survived a dragon, they'll be easy compared to that. We can get married in New Orleans."

"Whoa, wait a minute, I did not agree—" I sputtered, and he cut me off with another kiss.

"We can argue about it later. Now, I seem to recall you suggestin' that I help you get dirtier before you get clean."

Deciding that was a good place to end the discussion, I gave in to Lex's distraction.

# Chapter Twelve

The target dummy died a death most painful a dozen times over in the span of an hour, but that wasn't enough for the sadists who insisted I continue to murder it.

"I think you're gettin' better at this," Lex commented as I skewered it once more with my rapier.

"Good. So we're done then?"

"Nope."

"You're an evil bastard."

"That's funny, I seem to recall last night—"

"Don't even think about finishing that statement," I warned him. Straightening my top hat, I tugged my outfit back into place. Once again I was wearing my Renaissance faire/army surplus ensemble. It was functional and semi-comfortable, and considering the wide variety of fashions sported by my cousins, I blended right in.

Grinning innocently, Lex turned to Tybalt. "She still needs more practice, doesn't she?"

"Cat could use a few years of practice, but we don't have that kind of time." Scratching his chin as though stroking an imaginary beard, Tybalt studied me. "Her skills are showing some improvement."

"I'm so glad you're in agreement over this. I don't think I'm cut out to be a warrior princess."

"Well if you'd hit them with some destructive magic, you wouldn't have to be."

Sheathing the rapier, I placed my hands on my hips and frowned severely at the two of them. "We've already proved that I do as much damage to me as I do to them when I try that. I like this shirt. I don't want to light it on fire." It would be easier if I could pretend to be a sorceress and hail fireballs down on the vampires, but that wasn't me.

"We just need to work on your control. And pick a different element, for you've frost in your blood, not fire," Tybalt commented. "I know you hate to admit it, you've also sorcerer in your heritage, so I think it's possible for you to learn more effective offensive spells."

Before he could continue his speech a strange tearing sound split the air. A large rectangular glow formed on the surface of one of the stone walls of the courtyard near to us, and I realized someone must be opening a doorway into Faerie. The glow brightened and then vanished suddenly, leaving only a murky darkness in its place. Normally I'd expect someone to step through after that, but a thin round disk sailed out of the portal and bounced across the ground. It rolled to a stop a few feet in front of me, and I frowned down at it in confusion. About the size and thickness of a dinner plate, there was a dark rim that looked like a bent tree branch forming the edge, and a black tangle of string webbing in the center.

"What the—" I started, but was cut off as the disk shot up into the air. Hovering at eye-level it began to spin counterclockwise at a slow, mesmerizing pace. Entranced, I stared at it as a tiny rainbow light zoomed past me and danced around the edge.

"Tybalt!" Lex shouted. The alarm in his voice allowed me to tear my attention away from the spinning circle, but before I could turn toward Lex I spotted a new problem. Ponderously slow, dozens of magma elementals poured through the gateway, the sharp hiss of steam heralding their arrival as their feet melted the snow and ice of the courtyard with every heavy step.

"To arms!" Tybalt called out to the rest of the clan. Several choice expletives flew through my mind at the glowing, roughly humanoid invaders—they were the perfect enemies to pit against the Silverleafs, earth and fire to combat my cousins' mastery of air and water. My hand shot to the hilt of my rapier, but I didn't draw the weapon. The thin-bladed sword would be useless against them, melting to slag after the first swing. Unsure of what to do, I put my shields up and struggled to come up with a plan.

Wasting no time, Lex leapt into action. To my surprise he

didn't draw his short swords, and instead pulled a weapon out of thin air, literally. Now wielding a silver spear, the guardian attacked the nearest creature, ramming the weapon squarely into the elemental's chest. Though its blank expression didn't change, the fiery glow faded from its body, and it crumbled apart in large chunks of smoking rock.

The surrounding mob quickly focused its attention on Lex. It seemed odd that they ignored me—after all I'm sure they'd been sent here for me. Then a black-cloaked figure stepped into view and the portal closed behind him.

It was my father.

Strangely silent for once, Dorian strode toward me, weaving his way through the mob of steaming, swaying magma men, and I noticed that in addition to his clichéd black robes he'd added a sorcerer's staff. He waved the staff at me, and as a blast of unseen force hit me I sailed backward and smacked into a wall. My top hat popped off as my head collided hard against the stone. Falling to the ground, I landed in a small snowdrift and the air exploded from my lungs. The courtyard faded in and out before me in a nauseous wave as pain throbbed through my head.

"Bloody hell," I slurred as I drew my rapier. I was more than a little irritated that my shields had fizzled out for no apparent reason, and I intended to take that frustration out on him. Dorian's molten minions might not bleed, but I was willing to bet he would. He stood motionless as I charged toward him, ready to plunge my blade into his chest. The tip of my rapier bounced off his shield only a few inches away from his heart. Rookie mistake—just because necromancers aren't good at shielding, doesn't mean they don't have any at all.

With a cold smile he waved the staff, and I found myself airborne again. This time I flew in a new direction across the courtyard, landing with a bone-jarring thud in the middle of the battle of fire and ice. Our side wasn't doing as well as we should be—the faeries should've wiped the floor with the invaders in a matter of moments. This was their home turf, and yet somehow they were losing.

I was hauled to my feet and found myself standing next to Tybalt. "You're bleeding," I blurted, shocked. A blackened streak and a stream of blood flowed down the side of his face, a startling contrast against the frost-white of his skin. Concerned,

I touched the wound upon his brow in an attempt to heal it, but nothing happened.

"So are you. Leave it be, it's not bad. Give that here." Tybalt reached for my weapon and I handed it over. A line of frost and ice instantly coated the blade when the faerie touched it, along with a soft white glow.

"Thanks. Will this get through Dorian's shield?"

"I'll take care of that bastard. You get yourself behind your guardian and stay there," Tybalt ordered. "Now go!"

The faerie charged off in the direction of my father, and I looked around for Lex. Hurrying, I stumbled in the direction I'd last seen him, dodging flailing limbs and fluttering wings. A hulking elemental loomed in front of me suddenly, reaching out with red-hot arms to grab me. I jerked backward and almost lost my balance, and the creature swiped at me again. Before it could launch another attack the silver tip of a spear exploded out of its chest. With a smoking sizzle the weapon withdrew, leaving a hole burned through it. Like a broken doll it crumpled to the ground in a heap of glowing coals, and Lex stood on the other side of it looking like the modern incarnation of a god of war.

"You're bleeding," he said, concerned. Crossing over to me, he grabbed my chin and turned my head, searching for the source of the blood.

"Yeah I noticed. Tybalt's gone after Dorian, we have to help him."

"This way." Lex motioned for me to follow him, and he wove his way through the melee, knocking the occasional intruder out of our path. My cousin and my father struggled against each other, squaring off near the strange spinning web. Lex and I drew to a halt in front of it, and I was surprised at the sheer volume of tiny lights that whizzed around it like a thick cloud of angry fireflies.

"It didn't look like that before." I resisted the urge to reach out and grab it, reminding myself that it's a horribly bad idea to touch strange magic. Instead, I thrust the point of my rapier at the center of the web, but it bounced away, tearing the weapon's hilt from my grasp. The rapier flew into the crowd and I lost sight of it.

"Stop them!" my father's voice bellowed above the crowd.

My arm was nearly wrenched from its socket as something

grabbed my forearm and pulled, searing agony shooting out from where it gripped me. Following the momentum, I fell toward my attacker, hoping to break its hold, but before I could show off my self-defense skills Lex thrust his spear through the creature's neck. My skin was blackened and blistered where it had touched me, and the edges of my shirt smoked and smoldered around the wound.

"Where're your shields?" Lex asked. I ducked behind him as he fended off the elementals shambling in our direction.

"No idea. Not working," I said through gritted teeth. Biting back any further comments, I turned and stared at the hovering web. Any spell that's been cast can be undone, provided you know what kind of magic was used. From the general design of the thing I figured it was a dreamcatcher gone horribly wrong—instead of being used for protection through trapping negative energy, it'd become a weapon that drained our strength. Everyone but Lex's strength, that was. Why wasn't it affecting him?

"Hey, Lex—" I started, turning toward him. With amazing speed and skill he kept our attackers at bay, and a pile of crumpled, broken earth formed a half-ring around him. Suddenly the crowd parted and I saw Dorian striding toward us. "Look out!"

Once more he swung his staff, but this time he aimed it at Lex. The impact wrenched the spear from the guardian's hands and sent him flying past me, and I shrieked in terror as Lex smacked hard into the far wall of the courtyard and fell limply to the ground, where he lay in a motionless heap.

"Lex!" My heart fluttered with fear, but before I could move to help Lex, Dorian raised the staff for another strike. This time I ducked and covered, letting my arms take the force of the blow. The wave pounded against me and rushed over my body like a blast of hurricane winds. The soles of my boots dug into the snow, and I could almost feel the bruises forming.

"Just give up, Catherine. There's no one left to protect you," my father mocked. A nearby elemental took a swipe at me, and the blow sent me rolling across the ground. When I came to a stop I spotted the silver spear in the snow a few feet away, and I lunged for the weapon. The electric buzz of powerful magic shot up my arms as I picked it up and gripped it tightly. There were two options left to me: I could try to fend off the monsters closing in around me, or I could take out the disk and hope that its destruction would turn the tide of the battle.

Clutching the spear, I staggered to my feet and rushed toward the web. With a loud battle cry, I stabbed the spear through the center of it.

The lights shot out from it in an explosion of blinding rainbow sparks, and the rim hung limply on the end of the weapon. Shaking it off, I stomped on it for good measure. Satisfied that it was dead, I turned back to Dorian, but he'd disappeared. Without waiting to see where he went, I ran to the spot where I'd seen Lex fall. A magma man shuffled toward him, slow and menacing, and with a battle cry that would have made Xena proud I stabbed the spear through it. The shaft of the weapon bucked in my hands as it shoved through stone, and pain from my burn surged up my arm. I had a moment to ponder the fact that it was nothing like stabbing a target dummy with my rapier before the elemental fell forward and almost tore the spear out of my hands. Wrinkling my nose in disgust, I yanked it free and turned my attention to Lex.

"Are you okay?" He looked bruised and a little bloodied, but otherwise intact. Lex stared up at me as though I'd announced I was an alien queen here to abduct him. "Umm, here's your spear back." Sheepishly I held it out to him, and he stared at both it and me for a long, strange moment.

A series of loud, rumbling thumps echoed through the courtyard, and I turned to see the members of the shambling horde collapsing like marionettes with their strings cut. My father was nowhere to be seen, and the place was filled with battered but victorious Silverleaf faeries. Lex got to his feet and stood next to me, gently taking his weapon from my grasp.

"Thanks, Cat." The spear melted from view, returning to the thin air it had been drawn from. Taking my hands in his, he turned them over and examined them closely.

"It's not that bad," I said, assuming he was looking at the forearm burn. He nodded, distracted, but before he could reply Lex was cut off by a piercing shriek that made me shudder. A heartbroken wail filled the air, and I instinctively hurried toward it, spotting Portia crouched over something across the courtyard, her frosted wings drooping with sorrow. I stopped next to her and stared down at the figure cradled in her arms.

Tybalt.

"Oh no," I said, my throat squeezed tight with emotion. "Lord and Lady, no."

Portia sobbed hysterically as she hugged her brother's body. Tybalt's head lolled at a very unnatural angle, and I realized Dorian must have snapped the faerie's neck with that damned staff of his. My knees wobbled and Lex wrapped his arms around me. Resting my head against his chest, I wept bitter tears, and wished none of this had ever happened.

# Chapter Thirteen

For the first time since the formation of Faerie, the Silverleaf clan buried one of their own.

The call for vengeance was immediate and unanimous. They were eager to execute some vampires, and from what I could tell they intended to kill every vampire and necromancer connected to my father, from Lovely Laura on down to the lowliest minion she controlled. The scary part was that they could do it too, which made me wonder why Dorian had been stupid enough to try to attack me while I was within Castle Silverleaf. Sure he might ensure his position as Oberon if I was out of the way, but what good is the position when everyone he associates with is dead? All-the-way dead, not the average, everyday vampire dead.

My cousins were busy planning their elaborate revenge, and I had to admit that angry, bloodthirsty Portia was the most frightening thing I'd ever seen in my entire life. Listening to her describe their plans in her sweet, sing-song voice was even more disturbing than watching the glee in the imp's beady eyes as it recounted the plane crash it'd caused.

They were going to kill everyone, and it was going to be glorious.

My weapon training continued, but my heart was no longer in it. Lex spent most of his time with me, consoling me when I needed it and just generally keeping me sane—which was a tough job considering all the worries buzzing around in my brain. I wondered if I had gone after Dorian, would Tybalt still be alive? What if I failed the third test? What if Dorian became Oberon? Would I have to spend the rest of my life in Faerie, hiding from him? Would the vamps infect Faerie and spread through it like a plague?

All that stood between me and the answers was the final test.

One moment I was enjoying a peaceful sleep, safe in my bed, wrapped in my lover's arms, and the next I found myself standing in the middle of the earthen room beneath the faerie mound of the Underhill clan. For a heartbeat I thought it was a dream—one of those horrible walking-down-the-hallway-of-your-high-school-while-naked-without-your-homework nightmares—but with a quick glance down I discovered I was wearing my usual clothes, and with a pinch to my arm I proved to myself that it was real. After adjusting my top hat I let my hand rest on the hilt of my rapier as I surveyed my surroundings.

This time the cavern had been lit with a series of glowing spheres floating along the ceiling throughout the room. There wasn't a dragon, but three other people stood near me, one of which was Lex. I reached out and took his hand, and he gave mine a reassuring squeeze. Cecelia of the Silver Crescent stood in front of us, looking as serene and perfect as ever, and on the other side of her stood my father, dressed in his somber black robes with a dour expression on his face.

I snarled at him, filled with rage and grief, and Lex tugged me closer to him before I could do anything. I wanted nothing more in the world than to fulfill my oath and see Dorian dead.

"Stay where you are, Catherine," Cecelia warned. There was a subtle threat in her voice that made me pause. Balling my free hand into a fist, I took a deep breath.

"What is *he* doing here?" Dorian asked, pointing an accusing finger at Lex. "He has no right to be here."

"Actually, he has every right to be here, but that is not your concern," Cecelia informed him. "Each of you has progressed this far. This will be the final trial. Recent events have reminded the council of an important aspect of the position of liaison: the ability to survive an attack by one's enemies. Your objective here is simple: to live. The test begins now."

"What the hell—" I began to protest, but Cecelia vanished from view. Dorian wasted no time in turning on me. Without a staff this time, he conjured a ball of fire and whipped it at me. I flung my arms up to protect my face as my shields snapped into life, surrounding both me and Lex and deflecting the fireball so that it bounced back at him.

"Dumbass!" I shouted as he dodged out of the way. Shoving my anger down into the pit of my stomach, I resisted the urge to draw my sword, and instead poured more strength into the protective barrier.

"Now that's just mean spirited, Dorian," Lex scolded. The silver spear appeared out of nowhere again, and he held the weapon in front of him. One by one the glowing lights overhead winked out, plunging the room into darkness. "Guess they forgot to pay the bill."

"Looks like it," I agreed. I moved closer to Lex, and we stood together in the darkness as I debated our options. I could cast a light spell, but it'd weaken my shield. Sadly my lightstone was sitting in my apartment with a lot of my other trinkets, so that option was out. Though the darkness was terrifying, we were safe in my magical bubble, and if we were real lucky some big bad monster was out there eating my dad in one tasty bite right now. That deserved a victory cigarette, didn't it?

Dragging my smokes out of my pocket, I placed one between my lips and then held up my lighter, flicking it on. The small circle of light revealed my father inching close, a dagger in his hand. Startled, I forced myself not to flinch, and continued to light the end of my cigarette, blowing a stream of smoke in his direction. The smoke hit the invisible wall of my shield and curled back toward me, and I smiled.

"If you light yourself on fire again, I'm not pattin' you out this time," Lex warned me dryly.

"So noted," I replied. "Careful, Dorian. You might hurt yourself with that thing." Dorian lunged toward me, swinging his weapon, and it bounced off the barrier with an audible crackle and a small flash of light. "Not so tough without your evil trinkets, are you?"

"Your mother thought her shields would keep her safe. She was mistaken," he informed me in an annoyed growl as he rubbed his wrist. "It takes more energy to protect two people. You'll tire soon enough."

My anger surged and the flame of my lighter shot two feet high. I nearly dropped it in response, but instead I took my thumb off the button and killed the fire. "Well, my shields are plenty tough, and you're out there in the dark, completely unprotected, with whatever icky bad the faeries decided to throw at us. I'm just gonna stay in here and enjoy my smoke. I may even conjure up some popcorn while I wait."

"How do you know they put anything in here with us? Maybe we're meant to kill each other." His voice circled me, and I tried to follow the source.

"Works for me, I'm all about killing you. But I'm still willing to put money on the icky-bad theory, say, fifty bucks? Hey, how fried did that dragon leave you? Original recipe or extra crispy?"

An annoyed hiss sounded in the shadows, and I knew I'd hit a nerve. Another flash of light and a crackle of energy behind me alerted me when he took a second swing at my shield. Still no damage. If the darkness didn't attack him soon, it was going to be a really long test.

"Well, I guess it doesn't matter. Even if the monster out there in the dark doesn't get you, the Silverleafs will. They've got extra excruciating plans for you and all your fanged friends."

Dorian's stinging retort was interrupted by a loud roar that shook the ground and echoed off the walls. I paused, blinking in surprise, and then slowly lifted the cigarette to my mouth and inhaled a long drag. "Ooh, that sounds bad."

"Cat, I think your daddy owes you fifty bucks." Lex chuckled.

I doubted it could be another dragon lurking in the dark. The council wouldn't pull the same trick twice. Puffing away at my cigarette, I listened intently for a clue as to what was going on outside the safety of my shields. The low drone of chanting indicated that my father was casting some sort of spell, and the awful stench of necromancer magic wafted toward me.

"You smell that?" Lex asked me, his voice low.

A new scent wove its way through the smoke and necromancy, surrounding me from all sides. I wrinkled my nose in disgust as I sniffed the air, and it took me a moment to identify the unfamiliar and unpleasant aroma.

"Yeah. Sulfur." It's not magic, but instead it's a smell that clings to summoners who delve too deeply into their art, desiring faster, more potent power. The mark of demonic taint. This changed the game—I'd never tested my shields against such concentrated evil, and there was an excellent chance they wouldn't hold against a demon. What the hell was wrong with the Council, anyway? Letting demons loose in Faerie, had they completely lost their minds?

"We're going to need some light to work with," Lex informed me.

"Right." Dropping the butt of my cigarette, I ground it out beneath my boot and wiped my hands on the legs of my cargo pants. Rummaging through my pockets as the gloom pressed in around me, I found my box of matches and struck one against the side of the box. A tiny flame leapt to life, and I held it aloft above my head.

*"Light of life, of right, and pure,*
*Push back the night, let good endure.*
*Burn bright for everyone to see,*
*As I will, so mote it be!"*

A sphere of pure white light swelled from the tiny match and then hovered like a spotlight above our heads, illuminating the entire room. My father stood several feet away, two skeletons at his side. It was obvious he'd raised them with some components he'd carried with him, they couldn't have been native to the area. Their bones were bright white, as though bleached, and they swayed back and forth with soft creaking sounds as the bones rubbed together. Awaiting their orders, no doubt. Disgusting.

A trio of oily shadows loomed behind them, gliding forward, and I screamed in reflex. The demons hadn't taken a form, and really hadn't needed to while concealed in the dark. Realizing they had an audience, the creatures began to form arms and legs, heads and necks popping up out of their torsos like macabre toasters. My stomach flip-flopped and I turned away from the sight, only to discover half a dozen shadowy figures forming behind me.

Lex charged the demons, stabbing his spear through the closest one. There were a lot of them, and I knew I had only a few moments before one got past the guardian. I needed extra help if I was going to stand a chance against them. With shaking hands I fumbled through my pockets, grabbing a pouch of salt and a flask of water. Pouring the salt and water into my cupped left palm, I drew my rapier and sliced the blade through the mix. Blood welled as I broke the skin and it stung so badly my eyes watered, but I coated the entire length of the blade with the combination of blood, water and salt. Heart pounding, I held the sword before me and attempted something

I'd never done before: I invoked a goddess of battle.

*"I call the Morrigan, great Raven of Battle,*
*Bringer of Death,*
*Guide now my hands, my blade, and my breath.*
*Let my weapon be blessed, let it strike true,*
*Bring an end to the shadows, their evil undo.*
*Your daughter invokes you, your favor be won,*
*Heed now my call, let my will be done!"*

My breath hitched in my throat for an anxious second, and then power slammed into me so hard and fast I staggered and nearly fell. The blade of my rapier glowed with mystical fire, and I heard the screeching caw of a raven echo around me, strident above the noises of battle. I tightened my grip on the rapier's hilt, let my shields fall away, and charged the nearest demon with a bellowing battle cry.

As I'd been trained to do against vampires, I stabbed for the heart of the torso, but the oily shadow seemed oblivious to the hit. Demons can't be killed, only banished back to their realm, and that required words in addition to weapons.

"Go to hell!" I shouted, drawing my blade down through the torso with all my strength. The edges of the cut hissed and smoked, and finally the demon dissolved into icky black ooze that puddled tar-like on the ground. I turned toward the next demon and was struck hard in the shoulder, knocking me several steps back as I struggled to regain my balance. I caught a glimpse of my father battling his demon, and one of his skeletal minions clattered to the ground in a useless pile of brittle bones.

Lunging forward, I stabbed at the shadow, missing it as it danced out of the way. The dark figure continued to improve itself as time passed, looking more and more human in shape and form. It eluded my attacks, swiping at me and managing to catch me soundly across the jaw once. Black, unseeing eyes formed in its face, and fangs in its mouth. *Vampire*, the old fear shivered down my spine, and the demon took the opportunity to sweep my feet out from under me. I hit the ground hard, and my breath whooshed out of me in a painful rush. The rapier fell from my grasp as my top hat tumbled from my head. Unable to move fast enough I stared up at the monster as it leapt on top of me. It snapped its fangs at my face like a rabid dog and I struggled to push it off.

I shoved my injured palm against its face and grunted, "Get out." The demon's greasy flesh smoldered and smoked as the last one's had. Pushing hard, my hand sunk into its skin, almost burning through its skull.

"Say goodbye," I said. The demon began to collapse, and I rolled out from under it, scraping the disgusting ooze off the front of my clothes. Lex struggled with three demons off to my left, and I glanced around to see how my father fared in his fight, but I only spotted a second pile of bones with an oil slick next to it.

"Goodbye," Dorian said from behind me. Before I could react I felt the blade of his dagger stab through the small of my back, all the way to the hilt. "I had hoped you would be a greater challenge than your mother. How disappointing."

I would've screamed if I hadn't been so surprised. He withdrew the blade, which hurt as much coming out as it had going in, and I collapsed face forward into the dirt. For a moment I lay stunned, unmoving, and then a sharp kick to my side rolled me over onto my back. I stared up into the face of my father as he knelt down and buried his blade deep into my stomach, a pathetic gurgle my only reply. As he looked down at me I could see myself in his face—the brown of his eyes, the arch of his brow. There were no happy memories associated with the face of my father, no dimly remembered holidays or birthday parties. I knew he never loved me. There was no sorrow there, no pity. No mercy.

Out of the corner of my eye I spotted Lex struggling to finish off the final demon—his back was turned to me, and he had no idea I'd fallen. Dorian left his dagger buried in my belly as he stood, and I reached weakly for it. "You thought you could be Titania. Stupid witch, your kind isn't strong enough to hold it. Maureen certainly wasn't."

"At least I'm not a monster like you," I countered, my voice weak and strained. My fingers fumbled as I tried to grip the hilt of the dagger, and he began to speak the words of a spell—a killing curse that would end this and make him Oberon. I'd come so far, only to lose here.

Suddenly he broke off and dodged out of the way as a silver spearhead split the air where he'd been standing. Furious, Lex moved in a blur as he drove Dorian away from me. The only thing that kept my father from becoming a necromancer shishkebab was his shields, and I knew those wouldn't last long.

I tugged on the hilt, but I couldn't remove it, my hands too slick with blood... Blood. Dammit, I was a witch, I could fix this. *Heal*, I thought as I tugged the dagger free. *Heal*. The word repeated over and over through my mind. Blood flowed from the two wounds, but I was sure I could feel them beginning to close with a wave of stinging energy. I lurched to my feet and snatched up my top hat and rapier, the blade still glowing with divine magic. With the hat mashed securely down on my head, I stumbled toward Dorian.

The demons were gone. Lex must've finished off the last of them while Dorian was stabbing me. Too focused on each other to notice my approach, the guardian and the necromancer faced each other, trading snarled threats. I edged close to them, raised my rapier, and shouted my father's name. Surprised, he whirled toward the sound of my voice, and I stabbed my father through the heart.

The rapier hesitated for a moment at the barrier of his shield before plunging through and piercing his chest. Black fire spread from the blade and engulfed him in a hissing whoosh. Withdrawing the weapon, I watched as Dorian collapsed to the ground, writhing in the throes of terrible agony. Screaming, he tried to extinguish the magical flames.

"I am not my mother. My will is stronger, my blood more potent." I stood over him, and I took a long look at the rapier. The blade continued to glow with ethereal fire, and I turned my gaze back to Dorian. "I am Titania, and I am your judge. You murdered my cousin because you wanted this position. You murdered my mother because she hindered your plans to live forever. This ends here."

Lunging forward, I plunged the rapier through his chest and pinned him to the ground, ceasing his attempts to fight the flames. I wavered, unsteady from my injuries, but then I felt Lex slide a steadying arm around me. Dorian looked up at us in terror, and I watched him with grim determination. Without remorse I spoke the spell that sealed his fate:

*"The laws of nature you sought to breach,*
*Now your judgment you have reached.*
*Punishment for your evil deeds times three,*
*To set the spirits of the wronged free.*
*The end of your life's thread has come,*

*Let Titania's justice now be done."*

It was not a peaceful death by any means, but Dorian had no right to one. Plucking the Justice card from the band of my top hat, I dropped it onto my father's chest and the edges curled and blackened. I left the rapier and stepped away from the body, leaning into Lex. My legs buckled, and he scooped me up.

"Hold on, honey, I'm gonna get you out of here," he assured me. I closed my eyes and gave a silent prayer of thanks to the Morrigan for her aid, and when I opened them again we were in the Underhill great hall, standing in front of Cecelia and the council.

# Chapter Fourteen

"Help her, she's wounded," Lex demanded. He laid me down on the floor and I watched the earthen ceiling spin above me, reminding me of my first appearance in this room.

Cecelia turned to the faerie on her right. "Horatio, if you would be so kind?"

Horatio stood and walked over to me. He was short, squat, with rough brown skin that indicated an earth faerie of some variety. For a moment he looked me over, and then nonchalantly waved a hand above my body. Warm, soothing energy spread through me, and the pain and faint feeling faded away.

"Thank you," I said softly. The faerie's head inclined slightly at my words as he returned to his seat. Lex helped me to my feet, and we stood together in front of the council.

"Congratulations, you've both performed well during the trials," Cecelia announced, and I frowned. *Both of us?* "Catherine Marie Morrow, it is the belief of this council that you have proven yourself to be able to adequately perform the tasks of Titania of your region. We offer you this position, and if you accept it you will be initiated during the next full moon of your realm. Do you understand?"

"I do."

"Do you agree to these terms?"

"Yes."

"Very well," she replied, nodding in satisfaction. Cecelia turned to Lex. "Alexander Duquesne, when it became apparent that you are Miss Morrow's soul mate we endeavored to include you in the testing process. Though you did not participate in the first test, it is the belief of this council that you have proven yourself adequate to perform the tasks of Oberon for your region. You will serve as Oberon jointly with Catherine as Titania, but you cannot be both guardian and Oberon. Therefore, if you accept this, you must forfeit your position as guardian and the abilities that accompany it. We offer you this position, and if you accept it you will be initiated during the next full moon of your realm. Do you understand?"

Silence hung heavily in the air for a long, numb moment. The words "soul mate" stuck in my thoughts, tumbling over and over. Lex had said that we shared a connection, but it hadn't occurred to me that it was a *connection*. Soul mates are a rare thing—a person might live through several life cycles and never come across their soul mate. The idea that I'd found mine was shocking, and the idea that I'd almost let him slip away from me was even more so. Glancing over at him, I saw his expression was carefully controlled, not letting any hint of his thoughts show through.

"If I refuse, will Catherine still become Titania?"

My heart sank—he didn't want to work with me. I suppose I should've expected that. Lex hadn't been willing to jeopardize his position for me before, I guess it'd been foolish to hope he'd be willing to do it now, soul mates or not. I was such an idiot for trusting him again.

"Yes. Though I feel I should warn you that her position will be weakened if you choose not to become Oberon. Do you agree to these terms?" Cecelia asked.

"I need more time to consider."

"Very well. You will have until the full moon to make your decision. Until you make your choice, you will not be allowed use of your guardian powers or responsibilities, as they may unduly influence you. You both may go now, blessed be." With a very slight bow of her silvery head she dismissed us, and we were transported into my apartment. Lex and I stood in front of the mirror in my bedroom.

Tossing my top hat onto the bed, I crossed the room and snapped on the lights. Opening the door, I headed into the kitchen, where I turned the lights on and started to wash the blood from my hands. I didn't turn to see if Lex followed. I wasn't sure what I'd say to him at the moment.

It was strangely quiet in my apartment. The air conditioner

in my bedroom was off, and my cats were still in Faerie. Once my hands were clean I looked down and noticed the bloody stab wounds in my shirt. "Great," I muttered. I really needed to add some Kevlar to my wardrobe.

Returning to the bedroom, I found Lex still standing where I'd left him. His lost, haunted expression was almost enough to suck all the anger right out of me. Almost.

"You gonna stand there all night?" I began unlacing the cuffs of my swordswoman shirt. I needed a shower to clean up. I had a feeling that either we were going to be showering together in a fun way, or we were going to have a big fight and I'd be crying alone in the shower afterwards.

I wasn't giving myself good odds on the fun option.

"You're going to turn it down, aren't you?"

Looking up at me, he frowned. "It's not a simple decision, Cat."

"No shit, Sherlock, but everybody around me bullied me into trying to be Titania. *Oh, you'll be so good at it, it's for the good of the region.* Blah, blah, blah." With the cuffs unlaced, I started on the collar of the shirt. "Not so fun when the shoe's on the other foot, is it?"

"This is different." He slowly flexed the fingers of his right hand, staring down at it as though it'd fallen asleep and he was trying to restore feeling to it.

"No it's not."

"You're asking me to—"

"To give up your life? The thing that makes you special? To be outcast from your family and friends?" I interrupted. "Gee, sounds familiar somehow."

"That's not funny."

"I'm not laughing, Lex." Tugging the shirt off, I held the garment up to the light. It looked like a piece of evidence on a crime show. I almost considered keeping it as a souvenir, but decided to toss it instead. I started to walk out of the room to pitch it into the trash in the kitchen, but I paused as I passed Lex. His magic smelled different—instead of the muddled mix I associated with guardian, he now had the sharp winter chill of an ice sorcerer.

"At least you still have magic," I commented. "Was your family made up of sorcerers before they became guardians?"

"How'd you know that?" he asked, surprised.

I shrugged in reply, and then continued out into the kitchen and tossed my shirt into the garbage. Lex followed me this time and stood hovering in the doorway. "Bein' a guardian is more than a position, it's my entire life. It's who I am. Duquesnes have been guardians for generations. There was never a question of what I'd be when I grew up, only a question of where I'd serve. You're askin' me to give all that up, and not only for me, but maybe even for my children."

*Our children,* I corrected silently. My eyes stung and I turned away, standing over the sink as I fought to keep my composure. There's very little sunshine and rainbows in being a magician—being able to do magic makes your life harder, not easier, and finding your soul mate isn't a guarantee for a romantic happily ever after. My odds of a happily ever after seemed to be shrinking by the minute. Taking a deep breath, I turned and faced him again.

"Look, I know you didn't know this was coming, and I'm sorry. I had no idea about the soul mates thing, and even if I did, I wouldn't have expected this from the council. I've never heard of anything like it before," I said, trying to placate him. Crossing to the kitchen table, I plopped down into a chair, intending to remove my boots, but then I noticed an odd expression on Lex's face. He was hiding something. "You didn't know, right? That this was coming? Did you?"

"I didn't know that they'd offer Oberon to me."

"But you knew about the soul mates?" I asked incredulously, and he nodded. "For how long?" Annoyed, I unknotted my bootlaces and started loosening them.

"Since the attack at Silverleaf castle, when you picked up the spear. There're protective spells on it—only a guardian can handle a guardian's weapon. Anyone else who tries is wounded when they touch it, but you weren't. It didn't harm you 'cause your aura's in tune with my magic. It's the same reason I keep gettin' past your shields."

"Why didn't you tell me?"

"I don't know. I guess I thought you had enough to worry about right now without hearin' that too. Would it have changed anything?"

"I had a right to know." My fingers clenched around the chunky heel of my boot as I seriously considered hurling it at his head, but then I forced myself to drop it. The boots hit the floor with a loud thump, one after the other. I could not *believe* that he didn't tell me something that important.

"What are you doing?" Lex raised an eyebrow, seeming confused.

"Gonna take a shower."

"Don't you think you should—" he paused, and then frowned.

"Should what? Wait for you to stop being a jerk about this? Then I'd never get to shower." Hell might freeze over before he stopped being a jerk.

"I'm not—"

"Lex, when you were picturing our future together, did you see yourself making any changes at all? Or did you just move me into your house and expect I'd go with the flow?"

His gaze dropped to the floor and he ran a hand over his hair. "I guess I did. Cat, this is what I am. Bein' a guardian is all I know how to be."

"Yeah, well, being a witch is all I knew how to be, and when I was cast out, I got through it. I learned how to live as something else, and now I'm going to learn how to be Titania." I peeled my socks off and plopped them into the boots, and then shoved them under the table. "When you figure out what you want to do, you let me know, but in the meantime I think it's best that you leave." Standing, I placed my hands on my hips and stared him down. It was a toss-up whether I was angrier with him than I was at myself. I was such an idiot, I couldn't believe I'd fallen for him again, only to be reminded that I'd always place a distant second to his guardian responsibilities. Apparently even something as momentous as finding his soul mate wasn't worth interfering with them.

"Cat, don't be that way." He sighed.

"What way? Is it really so much to ask that just once I be worth sacrificing something for? My father wasn't willing to give up his search for power to be with me and my mother. My mother wasn't willing to give up on getting my father back and just take care of me. You weren't willing to risk your position to keep my secret safe from the council. Just once, I'd like to be enough, you know?"

"Cat."

"Just go. Please," I said, leaving no room for argument in my tone.

He left.

# Chapter Fifteen

"I really think you should call him, Kitty."

It was the third time the faerie had offered that particular bit of advice in the last ten minutes. Pausing, I flexed my fingers as they hovered above my keyboard, and took a calming breath. Portia was just trying to help. Really. She had no idea that she was quickly driving me nutty bonkers.

"I. Am not. Calling. Lex."

Oblivious to the annoyance in my tone, Portia continued flipping channels. On the surface, everything appeared normal. It was amazing to me how disturbingly normal my apartment felt when I returned home. After all I'd been through, I expected something to be different. I had changed, it should too. The only obvious developments that had occurred in my absence were a few days' worth of dust, a full mailbox, and a ton of new email. Merri and Pippin wasted no time in settling back in once Portia brought them over, and the sounds of scampering feet chasing the ever-elusive catnip mouse echoed throughout the apartment. Though she didn't need to, Portia lingered after her feline delivery. I had a feeling she didn't want to go home. Tybalt's death made Castle Silverleaf a somber place. The brisk, lively cheer had been drained out of it, leaving a chill melancholy in its wake.

I wanted to go into work, but the café was temporarily closed. I filled the free time with surfing the Web for a new job. I couldn't keep working at the café without Mac being there—even if I managed to keep my job, it would never be the same. Besides, it'd just be weird. The customers who saw me as a plain, simple waitress would have no idea that I was Titania, or what that meant. I was an outcast witch who had murdered, and worse, that murder had made me a kinslayer—somehow I doubted Dorian would've struggled with that title if he'd succeeded in killing me. I couldn't stay here, expecting my old life to change to fit my new one. What would I do, hear people's grievances after the café closed while I waited for the pan washer to finish one load and start another?

"Maybe I should talk to Lex," Portia offered.

"Absolutely not. No one is talking to Lex." *Ever again,* I added silently. *Fool me once, shame on you...*

Rain lashed the windows as the summer storm voiced its opinion, and thoughts of the last rainy night I'd spent in my apartment kept buzzing around in the back of my mind. Pulling out my smokes, I lit a cigarette and sighed as I exhaled.

"Well *someone* clearly needs to talk some sense into him—" Portia started, but was interrupted by a loud knock at the door. Frowning, the faerie zipped up from her perch on the couch and flew over to the door. Hovering in midair, she peered through the peephole out into the hallway. "Lord and Lady, what is *he* doing here?"

"Who?" Smashing out my cigarette, I got to my feet. I sniffed the air for magic as I approached the door, but only caught the scent of cinnamon wafting off Portia. "Lemme see," I ordered as I less than gently nudged her out of the way. I spotted a stranger on the other side of the door. A slender young man in a dark gray suit tapped his foot as he waited, glancing about the hallway. Short black hair stuck out in all directions in small spikes, and his eyes were hidden behind round sunglasses with smoked lenses. I sniffed the air again, expecting to catch a whiff of sorcerer, but still only smelled faerie. He looked vaguely familiar, but I couldn't place him.

"Yes?" I called out.

"Miss Baker?"

"Don't talk to him," Portia demanded in a loud stage whisper.

"Why not?" I asked.

"Because he's a *shadowspawn.*"

"What's a shadowspawn?" I'd never heard the term before, and it didn't sound pleasant.

"A faerie who has been outcast for doing acts of great evil."

Evil faeries, just what I needed. Well, at least he hadn't called me Morrow. I'd had more than enough of that from

Cecelia lately. "What do you want?" I asked him through the door.

"May I come in?" he replied.

"Why?"

"I believe we have something important to discuss." Pulling his hands out from behind his back, he held an object up so I could see it: a black felt fedora, slightly sweat-stained around the brim.

I unlocked the door.

"Kitty!" Portia gasped in shock. I couldn't blame her, I was vaguely surprised by my stupidity as well, but I had to know why the stranger had Mac's hat.

The shadowspawn faerie breezed past me into the living room, twirling the fedora in his hands. I eyed him warily—he was certainly no cousin of mine, but I had no idea what clan he belonged to. Though he smelled strongly of faerie, leaving no doubt as to what he was, he seemed faded somehow. Less vibrant.

"Ah, I see you are a smoker. May I?"

"No," Portia answered, hands on her hips.

"Sure, go ahead," I said. "So, who are you?"

Setting the hat on my coffee table, he reached into his jacket and withdrew a black and silver cigarette case. "You may call me Faust. I am here on behalf of my employer, who wishes to extend an invitation to you to meet with him." Selecting a slender black cigarette, he placed it between his lips and the end spontaneously ignited with a tiny pop of magic.

"Who's your employer?" With a name like Faust, I was pretty sure he wasn't working for the good guys. Faust exhaled a stream of smoke that was bright green, and I blinked at it in surprise.

"Zachary Harrison. I believe you've met."

"I'm not surprised," Portia said archly. "His entire family was exiled from Faerie, no wonder they've taken up with monsters."

"Your family's history is not as pure as the driven snow as you would have others believe, Silverleaf. You should be careful who you insult."

"How dare you!" she snapped. The temperature in the living room dropped, as though I'd suddenly come into the possession of an industrial-grade air conditioner.

"Hey, cut it out, both of you. Now I remember, you were in the Underhill's great hall. You sponsored Dorian, didn't you?"

"I did, yes."

"Guess you backed the wrong horse."

"It would appear so," Faust said, smiling thinly.

"So what does Harrison want?"

"To meet with you, nothing more. He promises you safe passage to and from the meeting, and that you will not be harmed at any time."

"A vampire's word has no weight, they have no honor," Portia hissed.

Ignoring her, I eyed Faust. "Uh-huh. And why would I want to meet with him?"

"Because he is in possession of something you hold dear, and if you don't meet with him, the consequences will be...unfortunate."

Suspicious, I glanced at the hat on the table. "He has something of Mac's?"

"In a manner of speaking."

"A manner of speaking?" I repeated, raising an eyebrow.

"Come now, Miss Baker. It was my understanding that you are a clever girl." Picking up the hat, he handed it to me. The fabric was wet from the rain. Cigar smoke and the dry papery smell of librarian clung to the fedora, but there was something else as well, a sharp, coppery tang. I turned the hat over in my hands and noticed that my fingers were stained with blood. Startled, I gasped.

"But...how?" It couldn't be Mac's blood, not this fresh, after all this time. This was a trick, had to be. I handed the hat to Portia to get her opinion, and her deep blue eyes widened in surprise the moment she touched it. From her expression alone I knew—Mac was alive. Alive, and bleeding.

"They never found the body, did they?" Faust asked, and I shook my head. "There is a car waiting outside for you."

"Give me a few minutes to grab my stuff."

The faerie vanished, leaving only a cloud of green cigarette smoke in his wake.

"You are not going with him," Portia ordered.

"But Mac—"

"We can find Mac and rescue him."

"Before they can hurt him? Or kill him? What if they're holding him somewhere you can't go?"

"Well...then..."

"Then I'm going. And you can rescue me later."

Surely it was a trap of some sort, but I wasn't willing to risk it. If Mac was alive I couldn't abandon him. Rushing around my apartment, I threw on as many charms and talismans as I could manage, filled my pockets and my purse, hugged my cousin goodbye and then headed out into the night.

Of course I hadn't thought to bring an umbrella in my hurry to leave, so I wandered out into the downpour unprotected. I don't mind a good storm, and as a water sign I usually enjoy them, but I started to look like a candidate for a wet T-shirt contest in short order. With my head tilted down to keep the brunt of the drops off my glasses, I concentrated on running to the waiting car. As I soon realized, car was really an understatement, because it was in fact a white stretch limo. The driver opened the door for me and I ducked inside.

The interior was leather, the cabin was spacious, and I thought I spotted a bar off to my left. Good, I could use a strong drink. Faust popped into the seat next to me, and I noticed there was a woman sitting across from us. She was pale, bright like a ghost in the night, and hair so blonde it had to come out of a bottle hung straight down her back.

The all-white outfit made me realize who she was: Lovely Laura Barrenheart. White was her trademark—it made her stand out among the other vamps who preferred black, black, and more black in their wardrobes. I blinked at her, wondering what the hell she wanted. Maybe to complain about how I'd killed her pet, but surely my father hadn't meant that much to her. Laura was a council member—she probably couldn't take a step without tripping over one of her toadies.

My shields snapped in place around me. "Well, if it isn't the Wicked Bitch of the Southwest Side. What the fuck do you want?" I asked. Faust made a noise that sounded almost as though he'd swallowed a bug, and then started coughing. Laura's gaze darkened, which was quite a feat considering her eyes were the palest gray I'd ever seen, so much so they were almost colorless.

"Watch your language, Miss Morrow," she warned. Those

pale gray eyes looked me up and down, appearing extremely disappointed by what they saw. "You do not look much like your father."

I studied her in return—she was beautiful, in a Nordic ice-princess sort of way. After getting a better look at her light lashes and eyebrows I had to grudgingly admit that her platinum blonde hair was natural, and not bleached. I don't think I've ever seen anyone naturally have hair that shade, and it made me hate her just a little bit more. What I wouldn't have given in high school for hair that color, instead of the boring brown I'd been cursed with.

"You killed my servant. By our law, that makes you indebted to me."

"Yeah? Well, you killed my mother. I say that makes us even," I countered. Laura shifted in her seat, her thin lips pressed into a firm line. "Not even going to deny that one, are you? Did the council send his body back to you, sword and all?"

Laura growled low, and Faust cleared his throat. "Perhaps it's best not to antagonize her, Miss Baker."

"I doubt she's gonna shed any tears for old Dorian. Laura's gone through more men than a botoxed Hollywood cougar on a bender."

Apparently Laura wasn't used to being mocked, or she had a very short temper, because she lunged across the seats in a blur of motion and attempted to attack me. Her well-manicured claws bounced harmlessly off my shields, and I smiled sweetly. "Gee, blondes really are that dumb."

"That's enough, from both of you." Faust tsked, sounding weary as Laura was thrown back into her seat by an invisible force.

"Sure, whatever you say," I said.

"She was guaranteed safe passage," he scolded the vampire.

"Zachary promised her that, not me. I will not be ordered around by him."

"This brings dishonor to you both, councilwoman," Faust said pointedly.

"That whelp killed my Dorian, I don't care what she thinks."

Her Dorian, huh? Nice.

Deciding I'd had enough excitement for now, I sat back in silence and watched the passing scenery through the tinted windows. The route was familiar enough despite the fact that I don't drive when I travel downtown—I don't own a car, and the train's faster anyway. Plus there's the fact that I don't go downtown very often, which is really just a crime. Chicago's got everything: museums, fine dining, great theater, sports, shopping, and so on. I just don't take the time to fit any of it into my routine, and I made a mental note to rectify that mistake should I manage to live through this meeting.

The limo carefully navigated the rainy streets, and Faust interrupted the quiet. "Well, this is where I leave you. Lady Laura, I do suggest you try to keep your temper in check. Good evening to you both."

The faerie vanished, leaving me alone with Lovely Laura. Heavy silence hung in the air until the limo finally pulled into the parking garage beneath the building. The Harrison building is one of the larger structures downtown, a brand-spanking-new high-rise office building. A gleaming, sleek structure, it was only one of the many Zachary Harrison was reported to own—it wasn't on the scale of the Sears Tower or the Hancock, but still very impressive.

The parking garage was empty, and our footsteps echoed loudly as we walked toward the shiny silver doors of an elevator. As I glanced around I noticed that the place was pristine, clean like no other parking structure I'd ever seen, and the air was surprisingly fresh. When we reached the elevator Laura stepped inside with me, and I tried to stand as far away from her as I could. With the amazing speed of modern technology the elevator whooshed up, whizzing past floor after floor and making my ears pop.

The doors opened on the very top floor—the penthouse of course. Stepping through the doors, I entered a large, open room. Sparse decoration was scattered throughout the area, a Spartan black and chrome design that communicated the modern ideal of "I'm so wealthy I can afford to waste all this space in a city this crowded." Everything around me shone with a high polish, and I felt very small and dirty as I tracked rain and mud on the black marble floor.

Zachary Harrison was seated at his desk, another boring, bland piece of furniture I wouldn't have bought for my apartment no matter how cheaply it was on sale. Maybe I was showing my bourgeois roots, but if I had enough money to buy my own island I'd want some bling in my décor. Since I'd seen Harrison before I was somewhat prepared for the experience. The man really was gorgeous—if you ignored the fact that he was a walking corpse, but the non-magical world had no knowledge of that. The media *loved* him, the paparazzi followed him around everywhere he went, he'd been voted world's sexiest bachelor or something like that by some magazine three or four times. Harrison was rich, handsome, famous, intelligent, always impeccably groomed and dressed, and he would be young and beautiful forever.

The vampire was too enthralled with his computer to bother to look up as I entered the room, and I was too irritated to wait for him to pay attention to me. Laura sauntered over to one of the enormous windows and stood looking out over the city, ignoring both me and Harrison. I headed over to his desk and plopped into a chair across from him.

"If this is the famed Harrison hospitality I've heard of, forgive me if I don't pick one of your hotels for my next vacation."

Harrison's fingers paused above his keyboard as he glanced up at me. "Were you mistreated?"

"Your girlfriend tried to rip out my throat, but it's okay, her claws bounced right off my shields. Oh, sorry about the floor." I waved my good hand at the trail of wet footsteps behind me. "You can put it on Laura's bill."

Anger flashed across his face, quick and terrible, and the scent of new smoke rose around us like a stinging cloud. "Please accept my sincere apology for her behavior, Miss Morrow."

"Don't apologize to that brat," Laura demanded.

"Don't call me a brat, you skanky whore," I countered.

Laura charged at me but, moving in a blur, Harrison zipped around the desk and intercepted her. Scooping her up, he flipped her over his shoulder like a sack of potatoes and carried her to the elevator. She kicked and screamed the entire way, shouting obscenities that even I would be hard-pressed to match. Harrison deposited her in the elevator, and her screeching was cut off once the doors closed, leaving the room in blessed silence.

It gave me a moment of pause—Harrison had just dealt with a member of the vampire council as though she were a cranky toddler on her way to a time-out. I tried to picture someone treating Cecelia of the Silver Crescent that way, and my brain almost bruised itself trying to conjure up that image.

"I didn't send her, I knew she wouldn't behave," he explained as he returned to his desk. "I didn't find out that she'd invited herself along for the ride until after the limo had left." Pausing, he stood in front of me and leaned back against the front of the desk.

"Uh-huh. Where's Mac?"

"He's in good hands. You'll see him shortly, after our discussion."

My heart leapt at the idea that Mac was alive—at least I hoped he was alive. I was gonna be real annoyed if they'd made him a vampire. "What discussion? If you're asking me to call off my cousins, lemme just say right now you're wasting your time."

"I would like the opportunity to speak with your family. However, I invited you here to discuss the possibility of a business arrangement between us."

"Really?" I raised an eyebrow. "You need a waitress that badly? You know there're plenty of good ones looking for work out there, especially in this economy."

The vampire smiled politely. "No, no. This concerns your new position as Titania for our region. My congratulations on gaining the position, by the way. I understand your trials were particularly difficult. I supported Dorian as our candidate, of course, though ultimately I did think him unsuitable for the position."

"Then why support him at all?"

"Better the devil you know than the one you don't," Harrison answered. "At first we were unsure who the other candidates would be, and then once we found out, Dorian continued to be our best answer. We were quite surprised when you became a candidate, and considering your history, I was certain you would not be open to the prospect of working with us."

"Oh gee, why not? I mean, you only murdered my mother and tried to kill me. You invaded my clan's home and killed one of my cousins. Not the brightest thing you've done, because they're going to kill Laura and every damn vampire she's ever made, and every necromancer she's ever recruited. And their families. And their friends."

"That was Dorian's doing, not mine or hers. No one authorized it."

"I don't believe you, and they don't care."

"Dorian tended to solve problems with a slash-and-burn mentality. You will find that I'm much more diplomatic about such things," Harrison replied with a nonchalant wave of his hand. "I would welcome the opportunity to attempt to make amends with your family for his crime."

"Fat chance." I snorted. "Look, just get to the point. What do you want?"

"Your cooperation. We would like to open a dialogue with the residents of Faerie."

I barked a short, derisive laugh. "Yeah right. They won't talk to you, especially now."

"I'm sure they could be convinced to listen, if the subject were interesting enough."

"Well, unless you vamps somehow managed to overcome your abomination status, I don't see how they're going to be convinced to listen to you." I didn't care what his offer was, because the faeries weren't going to take it. Any idiot magician could tell them that.

"They will want to listen to this. We need the help of the faeries. All of us, not simply the vampires. Magicians have lived well while we have been hidden, and better still while the majority of mankind simply does not believe we exist. However in these modern times the voids come ever closer to rediscovering our existence."

"Voids?" I asked, confused. I hadn't heard the term before.

"Humans devoid of magic—straights. Each of us has our own methods for preventing detection, and they have worked well thus far, but in the past few years it has become almost impossible to keep things secret. The government searches for terrorists, and instead they uncover necromancers, shapeshifters, witches and sorcerers. Those of us who are able have been spending a great deal of time and effort to ensure that the investigators come up empty-handed, but there is only so much we can do. Eventually, they will find us, and once the public gets a hold of it...well, as a witch I'm sure you're familiar with the history of the Burning Times."

The blood drained from my face. Thousands, perhaps even millions of magicians were killed during the Burning Times. It was a dark span of our history, when the church declared open war upon our kind. As pacifists, witches suffered the brunt of the attacks. We let ourselves be slaughtered. Martyred.

I licked my lips. "Where do the fairies come into this then? They aren't a part of this world, and they can kick out any fool who tries to invade theirs."

"I think that if given the opportunity, they would like to play a greater part in this one again. To do more than play pranks, cause mischief, and seek out dalliances with the mortals. If they join with us, they can have a solid place in our world again. Perhaps even regain their lost fertility."

That was definitely a carrot that would catch the faeries' attention if dangled in front of them. No offspring of any sort had been conceived in Faerie since Faerie had been conceived itself.

"To what end?"

"My associates and I are of the opinion that we should take the initiative and inform the public of our existence before they stumble upon it themselves—after we take necessary steps to ensure our safety, of course."

"So you want me to tell the faeries about your cunning plan, so they can help you expose all of us to society?" I asked, raising a skeptical brow.

"Essentially, yes."

"Why don't you ask them to help keep us hidden instead? Living with the straights didn't work out before, that's why we went into hiding in the first place."

"This will be different from what came before."

"Why, because society is so much more tolerant than it used to be? Have you looked at the news lately? We'd just be another group for everyone to hate."

"Are you familiar with Machiavelli's work *The Prince*?"

"Sure, read it in college, why?"

"Then you know the theory of how it is better for a leader to be feared than loved. When we lived side by side, we appealed to the populace by helping them. We healed them, we protected them, we educated them, and they repaid us by slaughtering our kind in droves. I propose that this time we rule them, as we are uniquely equipped to do so, and that we be the ones who deal out the death when necessary."

I blinked at him, horrified by his matter-of-fact tone—he would make tyrants out of us. "Oh hell no."

"I assure you, Catherine, it is the only way. I need you to help me set things in motion."

"Absolutely not," I spat.

"I thought you might feel that way, at first. Given time, you'll come to agree with my point of view." Standing, he circled around behind his desk and sat in his chair. Harrison tapped out something on his keyboard for a moment, and then leaned back in his seat.

"Yeah, right, so not going to happen."

"I wish you to stay here until your initiation ceremony, so that we may discuss this further. Will you agree to this?"

"No."

"You may want to hear the second half of that offer before you turn it down," he advised. From behind me I heard the sound of the elevator doors opening, and I turned toward them.

"*Mac,*" I gasped. Leaping to my feet, I ran to meet him, and he'd only taken a few steps out of the elevator when I threw my arms around him in a crushing hug. I'd never been so happy to see someone in my entire life.

"Oof! Glad to see you too, Cat." He was too pale, and seemed thinner than usual, but he was alive. *Alive.* I sniffed him to make sure he wasn't a vamp, and much to my relief he still smelled like librarian. Sweaty librarian, but definitely not a vampire or necromancer.

"What happened? Your plane—everyone thinks you're dead."

"Never got on the plane, they nabbed me before I even got to Midway," Mac replied.

"But why?"

"Insurance," Harrison answered, still seated at his desk. "In case Dorian failed, we wanted to make sure that we had something you valued for negotiation purposes. We had no idea that his plane was going to crash, but it does create an interesting dilemma."

"What kind of dilemma?"

"Well, the world believes that Mr. MacInnes is deceased, because we arranged for the computer records to indicate that he got on the plane. When the plane crashed, he was counted among the dead. To the rest of the world, he's already a dead man. If you do not agree to my terms, Miss Baker, I will kill your friend."

I stared at him, horrified. "And if I agree, we'll both go free and unharmed when the time is up?"

"Of course," he replied, nodding. "We'll even compensate you financially for wages lost while in our company."

I swallowed hard. There were many words rushing through my head, many of them involving four letters, but I choked my anger down and nodded. "All right, you win. I agree to stay until the time of my ceremony and listen to your plans."

"Excellent. For now, I'm sure you could do with some food and rest. And before you try calling your cousins to your rescue, I should also point out that this entire building is triple warded against faeries. They can't hear you, nor will you be opening any portals to Faerie from here," Harrison advised. "I suggest you enjoy your stay for the time being. We will discuss matters further tomorrow, over dinner." He smiled at me, and I really hoped that I wasn't the one on the menu for the meal.

The vampire motioned toward the elevator and I turned to see the doors open, and two giant thugs stepped out. "Please escort Miss Baker to the room that has been prepared for her, and escort Mr. MacInnes back to his room as well. They are not to be harmed in any way, or you will answer to me."

Mac and I entered the elevator, and I clung to his hand like a nervous child. Everyone was silent during the short ride, and then the doors opened to reveal a hallway decorated in warm earth tones, lined with doors on each side and the occasional decorative potted plant.

"This way, Miss Baker," one of the thugs intoned.

I hugged Mac and whispered, "Love you, hon. I'll see you later." Mac gave me a weak smile in return, and then I stepped out into the hallway. The thug led me down a maze of halls until he finally stopped in front of a nondescript door and opened it, ushering me through. Once I was safely inside he shut the door behind me, leaving me alone. Though I had a feeling the effort was futile, I checked to see if the door was locked. Of course it was.

I stood in a short hallway that angled off a few steps away from me. Compared to the cold, barren feeling of Harrison's office, this décor was much more my style—cream wallpaper adorned the walls and the rich burgundy carpet was so thick and plush my shoes instantly sank into it. I looked down at my muddy white sneakers and scowled. With one hand leaning against the locked door for balance, I toed both shoes off and then tugged the damp socks off afterwards. My toes wriggled happily in the unfamiliar feeling of clean, new carpeting, and I walked forward to explore the place further. After the bend the hallway opened up into an enormous room.

"Lord and Lady." I whistled, impressed. Off to my left was a bar, an honest-to-goodness bar stocked with a variety of glasses and bottles of expensive liquor, with three barstools lined up in front of the highly polished dark wood. To my right was a round dining table with four chairs around it, and the room stretched out past the table to include a sitting area with couches, tables and a ginormous flat-screen television hung on the wall. A door across from me led into what I assumed must be another room, and I headed toward it.

The bedroom was also huge, complete with an orgy-sized bed like the one I had in my room in Castle Silverleaf, though this was a much more modern design. The headboard was the same glossy dark wood as the bar and tables in the previous room, and a mountain of pillows were arranged at the head of the bed. An overstuffed easy chair sat in the corner with a table and reading lamp next to it, and there was even a bookcase along the wall next to it. Curious, I crossed to it and examined the titles. They were all books I owned, an eclectic array of the works of my favorite authors. I frowned, concerned. How long had the vamps been planning my stay here? Since they nabbed Mac? Since the moment they heard of my father's death? I supposed it wouldn't be too difficult to find out my reading habits, they only needed to look at the history of my credit card, and that would be a ridiculously simple task for someone like Zachary Harrison.

On to the next room, I decided. The next door was to the right of the door back to the sitting room, and it led to a walk-in closet complete with dressing table and a lighted mirror that took up a good portion of the wall. I jumped, startled by my bedraggled appearance—rain and my hair do not mix well. In the reflection of the mirror I spotted clothes filling the racks behind me. I was willing to bet they were all my size too—there seemed to be a running theme with people feeling the need to makeover my wardrobe. First the faeries, now the vampires. Frowning, I opened one of the drawers and discovered a rainbow of satiny, lacy undergarments.

"Not a chance." I shook my head firmly and slammed the drawer shut.

An assortment of perfume bottles and cosmetics I didn't recognize were spread across the top of the dressing table—I don't generally wear makeup either. I guess I'm just bad at being a girl. I sniffed in their direction and sneezed at the floral mess that assaulted me. Yuck. No way I was touching any of those.

I was willing to bet the door on the other side of the closet connected to the master bathroom, and I confirmed my suspicions the moment I opened it. This was nothing like the one in my apartment, oh no. The room was like having your own personal spa. A marble Jacuzzi tub took up one corner of the room, there was not one but two sinks, and a shower area—I hesitated to call it a stall, it was simply too large—complete with a zillion water jets guaranteed to spray you from every conceivable angle. More bottles of obviously feminine things I had no knowledge of lined the counter of the sink closest to the tub.

Apparently being imprisoned in the head Dracula's tower wasn't going to be as bad as I thought. Probably a good thing, considering I was going to be here for about two weeks. I decided to test Harrison's claim that the place was faerie warded. I called out Portia's name several times, to no avail. I walked over to a mirror and examined it. I wasn't sure if there were any sharp implements about to cut myself with, but then again the place was filled with beauty products, there had to be some clippers or scissors or a razor somewhere.

For several minutes I searched through the bathroom drawers, increasingly appalled by the sheer enormity of the items stored within them. Did women really use all of this stuff? Finally I found a petite pair of silver scissors in a drawer full of nail polish, and I sliced a small cut into the palm of my right hand. Holding my palm flat against the glass, I chanted an invocation:

*"Through ward and steel I punch this door,*
*A portal to home create once more.*
*With blood as key, to set me free,*
*As I will, so mote it be."*

The image shimmered with a faint, anemic glow and then returned to normal. I swore at it loudly and soundly before washing my hands in defeat. It looked like I was good and stuck.

Damn vampires.

# Chapter Sixteen

I thought that I would be much too paranoid to let myself fall asleep in Vampire Central, but as soon as my head hit the pillow I passed out. Admittedly the combination of a relaxing shower, a feast of gourmet food, the softest most comfortable pair of pajamas in the continental United States, and *Casablanca* on DVD might have contributed to my sleepy state.

I drifted into the dream, the transition from sleep smooth and pleasant. The grass was cool and damp beneath my bare feet as I walked into the center of the grove. Soft moonlight pushed back the shadows that lurked between the surrounding trees, and lazy fireflies pulsed on the summer breeze. I felt calm, serene. Powerful. As I smoothed the skirt of my robes the first note of warning chimed in the back of my brain, reminding me that I'd never be caught dead in a set of long, flowing robes while awake, not even if they were a very complimentary shade of emerald green.

Frowning in confusion, I studied my surroundings again, looking for any familiarity, and an approaching rustle of leaves caught my attention. I turned in the direction of the sound, and my heart leapt at the sight of Lex walking toward me. He'd been spared the indignity of dorky wizard robes, but not given the benefit of a shirt—not that I was about to complain about that detail—wearing only a pair of black leather pants.

Apparently this was going to be a good dream.

Without a word Lex drew me into his arms and gave me a long, lingering kiss. When he pulled away, he gazed down at me. "Where are you, Cat?" Confused, I glanced around at the unfamiliar setting. "No, not here. Where did the vampires take you?"

It took my brain a moment to realize what he was talking about and remember the events of last night. The shock of it almost woke me up, but Lex kissed me again and kept me anchored in the dream. "Where, Cat?" he repeated.

"The tower," I finally managed to answer. "Downtown. Ask Portia, she probably followed me."

"She tried, but Faust was blocking her. Is it Harrison's tower?" he asked, and I nodded. Lex stepped back and ran his fingers over my throat, looking for injuries. "Did he bite you?"

"No. Laura tried to tear my throat out, but she just bounced off my shields. Was kinda funny." I tried not to shiver at the sensation of Lex's touch, but failed miserably. Reminding myself that I was supposed to be annoyed with him, I took a step back.

"Don't let him bite you."

"Why do you care?"

"Cat, I don't want to fight."

"Fine. I don't intend to let him bite me," I assured him. "I think he's going to insist, though."

"Don't let him," Lex repeated, more forcefully this time. "I'll get you out soon."

"But you can't, they'll kill Mac," I protested.

"Mac?"

"Mac's alive, he never got on the plane. The vamps took him as a bargaining chip, and they'll kill him if I don't listen to Harrison's stupid plans."

"Then I'll get you both out."

"But you don't have your guardian magic, and I agreed—" Before I could continue a loud crack of thunder interrupted me, and the dream suddenly ended. I found myself wide awake, staring at the ceiling of my suite, wondering what to do. Though I couldn't be certain, for a moment I thought I caught the faint scent of dying smoke lingering in the air.

Aside from last night's rocky start, the bad guys were pretty much refusing to be bad, and it irked me. I was further irked by the idea of having dinner with a man who some trashy gossip magazine had proclaimed one of the most eligible bachelors alive. First of all, the man wasn't alive. Second, I wasn't looking forward to having the head vampire try to sell me some crazy plot to take over the world between dinner courses. I wasn't buying. Period. I didn't care how rich he was, how handsome, polite, powerful, dangerous, blah blah blah. I wasn't my father's daughter, I wasn't going to be swayed to the Dark Side by a good sales pitch and an enticing benefits package. I'd rather serve coffee to cranky people in the Three Willows and barely scrape by than sell my soul to Mr. Sexy Corpse. I'd get out of this, both Mac and me.

Unless, of course, Lex charged in and rescued us. Honestly though, I knew he couldn't do it. He wouldn't have legal grounds to barge into the Harrison building, and I knew all too well how unwilling he was to break the rules on my behalf. I'd voluntarily agreed to stay, more or less, and if I did manage to escape I'd make myself an oathbreaker in addition to being a kinslayer, which would pretty much ensure that no one in magical society would want to deal with me ever again. No point in being Titania if no one would talk to me.

I stood in front of the wall o' clothes in the walk-in closet and wondered what the hell I was going to wear to dinner with Dracula. There were several dresses, ranging from airy sundresses to formal evening gowns, but there was no way anyone was getting me into another dress so soon after Portia's stint as my Extreme Makeover Fairy Godmother. Not a single pair of blue jeans to be found in the whole mess, which I thought was proof of Harrison's un-American activities. It appeared as though I would have to settle on a suit of some sort. There were plenty to choose from, so I picked out a deep blue suit jacket and matching conservative skirt, pairing it with a semi-ruffled white silk blouse.

Unsure of just when Harrison was going to drop by, I settled down in front of the beautiful giant television and started flipping channels. It had every channel imaginable—movie channels, sports channels, pay-per-view, everything. My heart sank as I flipped past the Game Show Network, wondering if Portia was perched on my couch right now trying to figure out the mysteries of the remote without me. It sank further at the thought that Tybalt would never again sit next to his sister, enthralled by the television.

Out of the five million channels I picked a special about baby tiger cubs in an animal refuge. Harrison arrived as the young tigers were gnawing on the legs of the refuge owner's kitchen table, and I barely waved at him in greeting, mesmerized by the cuteness in high definition in front of me.

"I trust you find the room to your liking?"

"It's very nice. I hope you're not billing my charge card for it though, you'll put me right over my limit."

The vampire crossed the room and sat next to me on the couch, watching the screen with a bewildered expression on his face. "What *are* you watching?"

"Baby tigers." He frowned at me, and I rolled my eyes at him. "What? You know there is life outside of FOX News."

"Apparently so. What would you like for our dinner this evening?"

"I'm not on the menu, right?"

"I have no intention of harming you, Catherine," he assured me.

"That's avoiding the question, since I know full well you could bleed me and not cause any harm." Harrison refused to dignify that with a reply, and I shrugged. "What are my options?"

"Whatever you want."

"Anything?"

"Anything."

"So if I asked for a Big Mac and fries, we'd eat McDonald's for dinner?"

The question seemed to throw him. I doubted Zachary Harrison had ever eaten McDonald's in his entire life. He had been born into money, coming from a long line of wealthy businessmen with a somewhat sordid reputation—think "robber baron". "If that's what you wanted, yes." He nodded firmly after a moment's thought.

"Do you even eat? Vampires, I mean." I tilted my head to the side as I regarded him. I knew they needed blood to survive, but I'd never found out if they were completely restricted to that liquid diet. Did they gain weight? Were there fat vampires out there somewhere, binging on doughnuts after feasting on the blood of the living?

"We can eat, but food no longer provides sustenance and isn't easily digestible. Most consider it a nuisance and only eat when an occasion calls for it to keep up a mortal appearance."

"A *mortal appearance*?" I snorted. "Oh, please. You're not

immortal. You're just harder to kill."

Dracula did not look pleased by my comment and again decided not to justify it with a reply. Apparently he'd been brought up better than I had. He definitely was more well spoken. Harrison sounded like the narrator for *Masterpiece Theatre*, and I sounded like a guest on Jerry Springer. Well, maybe not Springer, but something on daytime television.

"I don't suppose we'll be leaving the building for our dinner experience?"

"No, we'll be dining in this evening."

"I'm not really hungry."

"You're not going to attempt a hunger strike, are you?" Harrison raised an eyebrow, appearing amused by the idea.

"No, I'm not." Though my hips could certainly stand a day or two without food, the only person I'd be hurting with a hunger strike would be me.

"You disapprove of the company then?" The vampire actually appeared hurt by that idea, and I blinked at him in surprise. I was hurting Dracula's feelings? Go me. No, I meant bad! Bad Kitty! I needed to be on Harrison's good side if I wanted to remain alive and in one piece. The problem was I didn't think I had it in me to be nice to him. Sure, he was the prettiest man I ever did see, complete with good manners and a pleasant voice, but he was still a damn vampire. The best I could handle was to not light him on fire or stab him in the chest with a leg from one of the expensive wooden end tables.

"Why do you hate all necromancers?" he asked. The bluntness of the question made me pause.

"Because vampires destroyed my family."

"A few unidentified vampires killed your mother, and that's an excellent reason to hate those individuals, but why do you blame all of us?"

On the surface it seemed like a valid question that made me out to be some sort of supernatural racist, but I had no intention of letting it throw me. I sat up straighter in my seat and squared my shoulders. "Because you're evil dead things who feed on the blood of the living and are a horrible crime against nature."

"That's quite a list of indictments. I take it you must be a vegetarian, who recycles, saves the rainforest, and drives the speed limit in a hybrid."

"Very funny." I frowned. "It's not the same thing. You purposely and selfishly take yourselves out of the wheel of life. That's a big karmic no-no."

"If it's such a 'karmic no-no', wouldn't we have been punished by a higher power when the first vampire was created, instead of being allowed to flourish throughout the ages?"

"Oh, please. I can think of a lot of bad things that should've been destroyed on creation and weren't. Like serial killers, or disco," I countered with a roll of my eyes. I wasn't about to accept the idea that vampires were okay just because they hadn't been wiped off the face of the earth in a hail of holy vengeance. There were plenty of evil things out there that deserved to be smote into oblivion and yet weren't. It's almost as though the higher powers have a policy of "it's your mess, you clean it up."

"Well then, what makes you believe that we are incapable of doing good?"

"Your track record, for one thing, and just because you donate money to your family tax write-off charity doesn't mean you're a good guy."

"Not even when that charity helps thousands of people throughout the world every year? I think you're being a bit harsh, Catherine."

"Aren't those the same people you want to rule over with an iron fist?"

The vampire nodded, smiling dryly. "Yes, though that is not entirely accurate. I don't propose that we crush the voids beneath our boots, I'm merely proposing that the magical races should be leaders, in the forefront of society. Not the mystic healer pushed away to live at the fringe of a village, the monster under the bed, or the martyr who chooses to burn rather than to fight back. We can't trust the voids with our lives, not after the way they treated us in the past." Seeing that I wasn't convinced, he sighed and folded his hands in his lap. "Will you at least allow me to prove to you that I am not worthy of your hatred?"

"Umm, you kidnapped my best friend because you wanted him to be 'insurance'. That doesn't really inspire trust."

"And he's alive because of it, isn't he? And unharmed as well."

"There was blood on his hat when your faerie buddy

showed up at my apartment."

"I knew you would require proof that we did indeed have Mr. MacInnes. It was a painless blood draw, no worse than donating to the Red Cross."

"Huh."

"Would you like a glass of wine while you decide what you would like for dinner?" he suggested, and I nodded. He rose to his feet and crossed the room to the bar. He opened a bottle of white—smart move, I don't drink red unless it's a dessert wine—and to his credit he didn't slip anything into the glass as he poured it. When Harrison returned I took the glass and thanked him, and he sat next to me on the couch again.

"Let me guess. You do not drink...wine..." I commented with a bad Béla Lugosi impression.

"Not generally, no." He chuckled. "Have you decided, or should I order something to match the wine?"

I'm not exactly an expert on what matches with food. White wine went with fish? Maybe? Chicken? Letting the vampire pick would probably make him happy. "Sure, you can order."

We chatted politely until dinner arrived, and then we moved to the suite's table. I wasn't sure what it was I ate—a series of fancy courses of tiny portions of strange cuisine. I almost felt like a judge on one of those gourmet cook-off shows. *Yes, the presentation is lovely and the taste is subtle, yet profound.* Not the sort of food my palate was accustomed to, working at the Three Willows and living on a diet of grease, salt and cheese. The vampire didn't eat, which I expected but was still somewhat unnerving, and he continued to engage me in chitchat throughout the meal. This was the charming gentleman I'd seen in interviews. He was cultured, well-mannered and seemed genuinely interested in everything I had to say. If I didn't know he was king of the undead castle, I'd have been very flattered by all the attention.

When dinner was over, Harrison decided to mix me up a cocktail while I sat at the bar and watched, surprised and impressed. I'm sure the man had a legion of people to do this sort of menial labor for him, yet he performed the task with efficient skill. As I sipped the drink, some sort of heavenly chocolate martini concoction, the vampire eyed me.

"Why Baker? I understand not keeping your father's name, but Baker is not your mother's maiden name."

I wasn't prepared for the question—no one had ever asked that before. "I wanted something that I felt represented me, and baking is something I'm good at. Baking cookies with my mom on the weekends was my favorite thing to do as a kid. I make awesome chocolate chip cookies."

"I don't doubt it."

"That's one thing I love about the café: I'm a big believer in the healing power of food. A good burger can cure what ails you. It's not an accident that my butt's so big," I joked.

"I wouldn't call it big."

"No?"

"No. Lovely would be a better word."

I rolled my eyes at the compliment, and he shook his head at my reaction. "You still don't like me very much."

I blushed, feeling a bit bad that I was so transparent after he'd gone through the effort of being a courteous host. "No. Well, yes, but we aren't working under ideal circumstances here. You're Mr. Rich and Pulseless, and I'm just a waitress from the suburbs. A waitress who just happened to find her mother ripped apart by vampires. No matter how friendly you are, I can't have a warm fuzzy feeling to all this." I waved a hand at the gorgeous room around me for emphasis. "I'm not exactly here on vacation, considering you blackmailed me into staying."

"Regardless, you are my guest, and I wish you to be as comfortable as you can be while you are here," Harrison said, attempting to placate me. "And for the record, I do have a pulse."

"You do?"

"See for yourself." Pushing back the cuff of his sleeve, he bared his wrist and held it out to me across the polished wooden top of the bar. I eyed it warily, expecting some sort of trick. I reached out two fingers and lightly placed them against the vampire's skin. He was cool to the touch, as though he'd been sitting under an air-conditioning vent for too long, but he wasn't a popsicle. Not cold enough to qualify as a corpse, but still abnormal. Trying to remember back to my Girl Scout days and my first-aid patch, I felt around for a pulse. I found a slow, sluggish beat beneath my fingertips, like the sleepy tune of a waltz. I frowned, somewhat surprised, and then I caught the scent of smoke as I felt an electric line of heat shoot up through my fingers and zing through my body.

"Whoa!" Snatching my hand away, I glared at him. Rising to my feet, I stepped back from the bar.

"My apologies, I didn't mean to harm you."

"What'd you do?"

"Increased my heartbeat to raise my body temperature. I didn't realize you'd be affected by it. Actually I'm quite surprised you were able to sense it at all." Harrison seemed impressed by my abilities. "You really are quite remarkable, Catherine."

I opened my mouth to correct him, to tell him to call me Cat, but my good sense kicked in and reminded me that I didn't want to be on a chummy, nickname basis with Dracula. Instead, I shrugged and thanked him.

"Well, now that I've made you uncomfortable I suppose this is a good point to end our evening," Harrison said, smiling dryly. Stepping out from behind the bar, he crossed over to where I stood, and taking my hand, he raised it to his lips and brushed a light kiss across it. "Thank you for a lovely evening, Catherine."

A faint blush stained my cheeks as I struggled to come up with a reply. It was most tempting to ask if I could go home now, but I had a feeling it wouldn't go over well. Flustered, I stared up at him. He had stunning green eyes, the same shade of emerald green that my robes had been in my dream. Lex's warning leapt into my thoughts, as though he stood behind me, speaking the words aloud. I backed away, but the vampire tightened his grip on my hand and pulled me tight against him.

The magic washed over me in a wave of smoke and lust, and I recognized it as the same seductive spell Simon had placed over me. My heart did a startled flip, and though my brain warned me to back the hell away, my body seemed to be happy right where it was. With one hand firm against my back, Harrison placed his free hand under my chin and turned my gaze up to his. The color had somehow drained from his eyes, making them a pale, watery green. The smoky smell intensified, and what little part of me that hadn't been inundated by Harrison's magic cringed in anticipation of being bitten.

And then he kissed me.

The sheer shock of it allowed me to shove more of his influence away, just enough to let me struggle in his arms. I felt a small but sharp nick of pain on my lower lip, and dimly recognized the faint taste of blood in my mouth. Aside from the bloodshed, Harrison was quite a talented kisser—I'm sure he had a lot of practice with the never-ending parade of models and Hollywood starlets the man dated. Yet aside from the spell I felt nothing, none of the fire and emotion I felt with Lex. This was empty, hollow. Fake.

I managed to turn my head away and break the kiss, but the vampire took that as an opportunity to plunge his fangs into my exposed throat. I shuddered and my legs went weak at the knees as another wave of power rushed through me. I didn't think it possible, but the sensation was even stronger than Simon's bite had been. The realization frightened me. I'd let Simon bleed me into unconsciousness, would I let Harrison bleed me to death?

Harrison moaned against me, like a diner appreciating exquisite cuisine, and I gathered my resolve to fight. His effect on me was magic, nothing more, and having experienced it before I was pretty sure I could fight it off if I concentrated hard enough. Focusing on the memory of Lex's voice telling me not to let the vampire bite me, I gathered a wave of energy and shoved Harrison away with my shields. The energy fizzled and faded after a moment, as I was too scattered to concentrate enough to keep them up, but they'd helped. Harrison stared at me, almost slack-jawed with amazement, and I took the opportunity to haul back and slap him hard.

"I. Am not. For dinner," I informed him, my voice weak and breathy. Staggering away, I backed toward the bedroom. It made no sense to try and head for the hallway—I'd only run right into the security guards and I doubt they'd be sympathetic to my plight.

"How did you do that?"

"Magic," I said snidely.

"You severed the spell, that's not possible." The vampire glided toward me, the expression on his face reminiscent of a scientist studying a specimen under a microscope. I turned to bolt into the relative safety of the bedroom, but he moved with frightening, unnatural speed and caught my arm, hauling me back against him.

"It is too possible, you're just used to easy women." Wriggling and squirming, I tried to fight my way out of his iron grip. The stench of vampire magic rose around me so strong that my eyes watered, and it triggered a sneezing fit. Either it's difficult to bite a girl who's sneezing like someone with cat allergies standing in an animal shelter, or Harrison was just too shocked by the reaction to respond, because my neck remained fang free long enough for me to manage to put up my shields and shove him away again.

Like a terrified bunny I bounded through the doorway to the bedroom and cut to my left, through the closet and into the bathroom. Slamming the door behind me, I locked it and turned to my reflection to see how bad the damage was. My throat hadn't been ravaged or anything, but there were definitely two bleeding holes in the side of my neck that would make a horror film director proud. With some arterial spray I'd qualify for a Tarantino movie.

"Catherine!" Harrison called from the other side of the door. The knob jiggled but refused to open. Thank goodness the man demanded quality construction in his buildings. I wiped my right hand over the wounds and placed my open palm flat against the door, drawing a sloppy protective pentacle.

"*Open only for light and life, seal thyself from death and blight,*" I breathed a quick impromptu spell. The smeared symbol glowed brilliant white for an instant, burning its image into the wood. An indignant, inhuman howl sounded from the other side of the door, and I drew myself up in satisfaction.

"*I am not on the menu,*" I yelled at the very top of my lungs. "Now get the fuck out!" Deciding to make my point clearer, I grabbed the nearest bottle of bath oils and hurled it at the door (after I'd backed away far enough to avoid the glass that exploded everywhere on impact). "Out, out, *OUT!*" I screeched, throwing another bottle with each word. The room filled with a horrid mix of floral scents, but I was really more concerned with the scent of dying embers that seeped in under the bottom of the door. It rattled on its hinges but stayed shut, and a long string of curses followed. I responded to said string of curses with one of my own, a parade of colorful metaphors commenting on Harrison's parentage, breeding, manners and various suggestions of just what he could go do with himself.

Sitting as far as I could from the door, I snatched up a washcloth and held it to the side of my neck to staunch the bleeding, and then curled up and hugged my knees to my chest. I supposed it was a petty female thing to hide in the bathroom and throw things, but if being a petty female kept me from being on the dinner menu then I was all for it. Course I had no idea what I'd do when someone managed to open the door. I'd deal with that problem when it occurred.

# Chapter Seventeen

The spell proved powerful enough that it kept out maintenance men as well as vampires, which made me wonder what sort of people Harrison hired to maintain his building. It didn't help their cause that the hinges were on my side of the door. As far as I could tell, no one with an impure heart was getting through the door thanks to my improvised spell, and a magical locksmith with a pure soul is something you just don't find advertised in the yellow pages.

I'd made a good choice by picking the bathroom to barricade myself in. I had water, a toilet, plenty of fluffy towels, and my toothbrush. My fat ass could use a day or two of starvation, so I was all set. After arranging a nest of towels into a makeshift bed, I fell asleep on the floor. Insistent knocking woke me from a deep and dreamless sleep, and I mumbled several unkind suggestions in the direction of the noise. Blearily I glanced at my watch and noted that I'd been left in peace for several hours, a pleasant surprise.

"Cat, honey? You okay?" a familiar voice drawled from the other side of the door.

"Lex?" I squeaked.

"Yeah it's me. You gonna let me in?"

I fought back the urge to leap to my feet and throw the door open. Was this a trick? A sneaky ploy by one of Harrison's minions to get me to open the door? Wouldn't surprise me. I approached the door and sniffed it—the air was still so thick with vampire magic it triggered a sneezing fit. "How do I know it's really you?"

"Should I slip my driver's license under the door?" he asked.

"No. How'd you get here?"

"Drove."

"That's not what I meant." The man was irritating enough to be Lex, that much was sure. "How'd you get past Dracula and his thugs?" Images of Lex opening up a can of whup-ass inspired by the many blockbuster action movies I'd seen zoomed through my thoughts. Maybe it was my lucky day and Lovely Laura had lost her head, literally.

A chuckle sounded on the other side of the door, and I pictured him smiling and shaking his head. "They had to let me in to check on the health of the Titania. Kinda like havin' a search warrant. Now are you goin' to open the door or am I goin' to have to pick the lock?"

"I want proof you're really you."

"Thought you might say that. I have chocolate chip pancakes for you."

I unlocked the door.

Lex grinned at me as he leaned against the dressing table, looking out of place surrounded by the girly glass perfume bottles and the lighted mirror. Of course I did the sensible, composed thing, and threw my arms around him and kissed him as though I was afraid he'd disappear when I stopped.

"It's okay, honey, you're all right," he murmured once he pulled away. With an enormous amount of effort I swallowed the urge to burst into tears and buried my face into his chest. Lex continued to murmur to me for a few more moments as he held me close, until he finally turned his head and spoke to someone standing in the doorway to the bedroom.

"She's leaving with me." There was a steely, almost frightening tone in his voice. It was so different from his normal easygoing drawl that if I hadn't been pressed against him I wouldn't have known it was Lex talking. I turned to see who was the intended target of the scary voice, and a rush of anger sizzled through me as I spotted Harrison. The vampire was dressed in a new expensive suit, and he watched us with an intrigued expression. Said expression turned to surprise when I moved with speed that shocked even me, snatched up the nearest perfume bottle, and hurled it at him. The delicate glass cylinder shattered upon impact and splattered the front of his suit with a strong, obnoxious floral scent.

"You son of a—"

Lex grabbed hold of me and prevented me from showering the head vamp with more perfume retribution. That didn't stop me from cussing Dracula out though, and two light bulbs exploded over the dressing table, victims of my fury.

"You said you wouldn't bite me," I snapped.

"No, I said I wouldn't harm you, and I haven't." Harrison made a great show of slowly brushing away the remnants of the bottle, refusing to let his calm be ruffled. Turning me toward him, Lex peered at my bloodstained clothes and the twin bruises on my neck, and then he ran his fingers over the marks to better gauge how bad they were. I resisted the urge to flinch, but honestly it didn't hurt a great deal. Harrison's bite had been fairly neat and the holes had healed shut. Normally a wound that small would've been completely healed by now, but I had a feeling that because magic was involved it interfered with the healing process.

"This looks like harm to me," Lex accused.

"Miss Baker suffered no permanent damage. She is not leaving with you, because she agreed to stay here until the full moon. You are only here to observe her condition, as was agreed. Though I must admit after tasting her blood I'm considering keeping her as a pet," the vampire commented, his tone as casual as if he were remarking about the weather.

"Oh hell no." There was no way I was allowing myself to be signed up as a permanent menu addition. Ever.

"Catherine is Titania for the Midwest. She serves Faerie, not you. You can't keep her here once the agreed upon time is over."

"Miss Baker has not been officially appointed Titania as of yet. That makes her fair game. Besides, she may very well wish to stay once the time is over."

"I'm not anybody's game," I growled. Harrison ignored me, and it made me long for my lighter. I bet he'd respect me more after I lit his undead ass on fire. Temper sizzled through me and the rest of the bulbs around the mirror began to flicker and buzz ominously.

Before I could continue destroying innocent lighting fixtures, Lex drew me against him and gave my arms a squeeze to remind me to control myself. "This isn't a fight you want to pick, Harrison. You already put her clan on the warpath, and they can wipe out every vampire from here to Miami if you give them reason to."

"But they won't, not for a cousin, and someone who hasn't yet been crowned Titania." The vampire smiled, a sly expression that made my stomach roil and my fists clench. "Miss Baker stays here for now."

"For now," Lex replied. "But Catherine is my soul mate, and when your agreement is over, she'll be leaving with me. If I hear that you laid a hand on her during her stay, I'm gonna take it personal."

"Is this true?" Harrison raised an eyebrow at me.

"Yes," I answered. The vampire looked royally annoyed by my statement, and I had absolutely no sympathy for him.

We glared at each other in strained silence, but then he shrugged nonchalantly at the idea. "Very well. Catherine will continue to enjoy my hospitality for now, after which I will return her to you."

"Your hospitality hasn't been up to par, Harrison," Lex warned, cutting me off before I could launch into a hailstorm of expletives.

"A lapse in judgment, for which I apologize. You have my word that Miss Baker will not be harmed or bitten against her will." It wasn't much, but it was something. I turned my attention back to Lex and stared up at him.

"You'll be okay, sugar. I'll see you soon, I promise," he said softly. Something in his eyes made me want to burst into tears, and I choked the feeling down. All I could manage was a nod and a weak smile. Lex turned toward Harrison, looking grim and determined. "Don't cross me, Harrison. You don't want to pick this fight."

"Duly noted. Now if you would be so kind..." The vampire extended an arm toward the exit.

After a long parting kiss Lex walked away from me, and for a tense moment it looked as though he was going to take a swing at Harrison. Instead he kept his temper in check and glared at the vampire. "If you put your hands on her again, I will end you," he said, his voice so low I could barely hear it across the room.

Without waiting for a reply Lex turned and disappeared from my sight. Harrison followed, leaving me alone and unsure of just what to do with myself. Since I was already in the closet I decided now was as good a time as any to grab a new change of clothes, as the sensible blue suit I'd chosen for dinner last night was a tad bit on the rumpled and bloodstained side. Yet another outfit I'd been extra hard on—guess I wasn't a friend to fashion anymore. Not that I had ever been in the first place, but until recently my previous clothing destruction experiences had all been of the tragic waitressing-accident variety.

There was still not a pair of blue jeans in sight and it was downright un-American. If I was going to be trapped in the tower, I needed comfortable pants. I stood with my hands on my hips and surveyed the selection. Eventually I heard a soft step in the doorway. Harrison had returned.

"I'm not talking to you," I informed him.

"Catherine, I apologize for my behavior last night, it was inexcusable."

Pausing in my search, I glanced over at him. His expression seemed sincere but there was no way I was going to buy that. Vampires don't apologize for being predators—it's like a lion feeling remorse for the gazelle it just brought down. He must have realized from my less-than-pleased reaction that putting the bite on me wasn't going to endear me to him, and now he was doing damage control. Right, good luck with that one, fang-face.

"Please, hear me out," he said. Emphasizing my displeasure, I ignored him and concentrated on rummaging through hanger after hanger of endless blouses. "I'm not leaving until you've heard what I have to say." Apparently Harrison was still not entirely clear on the concept of "no", and I wouldn't be rid of him until he'd spouted whatever apologetic speech he'd prepared.

"Fine, what do you want?"

"A second chance."

I barked a short, bitter laugh. "That's nice."

"We still have several days to spend together. It will be easier if you will at least listen to what I have to say."

"Uh-huh."

"Need I remind you that part of our agreement involves you listening to what I have to say? If you refuse to hold up your end of our bargain, I have no reason to uphold mine," he informed me.

A chill ran down my spine—I *had* to listen to Harrison, Mac's safety depended on it. "Okay, okay, I get it." Checking the tag on a blouse, I sighed in disappointment when I couldn't find the type of fabric listed anywhere, only some fancy designer name embroidered in a flowing script. "If I didn't know you had more money than some countries, I'd suspect you of being a communist."

"What makes you say that?"

"No jeans. Denim is the American way. They do make designer jeans, you know. Not that I own any," I trailed off. "And exactly what do you have against white cotton socks?"

"My apologies, I did not choose the wardrobe."

"Oh yeah? Who did?"

"Ms. Barrenheart."

"Figures." I snorted derisively. "So what's her real name anyway? I bet it's long, contains a ton of consonants, and ends in -ski." Tossing the blouse over my shoulder onto the floor behind me, I looked for another candidate. If Lovely Laura had picked these clothes out, I was going to be extra mean to them. A couture bonfire might be in order.

Harrison changed the subject, wisely avoiding answering any Laura-related questions. "Catherine, I am truly sorry for my actions. I was surprised by your abilities and I let my curiosity get the better of me."

"The old 'curiosity killed the Cat' story. Very original. Never heard that one before."

"It's the truth," Harrison insisted. "I've never encountered anyone like you."

I pitched another blouse onto the floor and glared at him. "You just aren't used to people telling you no. I'm sure you have at least heard of the word before."

"Well, yes."

Chuckling ruefully, I shook my head at his confused expression. It was likely the sad truth, after all he had been raised a spoiled little rich boy who grew into a spoiled rich man. Zachary Harrison was the very definition of privileged. I doubted there were many people with enough spine to refuse him anything.

"Yeah, well, I'm sure all the girls just throw themselves at your feet and are more than eager to open a vein for you. Not this girl."

"Which is what I don't understand."

"What don't you understand?"

"How you can be immune." Slowly Harrison stepped toward me, cautious not to spook me. I watched him like a bunny eyeing a snake, but I resisted the urge to bolt since just moments ago he had given his word to Lex that I wouldn't be harmed, and I didn't think he was going to go from businessman to oathbreaker in that short a time span.

"May I?" he asked.

"May you what?"

"A small touch, nothing more."

With Mac's continued safety in my thoughts, I nodded a grudging reply, and Harrison reached out and took my hand in his. I felt a sizzle of spell at the contact, but I was prepared for it and pushed his magic back and refused to let it affect me. The vampire seemed amazed by this and turned my hand over, peering at it as though my skin would reveal some vital clue as to why I hadn't been reduced to a panting puddle of lust on the floor.

"Here's a hint: magic," I explained, drawing my hand away.

"I have encountered witches before. I also deal with sorceresses on a regular basis, in fact. Nothing like this has ever occurred."

"How many of them hated vampires?"

"None, I suspect."

"There you go."

For a moment we sized each other up. I was surprised he wasn't angry about it—I almost expected a frustrated temper tantrum, but Harrison seemed too polite for that. Instead he tilted his head to the side, looked me up and down, and then picked out a deep green silk blouse and held it out to me. It was the most acceptable shirt I'd seen thus far, but I tossed it over my shoulder and added it to the pile. I grabbed a white cotton shirt instead.

"I'm not buying the apology, Harrison. You wanted to butter me up and put the orgasmo bite on me so I'd be all about your fiendish master plan and get you the faerie hook-up. The bite backfired and now you've dug yourself into a pretty deep hole. I don't think you can climb out of this one."

"I'm willing to try," he said, sounding awfully sincere. As if punctuating his good intention Harrison handed me a pair of plain black pants and loafers, exactly the sort of clothing I was looking for next.

"Uh-huh. Well then we're going to get one thing straight right now." I scowled, placing my hands on my hips. "Since you're obviously not familiar enough with it, let's go over the meaning of the word no. *No* means stop. It means *don't.* It means I'm *not* okay with what you're doing, and you need to cease and desist said activity. *No* is not an invitation to try and change my mind to yes. *No* does not mean ply me with more alcohol until I'm too drunk to speak coherently or become unconscious. You were a frat boy in college, weren't you?"

"It was expected as a family tradition." Though he was listening to me, I had the impression my speech wasn't really getting through to him, and I sighed in disappointment.

"Why am I not surprised. Look, I don't want you to bite me. Period. Not under any circumstances."

"I gave my word that you would remain unharmed."

"Yeah, you also said you had no intention of harming me before you bit me, so I'm not real convinced by that."

"I had no idea you would find it harmful, no one else has," he reasoned.

"Well I do."

"Now that I know that, I will make sure no one lays an unwelcome fang upon you, Catherine." There was amusement in his expression, and I shook my head in annoyance. I didn't find it funny at all.

"Okay. Now leave so I can change, please."

With a polite bow he turned and left, shutting the door behind him. I wasted no time in shedding my clothes and donning the new ones. I considered taking the time to shower, but I wasn't sure if I trusted my surroundings enough to be that vulnerable at the moment. Instead I searched the bathroom for something to clip my hair up with, and found some hair sticks that let me twist it up into a bun.

When I emerged into the sitting room the chocolate chip pancakes Lex had tempted me out of the bathroom with were waiting for me on the table. Unfortunately Harrison was also waiting for me, seated across from my plate as he had been at dinner the night before. Well, I wasn't about to let him keep me from eating, so I took a seat and dropped the white linen napkin into my lap. I picked up a glass of orange juice and took a cautious sip.

"Is there anything I can get for you?"

"A cab ride home," I quipped, and he smiled dryly.

"I'm afraid I can't do that. Anything else?"

"You could leave," I suggested, and he ignored the request. Hungrily I began slicing the pancakes as I considered his offer. There were a lot of things that came to mind, but many of them revolved around food in my famished state. I could use some email access. Lock picks. Maybe something to dig an escape tunnel with.

"I wanna have dinner with Mac. And not you," I blurted after swallowing a mouthful of pancake.

"Pardon?"

"Tonight. I want to have dinner with Mac. Just me and Mac, so I can catch him up on the gossip. Oh, and I'll need a Sears catalogue too, 'cause I'm not wearing Laura's clothes."

"Very well, I will arrange that. I must insist on dinner tomorrow evening, however. Oh, I would have appreciated being informed of the fact that Alexander is your soul mate before our dinner last evening. It's a foolish man who allows himself to get on the bad side of a Duquesne. I was prepared for him to be involved professionally with your stay here, but his personal involvement is another matter entirely."

"I thought you knew that, because they offered him Oberon."

The vampire's eyes widened, and I could've sworn his jaw dropped at my words. "The council offered him Oberon?"

"Yeah. You didn't know that, oh great and powerful Lord of the Tower?" Harrison seemed to know everything else about my business, it seemed odd he hadn't heard about that particular detail.

"No."

"Huh. They announced that I agreed to be Titania though, right?" I questioned, and he nodded. "Maybe they didn't say anything because Lex didn't—"

"Didn't agree to it?" Harrison finished.

"Yeah."

"Interesting. Well, *bon appétit.*"

Harrison smiled as he rose from the table. I gave him a weak parting wave in reply as he left the room. I finished the pancakes in silence, enjoying the fang-free time. Unsure of what to do with myself when I was done eating, I decided to shower. After all, I might as well be neat and clean for whatever drama bomb exploded in my lap next.

I read for the rest of the day instead of parking myself in front of the TV again. Even my favorite book couldn't lift my spirits. I found myself making snide remarks at the hero and heroine instead of enjoying the romance. My mind kept drifting back to Lex and I in the snowy courtyard of Silverleaf castle on the night of my celebration ball. *It was my fault that you were attacked that night. I should've been there...* Well if he'd been in my apartment when Faust showed up, I wouldn't be here, either. Sure I was glad that he'd showed up to check on me today—I hadn't expected it—but it would've been better if I'd hadn't been lured to Vampire Central in the first place.

Mac showed up promptly at six o'clock. He stood near the bar, glancing around the suite as a waiter set the table for our dinner. I wasn't sure I could take another gourmet experience, but when the dishes were uncovered a simple meal of pasta was revealed. The waiter left, and Mac ducked around behind the bar.

"Nice place. What do I have to do to get my own bar?" he joked. Choosing a bottle of wine, he searched for a corkscrew.

"Let the head vampire molest you," I replied.

"I'm fine with that, he's gorgeous. I don't think I'm his type though. Pity." Tugging the cork free of the bottle, he crossed to the table and poured us each a glass of wine.

"He's pretty, but he's a jerk. Have they been treating you well since they nabbed you? Not using you for a blood donor?" Flopping down into the chair, I sipped at the wine. Not bad, but then again I knew Mac had better taste than I did.

"No. Most vampires aren't interested in dining on librarian. I've heard we taste too dry for them."

"So, what've you been doing?"

"Reading, mostly. They let me borrow some interesting texts about the history of a few of the Italian sorcerer families, which are completely sordid in a very daytime-television kind of way." Mac sat across from me and dropped his napkin into his lap. "I have to say, the food's not bad. I'm thinking of adding risotto to the dinner menu at the café."

"I have to get us out of here soon. The café's been closed. Your family's not sure what to do with it."

"We're out of here on the full moon?" he asked, and I nodded. "Well, that's good. I was a little concerned that they'd keep me here indefinitely. Congratulations on becoming Titania, by the way."

"I'm not Titania yet. Soon-to-be-Titania. They offered Oberon to Lex, he turned it down." I took a long drink of wine, emptying half the glass in one long gulp, and Mac stared at me.

"They did *what?* Is that even possible?"

"Apparently so. The council figured out that Lex and I are soul mates, so they offered to let him be Oberon to my Titania. Okay, technically he hasn't turned it down yet, but he said he'd think about it, and I know he's going to say no. He's not going to do anything that would jeopardize his guardianship. Guardianness. Guardianocity. Whatever."

Pausing with his fork halfway to his mouth, he slowly put it back down on his plate. "Soul mates?"

"*I know.* And he *knew.* He knew when I touched his magic spear thing and he didn't tell me. Because he's a big dumb *jerk.*"

Mac raised his eyebrows, surprised, but then he grinned. "You touched his magic spear? I'm assuming that's not a euphemism for something lascivious."

"Mac!" I gasped, and he laughed.

"Sorry, hon, I couldn't resist. Well, it's probably for the best. You knew he'd be moving on after this assignment anyway," Mac assured me. Looking down at my plate, I pushed the pasta around aimlessly. Ravioli in some sort of cream sauce—it smelled delicious, but I was rapidly losing my appetite. "Okay, Cat, spill."

"Lex and I...guess we kinda got back together for a bit. He started talking about plans for the future. Having me meet his family, get married in New Orleans, that sort of thing. Then they told him he'd have to give up being a guardian if he wanted to be Oberon. I'm sure you can guess how well that went over."

"Like a lead balloon. Do you want me to have a talk with him?" Mac's shoulders straightened as he sat up in his chair, sounding like an overprotective older brother. "Or maybe Tybalt should speak with him."

At the mention of my cousin's name I reached out, picked up my glass of wine, and drained the rest of its contents. "There was an attack on the castle, Tybalt was killed during it. By

Dorian. Dorian really had a lot to answer for, I hope he's rotting in hell."

"I'm sorry to hear that. I liked Tybalt. Well, let's drink to Dorian rotting in hell," Mac suggested, refilling our glasses.

The rest of the evening was spent trading gossip and making plans. Words could barely describe how grateful I was just to spend time with Mac. It felt like a miracle that he was alive and well, like I'd been given a second chance to appreciate our friendship. We drank wine, watched trashy tabloid television, and did our best to pretend that we weren't the unwilling guests of some of the most powerful vampires in the United States. When his escort showed up at ten to take Mac back to his room, I gave my friend a long hug and silently promised that I'd make sure we both got out alive and safe.

# Chapter Eighteen

After Mac left, I stayed up later than I should have, enthralled by nature specials in high definition and surround sound (nothing quite like hearing the sharp snap of bones when a lion snacks on a wildebeest). When I went to bed I considered dragging the reading chair across the room to barricade the door, but it was too heavy and I was too tired to deal with it.

Drifting off to sleep, I soon found myself standing in the grove once again. Turning, I spotted Lex standing a few feet away, his back to me. He was shirtless, and I could read his tension in the pinched muscles of his shoulders.

"I thought I told you not to let him bite you," he said, his voice accusing.

"*Let* him bite me? You think I *let* him do that? Like I was bored and just decided to open a vein for the hell of it?" I snapped in reply, offended.

Lex whirled around, crossing to stand in front of me in quick, angry strides. "Why not? You agreed to stay with him 'til the ceremony."

"Because he has Mac. He'll kill him if I don't cooperate."

"You could've called me, we could've gotten Mac out together. It's dangerous, Cat. You don't know what a vampire that powerful can do once he's tasted your blood."

A chill ran down my spine, and I rubbed my arms in reflex. It was true. I didn't know what sort of things Harrison could do to me, only rumor and old wives' tales. Vampires don't feed on the blood itself, but on the magic within it. I wasn't sure if that could be used against me.

"I couldn't call you, Lex," I replied, shaking my head.

"Why not? Why couldn't you call me?"

"We didn't exactly part on good terms. Besides, you're only there for me when it doesn't risk your reputation. You don't ride to my rescue unless it's convenient, or you're ordered to." I felt guilty the moment the words left my mouth, and I glanced away, unable to meet his eyes. Lex growled in annoyance, and then drew me to him. He kissed me, fierce and possessive, his fingers tangling in my unbound hair. I leaned into him, too weary to fight and too hungry for his embrace. After several long moments his hands fell to my waist, intent on untying the cord that belted my robes.

"Don't," I said, pulling away.

"Why not?"

"Because when I wake up I'll still be in the tower, and you still won't know whether or not you want to be with me."

"Then shouldn't this be a good dream?" he countered.

"I need more than a dream. I either need you with me, or I need you to leave. I can't live on the hope that maybe you'll find a way to work me into your life."

"I love you, Cat."

"I know. But that's not enough. It never was."

I turned to walk away, and the dream faded. The rest of my dreams after that were a jumble of images. Cool hands slid over my bare skin, Harrison's voice whispered to me, assuring me that everything would be better if I just stopped fighting. When I awoke I discovered a Gordian knot of sheets tangled around me, drenched with sweat, and the taste of blood in my mouth. A panicked dash to the mirror revealed that I'd bitten my lip, and because my neck was free of marks I let myself relax. The blood was just part of the dream, nothing more. I even managed to heal my lip completely by the time I was out of the shower.

After my shower, I emerged from the bedroom to find a gift bag tied with curling red ribbon next to my plate of pancakes. Fruit pancakes this time, I noted as I crossed over to the table. Untying the ribbon, I discovered several department store catalogues. Sitting down, I plopped the napkin into my lap and divided my attention between my food and the catalogues. Attached to the top one was a note, and I opened the envelope.

"Nice stationery," I commented to the empty room. Even Harrison's penmanship was polite. I'd never seen a man's handwriting be so legible. The letter was short and to the point: Harrison requested the pleasure of my attendance at dinner at six o'clock that evening. I hoped Harrison would be well behaved after Lex had promised to kill him if he laid a hand on me. While I couldn't speak for the vampire's ability to restrain himself, I was pretty damn sure Lex could take him in a fight. Well, he could if he still had his guardian abilities.

Alone again with nothing but the television to entertain me, I looked through the catalogues and wrote up a ridiculously large order. Not that I expected to need that many outfits, but I was about halfway through destroying Laura's fashion choices and had every intention of making Harrison replace everything I shredded.

I didn't want to have dinner with Harrison again. I really, really, *really* did not want to have dinner with him again. It would only end badly. I had almost no faith in his assurance that I would remain unmolested. He simply couldn't help himself—I was too much of a curiosity for him. I'm sure the supermodels he kept around as arm candy were more than happy to fall on their backs with their legs spread wide, and yet mousy little me couldn't stand the sight of him. Harrison probably felt like he was living in the Twilight Zone.

Well, I wasn't about to wear anything even remotely revealing. Hell, I would've worn a turtleneck if there'd been one in the closet. I settled on the most prim, proper, dowdy schoolmarm look I could manage with the wardrobe. Boxy khaki slacks, penny loafers, and a plain white long-sleeved blouse, buttoned as high as it would go. The white fabric washed all the color out of my face, not that there was much to begin with. I left my hair down for maximum neck coverage, and it looked limp and lifeless, as horrid as the "before" picture in a shampoo commercial. Gazing at my reflection, I decided I looked like a soccer mom out for dinner at a family restaurant chain. Fabulous.

I dreaded the arrival of six o'clock. Nausea invaded my stomach and camped out, refusing to leave no matter how much calm I mustered up. A few minutes before six the door opened and revealed, much to my horror, Lovely Laura Barrenheart.

"The hell do you want?" I asked, surprised.

Laura crossed the room and paused next to the couch, scrutinizing me with distaste obvious in her cold gray eyes. The vampire stood perfectly still, looking like an ice statue ready for a night on the town in a sparkling white cocktail dress. From her elegantly styled hair to the tips of her killer high-heeled shoes, Laura was the essence of grace and beauty. It was damn intimidating.

"I'm here to escort you to dinner." Something in her tone hinted that she'd enjoy escorting me down a flight of stairs, face first. "You're not wearing that."

"Why not? The invitation didn't mention a dress code."

"You look terrible, it's insulting to your host," Laura said.

"Which is exactly what I'm going for."

The vampire rolled her wintry eyes at me and turned, gliding toward the bedroom and the closet she had stocked with what she considered appropriate attire. Boy was she ever in for a surprise. Shutting off the TV, I got to my feet and followed her, eager to see her reaction to my closet renovation efforts.

Pausing in the doorway, the vampire gazed down at the pile of mangled fashion on the closet floor. I tried to destroy at least one article of clothing per commercial break, and it had been an advertising bonanza that day. Tension pinched her shoulders, and Laura turned toward me slowly. Expecting a fight, I'd put my shields up the moment she first entered the room, so I was prepared when she tried to slap me. Her hand bounced away, harmless, and I smiled broadly at her like a toddler inappropriately proud of the mess she created.

"We're going to be late for dinner," I pointed out. The vampire glared at me as though she hoped she could burn holes through my shields and reduce me to a smoking pile of ashes. After a long, tense moment, Laura sighed and walked around me into the suite's sitting room. I followed her, slowed by the effort of keeping the shields up and hoping to give her some space.

Opening the door to the suite, she paused in the hallway. "This way please." Laura motioned down the hallway, indicating that I should go first. Yeah right, like there was any way I'd let her get behind me.

"Oh no, after you." I smiled thinly, and the vampire smiled with equal derision and strode away. The hallway looked pretty much the same as I remembered it: earth tones, unremarkable decorations, soft lighting. I tried to remember the turns as we moved from hallway to hallway, but there was just no way I'd manage to memorize it. The décor all looked the same, and there were no visible numbers on the doors like you'd expect in a hotel setting. We reached the silver elevator and stepped inside, her high heels clicking sharply on the floor. Laura continued to remain silent, probably plotting my slow and painful demise, and I continued to concentrate on keeping my shields up to prevent said painful demise. The elevator moved down, which surprised me as I'd been assuming we were headed up to Harrison's penthouse office. Great, maybe she was taking me down to the parking garage to beat the sass out of me.

It was going to be a long night.

"Exactly how does a council member end up as an errand girl for a vamp who's got to be, what, no more than five years dead?" I asked, my tone light and casual. The sting of dying smoke filled the elevator as Laura struggled to control her temper at my rude outburst, and I held my hand under my nose to stave off a sneeze.

"I am no one's 'errand girl'," Laura replied through gritted teeth. "Zachary asked that I do this as a favor to him."

"You don't strike me as a woman who does a lot of favors for people."

"Zachary is special, a fact which you would do well to realize, Miss Morrow."

"I have enough special people in my life already, I don't have room for bloodsuckers."

"Typical. You witches are so disappointing, so much wasted potential. All that power, and your greatest desire is to have a home and a few squalling, needy brats to cling to your skirts. Pathetic." Laura scowled, her voice dripping with loathing.

"Yeah, well, the market on villains was already cornered by you undead assholes."

"There is nothing evil about pursuing power. In fact I've always thought it rather sinful to let your God-given abilities be squandered. I won't expect you to understand."

"You know what they say about absolute power," I muttered. The elevator doors opened and Laura stepped out. A short hallway ended in a pair of heavy wooden doors, and Laura opened them without hesitation. The room we entered was large and had a definite male feeling to it—dark wood, deep colors, lots of shiny, expensive electronic gadgets scattered around. A pinball machine and an old-school video arcade game were tucked into a far corner. There was a dining table set up in the same formal, overdone setting I'd come to expect of meals in Vampire Central. Laura drew to a stop next to the table and peered around, looking for Harrison.

"Good evening, ladies." We both turned toward the sound of his voice, and for the first time Lovely Laura and I had the same reaction to something: shock. Zachary Harrison, multi-zillionaire businessman and king of the undead castle, was wearing blue jeans and a plain white T-shirt. It was obvious from the cut and the color that these were designer jeans, and someone had taken time to distress them instead of letting wear and tear rough them up. Still, it wasn't a suit. He looked really good for a dead guy—like someone who might stop into the Three Willows for a sandwich on his lunch break, who I'd flirt with while refilling his coffee.

"What has she done to you?" Laura asked, horrified.

Harrison chuckled, shaking his head in amusement. "I was reminded that denim is the American way."

The corners of my mouth crept up in a slight smile. As much as I hated him, it was damn amusing to watch Lovely Laura squirm in her pretty shoes. With a sound of disgust, she folded her arms across her chest.

"Which would explain why American fashion is tedious and inferior," she countered icily. "I'll leave you two to your evening." Nodding at Harrison, she turned and strode out of the room, her high heels clicking angrily on the hardwood floor.

"Gee, I think we're both in trouble now." I raised an eyebrow at her exit. "You might be grounded."

"It would appear so. Do you approve of the outfit?"

"Not bad." I shrugged, looking him up and down thoughtfully. "It gives you the false illusion of being a nice guy."

"I am a nice guy," he protested, appearing hurt.

"No you're not. Besides, even if you were nice for a vampire, that's like being nice for a shark or a crocodile. You're still a predator in designer jeans."

Harrison winced, seemingly wounded by my frank assessment of him, and I almost felt bad. The memory of locking myself in the bathroom and sleeping in a nest of fluffy white hotel towels kept me from believing his act. Nice guys don't drink blood, period.

"What do you want?" I asked.

"That's a very broad question."

"I thought you were going to leave me alone."

"I agreed not to harm you. I see no harm in having dinner and engaging in polite conversation."

"There wasn't any harm in it last time either until you decided to have me for dessert." I scowled.

"A mistake which I have apologized for, Catherine. Repeatedly. I didn't bring you here to bite you, I merely want to get to know you better." Spreading his hands wide in a placating gesture, he stepped toward me, sincerity shadowing those lovely green eyes. I stood my ground, watching him as he drew closer. I'm sure he intended to give my shoulder a comforting pat or some other benign social contact, but much to his surprise he collided with my shields instead. Blinking, he gazed at me in surprise, and I smiled sweetly. Harrison rubbed his hand where it had come in contact with the energy. His pride probably hurt more than his hand did.

"You don't trust me not to harm you, even though I gave my word."

"I don't trust you at all, Harrison," I replied, my hands on my hips.

"Zach," he said, and I frowned. "Call me Zach, please. I'm only Harrison during work hours." With a charming smile, he turned and pulled out one of the chairs in an invitation for me to sit down. "What would you like to drink?"

"A glass of wine, please." Reluctantly, I sat down and let him push my chair in. I wasn't going to win this argument, and since I was safe behind my shields I might as well play along with his plans. Zach nodded and crossed to the bar, producing a bottle from beneath it. After uncorking the bottle he poured the contents into a glass. I had a feeling the wine hadn't been on sale at the corner store, but I'd never be able to tell if it was fine wine or not.

"I took the liberty of ordering dinner. It should arrive soon." He set the glass down in front of me and then poured one for himself. "In the meantime, there are a few things I would like to discuss with you."

"Great." Sipping my drink, I eyed him, knowing I wasn't going to like whatever he had to say. Taking the seat across from me, the vampire leaned back into his chair and folded his hands in his lap.

"I know you don't approve of my plans for the future of magician society, and I agree they may seem a little radical on the surface. I'd like the chance to work with you on this subject. Perhaps we could develop a new strategy together." Unimpressed, I waited for the punch line, because there had to be more to this story. "You must agree that things can't continue as they have been, not in these times."

"I've been getting along well enough."

"Have you? I'm sure you noticed that your room was stocked with your favorite books, clothing in your exact size, we even picked your preferred brands of liquor for your bar. How do you think we found that information?"

"I figured you hacked into my credit card history, and probably my discount cards for the grocery store I go to, and the bookstore too. It'd be easy enough for you, it'd only take a mediocre computer nerd to find that stuff out and you can obviously afford better than average."

"Then you wouldn't be surprised to learn what else we found. A record of every candle, oil, crystal and herb you've bought within the last five years. A list of the 'questionable' reading material you own, the pagan websites you visit on a regular basis, and the associates you communicate with who share similar interests. Catalogued, indexed and recorded in a government database."

My mouth dropped open and my jaw worked a few times as I struggled to find the words to respond. "But...why? It's not a crime, that doesn't make any sense. Why should anyone care?"

"Because religion isn't as free as it used to be. Magicians who haven't been careful about concealing their beliefs, like yourself, have been designated as potential threats by the moral majority."

"Potential threats doesn't mean they're about to round us up into internment camps."

"They already are," he replied. I choked on a sip of wine.

"*What?*"

"Shapeshifters have been disappearing across the country for the past few months. A few here and there, not enough to raise an alarm."

"Then how'd you know about it?"

"I have my sources," Zach replied mysteriously.

It seemed far-fetched to me. Shapeshifters live on the edges of magician society, rarely interacting with others. I couldn't imagine them calling up Harrison to rescue them from some shady government bad guys. I scowled at him in annoyance, but my chance for a stinging retort was foiled by the arrival of our food. The waiter removed the silver dome atop my plate and revealed an enormous cheeseburger and a stack of French fries. Before disappearing, the waiter placed a bottle of ketchup next to my plate, and I stared at it in equal wonder. Fast food was the last thing I would have expected for dinner, especially considering that during our last meal together I'd barely recognized the food I'd been served. I looked up at my host, wondering if it was too good to be true, and he chuckled at my reaction.

"It's safe, don't worry. I thought you would appreciate something similar to the food in your café."

"Oh. Thanks." Picking up a fry, I took a tentative bite, and it was just the right balance of grease and salt. "So basically what you're telling me is that the man is planning to keep us down, and I should join with you so we can stick it to him," I commented as I reached for the burger.

"Something along those lines."

"Would we be equals in this effort?"

"Of course."

"Really. 'Cause I seem to recall you mentioning something about making me into a pet. I'm sure there's a cat joke there just waiting to happen." Giving him an indignant glare, I took a bite from the burger, which was as wonderful as the fry had been. Apparently Zach had realized that the way to my heart is through my stomach. I'm surprised he hadn't started with chocolate chip pancakes after Lex had revealed that particular weakness.

"I said that to annoy Duquesne, and it worked perfectly. You are much too precious to keep as a mere pet, Catherine." He smiled, and the expression did not make me feel better.

"Then what were you planning on keeping me as?"

"A friend, nothing more. I find your company rather entertaining. For now, I think we should enjoy our evening." Raising his glass in a toast, he gave me a dazzling smile, the sort that could melt the average woman into a quivering puddle. Luckily I wasn't an average woman, and I rolled my eyes in response.

The vampire behaved like a gentleman for the duration of dinner. No sudden moves, no attempts to break through my shields and put the bite on me. It was a pleasant change. When I finished eating he gave me a tour of his place, and I immediately noticed a running theme throughout the various odds and ends he collected: rare or one-of-a-kind. Sports and movie memorabilia, modern artwork, even the liquor in the bar was unique or hard to come by. Zach explained the history of his collection to me, and it was vaguely interesting in a museum kind of way, and had the added bonus of keeping him from misbehaving. Afterwards he decided we should watch a movie, and I went along with the idea. Hey, safe inside my shield the vamp couldn't even get away with something simple like the old yawn-and-put-your-arm-around-the-girl trick. We sat on opposite ends of the couch, reminding me of a few awkward first dates I'd experienced in my distant past, and tried to concentrate on the movie.

His cell phone rang as the credits were rolling, and he ducked into the other room to answer it. Left alone, I wandered around and took another look at his collection of random stuff. Just one of his signed baseballs was probably worth more than all my worldly possessions. When he returned to the room Harrison seemed disturbed, and I frowned at him.

"What's wrong?" I asked.

He glanced at the clock, scratching his chin. "There's someone I want you to meet, but it's late for you and I'm sure you must be tired, so it can wait until tomorrow afternoon."

"Harrison—"

"Zach, please," the vampire corrected me. Picking up the remote, he shut off the television, and then he walked out of the room again. I wondered what was on his mind, and against my better judgment I followed him.

A sharp pop greeted me as I stepped through the doorway, and I froze at the sound. Across the room Harrison stood at the bar with a champagne bottle in his hand, two crystal flutes set in front of him, and a tray of chocolate-covered strawberries next to them.

"Are we celebrating something?" I asked, suspicious.

"No, I just thought you might enjoy champagne with your dessert," he replied, motioning to the strawberries. "Although it could be fair to say that we are commemorating a new beginning."

"What new beginning?"

"Of our partnership." With a friendly smile he held the champagne out to me. "You can stop shielding, I promise I'm not going to attack you."

"Forgive me if I don't believe you."

"That's understandable, I suppose. I've also told you, more than once in fact, that I won't bite you while you are opposed to it. I don't want to force you to do anything. It would only damage our relationship."

"You sound like a therapist."

Harrison chuckled. "Perhaps, but it is the truth. I behaved badly and I apologized for that, it won't happen again."

"Listen, Harrison," I began and he opened his mouth to correct me. "Zach, right, whatever. Listen, Zach, I'm not going to trust you as long as you keep me locked up here."

"You won't be here permanently. The full moon is not so far away." Again he offered the champagne to me, and against my better judgment I let my shields slip away and I took the glass from him. Zach raised his glass in a toast and tapped it against mine, smiling at me with his perfect white teeth.

Reaching under the bar, he withdrew a slim silver cigarette case, opened it, and held it out to me. "I thought you might need one by now." Greedily I snatched up a smoke, and my hand nearly shook as I held it. Nicotine withdrawal? Just a bit. Zach pulled a matching silver lighter from his jeans pocket and lit the end of my cigarette for me. I fought back the instant temptation to try lighting him on fire with it—I wasn't sure I had enough control to do it, and I had no idea what I'd do after I lit the vampire king up, aside from a happy dance. For the moment I decided to be content with my smoke as Zach placed an ashtray in front of me.

"You're being too nice, what's the catch?"

Watching me, he sipped his champagne. "If I let you leave right now, what would you do? Where would you go?"

"Home."

"To your one-bedroom apartment by the train tracks."

"There's nothing wrong with that." Frowning, I blew a stream of smoke in his direction.

"No, but you could have much more. You don't have a car."

Zach ticked further points off on his fingers as he continued. "You have no savings to speak of. You've barely traveled out of state, and never out of the country—unless you count your trips to Faerie and back. You work ten, twelve hour shifts for little more than minimum wage, and now you'll be adding all the work of a Titania for no additional pay at all."

"Hey, I make plenty more than minimum wage. And so what? You'll snap your billionaire fingers and fix my financial problems if I agree to abide by your unholy will?" I raised an eyebrow.

"From what I've seen thus far, I can't imagine you abiding by anyone's will but your own. Though if I put you on my payroll I would request that you at least *try* to follow the terms of your contract."

"What terms would those be?"

"Nothing too difficult. A little spellwork now and then—it wouldn't violate any of your witch rules, not that you have to worry about that anymore. Once in a while I'll ask you to attend a gathering with me. We can continue to discuss proposals for the future of magician society and work for the betterment of us all." Zach appeared blasé about the idea—I'm sure the devil is always nonchalant when contracting for your soul.

"Right. And if I say no?"

"I will be very disappointed."

"Disappointed?" I repeated. A disappointed vampire could mean a lot of things, none of which were pleasant.

"But why would you say no? Am I really asking too much of you? I'm offering comfort and financial stability—"

"And all I have to do is ignore the fact that I'll be at the beck and call of the same people who turned my father into a monster and murdered my mother and cousin," I snapped at him. "I don't need a savior to drop into my life and make it all better."

"Isn't that what your guardian intended?" Raising a cool eyebrow, he ignored my temper as usual and drank his champagne. "To move you into his big house in the suburbs, pay off your debts, take care of you? Like a good little housewife?"

"That's not the same," I grumbled. Like a sulking teenager, I trailed off into uncomfortable silence. As much as I hated to admit it, Zach had a point. Hunching over the ashtray, I ground out the cigarette and unhappily sipped my drink. "Besides, that's your fault. Lex wouldn't have entered the picture again if you hadn't put a hit out on me."

"I wasn't responsible for that."

"Lemme guess, it was Laura's idea?" I asked, and Zach nodded in reply. "There's a big surprise. Doesn't she outrank you, vampire-wise? What's stopping her from taking me out whenever her panties get in a twist?"

Zach chuckled, apparently amused at the image. "I won't let that happen."

"Exactly how are you going to stop her? Sure, you've got more money than some third-world countries, but you're just a baby by vamp standards. I'm surprised she listens to you at all."

"Because I am stronger than she is, but it's nothing you need to be concerned about. I'll escort you back to your room now. I'm sure you'll need time to think things over. Would you like to take the strawberries back to your suite?"

I eyed them for a moment, and then decided it would be a crime to let them go to waste. "Sure."

The trip to my luxury cell was silent, and I still couldn't memorize the twists and turns of the hallway maze. Something about the faerie ward must have messed with my internal sense of direction. I wasn't sure what Zach intended to do once we reached our destination, and to my surprise he walked into the suite behind me, set the tray of strawberries down on the table, and then stood gazing around the room.

"If you're looking for the disaster area it's in the closet, otherwise I've been very well behaved." Folding my arms across my chest, I followed after the vampire as he went to investigate my destructive tendencies. Unlike Laura's somewhat violent reaction, Zach merely surveyed the slaughter with quiet curiosity.

"Nice." He shook his head, bemused.

"You're taking it much better than Laura. She tried to hit me."

"Did she?" Zach turned toward me. Touching my chin, he tilted my face from side to side as though checking for bruises he hadn't noticed before. "Obviously she only encountered your shields. You should consider yourself lucky. Laura isn't a woman easily trifled with."

"Hmph, if I were lucky I wouldn't be here in the first place," I muttered. When he didn't remove his hand from my face I leaned away from his touch.

"Have we been so cruel to you?"

"You *bit* me."

The vampire sighed. "Aside from that incident, has your stay truly been that bad? Were you dressed in rags and chained in the dungeon with only bread and water to survive on? Tortured? Interrogated?"

"No." I squirmed under his regard.

"You look at me and you see the demons from your past, but I am not the monster you would make me out to be," he said quietly. "Is that so difficult for you to accept?"

"Yes, it is."

"There are those who would not be so accommodating in this situation, vampires who are truly worth your ire. At the very least I want us to be able to work together peacefully."

"At least? What more do you want?" I frowned up at him, and he slowly leaned down toward me. I backed away and bumped into the doorframe that connected the bedroom and the closet, and I winced as I struck my head against the wood.

"I'm not going to bite you or bespell you," he assured me before I attempted to put up my shields.

"What are you going to do?"

"Kiss you."

Before I could argue, he moved forward and pressed his lips against mine. I prepared myself to fight off a wave of vamp magic, but none came. Instead he simply kissed me. For a second I stood stunned, because while I expected him to try magic and trickery, an average, everyday kiss was a complete surprise. Okay, to be honest *average* is probably a poor word choice. Though Zach was more forceful than I'd like, the man definitely had skills, but I probably should have expected that considering his nature. Like the kiss he had stolen before, there was no spark, no electric zing or heady tingling response that I felt with Lex. It only made me feel uncomfortable, like the awkward ending to a bad date. Sensing my unease, Zach pulled away and studied me.

"I really don't understand you," he said, shaking his head.

"Yeah I'm just full of mystery." I stepped away, putting safe distance between us. "I thought you were going to leave me alone to think."

"Of course. I will see you tomorrow afternoon."

"Right." I nodded unenthusiastically.

"Give me a chance, Catherine. You'll find that I'm not entirely terrible to be around. Rest well."

With that he left, and all I had for company were my troubled thoughts. I wasn't going to take his offer, no matter how *generous* it might be. The vampire was the serpent trying to tempt me into partaking of forbidden fruit, to toss away my morals and my better judgment and allow myself to be a pawn of the undead. A necromancer, like my father. Everything I fought against, everything I was opposed to, and yet living the straight and narrow life had netted me what? Years of hard work with little to show for it. Instead of a house in the suburbs with a white picket fence and 2.5 kids, I had a tiny apartment and two borderline obese housecats. Instead of a loving husband, I had a man who wasn't willing to change his life in order to be with me, and a gorgeous vampire offering me everything a girl could want in return for a little blood and sympathy.

All I had to do was give in to the dark side and I could live a life of wealth and ease. Happily ever after. Forever.

Frustrated and upset, I didn't sleep well, my dreams Lex-free and frightening. When I awoke the next morning I once again tasted blood, but this time I couldn't explain why, and that was even more troubling than the nightmares.

# Chapter Nineteen

The king vampire showed up at my door promptly at noon. His pretty green eyes were hidden behind an expensive pair of sunglasses, just as they had been when we met that day at the airport. I felt underdressed standing next to him. Zach wore another expensive dark suit, and I'd picked out a plain black blouse and slacks. I'd wound my hair up into a bun, and with the lack of color in my outfit it gave me a very rigid, severe look, like a Star Trek villainess. For a moment I'd worried that too much time in Vampire Central had been a bad influence, forcing me into an all-black outfit, but I hadn't found anything else in the closet I didn't instantly hate.

"Where are we going?" I asked as I followed Zach down the hallway.

"To meet some people. Be advised, we'll be leaving the building. I have a feeling your faerie family may make an appearance once we're outside the wards, and I'd appreciate it if you would calmly explain to them that you're here as my guest."

"Well I can't guarantee I can call off Portia before she stabs you in the chest. She's more than a little upset over losing her only brother." I folded my arms across my chest, and he nodded.

"Of course. As I've said, I had nothing to do with that, and I'm sorry for your loss."

"It's going to take a lot more than 'sorry' to call off my clan."

"I know."

We took the elevator down to the parking garage, where a black stretch limo was waiting for us. I climbed in, relieved that there was no Lovely Laura waiting for me in this one, and Harrison followed after me. The sun was shining brightly as we drove out into the street, though it was barely visible through the tinted windows.

"Doesn't this bother you?"

"What?" he asked, raising an eyebrow.

"The sunlight? It's noon. Shouldn't all good little vampires be a-snooze in their beds?"

Zach smiled, shaking his head. "I suppose that's your proof that I'm not a good vampire. But to answer your question, yes, it does bother me, but I can withstand it. There are a few powerful individuals who can endure direct sunlight for long periods of time."

"And you're one of them?" I asked, and he nodded. "But you're practically a baby, how does that work?"

"Good genetics," he replied, smiling his perfect smile at me. Before I could question him further, our conversation was interrupted by the arrival of Faust as the faerie popped into the seat on the other side of Harrison. "I thought I asked you not to do that."

Brushing at his gray suit jacket, as though his entrance had caused him to be coated in a cloud of pixie dust, Faust smiled. "There seemed little point to it, considering she already knows what I am, and it's faster this way. Besides, I thought it best I arrive here before—"

A flurry of things happened all at once, almost too fast for me to follow. Portia appeared in the seat across from us—a compact and ancient-looking crossbow clutched in her hands—and she fired a bolt at Harrison. In a blur of motion the vampire pulled me into his lap like a naughty secretary and surrounded us with his shields, so the bolt bounced off the barrier and buried itself in a nearby seat cushion. With a wave of his hand, Faust knocked the weapon out of Portia's grasp, and she glared at him. The two faeries hissed at each other in their language, looking as though they were two seconds from tearing each other's throats out.

"Hey! Cut it out!" I shouted, trying to interrupt them.

"You!" She pointed at Harrison. "Unhand her this instant!"

"She's fine right where she is," he replied calmly.

"*Portia.* What are you doing here?" I asked.

"Rescuing you from that vampire."

Said vampire was still holding me in his lap, using me as a

human shield to supplement his magical one. Curious, I reached up and poked the edge of the barrier. The energy swirled like smoke in dark gray whorls around the tip of my finger, which seemed like an odd reaction—but then again I wasn't familiar with vampire shields, they all might work that way. I wasn't sure how he'd managed to surround me instead of pushing me away. Vamp shields were probably designed to protect both the vampire and whoever is being snacked on at the moment.

"You don't need to rescue me, I volunteered to stay with him until the full moon."

"I know, but you won't have to stay with him at all after I kill him," Portia replied, the soul of sensibility.

"You can't kill him."

"Why not?"

*Yeah, why not?* I frowned, trying to think of a reason. Nothing really came to mind. Turning to him, I waited for him to supply a good excuse as to why we should let him continue his existence.

"Because it's in everyone's best interests that I not be harmed," Zach answered.

"Right, what he said. Now put me down."

"I rather like you where you are." The vampire smiled. Faust made a coughing sound, like he was swallowing a laugh, and I shot him an unfriendly look. "Besides, I think it's best that you stay where you are while your cousin is here, in case she loses her temper again."

"Great." I rolled my eyes and then turned to Portia. "Look, he says he didn't have anything to do with the attack on the castle, and I believe him. But if you want to kill Laura, I'm all in favor of that. I can even start making a list of deserving minions for you while I'm stuck in Vampire Central."

Faust openly snickered this time, and he smiled. "Oh, I like her."

"You'll do no such thing," Harrison ordered me. "But since you're here, Mistress Silverleaf, you may as well hear what I have to say."

"I'm really not interested in anything you have to say, vampire."

"You'll find this more interesting, I think."

"I doubt that." She sniffed.

"We believe we've found a cure for the extinction," Faust commented idly, as though remarking on the weather.

"You? A vampire and a shadowspawn? You expect me to believe that? What sort of fool do you take me for?" Portia eyed them, suspicious.

"Only a fool would ignore a chance like this, Silverleaf," Faust countered. The temperature inside the limo dropped, and a line of frost spread across the window behind Portia's head.

Clearing his throat, Harrison interrupted before Portia could do anything violent, like encase the other faerie in a block of ice. "That's enough. Now, the fact of the matter is this: there is much more that faeries and magicians could be doing to help each other, but aren't. If we worked together, we could all be in a position of power in this world, and if Faerie was dissolved, your lost fertility would be regained. You would no longer face extinction."

"Faerie is safe. The elves thought they could survive in this world, and they were wiped out because of it," she argued, unconvinced.

"They also tried to fight humanity on their own. If we all banded together, and I do mean all varieties of magicians and magical races, then there is nothing that could stop us."

It was a very militant point of view, which didn't appeal to me but may have sounded appealing to Portia in her current martial mindset. Raising a thin, pale brow, she eyed the vampire.

As though sensing a weakness, Faust leaned forward. "Think of it. The opportunity to freely walk this world again. No rules, no limitations, no hiding. More importantly, to once again have the chance to hold a babe in your arms and not suffer the knowledge that the child will grow old and be gone in a blink of your eye. Doesn't it pain you to watch the generations of your bloodline bloom and then wither, like flowers cut before their time?"

Frowning, Portia turned her gaze to me. There was such terrible sadness in her eyes, and I wondered if the faerie blood in my veins was Portia's. I knew there was a Silverleaf somewhere in my mother's family tree, but I'd never asked who it was. Should I have been calling Portia grandmother all these years, instead of cousin? Or perhaps I was of Tybalt's line—a frail, tenuous link to the brother she'd lost. I opened my mouth to ask her, but the car pulled to a stop, and I found myself free of the vampire's lap as he nudged me back into my seat.

"We're here. Mistress Silverleaf, you're welcome to join us, if you'll attempt to behave yourself and change your attire to something more appropriate. This way, Catherine."

The door opened and he stepped out into the sunlight. I paused for a moment, glancing at Portia, and watched as the faerie's features and clothing changed, rippling like melting water and then reforming. With pale blonde hair and fair skin, she looked rather like a Nordic ice princess, which creeped me out as it reminded me a bit too much of Lovely Laura. Portia's icy wings vanished and her punk princess ensemble changed to a light blue sundress, complete with matching flip-flops. Silently hoping that she'd refrain from slaying anyone, I followed Harrison out of the car.

We were in a residential neighborhood—old Irving Park maybe, from the feel of it, but I didn't get a good enough look around to orient myself. The limo was parked in the middle of the street, and after Portia and Faust piled out of the car behind me the driver pulled away and left us. Harrison headed toward a nearby house. A small, two-story home, it blended into the row of brick bungalows that lined the street. Wilted flowers and a forlorn garden gnome decorated the front lawn, and the grass was overgrown and in desperate need of mowing. The vampire stopped at the top of the front steps and rang the doorbell, and then was ushered inside by a figure I couldn't see. Hurrying to catch up, the faeries and I trotted up the stairs and into the house before we ended up locked out on the front porch.

"—that you're here, Mr. Harrison. We've been so grateful for all of your help." An elderly woman stood in the center of a clean but well-worn living room, one gnarled hand restlessly running through her short silver hair. The musky smell of wet dog permeated the place, and I rubbed at my nose. Glancing around, I expected to find evidence of small, yapping dogs, but there wasn't a dog hair in sight.

Canine shapeshifters. Fun.

"How bad is this one?" Harrison asked, sounding genuinely concerned.

"Bad. Honestly, we're not sure he'll make it." Picking up a tissue from a box atop an end table, she wiped at her eyes.

When she finished she finally looked past the vampire and spotted the rest of us clustered near the door. "Oh, hello again, Mr. Faust. Who are your friends?"

"This is the new Titania, Miss Catherine Baker, and her cousin Portia," Faust explained, nudging me forward into the room.

"Pleased to meet you. Call me Dottie, everyone does. Are you a healer, Miss Baker?"

"I have some skill at it, I'm a witch. Or was a witch," I corrected. I'm certain I didn't sound as sure of myself as she would've liked, but she seemed encouraged.

"Come with me." Waving at me to follow her, she led us through a dining room and then down a flight of stairs into the basement. The smell of fur intensified with each step, and my eyes watered. "We only have one at the moment, which normally is a blessing, but this poor boy's in such awful condition. Well, we're very grateful for the aid that Mr. Harrison's given us, and it's been so helpful in buying medical supplies and the like, but we still can't find a good healer. There are so few among us, and not many more among his people."

I nodded in understanding. Not a lot of witches in the necromancer posse, I knew that much was true. Probably not many among the shapeshifters either, considering that once a person is infected with wild magic they tend to lose the ability to control their original magic.

The basement was set up as a sort of medical facility. Empty cots were arranged in rows, like a makeshift barracks. The sharp tang of antiseptic nosed its way through the shapeshifter musk, and it made me sweat. Nervous, I wiped my palms on my slacks as Dottie pushed aside a white sheet that hung from the ceiling and cordoned off a small corner of the room.

A figure lay limp and lifeless on a cot, an I.V. dripping an unknown liquid into his arm. From the body's broad shoulders and muscular build I guessed it was male, but the face was unrecognizable. Like the shifter I'd judged in the second test, this one was trapped somewhere between canine and human, but it hadn't gone as far. The nose and upper jaw jutted out from his face, forming the beginnings of a snout, and light gray patches of fur were scattered across his skin. The shifter's arms lay limply atop the blanket covering him, and his hands were curled into long, wicked claws. An array of bruises covered his skin—black, blue, purple and green—as well as a multitude of cuts and puncture wounds.

"Lord and Lady," I swore softly. "What happened?"

"The 'yotes raided a facility in Gary. This was the only one they found still alive," she explained.

"What kind of facility?"

"Government research. Something federal, small but well-funded."

"They've been experimenting on any shapeshifter they can get their hands on," Harrison commented from behind me.

"Why?"

"Various reasons. We think they're trying to find a biological source for magic, one they can use for military means. I'm sure you can imagine how they treat an uncooperative test subject."

"He's sedated," Dottie informed me. "Poor thing's in so much pain. He won't be able to heal this until he can think clearly, and he won't be able to think clearly until we can heal some of this damage. Can you help him?"

I glanced at him, uncertain. It was a tall order, but I could probably manage pain relief. Might be enough to let him heal. Of course I didn't have any of my tools with me, so I turned to Portia. "I need silver and moonstone."

"Okay. Hold out your hand." The faerie held her hand above mine, and a large moonstone the size of an egg attached to a braided silver chain appeared in my palm.

I wrapped the chain around my hand, holding the moonstone tight in my fist, and approached the shapeshifter's bed. Kneeling on the cold concrete floor next to the cot, I held my right hand over the shifter's chest. After a moment or two I decided on the words, and then I took a deep breath and centered myself. No pressure.

*"Soothe the wild, the pain will end,*
*Calm and mild, your wounds I mend."*

Over and over I murmured the words in a low, rhythmic chant. The magic spread in a fitful, uneven wave as I moved my hand above the injuries, fighting against the wild magic—it's called "wild" magic for a reason, it's unpredictable and hard to control. Like an untamed animal it fought my influence, but with persistent patience I waited it out. I wasn't sure how long I struggled, but it felt like hours. From time to time I heard the whisper of voices behind me, but they wisely didn't interrupt me. The cuts and bruises faded, and then, surprisingly, the canine features began to recede. I hadn't expected to fix those, but I wasn't going to argue. If my magic was able to go the extra mile, then go me.

My legs were numb by the time I sat back on my heels, finished with my task. In fact I was almost entirely numb, physically and magically, and I wobbled as I got to my feet. I felt a cool hand on my shoulder, steadying me, and was glad to see that it was Portia and not Harrison by my side. "You did good, Kitty," she assured me.

"Thanks." With a weak smile, I handed the pendant back to her.

"Oh! Amazing! It's like a miracle," Dottie exclaimed. "Thank you." Pushing past me, she leaned over the shapeshifter and examined him. "Truly remarkable. It would've taken days to accomplish this without you."

"You're welcome," I said, though it seemed like a lame reply.

"We'll let him sleep for now, I'd like the 'yotes to be here when he wakes up."

"Coyotes?" I asked, and she nodded. Most of the shifters who came into the café were coyotes. I took a good look at him. Now that he appeared human the shifter was barely more than a kid, obviously a teenager. Built like a linebacker, but he had a baby face that hinted that he probably couldn't even grow a beard yet. And someone'd tortured him 'til he was a walking bruise.

"C'mon, I'll take you home," Harrison offered. Portia and I perked up at the offer, and then he clarified his statement. "The tower."

The faeries were quiet on the ride back. I sat with Portia, Faust sat with Harrison, and the silence was heavy and strained. When we neared the ward around the tower, Portia gave me a hug and promised to see me at the ceremony. The two faeries vanished at the same time, leaving me alone with the vampire. Though I half expected him to drag me back into his lap and try to molest me, Harrison behaved himself. In fact, he didn't even say anything for the rest of the ride, and I nearly fell asleep. Once we were back inside of the tower I thought I'd be escorted back to my room, but instead the elevator opened to his floor.

"After you," he said.

"Why here? I thought I was going back to my room?"

"Not while you look like you're going to faint. I want to keep an eye on you until you've regained more of your strength."

"Was tougher than I thought it'd be. The kid's magic wasn't playing nice with mine."

"You did very well today, I was impressed."

"Thanks. I feel like hell though," I said, and then yawned. Following him into the TV room, I slipped off my shoes and flopped down into a chair.

"Understandably so. It had to be a very draining experience. Shapeshifters can endure a great deal of damage, which is probably how the boy survived. Most magicians would've died long before the coyotes discovered the facility... I've never met a witch willing to heal a shapeshifter. They seem to consider it beneath them."

"Yeah, well, I'm a bad witch. Maureen would've done it, though." Frowning, I looked up at him. Did he have anything to do with Maureen's death? Did I really want to know the answer to that question?

"What would you like for dinner?" he asked, changing the subject.

"Pizza."

Chuckling, he shook his head and withdrew his cell phone from within his jacket. I listened as Harrison called whoever it is he calls to feed me. The kitchen? A caterer? His secretary? His villainous sidekick? No idea. When he finished, he took a seat on the couch and turned on the television. After some debate we settled on a movie, but I barely paid attention to it. He kept me talking, making whatever conversation he could, as though I had a concussion and he was attempting to keep me awake. It was a good idea, because my thoughts kept wandering off and my eyelids felt very heavy. When the food arrived he encouraged me to eat more in a way that would've made an Italian mother proud. I felt better after I'd gotten some food in me, and I curled up on the couch to watch the remainder of the movie. The vampire sat next to me, his arm around me, and I didn't argue—it felt bizarrely comforting.

When the movie ended he gave me a speculative look. "Are you feeling better?"

"Much, thanks."

Zach reached over and touched the side of my face. "You still look pale."

"I always look pale." Suspicious, I moved away from him. "No offense, but I don't trust you not to take advantage of me."

"I did give you—"

"Your word, I know," I finished for him. "But you also have a habit of overstepping your bounds, and I do seem to recall being in your lap earlier."

"Yes, I'm sure it was a most horrifying experience." The vampire gave me a charming smile, showing off his perfect white teeth.

"Listen, I am actually considering working with you on a limited basis, but strictly business. That's it," I informed him matter-of-factly. "No one should have to go through what that poor kid did."

"Agreed. But it's a shame not to mix pleasure with business. Do you really find me so unattractive?"

"You're rich, handsome, usually charming, well-dressed. It'd be an appealing package, but I already have one pushy, demanding man in my life, and that's my limit."

"Is he?"

"Is he what?"

"In your life?"

"Oh. Well..." I struggled to find the right words to say. I loved Lex, and I knew he loved me. He just loved his job more. Not unlike my father, who'd loved his magic more than his family, and look how well that turned out.

"You don't sound very sure of yourself. He did turn down the position of Oberon. That's not very encouraging."

"He didn't turn it down. He said he needed more time to think about it."

"Did he? If I were in that position, I would've agreed immediately."

"Like hell you would've. You'd give up being a vampire to be Oberon?" I asked, skeptical.

"Necromancer. Though I don't mind it, to be honest most of us consider 'vampire' a derogatory term. But if being Oberon meant being partnered with my soul mate, then yes, I would. A soul mate is the rarest of gifts. To deny it would be like second-guessing fate. What will you do if he rejects the offer?"

"I'm going to be Titania, with or without Lex as Oberon. It'd just be easier to work with him." I tried to sound nonchalant about it, but it was hard to pretend it wasn't like an ice pick digging around in my heart.

"He doesn't deserve you."

"Hmph. You sound like a jealous ex," I joked.

"Perhaps." Reaching out, he picked up my hand and held it in his. "You're a lovely woman, Catherine. I think the higher powers were unfair pairing you with someone who obviously doesn't appreciate that."

I tensed, expecting him to give me a magical nudge, but none came. Cautious, I raised an eyebrow. "And you would?"

"I wouldn't have handed you over to the witches' council, and I certainly wouldn't have abandoned you when you were most vulnerable." His voice was warm and soothing, and I found myself believing him. It was true, after all, wasn't it? Lex betrayed me, and left me alone and outcast. Somewhere in the back of my mind, my better judgment was trying to warn me that normally I wouldn't trust a damn word Harrison said, but it seemed faint and far away. There was such sincerity in his eyes.

Sliding closer to me, he raised my hand to his lips and brushed a light kiss across my knuckles. "I think you should give me a chance. We could do amazing things together."

"I think you're only interested in me because I'm going to be Titania, otherwise I'd never get a second glance," I countered, tugging my hand away.

Taking that as a challenge, Zach scooped me up into his lap as he had in the limo, except this time he turned me so I was straddling him. He kissed me senseless, leaving no doubt that he found me attractive. One hand rested on my hip, while the other slid up my back, drawing me closer. I should've fought him, zotted him with a spell that'd stand his blond hair on end, but instead I leaned into him. He continued to kiss me, hungry and eager, and then he moved to my neck. Lightly his lips brushed against my skin, and I nearly yelped with surprise, but he held me in place.

"Please, Catherine. Just a small bite," he murmured

against my throat. I shivered, frozen and afraid to breathe, struggling to find my voice. Taking my silence as permission, the vampire sank his fangs into my skin. Magic washed over me in a sharp, fast wave that made my back arch and hands clench into fists against his chest. The spell was stronger this time, and it completely overwhelmed me.

He drank greedily, though in my weakened state I probably tasted as appetizing as a flat diet soda left out on the counter all day. The hand at my hip slid up my side and caressed my breast through my blouse. My eyes closed as I let myself enjoy the sensations. I was so deeply enthralled, I didn't even notice that he'd stopped drinking until I felt his lips brush my collarbone. The buttons of my blouse were undone, and I realized my bra was soon to follow. The thought was sobering enough to finally give me focus.

"Wait. I can't—I can't do this," I stammered breathily.

"Why not?" His eyes had faded to a pale green, and it startled me. I suddenly became aware of the strong scent of smoke, and wondered how I hadn't sensed it sooner.

"I can't," I repeated, shaking my head. *What the hell are you doing?* Squirming away from him, I retreated to the other end of the couch and hastily buttoned my shirt. Frustrated, he ran a hand through his hair, and after a long moment he nodded.

"All right. I'll escort you back to your room, but this conversation isn't over."

Yeah, I was afraid of that, but at least the make-out session was over, and that was good enough for now.

# Chapter Twenty

I went to bed as soon as I could, eager to crawl under the covers and hide from the embarrassment. After drifting off to sleep I soon found myself in the middle of the grove once again. This time a large flat rock appeared in the middle of the clearing, and I sat perched atop it. I hugged my knees to my chest, and the skirt of my long robes was tucked around my feet. The sound of my weeping was the only noise in the summer night. I sobbed in confusion, regret and sorrow, as though my heart was broken. I didn't know what to do anymore—I had a knight in shining armor who didn't want to ride off into the sunset with me, and a vampire who wanted me to be his evil queen. Gods help me, but the vampire's offer was sounding more appealing with each passing day.

"Don't cry, sugar." Looking up, I saw Lex kneeling next to me, and he rubbed my back soothingly.

"You don't know," I replied, shaking my head.

"Know what?"

"What I..." I shook my head again, unable to answer. Lex frowned, and then he brushed my hair out of the way and examined my throat. I knew there weren't any marks—I'd looked—but he cursed as loudly as he would have if there'd been a stream of blood trickling down the side of my neck.

"Damn it, I told him to leave you alone," he growled.

"Why do you care, when you don't even want me?" Surprised, I clamped a hand over my mouth—had I really said that? Out loud? Lex looked about as startled as I was, and he rocked back on his heels.

"You know that's not true."

"Yes it is. Why aren't I enough for you?" I asked, the

question ending on a shrill, hiccuping sob.

"I never said that, Cat—"

"You don't have to, I know it's true." Rising to my feet, I glared down at him. "But that's fine. I don't need you."

A loud crack of thunder startled me, and a chill wind blew through the grove. I looked up at the night sky, expecting to see rain clouds rolling in, but the stars were still bright above us.

"You don't mean that," Lex said. He gazed up at me, confused, and I folded my arms across my chest.

"I won't waste my life waiting for you to decide what's most important to you."

"I've already made my decision. Marry me."

I blinked, startled. "What?"

"Marry me. In fact, why not right here and now?" Rising to his feet, he took my hands in his.

"Because we're in the dream realm. Nothing's binding here, don't be silly." Frustrated, I tugged my hands away.

"'Why should Titania cross her Oberon?'" he quoted, smiling slyly.

"Because I can't trust you. You'll just end up resenting me and then you'll leave. Titania and Oberon aren't exactly a healthy example to base a relationship on."

"We'll work it out."

"Yeah, 'cause that worked so well before," I snapped, scowling at him. "You're not my Oberon. You never were. Just leave me alone."

The wind picked up, whipping my hair behind me as another rumble of thunder sounded. Lex glanced around and then cursed viciously. Lightning flashed, splitting the sky, and my heart beat wildly. He stood ready to protect me from the danger invading our grove, and then he turned and gripped my arm.

"Don't let him bite you again, Cat. It's poison. He's trying to control you—"

And just like that the dream was gone, and the rest of the night was quiet and empty.

In the morning my clothing order arrived, including a few items I knew I hadn't requested but apparently Zach thought I needed. At least his fashion choices were more conservative than Laura's, so I let it slide. True to his word, Zach showed up to take me out to dinner that evening. The vampire continued his attempt to convince me that he was Prince Charming instead of the Prince of Darkness, probably hoping that if he won my heart I'd continue speaking to him after I left. I learned that part of his master plan included escorting me to the opening of the new show in his art gallery the night before the full moon, where I'd get to do my best arm-candy impression in a dress that cost more than my last semester at college.

Harrison spent the majority of his free time trying to romance me. More dinners, more movies, a thrilling tour of Vampire Central and the many luxury amenities within it, all with magician political commentary and the things we could do together to change things for the better. It began to make sense—I could see myself working with him, using my influence to impact the future of magiciankind.

Though I was loathe to admit it, with all the time we spent together I started to tolerate him a bit more. I even let him kiss me good night at the end of our pseudo-dates—it seemed reasonable that if allowing the vampire kiss me kept him happy enough to keep his word and let me and Mac leave when the moon was full, then I should just endure it. And as much as I complained about Zach's status of walking corpse, the kissing wasn't a horrifying experience. For the most part, if I didn't already know he was a vampire, it'd be hard to tell. Zach kept himself reasonably warm to the touch, the miracle of spray-on tan gave his skin a healthy glow, and his smile was harmless since real vampires don't sport constant fangs like movie monsters. When he wasn't attempting vamp magic he smelled only of cologne and a slight scent of soap. If I didn't have such a scarred past and a turbulent present, I could have fallen for Zach's act. He'd even worked his way into my subconscious, because now when I dreamed, I dreamed of Zach.

In his lair again (though in my opinion anything called a lair ought to have torches, cobwebs and a coffin), Zach sat next to me on the couch as we watched another movie. An action-packed thriller, it featured lots of explosions and car chases that took full advantage of the big-screen TV and surround-sound system. He slid his arm around my shoulders halfway through the film, and turning toward him, I raised an eyebrow, looking from the encroaching arm to those gorgeous green eyes.

"You're invading my space. Go watch the movie on the other end of the couch."

"No."

"No? Okay, I'll go watch the movie on the other end of the couch then." Rising to my feet, I tried to walk past him and found myself suddenly tugged into his lap.

"There, much better." Zach grinned.

"Oh no it isn't, we've been over this before, now let me go." I sighed, trying to escape, but Harrison shook his head and held me in place. Reaching up, he caressed my cheek, and then trailed his fingers down the side of my neck.

"Don't," I warned him.

"I'm not going to bite you."

I started to argue but was cut off when he kissed me. By now I'd gotten used to Zach and his demanding, intense kisses—at the end of the night he kept expecting me to melt into a puddle of willing goo and invite him into my suite, and I kept rebuffing his efforts and closing the door in his face.

When it became apparent he wasn't about to let me go I decided to give him a no-nonsense magical shove to get my point across. To my immediate surprise my shields didn't snap into place as I expected. They formed around me, but they stretched to include Harrison. Just like they did with Lex.

Sensing the change, the vampire pulled away and looked deep into my eyes for a moment, and he smiled. The expression frightened me more than if he'd flashed fangs at me.

"How...how did you do that?"

"You can't keep me out, Catherine. Not anymore." Though his voice was still soft, his tone had a threatening edge to it, a hint of the predator that lurked beneath the benign smile.

"What did you do?"

Harrison continued to smile, ignoring my discomfort. "Would you like something to drink? A glass of wine, perhaps?"

"Sure, wine is good," I lied. Anything to get away. He released me, and I squirmed away from him and retreated to a safe distance. I had no idea how he'd managed to get around my shields. Sure, he'd surrounded me with his shields in the limo when Portia tried to shoot him, but that was different. I followed him to the bar, and he poured a glass of deep red wine.

"There's dessert here as well, chocolate-covered

strawberries." He waved at a covered plate next to where he stood. Though I certainly had no appetite at the moment I removed the cover, discovering an arrangement of fat, luscious-looking berries decorated with intricate designs in white and dark chocolate. The vampire held the glass out to me, reaching through my shields as though nothing was there at all. Glaring at him, I took the glass and backed away.

"How are you doing that?"

"It's very simple, actually. We're connected, you can't keep me out."

"How are we connected? We weren't connected before. I could keep you out a few days ago, what changed?"

"You have," Zach answered. "Is the wine not to your liking?" I glanced down and sniffed at the dark liquid, almost expecting to see an ominous skull and crossbones swirling within the glass. When I couldn't find anything obviously wrong with it I took a sip—raspberry wine, one of my favorites. "It hasn't been tampered with."

"The wine hasn't, but I have?"

"I wouldn't put it that way, no. It's actually quite an honor among necromancers."

"I'm not a necromancer."

Shrugging, he surveyed the selection of strawberries, picked one up and bit into it. "Not bad, you should try one."

"Just explain what you did."

"We're attuned to each other now. You can't use harmful magic against me, but I can't use it against you either. I can't force you to do anything, but you can't keep pushing me away." With his usual calm, polite air about him he explained the situation while peering down at the tray of berries. "Together, however, we strengthen each other's abilities. With enough practice one can even tell what the other is thinking or feeling." Selecting one, he held it out to me and I glared at it, struggling to figure out exactly what he meant. I'd never heard of two people becoming attuned to each other in a magic-type sense.

"And how is that possible?"

"I'm afraid to admit that it is necromancy, a rarely used spell. It's usually a mark of trust between a master necromancer—or vampire as you're fond of calling them—and his or her favorite apprentice. But that's not important. What is important is that we share a bond, not unlike the one your guardian so easily tossed aside. I can't hurt you now, I couldn't even if I wanted to. You have nothing to fear from me, so there is nothing to prevent us from working together."

"And it never occurred to you to ask if I wanted this?"

"You wouldn't agree."

"Damn straight I wouldn't agree, you manipulative bastard." I slammed the wineglass down, and red liquid sloshed over the sides. Furious, I hauled back and slapped him. The blow didn't faze him, but I suddenly felt pain zing to life across my face, mirroring where I'd just struck him. "What the hell!"

"I did warn you. Our pain is shared now, and you'd do well to inform your faerie cousins of that," he said coldly.

"This isn't fair."

"This is how the game is played, Catherine. A Titania should know that."

"It's not a game—"

"Yes, it is, and you'd best get used to it. You should be grateful for what I've done for you. There are those who wouldn't be as gentle as I have been, who would've capitalized even more on your mistakes."

"What mistakes?"

"For one, Maureen would never have agreed to stay here."

"Maureen wouldn't have left a friend to die," I protested.

"Yes, she would have. A Titania is expected to sacrifice her own needs in order to protect her people. You should have left your friend, but you didn't. You shouldn't have gotten involved in vampire and shapeshifter politics, yet you have. Your path was decided the moment you let Faust into your apartment."

"And what path is that, pray tell?"

"A greater path than that of Titania. You can be more than a mere go-between for magicians and faeries. You can be a great leader, and change the future of all magicians."

"But only if I work with you, right?"

"I'm the only one who will offer this to you. Duquesne certainly won't get involved. He's ignored this problem for far too long."

My heart sank. "Lex knows? About the government, and the experiments?" That couldn't be possible. It was Lex's job to protect magicians from that sort of thing. Wasn't it?

"Of course. As always, the guardians are unwilling to get

involved in mortal affairs. Oh, they'll protect us from each other, but not from the outside world."

Resisting the urge to squirm, I decided to move on. "So what happens next?"

"Tomorrow we'll attend the gallery event, and then on Sunday you and Mr. MacInnes will leave. After that, I would like you to return, of your own free will."

"Uh-huh. Leaving the 'oh hell no' of it all aside, my bills are probably piling up—"

"I've already taken care of those. I made sure your payments were made, including your rent."

"With what? I barely have anything in my savings." I blinked at him. Lord and Lady, my account was probably overdrawn by now. There were sure to be many angry messages waiting for me in my voicemail.

"If you remember, I did promise to reimburse you and your friend for the time you've both spent here, because it is my fault that you're losing wages by being my guests. I wanted to pay your debt off entirely, but I had a feeling you wouldn't thank me for that."

I nodded in response. The man was right—I probably would have told him off for interfering with my responsibilities.

"Oh. I still need to leave to be proclaimed Titania, they'll be waiting for me," I pointed out.

"This is true. When you're finished with that, will you come back?" Gently he stroked the back of my hand, his gaze imploring.

"No. I can't operate as Titania in a no-faerie zone."

"I own other buildings, you can live anywhere you want. A house in the suburbs, a condo on the lakefront, wherever suits you most."

"You can't buy my loyalty, Harrison. Look, I was seriously considering working with you, but now I don't know. I won't be pushed around like one of your minions. I need to go back to my room." My head hurt, and I needed space.

"All right." He reluctantly nodded. "Let's go then."

Walking around the bar, he took my arm and escorted me to the elevator. The ride up was short and silent. When we finally reached the door to my suite there was an awkward pause—I could tell Zach was considering kissing me good night as he'd become accustomed to doing. Instead, he looked at me with a terrible sadness in those striking green eyes, then opened the door for me. Without a word I walked into my room, and listened as the door shut behind me and the lock clicked into place.

Deciding on a drink, I headed immediately to the bar and poured a tumbler full of Irish cream—some people drink it by the shot, I prefer it by the glass, with a few ice cubes for elegant presentation. I took a long gulp and closed my eyes, trying to sort through the mess of thoughts flying through my head. Did Zach honestly expect me to come back to him? Even more frightening, was there a possibility I would? No, surely not. *No, you'll just go home to your tiny apartment and live the rest of your wretched life with only a series of housecats for companions.*

But I didn't have to live alone, I had a soul mate, one who'd been envisioning a happily ever after in our future until the faeries scared him away from it. Lex was out there somewhere, waiting for me, and from what he'd said in the last dream it sounded as though he'd decided to become Oberon. Once Zach let me go, I'd be free to run into Lex's arms and ride off into the sunset. All I had to do was be patient. Maybe Harrison's spell would wear off eventually...

I heard the door open and the sound of approaching footsteps behind me. Without opening my eyes I sighed wearily. "I so do not want to continue this conversation."

Before I could turn around my head was slammed forward, colliding hard with the top of the bar. An instant migraine exploded behind my forehead and then I was dragged backwards by my hair.

"I'll make this quick then," Lovely Laura growled at me. The room spun and tilted crazily around me, and as I struggled to stand the vampire grabbed for my throat. Her pale eyes almost glowed with hatred and her sharp nails dug into my skin. Terrified, I tried to break her grip, but she was too fast. Drawing her hand back, she tore deep slashes into my throat, producing a huge spray of blood. I grabbed at the wounds, hoping to hold together what was left, then Laura struck me hard and I sailed backwards. I'd have a spectacular black eye from it if I lived.

As I hit the floor with a bone-jarring thud, I thrust my shields out with all the control I could manage. The energy sparked, fizzled, and then faded as Laura kicked me in the stomach, and the breath rushed out of me in a guttural whoosh. I struggled to steady myself and try again, but everything was too scattered and hazy in my mind to attempt any magic, even something as simple as my shields.

"I don't know what he sees in you." Jamming the pointed toe of her high-heeled shoe beneath my chin, she turned my head from side to side. "You're homely, overweight, badly dressed. Ungrateful. Unworthy. Dorian should have drowned you at birth like a mongrel pup." Moving her foot, she stabbed my stomach with the sharp heel of her shoe, puncturing who knows what internal organs in the process.

"Fuck you," was the only stinging retort I managed. It was much too difficult to talk and I knew that was a bad sign. The wounds refused to heal, resisting my weak attempt to close them. Warm, slick blood gushed over my hands—I didn't have long left, and Laura was going to waste the last moments of my life with some bitchy speech.

"And you are crass as well," she added with another stomp. "What a fool, to think you able to lead. You're too weak for greatness. He'll be much better off without you."

The vampire stomped on me again and I fought the urge to giggle madly at the image of Lovely Laura and her "killer" heels. Ugh, death by bad pun, how cliché. Closing my eyes, I waited for the end, but to my surprise I heard a startled shout from the direction of the door. I dragged my eyes open again to see a Harrison-shaped blur streak toward her, grab her and throw her against the nearest wall with a resounding crack of broken drywall.

"What the hell are you doing?" he shouted.

"I'm altering your plan."

"Why, you think you can take her place?"

"She won't have you," Laura hissed in reply. "I won't let her."

*Gee, hell really doth have no fury like a woman scorned.* My eyes fluttered shut because I no longer had the strength to keep them open. I would've found the exchange much more interesting if I hadn't been bleeding out.

"Get out! Now!"

"No. I *made* you. I know what's best for you. She's too much like her mother, she won't be corrupted. That girl will never obey you. It's best to get rid of her now and make a clean break." Laura made me sound like some sort of untrainable puppy that needed to be put down, and I *really* wanted to light her on fire. Repeatedly. Instead I just gurgled piteously from the pain.

Next I heard a slap followed by an outraged gasp. "How dare you interfere," Harrison growled.

"Someone has to—you don't have even a fraction of my experience. I'm looking out for your best interests."

"No, you're looking out for your best interests."

"*I made you*," she repeated, her voice raising a screeching octave.

"But you can't control me."

For a brief moment I thought I caught a whiff of burning flesh through the stench of blood, but I couldn't be sure if it was my own imagination picturing Lovely Laura wreathed in flames. The smell was followed by a few gasping noises that sounded like they came from a female source. Good for Zach, I hope he snapped her skinny, pale neck.

Footsteps, a door slammed, and then Harrison hovered over me. He looked like hell—he had wounds that mirrored mine, but less severe. Zach murmured reassuringly, and though the words were beginning to sound fuzzy and incoherent I could hear ten shades of worry in his voice. He drew my hands away from my throat and started to heal the slashes with a wave of tingling, stinging magic. Unfortunately the pain didn't subside one bit, and the relentless press of unconsciousness crowded my thoughts. As my mind began to drift, I realized Zach was right—I really could sense his emotions. Staticky and faint, like being able to hear a distant radio station when the conditions were just right. Despite the angry words he'd exchanged with Laura I knew he was afraid, deeply terribly afraid.

"Catherine, look at me," he ordered, and I struggled to meet his gaze. Zach looked grim as he stared down at me, and I knew that couldn't be good. "I need you to drink." I frowned, confused, and watched in pained silence as he unbuttoned the cuff of his sleeve and rolled it up. The vampire raised his wrist to his mouth and bit through the skin. He moved to hold his wound against my lips and I tried to turn away. "Catherine, you have to drink, you'll die if you don't. The blood won't turn you, it won't hurt you, it will just help me heal you."

I had to believe him—I didn't have a choice. Death wasn't exactly an option I was open to, especially when I was so close to regaining my freedom, so I drank. The blood burned, feeling as though it seared a path of scar tissue down my throat as I swallowed. I'd never experienced anything like it. The sensation was like trying to describe how a nightmare would taste, or what flavor death might have. My body tried to reject the invader, and my limbs flailed and thrashed as though suffering a seizure. Zach pinned me down and held me still as best he could, continuing to pour the poison into me. I had no idea how it could be helping, it felt as though the blood was killing me faster.

Finally he removed his wrist and smoothed the fingers of his other hand over the torn skin, closing the wound. Then he pressed his hands against each of the puncture wounds caused by Laura's heel, one after the other. The pain was phenomenal, unimaginable, a spear of agony that sprung from my core out to my skin. I didn't remember it hurting that badly when she'd caused them in the first place. I screamed loud and long, the sound filling the room until I sank into the blessed oblivion of unconsciousness as my newfound talent for fainting finally resulted in something good.

# Chapter Twenty-One

The soft, rapid clicking of a keyboard woke me, and I dragged my eyes open to stare at an unfamiliar ceiling. By now I was getting used to the running theme of fainting and waking up in an unexpected place. I'd gone through most of my life without fainting a single time, and yet somehow during the past few weeks I'd developed the constitution of a Victorian heroine suffering from the consumption. If I survived this whole ordeal, I was joining a gym and toughening myself up. And quitting smoking. Again. For real this time.

Lifting my head, I studied the room. Yup, definitely not my suite, or my apartment, and also not Castle Silverleaf, though the bed was nearly as large. The place was the definition of master bedroom—it was probably larger than my entire apartment. Antique wooden furniture decorated the space, and a familiar vampire hunched over a laptop in an easy chair across the room, a stack of newspapers on the table next to him. Though Zach's hair was a bit mussed and the top buttons of his dress shirt were undone, it reminded me of when I'd arrived at his office here in the tower because he had the same intent expression as he studied whatever important work was plastered on the screen. The sight was somewhat of a relief. It was less embarrassing to wake up in Zach's bed when he was fully clothed on the other side of the room, engrossed in some business dealing. Curious, I glanced down at myself, easing the covers aside to discover that I was wearing a set of boring cotton print pajamas I'd ordered from one of the catalogues. While it was a little mortifying that he'd probably dressed me, I was pretty positive he'd behaved himself.

Sensing my movement, Zach looked up from his laptop,

seeming surprised. "You're awake," he said, setting his work aside. "How do you feel?"

"Like I got stomped on," I replied, my voice rough and gravelly. Everything ached, thankfully not as terribly as it ought to considering how close to death I'd been. Crossing the room, he picked up a heavy earthenware mug from the bedside table and moved to help me sit up.

"Here, drink this."

"No more blood," I protested in a piteous whine.

"No more blood, it's herbal tea. I added a potion to it that will help ease the pain and regain your strength more quickly."

I nodded my thanks and took the mug, holding it with both hands as I sipped at it. The liquid was dark and lukewarm, and it smelled faintly of mint. If there was a potion stirred into it I couldn't smell it, but then again alchemy is the most difficult magic for me to detect. Potions tend to smell like their ingredients, or whatever they're added to.

"You were an alchemist?" I'd figured him for a sorcerer, since so many necromancers start out that way.

"Yes. I'm the first magician in the Harrison family." He smiled dryly. "It was a bit of a surprise for my father."

I looked down at the tea and froze. Zach was an *alchemist.* "You put potions in my food, didn't you? To do the spell that bound us together."

"Part of it," he admitted. "Your weakness for sweets was very helpful. As was the fact that you're a heavy sleeper."

"You son of a—"

"Catherine, if I hadn't cast the spell, you would be dead right now. I wouldn't have known Laura attacked you until your body was found in the morning. Would that be better?"

"No." He had a point, as much as it pissed me off to admit it. "Thank you. For saving me, I mean. How did you do it, I'm not—I mean, I'm still...?"

"Alive? Yes, you are. It takes more than that to become a necromancer, and a lot more to become a master. You should get used to the terminology, by the way. Many of the elder masters consider being called vampire a grave insult, and they don't deal well with being insulted."

"Uh-huh. Why did I have to drink from you?" I wrinkled my nose at the very idea of it. Yuck.

"I'm sorry, but I couldn't heal you without it. Usually to heal a wound, like a bite for example, we use the magic within the person's own blood to do it. You'd lost so much blood that you didn't have the strength to repair that much damage. I had to give you mine so I would have something to work with. It won't happen again, I'll make sure you stay safe."

"Really. Did Lovely Laura suffer some sort of unfortunate accident while I was asleep?"

"No, she didn't, but she's not getting anywhere near you again."

"My hero. You know, I don't think these bruises will match my dress for the party," I joked half-heartedly.

"I'll find a makeup artist to cover it for you. You should be well enough to make an appearance, but we won't stay long at the opening."

"Is Laura going to be there?" There was no way I could deal with her after this—she was number one on my hit list now. Maybe when I got out I could join up with the Silverleafs and we'd slay her mightily together, one big, happy, vengeful faerie family.

"Yes she is, but if she even looks in your direction, she'll be asked to leave."

"Asked with extreme prejudice?"

"Yes. I'm sorry she attacked you, this is entirely my fault."

"You two were..." I paused, searching for a polite term, "...involved, huh?"

He shifted uncomfortably and then nodded. "I was one of her most prized pets, but that was years ago. Laura tends to go through men rather quickly."

"Like she goes through shoes?"

The vampire chuckled, but it was a hollow sound. I could tell there was a story there, but he wasn't going to discuss it. "Why'd she go after me like a jealous wife if you're not involved anymore?"

"Aside from the fact that she doesn't agree with my politics in this case, it's one of Laura's eccentricities. She has no problem moving on to a new pet, but she expects all of her former ones to pine for her for the rest of their lives. She hasn't cared as long as I've had short, empty relationships with other women."

"And I'm different?"

"You are, yes." Avoiding elaborating on that topic, he changed the subject. "Catherine, I know you must leave tomorrow, but you need to be careful when you do. Magicians who haven't become necromancers don't typically ingest our blood, and there can be dangerous side effects. Rare, but there is a risk."

I frowned down into my mug and considered his words. "I'll be careful."

"Good. Now, I'd like to test how steady you are on your feet."

For the next several minutes Zach let me lean on him as I tested my wobbly legs doing laps around the room. At first it was a struggle, but as we continued to move I realized most of the problem was in my head. Sure I had plenty of aches and pains, but he healed my injuries very well and they'd been reduced to bruises and sore muscles. Once he was convinced I wasn't going to crumple like a wilting flower, Zach gave me free reign of the room and also the ginormous master bathroom and retreated with his laptop into the main room.

When I was clean and clothed—he'd brought a T-shirt and jeans from my suite in addition to the pajamas I was wearing—I emerged into the main area of his lair to discover a feast fit for ten people waiting for me. I'd always wondered what it would look like if someone ordered everything on a restaurant menu, and thanks to Harrison I had my answer.

"I wasn't sure what you wanted," he offered as an explanation as I stared in amazement at the banquet.

"Right..."

Like a parent trying to keep an eye on his child without hovering constantly, he observed me from a distance for the rest of the day. While he took calls on his cell phone and worked on his computer, I lounged around and watched movies until evening began to draw near. True to his word, Harrison found not only a makeup artist for me but also a hair stylist, a manicurist, and a fashion consultant who brought enough clothing to fill the women's section of a department store. The four of them swarmed around me like stylish bees and whisked me back into the bedroom. It was an effort to find something that I looked good and felt comfortable in. The experience was even more overwhelming than Portia's stint as the Makeover

Fairy. My hair was trimmed and warm red highlights were added, and my poor, neglected nails were molested in some acrylic fashion the girl called "French tips".

The makeup artist was a woman named Willow, who was slightly older than me, with shocking purple hair and funky black rhinestone-studded eyeglasses. She clucked with disapproval as she examined the dark ring around my eye.

"Oh, honey, what happened?" she asked.

"The ex-girlfriend threw down with me. She won." It was both a simple and accurate explanation, and Willow sighed and shook her head.

"She must be a real bitch."

"You have no idea."

"Well, it's obvious you're the one he loves now, or he wouldn't be lavishing all this attention on you." She winked conspiratorially. I fought the urge to frown in response, uncomfortable with that idea, and she took my hesitation as uncertainty. "Don't worry, hon, we can see it in the way he looks at you. Right, Steph?"

The girl attacking my nails looked up and nodded. "Oh yeah, totally. You know we do weddings too."

"I'll keep that in mind." Great, a vampire wedding, just what every little girl dreams of. My stomach plummeted and hung out somewhere between my knees for the rest of the experience. By the time they were finished, I barely recognized myself in the mirror. My hair was curled and swept up into a million-and-one hairpins piled on top of my head, with a few soft, decorative ringlets cascading downward. The makeup was flawless, concealing my bruises and improving my features so I looked like a movie star. The consultant had chosen a long, draped dress made of an airy material that seemed to float around me as I moved. Shades of light, summery green that I probably never would have chosen actually looked fabulous with my highlighted hair and the spray-on tan Willow had assaulted me with.

I looked fabulous. I hoped it made Laura suffer.

When I emerged from the den of fashion and was free of the hovering stylists I found Zach waiting for me, dressed in an honest-to-goodness tailor-made designer tuxedo. I'd never seen a tux that wasn't a rental before. He looked damn good. *For a walking corpse, right?* Right, I meant damn good for a walking corpse.

This could only end badly.

"You look stunning. Ready to go?" he asked, offering his arm.

"Yeah, just walk slow. I'm wobbly enough without balancing on these stilts."

"Of course." Zach smiled. "I must apologize, though."

"For what?"

"Smudging your lipstick." Gathering me into his arms, he kissed me. Unsteady from the shoes, I couldn't do much other than cling to him. "I want you to stay here with me tonight." I started to shake my head, but he cut me off before I could protest. "Nothing improper need happen, I only want to make sure that you're safe and well."

Though his words sounded sincere, there was an intensity in his eyes that promised much more. "I'll think about it," I replied weakly.

With me holding tight to his arm we made our way to the elevator. After a short ride we emerged onto the floor of the art gallery, arriving at his super-secret ninja back way in, which I was rather grateful for considering I didn't want to make an awkward grand entrance from the main doors. Caterers, security and other random minions parted before us like the Red Sea as Harrison swept past them. We walked through a set of swinging doors into the gallery itself, and I was struck by the thick, roiling scent of mixed magic—some vampire, some shapeshifter, a little bit of everything but faerie.

"I thought this was a human party?" I asked between gritted teeth, a fake smile plastered onto my face as we gazed out at the crowd.

"What would you prefer, the rich and privileged or the fanged and furry?" he asked, guiding me into the fray.

"None of the above."

"Don't worry, you'll do fine."

# Chapter Twenty-Two

There were vamps at every turn, sipping wine, discussing the artwork, exchanging polite conversation with one another. A sprinkling of shapeshifters was mixed in with the walking dead, as well as assorted magicians—necromancers mostly, with a few sorcerers and thankfully not a single witch in sight. It quickly became obvious to me that the safest place to be when surrounded by a roomful of vampires is on the arm of the richest and most powerful one. I'd wondered what the other vamps thought of Harrison. He was practically a baby, yet he ordered around one of the three members of the Midwestern vampire council like she was his bitch. What's more, she actually allowed him to treat her that way. Considering that Lovely Laura Barrenheart was the only female vampire council member I'd heard of, she really ought to be one tough broad, because she'd beat out the old boys' network. Or she was a turbo slut who'd slept her way to the top, but that was a very un-feminist thing for me to think. As a result, I'd figured Harrison had to be pretty powerful and well respected.

Boy, did I ever call that one.

The vampires were easy to spot. It's the lack of sun that gives them away. Even in a world that believes in better living through chemistry old vamps don't seem to have heard of a tan in a bottle. I thought they'd be snide to Zach, talk down to him like they were old money and he was nouveau riche, but they didn't. The vampires liked him, and most were even happy to see him. They seemed to respect him, and I wasn't sure if I should be impressed or terrified by that. Probably both. It was strange to me. When people reacted to Lex they feared or respected him for being a member of the magic police, but Zach they treated like their favorite politician, the one they not only voted for but were willing to donate to his campaign fund as well.

Me they treated like arm candy. I was on display as much as the artwork while Zach showed off that the new Titania was his pet. I wanted to *strangle* him for it. At least he was introducing me as Catherine Baker, the name I actually go by but virtually no one had used once since I'd been drawn into the crazy Titania drama. It was the polite thing to do—broadcasting a person's True Name to the world is an enormous faux pas in magician society.

Slow and methodical, Harrison made the rounds of the gala, chatting with his guests, stopping to admire the artwork and explain to me each piece and its meaning and importance to the collection. Polite, attentive and witty, he was a perfect host. Were all vampire gatherings this calm and sophisticated? Even Laura was on her best behavior, keeping her distance and spending her time flirting with every male within ten feet of her. I wondered if she thought it would make Zach jealous? I doubted it, considering he was glued to my side and seemed to have eyes only for me. The flirtation was subtle—the light touch of his hand at the small of my back, a whispered comment in my ear.

"Would you like something to drink?" he asked as we stood studying a large bronze sculpture.

"Yes, I think so." I nodded, glancing around. People were giving us space at the moment, and I didn't feel quite as uncomfortable.

"Stay here, I'll be right back. Don't worry, no one would dare bother you. I'll just be a moment."

"All right."

Zach kissed me on the cheek before walking away, and I felt my face burn with an embarrassed blush. Considering the thick layer of makeup I had spackled on my face, I doubt anyone noticed the expression. Left alone, I studied the sculpture with a critical eye. I didn't understand it—it looked like a big misshapen lump to me.

"Good evening, Miss Morrow," a voice behind me greeted. Turning toward the speaker, I frowned, and after a moment I recognized him as Simon St. Jerome. It was the outfit that threw me—he was wearing a simple black suit, and without his

Dungeons and Dragons black wizard robes he really looked quite normal.

"Simon? What are you doing here?" The vampire hadn't struck me as the social type, and this was definitely a social gathering.

"I could ask you the same question."

I wondered what he must be thinking after seeing me on Harrison's arm all night. "That's a long story."

The vampire tilted his head to the side, studying me. "I'm sure it is. I would like to hear it one day. Are you well?"

"Well enough, no thanks to Laura," I replied with a grimace, reaching to ensure my throat was still in one piece.

"I take it she objects to your...new status?" Simon raised a finely drawn brow, and I frowned.

"What status?"

"As the Lady of Harrison Tower."

"Huh. Yeah, I'm about as happy to be here as the Lady of Shallot," I quipped. I knew he'd get the Tennyson reference, and Simon nodded in understanding. "You didn't bring your friends? Mr. and Mrs. Black?"

"Actually they're speaking with your associate Mr. MacInnes at the moment. Apparently he's a fan of Emily's writing."

Glancing around for Mac, I instead spotted Zach returning, holding a white china cup and saucer.

"Here you are, my dear," Zach said, handing me the cup.

"Thank you." I smiled. Coffee, perfect. Powered by caffeine, I can survive anything.

"I see you've met Lord Wroth. I must admit I am surprised to see you here, you almost always decline my invitations," Zach commented as he scrutinized him. Simon seemed nonplussed by the statement. I wondered if Wroth was his true name. If so, he was taking Harrison's rudeness remarkably well.

"You've created quite a stir, Harrison. I thought this gathering would be well worth witnessing."

"Really."

The two vampires sized each other up for a tense moment as I drank my coffee, and I put a calming hand on Zach's shoulder. The moment passed, and he smiled pleasantly at Simon. "Well, I hope you have a good view then."

"I always do." Simon smiled in return, and there was a sly edge to the expression. He nodded at me, and then bowed slightly to Harrison before walking away.

"I guess even the undead have paparazzi," I joked, trying to put Zach at ease. "How much longer do I have to stay?"

"Are you tired?" Concern crossed his face, and I shook my head. "Just a bit longer then. We have a few more people to speak with." He held his hand out to me, and I put my hand in his and let him lead me away to the next *objet d'arte*.

Everything was calm and quiet as we continued throughout the gallery. We met more people whose names I would never remember, and I saw more art I didn't understand. Not my kind of party, but I'd take boring over potentially dangerous any day. Zach and I stood in the gallery's main room, providing fodder for several groups of gossiping vamps around us. Then the conversation died as a commotion interrupted the polite mood.

Turning toward the noise, I saw the body of a member of the security team fly into the room, landing a few feet from the doorway he'd been thrown through. I couldn't tell if the man was dead, but he was certainly not moving. Harrison took a step forward to shield me from whatever danger approached, and he turned to one of the vampire bodyguards that had been less than inconspicuously hovering around us all night.

"Get the civilians out," he ordered. "Now."

The vamp nodded in reply and began speaking into his sleeve like a Secret Service agent. I set my almost empty cup of coffee on the nearest table, which was probably inappropriate considering it displayed a piece of art, but I wanted my hands free to deal with whatever the problem was. A few more grunts and yelps were heard in the direction of the main entrance as the bulk of the crowd was herded out of the room, and then the instigator sauntered into view—a familiar figure in his black duster, T-shirt and jeans.

"Lex?" I gasped in disbelief. Stepping forward, I tried to move toward him, but was grabbed by Harrison and shoved behind him.

"I know you were not invited, Duquesne," Zach warned.

The guardian glanced around the room and shook his head in disappointment. "It's not my kind of party. I don't mean to stay long."

"You aren't welcome here."

Again I tried to step forward, but Harrison tightened his grip on my forearm, almost painfully so. I opened my mouth and prepared to tell him off, but I paused as I caught a hint of his true emotion. Despite the fact he looked outwardly calm and more than a little annoyed, Zach was worried. Afraid even, just as he'd been after Laura attacked me. I blinked as I digested this information, and in a surprising show of tact I kept my big mouth shut.

"I'm just here to collect my Titania, and then I'll leave you to your soiree."

"We've already proven that you have no grounds to remove her, since she willingly agreed to stay here as our guest," Lovely Laura chimed in. With slow, echoing steps she crossed to stand near us. Yeah, Laura wanted me dead, but protecting the vampire turf was more important to her at the moment. We were in the middle of a room full of vamps Zach needed to impress—it would be an enormous sign of weakness on his part if he let me leave with Lex now.

"I'm takin' her home."

I felt Zach's mood shift again. He was still afraid, but now he was angry as well. "Perhaps she doesn't wish to leave with you."

All eyes turned to me, and I wanted to sink right through the floor. "Umm, could we possibly discuss this in private?"

"There is nothing to discuss," Zach countered, and then turned back to Lex. "I've kept my word. I haven't forced her, nor harmed her. Catherine chose to be here. Now, you are trespassing, and I see no reason not to remove you from our territory." He motioned to the crowd, and a sea of vamps surged forward to attack Lex.

"No!" I shouted, and was completely ignored. Turning on his heel, Harrison strode away from the fight, dragging me along behind him. "Damn it, Zach, don't do this. Let me go," I implored as I stumbled along. Determined, he continued through the now-empty gallery, headed toward the private entrance we'd arrived at. "Please, tell them to stop."

"I can't," he replied. I tried to give him a magical shove, and it didn't even muss his hair. I dug my heels in to slow him down, and one of the stilettos snapped beneath me, causing me to tumble to the ground. Zach stopped, an apologetic expression on his face as he looked down at me. "I'm sorry,

Catherine, I truly am," he said as he knelt beside me. "I can't let you go with him."

"Why not?" I asked, my voice tight with too much emotion. "You had to know I'd see him again when I left." I fiddled with the strap of my broken shoe, my manicured nails making the process difficult.

"This is different. Let me do that." Taking my foot in his hand, he started to undo the tiny buckles.

"How is it different?"

"It is," he explained, his voice low enough to be a growl. "He picked this fight, now he'll deal with the consequences." Removing the broken shoe, Harrison paused and looked up at me. "Would you go with him and leave me standing here alone?"

"Yes. I have to help him." Lex was facing a roomful of vampires, without his guardian magic to protect him. I had to get back there before they tore him apart.

Without another word Zach removed my other shoe, and then hauled me to my feet. Once again he tried to drag me along with him, but I put up a stronger fight now that I had more traction.

"Catherine, even if I could help him, I still would not let you leave with him, now walk."

Unwilling to leave Lex to his fate, I switched tactics, snatching up the nearest piece of sculpture and hitting Zach with it as hard as I could. He staggered and dropped my arm, and the sculpture cracked and broke into several large pieces. Really, for a few grand you think it'd be more durable. An echo of pain shot through my skull as fragments of the piece fell from my hands. Cursing, I whirled and ran back toward the fray.

A circle of wary spectators had formed around Lex and Laura, and as I shoved my way through the onlookers it looked like she wasn't doing very well. Wielding his two short swords, Lex kept her at bay. The blades were covered in a spiky sheen of ice, just as my rapier had been during the battle in the courtyard of Silverleaf castle. The two combatants were each cut up, but no major wounds. Damn impressive on Lex's part.

Laura's back was to me as she concentrated on Lex, and I paused, glancing around for a makeshift weapon. Snatching up a half-empty bottle of water, I whispered a quick spell as I formed a ball of ice in my hand. Winding up like a major league pitcher, I hurled it at her, hitting Lovely Laura in the back of her blonde head. The vampire stumbled, surprised, and turned to face me. She stepped toward me, hatred blazing in her pale eyes, and then those eyes widened in shock as the tip of one of Lex's swords erupted from her chest. Laura let out a squeaky wail of disbelief.

"Give my regards to Dorian," I said as I watched Lovely Laura Barrenheart crumple. The fiery hatred in her eyes faded as she collapsed, and I managed to get in one spiteful kick before I was shoved out of the way. I stumbled and fell, sprawled awkwardly on the floor.

"*No!*" Harrison's anguished cry echoed through the gallery. With the councilwoman fallen, the surrounding minions scattered from the room like rats escaping a sinking ship. Someone tugged me to my feet, and I looked up to see Mac standing behind me. He dragged me off to the side, ducking behind the dubious protection of Simon St. Jerome and his vampire friend Michael Black, who stood watching the drama unfold like two critics observing a play. Aside from Zach and Lex, we were the only people left in the room.

Harrison stood over Laura's body, torn between mourning her loss and keeping a wary eye on her killer. Lex circled him, waiting for an opportunity to strike.

"You have no idea what you've done," Zach said quietly.

"True, I'm sure you know her crimes better than I do," Lex agreed.

"What do you hope to accomplish here? Prove your devotion to your lady fair? Wouldn't it have made more sense to ride to her rescue a bit sooner than the night before she was free to go?"

"I heard you were goin' to show off Cat like the newest piece in your collection, so I wanted to make sure your vamp buddies didn't get the wrong idea."

"And you showed up to prove your ownership instead? How Cro-Magnon of you. Will you be dragging her back to your cave next?"

I hated to admit it, but the vampire had a point. "Will you both cut it out? The wicked witch is dead, she had it comin', I say we call it a night."

"No!" both men replied.

"Oh, for the love of—" I started, but was interrupted by the undead peanut gallery.

"Hmm. Harrison knows, and yet he's still fighting it," Simon commented to his companion. "I think that's very interesting, don't you?"

"Yes, quite," Michael agreed.

"Knows what?" I asked.

"That you and Duquesne are soul mates, of course," Simon answered.

"Well duh, apparently everyone knows that," I muttered, grimacing in annoyance.

"Lord Wroth, Mr. Black. I take it you are enjoying your view," Zach said dryly as he glanced at them.

"Indeed, though this is not terribly original of you, I have witnessed this sort of drama before," Simon replied.

"You have?" I'd hate to think my adventure was just another day at the vampire office.

"My apologies, Miss Morrow. The drama in question is not an unfamiliar story: A newly made vampire so terrified at the thought of eternity alone that he is desperate to keep his stolen damsel with him, even as her knight is pounding down the doors to his lair."

"I object to being accused of something so cliché. I think my reasoning is quite sound. I might add that you are treading perilously close to interfering, St. Jerome."

"I'm merely having a talk with the new Titania." Spreading his hands in a placating gesture, he smiled. "Though I should add that it is a rather despicable specimen who would knowingly keep a lady from her soul mate."

"I need her," Zach growled. A shiver ran down my spine, and I grabbed Mac's hand.

"For what?" I asked. "You already put the necro-whammy on me. You said I could leave, and now none of your guests are here to witness whatever happens. Just let us go."

"I'm afraid I can't let a council member's murderer waltz away from the scene of the crime," Zach argued.

"Well, then you'll just have to stop me," Lex countered, and then lunged at him.

The two men moved with inhuman speed, a blur in the center of the room. With no weapon, Harrison fought with teeth and claws, and for the first time I was able to see him as a true monster. Lex caught him high across the chest, tearing a slash through Zach's suit, and a line of pain seared me in the same place. Gasping, I fell to my knees, still clinging to Mac's hand.

"Cat!" Mac exclaimed. "What's wrong?"

I placed my hand above the plunging neckline of my dress, and slick, warm blood coated my fingers. Kneeling next to me, Simon drew my hand away and examined the wound.

"Of all the foolish, irresponsible—" he sputtered. "Idiot boy." Rising to his feet, he turned to Michael. "Duquesne needs to be stopped, or he'll kill her along with Harrison."

Those were words I certainly didn't want to hear—Lex was mad enough to send Harrison straight to hell, and I didn't want to get dragged down with him. I watched as the two men continued to fight, two black-clad blurs that darted back and forth across the floor. I wasn't sure if it was Harrison's blood in my veins or whatever attunement he said we shared, but I felt every scratch, every bruise, every wound that the vampire endured.

Lex's blade cut a deep slash across Zach's torso, and I doubled over in agony. A blast of arctic air crashed into Harrison, and the vampire tumbled backward. Clutching his stomach as he lay in a crumpled ball, Harrison seemed defeated, and Lex advanced to deliver a killing blow. Seeing an opening, I stumbled between them and threw my arms out wide.

"Stop it!" I shouted. "That's enough!"

Lex tried to move around me, but I grabbed him. "Lord and Lady, will you stand still. You're hitting me too, jackass."

He frowned, noticing my bloodstained dress. "Cat...what happened?"

"You can't kill him, apparently it'll kill me too. He did some weird vampire wooj to me and now we're stuck with each other."

Lex shot a wary look at the fallen vampire, and then sheathed his weapons. I threw my arms around him and he held me close. I felt instantly better, as though Lex's very presence chased away my aches and pains.

"It's a spirit link, in fact," Simon spoke up. "It's really quite rare. I've never heard of it being cast on one who wasn't a necromancer."

"And I'm seriously not a necromancer."

Harrison stirred, groaning as he slowly got to his feet. "You could be. You'd be powerful. It's in your blood."

"No. It's not," I said, shaking my head. "Okay, we're going to leave now."

"I can't allow that," Zach repeated.

"I'm takin' her home," Lex replied. "Just 'cause I can't kill you doesn't mean I won't handcuff you to a sculpture so we can leave."

"Try it," Zach suggested. He grinned, flashing bright white fangs, and I shuddered. We were at a standoff—Lex couldn't attack him, and he wouldn't let us go.

There was a distinct sigh from the direction of our undead audience, and then a streak of motion darted from the shadows behind Harrison. He turned toward it, and a dull pain exploded in my head as Zach fell to the floor, unconscious. Lex held me tight, reacting to the sudden buckling of my knees. When I recovered I saw Mrs. Emily Black standing above Zach's prone form. Emily wiped off the side of a leather handbag, appearing unaffected by her surroundings.

I blinked. "Did you just hit him in the head with your purse?"

"I thought it best. We'd better hurry before he wakes up."

"Sounds like a plan to me. C'mon, sugar, let's get out of here," Lex said.

I hugged him, feeling a little steadier, and he brushed a kiss against my hair.

"Damn, broke another one," Emily muttered. She upended the bag, and several broken pieces of brick tumbled out and fell to the floor. I peered incredulously at Emily—the woman was short and petite and certainly didn't look like the sort to have a weapon in her evening bag, and definitely not a chunk of masonry. I turned toward Michael and Simon.

"Cracking your host in the head with a brick seems kinda like interfering in vamp politics to me. Isn't that against your Order's rules?"

"It is, but while Michael is in the Order, Emily isn't. That is why she can aid in rescuing you while we are merely observing," Simon explained. Dusting himself off, he attempted to put his black suit back into order. "We'll have to use the stairs. The elevators are monitored and can be overridden by security."

We ducked into an emergency stairwell and began making our way down to the parking structure. Thankfully the art gallery wasn't as high up in the building as my suite was, and we didn't have a ridiculously far distance to travel. Lex held my hand tightly as we walked, as though he worried I'd try to bolt and run back to Harrison. Or maybe he was just happy to see me. Either way, I knew we'd have an interesting conversation once we were rid of our vampire audience.

"So, if you're not in the Order, aren't you still going to get into trouble for assaulting Zach?" I asked Emily as we trudged down the stairs.

"*Zach?*" she said, an inquisitive note in her voice. "Hmm, just how familiar are you with young Mr. Harrison?"

"I tried to get familiar with him, but apparently I'm not his type," Mac joked. My cheeks flushed and I whacked Mac in the ribs with my free hand. Lex made a noise that sounded suspiciously like a low growl, and I hoped he was just clearing his throat.

"You're avoiding the question," I said to Emily.

"So are you," she replied, amused.

"You'll have to forgive Emily, she's an insufferable gossip." Michael chuckled behind us. "The answer to your question is no, she won't. Emily's position is unique."

"Unique?"

"Quite," Simon chimed in. "I took Michael on as my student and inducted him into the Order. Since he and Emily are soul mates, we couldn't separate them—it would be extremely cruel, so he turned her. She isn't part of the Order, but she wasn't a necromancer and therefore holds no allegiance to their society."

"That's why I volunteered when Alexander asked Simon for help sneaking him into the building," Emily informed me. "I don't often get to aid in the rescue of a damsel in distress."

"My wife, the mighty heroine." Michael affectionately mussed Emily's hair.

Emily pushed open the door to their parking level, and we emerged from the stairwell. It wasn't as pristine as the spot I'd arrived at in the limo, but I could still catch a faint smell of fresh, damp air through the exhaust and spilled oil—it was raining outside. The sound of shuffling feet and muffled conversation echoed through the concrete structure. We rounded a corner just in time to see a handful of security agents spill out of an elevator, and they didn't look happy.

"Ah hell," I sighed. "So much for avoiding the elevators."

The men spotted us and ran in our direction, a few of them

drawing guns. We dove behind the nearest cars for cover as shots exploded in a series of sharp pops.

"There's only a few, we can take care of them," Lex assured us, and I shook my head.

"'We'? Some of us are a bit out of our league here," Mac piped up, and I nodded in agreement.

"Yeah, and that's a lot of bullets to dodge. I don't suppose you had anything else besides a brick in your purse?" I asked Emily.

"Sorry, it was the only thing that got through the metal detectors."

"Great. Ideas?"

"Hey, look up," Mac said, pointing at the ceiling near our attackers. A bright red sprinkler head jutted from the bland concrete. Water. I could work with that.

Staring hard at the sprinkler, I reached out with my magic and yanked on the water in the pipes, which then erupted in a fine spray. I chanted the same spell that'd let me bean Laura with an iceball, and the water froze into sharp spikes, sending a hail of icicles in every direction.

"Nice." Lex grinned, darting out from our cover.

Emily grabbed a hold of my hand and tugged me after her as she dashed back into the aisle. A few of the men were down, injured but alive, and the ones left standing looked bewildered by what attacked their friends. Lex engaged those closest to us, and drawing back her fist, Emily decked one and laid him out flat. Not bad for a little vamp in a cocktail dress.

Lex made quick work of the rest of them, but the last man standing turned toward us and aimed his gun at Emily. I stepped closer to her, and instead of throwing my shields out from within me I pictured a perfect sphere of water around us, drawing on energy from the gush spewing from the sprinkler. The energy pulsed bright blue around us a heartbeat before he pulled the trigger, and the bullet hit the barrier. For a moment it hung there, suspended in midair, and then slid slowly to the ground.

"Good work," she said, impressed.

Before the gunman could fire again, a ball of ice the size of a grapefruit struck him in the side of the head and sent him sprawling. Emily and I turned to our vampire entourage, and Michael held out his hands, attempting to look innocent.

"Freak sprinkler accident," he explained, pointing upwards.

"Of course it was, darling. Let's hurry before it happens again, shall we?" Emily suggested.

Before I could manage to ask where exactly the car was, I felt a wave of white-hot anger thrum through me, and I collapsed in a pile of twitching, flailing limbs.

# Chapter Twenty-Three

Emily bent over me as I thrashed and kicked, molten agony racing through my veins. A high-pitched scream tore from my throat, long and agonized. The vampire placed her hands on either side of my face, and she held me steady as she looked deeply into my eyes.

Lex knelt next to me, and then grabbed my hand and held it. Some of the heat subsided, enough to let me concentrate on Emily as she spoke.

"Catherine, how much did you drink?" she asked.

"What?" My breath was still too fast, too shallow—I felt like I was hyperventilating.

"How much did you drink from Harrison?" she asked.

"I don't know."

"Did he have you recite any spells? Any oaths?"

"No."

"Good. Alexander, you'll have to carry her."

Lex picked me up and held me close, and my thrashing quieted into mild shakes. Just his mere presence helped fight back the effects of the poison racing through my body. We hurried through the parking garage, and once we reached their car—a bright red SUV—I was dropped into the backseat as everyone climbed into the car.

"I'll take care of her from here, Alexander. You need to drive," Emily informed him, patting his arm. Lex appeared less than thrilled at being banished from my side, but he obeyed her command.

"What's happening to me?" My voice trembled as the heat suddenly turned to an icy chill, and I shivered. The engine

Robyn Bachar

revved, and I heard the tires squeal as Lex raced through the parking garage and out into the rainy Chicago night.

"Please have a care with my car. We're going to need a bit of stability back here," Emily warned him, and then she turned to me. "The blood you ingested has saturated your aura with necromancy, and it's allowing Zachary's emotions to overwhelm you."

Taking my hand, she turned it over and peered thoughtfully at my wrist. "How much did you drink? Was it more than one time? Did he force you?"

"No, Laura tried to kill me, but Zach chased her off. He said I had to drink or he couldn't help me."

"You lost a lot of blood?" Simon asked, and I nodded. "A mortal wound would have required a good deal of his blood to heal."

"Will it wear off? Zach said it was dangerous for a magician to drink vamp blood if they weren't a necromancer."

"Yes, it is." Emily sighed, shaking her head in annoyance. "Alexander, you'll need to take her directly to your home once we part ways. The farther away from here she is, the better. Young Mr. Harrison won't leave the safety of the wards on this building. He knows the Silverleafs have marked him."

"I'll be damned," Michael said softly. "That's brilliant."

"What is, darling?"

"He's bought himself immunity from the faeries—they can't touch him without risking the safety of their Titania."

"Well, there's nothing to be done about that now. Now, I'll do what I can to aid you, Catherine. I'm afraid this isn't going to be simple, or pleasant—"

"Em, I don't think you should try this," Michael interrupted.

"I'm afraid I'm the only one who can, darling. No more interruptions," she admonished him. Focusing her attention on me, she patted my hand gently. "Unfortunately, I can't remove the attunement. I can ease some of your discomfort by drawing out the worst of the necromantic magic, but I can't remove all of it. Losing that much blood at once would likely kill you."

Oh, that was comforting. Still shivering uncontrollably, I couldn't really argue with her plan. All I wanted to do was get away, far away as I possibly could, and sleep for a week.

258

"Emily," her husband intoned again. "This isn't safe." I glanced at him, noticing the deep concern in his expression.

"Why? What's wrong?" I asked.

"Nothing, he's just being overly cautious." She gave me a reassuring smile.

I wasn't convinced, particularly when Simon spoke up on the subject. "I'm afraid I must agree with Michael. We don't know how Harrison's magic will affect you, Emily."

Squaring her small shoulders, the petite woman drew herself up. "I'm sure I can handle anything from one of Laura's kept men. He's only a child." Waving her hand dismissively, she ignored their fears. "Now, Catherine, it will be easiest on you if you do not watch this."

*Like getting a shot—just close your eyes, slight pinch, and it's all over.* Too bad nobody was going to offer me a lollipop afterwards. Nodding my consent, I squeezed my eyes shut and turned my head away. Intent on ignoring the feel of her fangs piercing my wrist, I concentrated on the sound of the speeding SUV and the splatter of rain against the roof and windows. Emily used just enough of her vampire magic to dull the pain of the bite. It made me wonder if she knew what her buddy Simon had put me through, and what she thought about it.

The chill in my veins began to subside, and the shivering quieted. As the sensations calmed, I could distantly feel even greater anger from Harrison, now mixed with poignant anguish as he realized he was powerless to stop me from being spirited away. Even as I regained control of myself, Harrison continued to remain in the back of my thoughts. I wondered if I would ever be completely free of him.

I also wondered if Emily was going to drain me into unconsciousness as I felt increasingly lightheaded, but she finally withdrew her fangs and moved away. Opening my eyes, I studied the vampire's expression. A frown creased her brow, and her gaze was distant and glassy as though she was in some sort of trance.

"Emily?" I asked.

"Give her a moment," Michael said. "She's having a vision."

I nodded in understanding. Before she became a vampire Emily must've been a seer, the rarest breed of magician, and taking in Harrison's magic triggered some sort of psychic episode. After a minute or so passed, Michael reached over from his seat and tapped her shoulder, murmuring her name. For another long moment Emily continued to stare blankly, then she blinked several times and awareness filled her soft gray eyes.

"Are you okay?" I asked her, concerned.

"Yes, I am now. It was a bit...unexpected. But don't you worry, my dear. I'll see that young Mr. Harrison behaves himself in the future. Rest now, we'll take care of everything." Turning to her husband, I watched them exchange a look heavy with emotion, and I wondered what it was she'd seen.

I turned to Simon. "You know about this spirit-link thing, how it works?"

"I've heard of it. I've never attempted such a thing," he replied.

"Can it be undone?"

"I don't know. I can research the matter."

I frowned. "How much would that cost? After all this, my blood bank's closed until further notice."

The vampire smiled, amused. "That sort of research is expensive, but you have nothing to fear. I'm sure your Oberon will insist on payments that are...less memorable."

I nodded, too tired to press him further. I drifted off to sleep, waking only when we stopped to switch cars. Apparently the vampires were going to keep an eye on Mac for now, which might have made me nervous, but Emily assured me that no one in the Order would ever harm a fellow librarian. On one hand I hoped that Mac got to experience Simon's ridiculously extravagant library, but on the other hand I knew he'd never want to leave if he did. Lex tucked me into the passenger seat of his SUV, and I missed the rest of the ride to his place. When I awoke again I was being shaken gently.

"Cat, honey. C'mon, we need to get you inside and cleaned up. I'll even make pancakes for you."

Still half asleep, I smiled. "I love you, but we both know you can't cook."

He laughed, the first real laugh I'd heard from him in far too long. Sitting up, I stretched in my seat and undid my seat belt. Lex held the door open for me, and my bare feet touched down on the damp grass of the lawn.

"Can you walk?" he asked, and I nodded. "Hmm, better safe than sorry." Scooping me up in his arms, he hoisted me out of the truck and shouldered the door shut.

Too tired to argue, I let him carry me across the lawn. I hadn't spent much time at Lex's place. It's a long drive from my apartment—not that I had a car—and since it's a half-hour from the nearest shopping center it qualifies as country in my book. He's got a pretty good sized chunk of land, lots of trees, and it's along a river I can never remember the name of. Lex even has a speedboat, which I'd been out on all of one time—too loud and too fast for me. The house is really too large for one person, but he's got a lot of junk—sorry, important guardian equipment—so it balances out.

The moon, almost full, lit the surrounding yard with a soft glow. The motion sensors triggered the outside lights as Lex walked up the steps of the front porch, and I heard the sound of dogs barking within. He set me down, and the wooden planks of the porch were cold. "You better get behind me, or they'll knock you down and lick you to death," he warned as he unlocked the door.

"You got another dog?"

"Yeah, that's Cesár. He kinda adopted me while I was out on a call. Got more than enough room, so I brought him home."

Bubba, the German shepherd, bounded out of the door first, followed by a mutt of unknown but vaguely Labradorish descent. Both dogs bypassed Lex and sniffed me, tails wagging. "No, she doesn't want to play with you boys. Go on, get."

The dogs hightailed it out into the yard, and I followed Lex inside. He flicked the lights on, and I looked around the room. I couldn't shake the odd, out-of-place feeling. I'd never felt comfortable here, and I guess I wasn't about to start now. Turning to me, Lex kissed me hard and deep, reminding me in a rush of heat and passion just how amazing he made me feel. "Missed you," he said simply when he pulled away.

"Obviously."

Lex caressed my cheek as he studied the black eye peeking out from behind the makeup that'd been spackled over it. "Did he hit you?"

"Of course not. Laura, on the other hand, beat the everlovin' snot out of me."

"I missed a chick fight?" He raised an eyebrow, looking disappointed, and I couldn't help but laugh at his expression.

"It wasn't a fight, it was a beating."

Robyn Bachar

"We're goin' to work on your self-defense skills, sugar. But first, you need to eat so we can do somethin' about those wounds."

"I've eaten enough for a small army today, and it didn't do much."

"And your blood was full of vamp magic before, now it's not," Lex pointed out in reply.

The main room of Lex's place is a giant combination of living room, dining room and kitchen. He flipped on the TV for noise, and a twenty-four hour news channel droned on in the background. I took a seat at the kitchen table and watched as Lex cooked me an omelet and toast, which was the extent of his cooking skills. It was almost a crime that someone who had a kitchen as nice as Lex—granite countertops, stainless-steel appliances—had zero cooking skills. Then again, it might very well become my kitchen, if Lex was serious about becoming Oberon and working out our issues.

"What made you change your mind?" I asked as he set the plate of food down in front of me.

"About what?"

"You know about what. What made you decide to be Oberon?"

"I never said I wasn't goin' to take it, I just wanted some time to get used to the idea."

"Gee, it would've been nice to have some time to get used to the idea of trying out for Titania." Picking up my fork, I poked at the omelet. In the back of my mind, I heard Zach's voice assuring me that if it had been him, he would've accepted the position without hesitation.

"You thought I was walkin' away from you again." It wasn't a question. Taking the seat next to me, he leaned back in his chair.

"Yeah, I did," I admitted.

"You didn't trust me. That why you let Harrison bite you?"

Frowning, I set the fork down. "We've been over this already. I didn't *let* him do anything to me. I didn't even know what this weird spell thing he did to me was, or how he pulled it off, but it wasn't my idea. I didn't agree to it."

"I meant it when I said I'd kill him for layin' a hand on you. Looks like I won't be able to follow through on that one."

"Well, it's even worse than that, because now we're going to have to work on keeping him alive too. If he goes, I go."

"That won't be easy. I'm willin' to bet he'll go after Laura's council seat."

"Great... Did you know about the government going after magicians?" I asked, changing the subject.

Lex looked surprised. "He told you about that?"

"He took me to a place, kinda like a safe house, where I helped heal this shapeshifter who looked like a prisoner of war. Poor kid must've been sixteen years old."

Lex rubbed his eyes wearily. "I'm sorry you had to see that."

"Harrison wants me to help him overthrow the government and take over the world. Like a Bond villain, without an accent or a white Persian cat." I snorted. Pushing around the food on my plate, I paused and forced myself to continue eating.

"You think that's a good idea?"

"Oh sure, I'm gonna get a leather jumpsuit and change my name to Kitty Galore. What do you think?"

"That you'd look good in that jumpsuit," he replied, and I rolled my eyes at him. "Seriously, though, you know he's goin' about it the wrong way."

"Yeah. What are we going to do about it, though?"

"I'm not allowed to go after straights, Cat."

"Lex the Guardian can't. Oberon, on the other hand... I just feel like if I'm going to do this, I want to make a difference."

Lex eyed me silently, and I went back to pushing food around on my plate, and then he nodded slowly. "I guess you're right. C'mon, you're doin' more playin' than eating, so let's get you cleaned up."

Unwilling to leave me alone in case I had another seizure-like episode, Lex perched on the bathroom counter as I showered, ready to leap to my rescue if I looked wobbly. It took a ridiculously long time to scrape off the makeup and undo my hairstyle. When Lex got a real look at my bruises he cursed about three minutes straight in French, which was quite impressive.

I didn't have any clothes at his place so he gave me a T-shirt to wear as a makeshift nightgown. Despite the fact I was battered, bruised and in borrowed clothes, I felt better than I had in a long time. Lex drew me close to him the moment I slid into bed, and he kissed me.

"I love you, Cat," he murmured.

"I love you too. Go to sleep."

I didn't have a single nightmare.

# Chapter Twenty-Four

The need for coffee awoke me from my blissful slumber, and Lex mumbled something vaguely coherent at me as I slipped out of his arms. It was early, especially considering how late we'd gotten to sleep after our daring escape from Harrison tower, so I drew the covers up around him and told him to go back to sleep. Lex nodded, mumbling again, but this time I was able to decipher that he wanted me to take the dogs with me if I went anywhere outside.

I didn't plan on wandering around the property, considering my current ensemble was distinctly lacking in pants, but as the coffee brewed the idea began to sound more and more appealing. The morning was cool and clear, not a single cloud left in the sky after last night's rain. With mug of coffee in hand, I headed out into the yard. The nearest neighbors were far enough away that I didn't need to worry about being seen wearing only my borrowed T-shirt. The dogs ran past me once I opened the back door, and then they trotted around, sniffing and inspecting their territory to make sure nothing had changed in their absence.

Blades of wet grass stuck to my bare feet as I made my way down to the river. Everything was quiet at this early hour. The river was calm and placid, its surface smooth as it eased by. Later on in the day the water would be stirred up by boats, and choppy waves would lap against the concrete seawall that lined the bank. Weathered wooden planks made up the pier, and Lex's boat rested in its station next to it. I glanced over the speedboat as I cautiously made my way to the end of the pier. The craft was long and sleek as I remembered, but I spotted a new detail when I reached its stern: flowing script spelled out

"Catherine." Huh. I couldn't wait to hear the story behind that one.

When I reached the edge, I sat down and let my legs dangle over the water. Though the recent rain had swelled the river's water level, my legs were still too short to reach the surface. The German shepherd, Bubba, lay down next to me and plopped his head in my lap. I scratched behind his ears. Though I'm a cat person, I like dogs too. Cesár took a spot behind me and began gnawing on a large stick that must've blown down during the storm last night.

I sipped my coffee, enjoying the morning quiet. I had a suspicion that there weren't going to be many more quiet mornings in the near future. Faint and distant, Harrison's magic tugged at me, a light itch in the back of my mind. I didn't know what this connection was between us, but I knew it was going to be a problem.

The sudden thumping of dog tails and a slight shaking of the pier alerted me to Lex's approach, and I turned around to look at him. Shirtless and shoeless, he wore only an ancient pair of blue jeans that were so worn and full of holes that sheer willpower was probably the only thing holding them together. He carried his own cup of coffee, and when he arrived at the end of the pier he nudged Bubba with his foot.

"You're in my spot, Bubba," he informed the shepherd. Giving me a parting slobbery kiss, the dog got to his feet and trotted away. Grimacing, I wiped drool from the side of my face as Lex sat down. "Here, let me take a look at that bruise of yours."

"It looks better." Turning my face toward him, I let him run his fingers over the faded bruise. The combination of food and a good night's sleep had let my magic heal a good deal of it. By tomorrow there wouldn't be any left of it at all.

"We're goin' to work on your hand-to-hand combat skills next."

"What hand-to-hand combat skills?" I smiled dryly.

"Exactly." He put his arm around me and then began drinking his coffee. I leaned against him, and we sat in comfortable silence.

Lex brushed a kiss across the top of my head. "You ready for the ceremony tonight? I talked to Portia, she said the council wouldn't grab us 'til after nightfall, so we have the day to prepare."

"I'm ready. Are you?"

"Definitely." He nodded.

"You're not... I mean, you're okay with this? No regrets?"

"No regrets. I love you, Cat. Bein' Oberon is goin' to take some getting used to, but I think you and I are meant to do this. Together."

"Good. Well, then there's only one thing left to worry about."

"Yeah? What's that?"

"How are we going to convince our pets to live together?"

Lex threw his head back and laughed. "We'll think of something."

When the time came for the ceremony I fully expected to appear back in the great hall of the Underhill clan, but much to my surprise Lex and I were popped into a forest. The night air was a bit warm, and the scents of rich earth mixed with the smell of smoke from a nearby fire. Flickering light filtered through the trees in front of us, and faint music floated on the breeze.

"Nice change of scenery," Lex commented. Taking my hand in his, he gave it a reassuring squeeze. "Let's see what kind of party the council's throwin' us."

"Don't try to kill the hosts of this one."

Lex grinned in reply, and we started toward the light. We emerged from the dense wood into a grove—a suspiciously familiar grove, in fact. If I didn't know better, I would've sworn it was the same grove that we'd been in during the dreams we'd shared during my time in the tower. That was impossible, however, considering the wards around the building would have prevented me from drifting into Faerie.

Unlike the dreams, the grove was filled with people. A bonfire burned in the center, and the three council members stood in front of it, waiting for us. Off to our right, Portia and a group of my cousins were gathered, white and shining in the moonlight. To our left were five human women, one of whom I recognized instantly as Lex's sister Marie—the pink hair gave her away—and the rest had to be Lex's mother and his other three sisters.

Lord and Lady. I really hoped they weren't here to kill me for de-guardianifying Lex. I'd probably want to slay me if I were them—here I was taking the only man in their family and destroying his opportunity for carrying on the family tradition. Nervous, I nearly tripped over my feet, and Lex glanced at me, looking concerned.

"You still hurtin'?"

"Yeah," I grudgingly admitted. "Though that's not the problem. Did you call them?"

"Who?"

"Your family."

"Nope. Don't worry, they'll love you," he assured me. Before I could panic any further, we reached the waiting council. Cecelia of the Silver Crescent gave us both a long, measuring gaze, and then she did something I never thought I'd see: she smiled.

"We are glad that you both have weathered the storm," Cecelia informed us. "These are difficult times. The path that brought you here was not easy to tread, and though tonight is a new beginning, the road ahead will be long and arduous."

The faerie paused, and I fought the urge to sigh. Cecelia definitely wasn't going to win any awards for motivational speaking. She turned toward me and motioned me to step forward.

"Catherine Marie Morrow, do you accept the position of Titania, and agree to perform as liaison between the realm of the Faerie and the Midwestern region of the United States of the realm of Earth?"

"I do."

Cecelia turned to Lex, and he stepped forward. "Alexander Duquesne, do you accept the position of Oberon, and agree to perform as liaison between the realm of the Faerie and the Midwestern region of the United States of the realm of Earth? If you choose to do so, you agree to forfeit your position as guardian and the abilities that accompany it."

"I do."

There was no hesitation in his voice, no tinge of regret, and it made my heart flutter and my face flush—he loved me, he wanted to be with me.

Cecelia's eyes sparkled, and her smile widened. "Excellent. You have passed your third test."

"What test?" I asked, confused.

"Because Alexander did not participate in the first test with the other candidates, the council decided to give him a separate trial. We chose to test his willingness to make sacrifices for this position. Though you were willing to give up your guardian abilities, we have...negotiated on your behalf. You will be allowed to retain most of them, and as is tradition for guardians, your children will be born with guardian blood."

Lex and I glanced at each other in surprise. It looked like his family wasn't going to have to kill me after all. Though the prospect of trying to manage a herd of little drawling guardians was intimidating. Possibly even terrifying. But hey, if I can deal with Portia, kids should be a piece of cake in comparison.

"Now, shall we proceed with the handfasting?" Cecelia asked.

*Handfasting?* I didn't recall a wedding being a part of the process of becoming Titania...but then again our situation was unique, and we were already planning on the marriage thing, and our families were here.

Why not?

"I knew I should've worn a dress."

"You look beautiful," he assured me with a grin.

Smiling, I turned to Cecelia. "We're ready."

# About the Author

Robyn Bachar was born and raised in Berwyn, Illinois, and loves all things related to Chicago, from the Cubs to the pizza. It seemed only natural to combine it with her love of fantasy, and tell stories of witches and vampires in the Chicagoland area. As a gamer, Robyn has spent many hours rolling dice, playing rock-paper-scissors, and slaying creatures in mmorpgs. Currently she lives with her husband, also a gamer and a writer, and their cat.

You can learn more about her at robynbachar.com. Robyn can also be found on Twitter at twitter.com/RobynBachar.

*Saving the world is easy for a superhero—unless you're a fraud.*

# Blaze of Glory
## © 2010 Sheryl Nantus

Jo Tanis is a superhero, fighting evil on the city streets, using her ability to feed off electromagnetic energy and fire off charges—and it's all just a show. The Agency captures her and others like her when their powers begin to manifest, pitting them against each other in staged, gladiatorial fights. An explosive implant on the back of her neck assures she'll keep right on smiling for the camera and beating up the bad guys.

When Earth comes under attack, suddenly the show becomes deadly real. Unable to deal with a real alien, the "supers" are falling in droves. Millions of innocent civilians are going to die...unless Jo can cobble together a team from among the fake heroes and villains the Agency enslaved. Including Hunter, who not only promises to show her how to deactivate the implants, but seems to know more than he should about how the mysterious Agency operates.

Forcing a rag-tag bunch of former enemies to work together is the least of Jo's problems. The trick is determining if Hunter is friend or foe—and becoming the hero everyone thought she was before the world is destroyed for real.

*Warning: Contains superhero in-jokes, Canadiana and large alien craft shaped like avocados. Really.*

*Available now in ebook and print from Samhain Publishing.*